Robert Smythe Hichens, Wilson Barrett

The Daughters of Babylon

A Novel

Robert Smythe Hichens, Wilson Barrett

The Daughters of Babylon
A Novel

ISBN/EAN: 9783337032272

Printed in Europe, USA, Canada, Australia, Japan

Cover: Foto ©Andreas Hilbeck / pixelio.de

More available books at **www.hansebooks.com**

THE DAUGHTERS OF BABYLON

A NOVEL

BY

WILSON BARRETT

AND

ROBERT HICHENS

JOHN MACQUEEN
HASTINGS HOUSE, NORFOLK STREET
LONDON
1899

DAUGHTERS OF BABYLON

CHAPTER I

ELCIA sat by the well of Naomi. It was towards
evening, and the glaring heat of the sun was
tempered by a soft breeze full of the thrilling
coolness that only desert winds know. Through
the palms about the well the lemon light slanted
across the dark head, with its heavy mass of
hair, that was bowed as if in deep meditation or
in grief. In the distance, softened and sweetly
melancholy, there was the sound of singing voices.
For in the fields, among the flocks and the herds,
the people of Elcia's tribe, sons and daughters of
Israel in captivity to Babylon, chanted the hymns
of their ancient faith as they watched the grazing
cattle, tended the nibbling sheep, or wrought at
making packs for the camels in the doors of their
tents. These same tents were hidden from the
great eyes of Elcia, for the well lay apart, and, at
this moment, there were no stalwart shepherds or

herdsmen discussing the tributes paid to the Babylonish king, or, with lowered voices, whispering of
the hour when Israel should be free, and mourning
be turned into the joy that cannot live in slavery.

In such discussions Johanan, husband of Elcia,
loved to take a part. Young, ardent, and enthusiastic, the bondage of his people weighed upon his
heart, and his mind was ever occupied with that
desired future, in which captivity should be changed
into freedom, and the heavy burthen be lifted
from Israel's shoulders, never to lie on them
again.

But Elcia was a woman. She was in the dawn
of an opulent beauty. Her magnificent eyes,
deep and liquid with light, looked not to Babylon
with desire for its destruction. She dreamed
rather of love than of hatred, as is the way of
women, and, in her reveries, betook herself to
desires that were not broad and far - reaching,
national, and of consequence to the many, but
to those that were personal, limited, and of importance to herself, and to the one or two whose
lives were at this time bound with hers.

She thought not of the great and distant Babylon
now, as she leaned alone by the well, fixing her
liquid eyes upon its still waters, illuminated by the
growing fire of the sunset sky. She thought of
her own life and of two who stood within its
circle—Johanan, her husband, and Jediah, son of
Zoar. And it seemed her thoughts ran sadly, for
her beauty was shadowed by an expression of dim
anxiety, and in her eyes the tears were brimming.

For, of a truth, although Elcia thought not of Babylon, yet even now the Great City was stretching out its arms to her, unseen by her eyes. Its mighty voice was calling to her, though she could not hear it. Its life, with cruel subtlety, was mingling with hers. For Babylon's terror and magnificence, Babylon's oppression and cruelty, stood up like a shadowy wall between her and her husband, Johanan. She had loved him well, for he was goodly and of a noble bearing, and his brave and passionate eyes had spoken to her heart, and stirred all the tenderness of her nature. But that seemed already long ago, before he thought of Babylon, and was ever with his kinsmen, discussing the sadness of their slavery and laying plans to break the heavy chains that bound them. Then he thought only of her, and forgot that he was in some sort a slave, as he held her in his strong arms and laid his lips on hers. But now, although in truth he loved her no less, he was yet caught in the meshes of the net of a wide intrigue. His heart was hot with wrongs and iron with resolution. It beat for his downtrodden nation. Elcia wished it to beat ever and alone for her.

Jediah was often at hand to speak with her of this growing fanaticism of Johanan.

" He forgetteth thee when he remembereth our bondage," he said. " He forgetteth thee, Elcia. He saith naught to thee. But unto others "—

Jediah paused significantly, looking close into the eyes of Elcia. An expression of keen anxiety woke in them, a hunger of pitiful curiosity and eagerness.

"Unto others?" she said. "What meanest thou? What saith he unto others, O Jediah?"

"I scarce—nay, I desire not to tell thee," he answered, with an assumption of uneasiness. "'Tis better that thou should'st be ignorant of this matter. 'Tis not thy fault that thou art"—

Again he checked himself. But Elcia was not to be put off.

"Tell me, Jediah!" she cried, "for I will know, even though it hurt me unto death."

"Well, then—to others he doth groan and ever lament that his wife is barren," said Jediah slowly.

Elcia uttered a cry and hid her face in her hands. This reproach was like a sword struck down into her heart. She quivered with the pain and with the terror of it, and her cheeks grew hot with shame and anger.

Jediah was a man of importance in the tribe, a Lord and Judge in Israel, son of the aged Zoar, whose flocks and whose herds were mighty, and whose tribute to the Babylonians in sheep and in cattle, in corn and in oil, was heavy, by reason of his great possessions. All held Jediah in respect. But Jediah was by nature pitiless and lacking in bowels of mercy. He was the friend of Johanan, who trusted in him above all other men. Yet he often spoke with Elcia by the well at eventide, or, in a more removed place, among the thickets of palm trees that gave a soft shade from the heat of noontide. And always he spoke of Johanan, and of how his thoughts were with his nation and remote from his wife.

And Elcia listened, and looked into his fierce and bold eyes, until she heard and gazed to her undoing.

Even now, as the sun sank lower, and the distant songs of the Israelites rose up in the evening silence, a step sounded among the dry reeds that grew thickly near the well, and Elcia, looking round, beheld Jediah.

"Thou art alone, Elcia," he said. And he glanced cautiously behind him to see that no herdsman wandered near among the palms, that no women, bearing pitchers, drew nigh from the fields. "Thou art alone. But it is ever so. Johanan forgetteth thee. Even now he is with Ahira and with Adoram. And he speaketh not of thee, but of Babylon. He thinketh not of thee, but of the Great City and of the oppressors of Israel. Is it not so?"

And he drew close to her and laid his hand upon hers. She answered him nothing, but the shadow grew in her face.

"Should he be married who cannot hold close his wife, Elcia?" continued Jediah. "No child cometh to bless thy union and to bring joy unto thy tent. And this thing setteth thee far from thy husband, for he desireth ever to have seed that they may bear his name and live long in the land. Should a woman be true to one who ever leaveth her to mourn alone beside the water?

Thou answerest not. Then I will tell thee. She oweth him neither love nor faithfulness. Rather oweth she these things to him who truly loveth her, who would give his life for her sake, who would, ay, who would even let the cruel chains hang still upon the necks of his people rather than that one sad thought should be within her heart, or the dimness of tears rise up to hide the sunshine from her eyes. Elcia, Elcia, when wilt thou reward thy servant? When wilt thou flee with me that we may hide ourselves in Babylon, where alone is safety for our love, mine and thine?"

"Ah, my lord, speak not so to me," she replied, and her voice was low and broken. "I dare not, I dare not. And Johanan"—

"Cares not for thee. What is a woman to him who is full of vain dreams of glory? Nothing, Elcia, and thou knowest it."

She bent her head lower. There was a cruel jealousy in her heart, jealousy of a nation, jealousy of a city. For had not the Babylonish oppressors caught Johanan's soul from her in wrath? Had not Babylon itself drawn him from her in anger?

"Thou art no longer anything to Johanan, Elcia. Did'st thou die to-night, he would go up against the Babylonians to-morrow, leaving thy fair body unburied, thy lifeless heart unwept. But I"—

And he drew close to her and put his arm around her.

"Thou lovest me indeed?" she asked him slowly.

"So much that I am ready to leave all here for thee, and to follow thee to Babylon, where we may be together in safety, where we may love, watched by no prying kinsmen's eyes, babbled of by no heedless tongues. There, in the Great City, Elcia, will I make thee forget thy sorrow that now turneth thine eyes to mourning and thy heart to grief. Hearken unto me. Even to-morrow, at sundown, there passeth a caravan for Babylon. It carrieth heavy tribute to the young Lord Alorus. Disguise thyself, watch well thine opportunity; say to the master of the camels that thou hast need to journey to the city. I will speak with him. I will be the surety for any payment. I will tell thee whither thou may'st go when thou reachest the end of thy journey, and in some short space of time will I join thee there. Say, Elcia, wilt thou go?"

She shuddered by the well, as if the falling of the night had chilled her fair limbs.

"I dare not, Jediah, I dare not," she murmured. "I fear the city. I fear Babylon."

A fierce expression of contempt and anger passed over his face and was gone in a moment.

"Thou hast naught to fear when I am with thee," he said. "Wilt thou not go, Elcia? Thy husband will not miss thee, be sure. He concerneth himself with thee no longer. But I think of thee from the rising of the sun unto the going down of the same."

"Dost thou indeed love me, Jediah?" she asked him.

And she fixed her great eyes on his.

"So well that I will leave all for thee, if thou wilt but trust in me."

And he bent down and kissed her.

"Wilt thou go to-morrow at sundown?" he whispered.

She felt the strength of his arms about her, and she needed love. She thought of Johanan, her husband, ever brooding on the wrongs of his nation in bondage, ever speaking of deliverance with the brethren while she was left alone. She wondered if, somewhere, far off, in the great and mysterious city, she might not find the joy which she lacked here, among the fields, amidst a down-trodden people. Something, that seemed to speak defiantly and against her will, rose up in her and said—

"I will go, Jediah."

"To-morrow, at sundown?"

"To-morrow, at sundown."

"It is well, Elcia. In Babylon how I will love thee! Hush! I see Johanan. Get thee gone."

She rose and disappeared among the palms. As she did so, Johanan approached the well.

"That is Elcia?" he said to Jediah.

"Even so, Johanan. I have spoken with her of what thou toldest to me."

"And she hasteneth away when I come near."

The face of Johanan, strong, manly, and courageous, full of youth and of energy, grew sad, even bitter.

"It is as I thought, Jediah. Tell me! Elcia cares not for me?"

"I know not, Johanan. She is beautiful, but she seemeth strange and cold, like the wind that cometh out of the desert. Thou hast done well to follow my counsel and to let be. Importune her not. If she seeth that thou concernest thyself with other things, that thou art a man to lead the brethren, and, peradventure, to lift from their necks the heavy yoke beneath which they groan, then will she come to thee as to her lord. It is the way of women. They worship not those that think of naught but them."

"Is it even so? Thou said'st to her that thou knewest how dear was she to me? That weigheth with a woman when another man speaketh it, Jediah."

"I did say so, Johanan."

"And she—?"

"Smiled, and when she saw thee coming towards the well, got her up and hasted away. Better not speak with her till the mood passeth, Johanan. She will turn to thee again, but not now. But let us talk not of Elcia longer, but of this bitterness that oppresseth us."

He took Johanan gently by the hand, and they walked together towards the tents, talking of the Captivity of Israel. The stars came up in the clear Eastern sky. And all that evening Elcia sat apart in her tent, alone. Johanan came not. For indeed he was ever with Jediah, who left him not, but spoke with him of the wrongs of their sad nation, and of the joy that would come with the morning, when the captives would be free, and their long oppressors be trampled under the feet of God's ancient people.

The night fell, and at last Elcia laid her down and slept. Her eyes were still wet with tears when she dreamed of Babylon.

.   .   .   .

The day following, Elcia felt as one in a dream, vague, wandering, and helpless. She looked at all the familiar things around her—at the wide and hedgeless fields of grass and green corn; at the tall reeds that rustled, with a dry sound, beside the water; at the droves of camels kneeling to receive their burdens, or moving slowly with their fantastic gait in long lines towards the horizon; at the peaked tents round which the children played, the women gathered to chatter, and the lean dogs snuffed in search of fragments of forgotten food; at the men going forth to labour, wrapped in their long robes, with sombre hoods drawn over their heads to protect them from the sun. She gazed at the clusters of palm trees and at the mimosa bushes. She listened to the singing of the birds and to the murmur of the waters and to the voices that spoke around her. And always she saw things as in a dream, and she heard them as from very far off. Once or twice, at early dawn and in the dull heat of noontide, she met Jediah. He gazed at her with his fierce eyes, in which there dwelt to-day a deep anxiety. And he said to her—

"Thou wilt depart to-night, Elcia?"

And she answered him, scarce knowing, indeed, what she said—

"To-night I will depart, Jediah."

"Leave thy tent ere sundown. I will await thee in the thicket beyond the well of Naomi, to bid thee farewell and to tell thee what thou must do when thou goest to Babylon."

"To Babylon!" She shivered, as if from fear, and her heart was cold within her. She heard, a little way off, some women laughing. Their happiness seemed a strange and mysterious thing to her. Jediah watched her closely.

"Thou wilt not fail, Elcia?" he said. "Thou wilt not stay here with the man who heedeth thee not—who despiseth thee, and would fain seek another wife; one who would raise up seed unto him and bless his tent with children?"

And then she felt as if a vice tightened around her heart, and she answered—

"Ere sundown I will meet thee, Jediah, in the thicket beyond the well of Naomi. And I will journey to Babylon to wait thee there."

Then he smiled and went his way, and in his heart he laughed at the weakness of women.

Johanan, according to the counsel of Jediah, had scarce spoken to Elcia in the dawn when she woke within the shadow of the tent. He had gone forth early, saying—

"I have much to do this day, Elcia. A man

must not be slothful, staying ever with the women, else is he abominable in the sight of his kinsmen and of the God of his fathers. It is not the slothful lover of women who will deliver Israel out of bondage. The God of our fathers hath indeed set upon me this task, to aid in the deliverance of Israel. For He hath left me lonely. Other men have children to call them within the tent, to catch them by the hand with tenderness and bid 'father' stay when they rise up to go forth. But our tent is empty, Elcia, and no voice calleth me 'father.'"

She answered him nothing, for her heart was heavy within her. And he, coming upon Jediah, said to him, with bitterness—

"She loveth me not, Jediah."

"Be not afraid, Johanan," he answered. "Be a strong man in Israel, and she will surely love thee, ay, and worship thee, and be unto thee all that thou canst desire."

And Johanan said—

"Thinkest thou so? Thou speakest truth unto me, thou who art a Judge in Israel?"

Then Jediah smiled and answered—

"I speak truth. But, if thou wilt, ask some other man how thou shalt keep the love of Elcia."

And Johanan believed Jediah, and went his way heavy-hearted.

That day he had to go a journey with his camels, to bear a debt from his father to the tents of a neighbour. He would not return until the sun was down. Jediah knew this, and that the caravan that went this day to Babylon would be gone, and even far towards the desert, ere ever Johanan stood again in his tent door to call his wife Elcia.

When the evening drew on, but while the sun was not yet red in the west of the sky, Jediah went with cautious footsteps to the thicket of palm trees that stood beyond the well of Naomi. It was here that he would bid good-bye to Elcia and speed her upon her strange and lonely journey to Babylon. For he dared not go with her lest suspicion should arise. There was no one in the thicket, and he waited a long time, listening ever for the footsteps of Elcia that came not. While he waited, anxiety and a fierce anger grew within his soul. If she should not come! If some sudden weakness of resolution, some woman's feebleness of heart, should prompt her to shrink back from his persuading! He moved restlessly, pacing about like some wild beast to and fro upon the dry ground, his eyes turned ever towards the well of Naomi, or to the light in the sky that betokened the approach of the sunset hour. The caravan would soon be passing on its road towards the desert. And she came not. He passed from the thicket into the open ground about the well.

In his anger he was resolved to go to the tent of Johanan, but ere he reached the well he saw, far off, the shrouded figure of a woman coming towards him, with the noble bearing that set Elcia apart from all the women of her tribe. As she drew near she let the garment that was before her face fall, and he saw that she was weeping. When they were among the palms, he said to her—

" Why art thou so late, my Elcia ? "

" I feared to come, Jediah."

" What hast thou to fear ? Am I not with thee ? Shall I not follow thee to Babylon ? "

" But to leave all—this place, my people, the well beside which I dreamed in the days when—when Johanan "—

" When he loved thee. Those days are gone for ever."

She put forth her hand as one that is wounded, and from her lips there came a cry of pain.

" For ever," repeated Jediah. " Think not of them. Put them behind thee. Think of the days that are before. Thou shalt see the wonders of that city which is like magic to men when they dream of it. Thou shalt see its palaces, its towers, and the great river, even Euphrates. And I will open thine eyes to love. And perchance thou shalt be blest, Elcia, as other women are blest, even in the bearing of children, who shall cling to thee and call thee by the sweet name of ' mother.' Yea, I will open thine eyes to love, and give to thee all that a woman needeth and that thou hast lacked so long. But hark ! " He lifted his hand and listened. Then he ascended the rising land beyond the palms to a place from which he could see a great way off.

" It is the caravan," he said, returning. " I see it like a long shadow on the plain. I hear the cries of the drivers and the distant noise of bells. It is time for thee to depart, Elcia. Thou hast thy bundle. Here is gold. Buy all that thou needest in Babylon, and wait me in the house that I have told thee of. Fear not. In no long time I will be with thee."

She answered him nothing. For again the dream floated upon her, and all things present and future seemed unto her like a tale told in a dark night. And in the dark night she perceived, like terrible and watching eyes, the distant lights of the great and renowned city. And the power of Jediah lay on her like a spell. She had no will to resist him, but bent before him as before a sorcerer, come up out of the great desert. Already the tents of her people seemed to lie a long way off, and their hymns in the fields were like unto dying echoes. And the well of Naomi was like unto a tender thought of a thing that existeth no more.

When the sun was set, and the caravan departed towards the desert, there was a woman in it who wept as she journeyed.

.   .   .   .

In the darkness of night Johanan stood in the door of his tent. He was weary with the heat of day and with long travelling across the shadowless plains. He stood in the door and looked into the tent. The moon was up in the clear sky. Its light streamed into the darkness, illuminating the couch where each night Elcia laid her down to sleep. And the eyes of Johanan turned towards this spot with longing to see if the woman he loved waked, waiting for his return. There was no one upon the couch. The tent was empty.

Johanan stood still for a moment in perplexity.

The hour was very late. No one was stirring. No women were about. All was quiet. There was scarce a breath of wind to rustle in the wide leaves of the palms. He entered into the tent, thinking that peradventure his eyes tricked him. He approached the couch and bent over it. No one was there, or had lain there that night. Then a great fear came to his heart, and he rushed out from the tent into the night. At first he had a wild impulse to search for Elcia among the palms and by the water, and his heart was alive with jealousy. He hastened on like a man drunk with wine, and scarce knew whither he went. He called aloud in the night, " Elcia, Elcia, where art thou ? " But no voice answered. Then he paused, and tried to think. Could she, perchance, have wandered forth, thinking to meet him on his returning way ? Or could she—and his heart grew cold—have been led by a dream down some strange path in sleep ? He went to and fro, seeking her. He came to the well of Naomi. The moonlight glittered upon the water, and he seemed to see Elcia's face there. But he found her not. Then he bethought him of his friend Jediah, the man in whom he trusted ; and he ran to Jediah's tent and found him wrapped in profound slumber. He caught him by the shoulders and waked him.

" Jediah," he said, " Jediah, knowest thou aught of Elcia ? "

Jediah gazed at him with eyes that seemed heavy with sleep.

" Elcia ? " he asked, in the drowsy, inward voice

of tired men. "Elcia? What should I know of her? Is she not thy wife, and in thy tent?"

"She is not in the tent. And it is deep night. O Jediah, what evil hath befallen me?"

Jediah rose up from his couch.

"Elcia is not with thee?" he said.

"Nay. I returned but now from my journey, and when I stood in my tent door she was not within. I have called on her. I have sought her. Whither is she gone, Jediah?"

And he trembled in all his limbs, and seemed like to fall.

"I know not," Jediah answered. "This is a strange thing, Johanan. Did'st thou part from her in anger when thou setted'st forth?"

"Nay, but I spoke to her of our unblessed union, and I did show unto her how sore was my heart that we were ever childless. Ah, it was cruelly done! O Elcia! Elcia!"

"Let us seek her, Johanan. Let us seek her together," said Jediah. And he wrapped himself in his garment, and they went out into the night.

CHAPTER II

ABOVE the great plain in which lay the mighty
city of Babylon the sun blazed almost cruelly in
a sky that seemed made of brass, pitiless, fierce,
and hard. It was nearly noontide, and across
the plain, beyond the huge walls which enclosed
the city, a caravan travelled slowly towards the
western gate. The long lines of camels, heavily
laden with merchandise of spice and of ivory, of
perfumed oils, of alabaster and of fine linen, moved
onward with a fatigued and grotesque gait,
snarling in the sultry heat, and, with heavy and
irritable eyes, gazing askance at the Nubians, who
drove them forward. Round about them hovered
swarms of flies, which buzzed incessantly, and,
alighting upon them in thousands, crept towards
their eyelids, as if drawn thither by a magnet.
The drivers called to each other as they ran, and
cracked the stout thongs of the whips they carried.
And as the caravan approached the city, and the
mighty palaces, standing upon lofty platforms of
brickwork, the temples, and the endless rows of
dwelling-houses came more clearly to the view,
an excitement dawned in the faces of those who
accompanied the caravan.

Dark-eyed traders, swinging to the movement of the dromedaries, spoke together of the fabulous wealth of the city, of the huge sums given by its citizens for the pleasures that made glad their hearts, of the lavish extravagance of its women, who walked in the hanging gardens loaded with rare jewels, having their hair bound with bands of heavy gold and their fingers covered with rings, while their long robes, embroidered in a thousand hues, rustled till the scented air was filled with music to wake the souls of men. Within those gigantic walls that stretched for miles were surely hoarded riches such as the world had never known before in all its history—pearls brought from the fisheries of Bahreim, and perchance from the deep waters of Ceylon ; ebony and frankincense, bronze and gold, glimmering silks and odorous cedar, cottons dyed the hues of all the birds, ivory smooth as the cheek of a maiden and hard as the heart of a warrior when he goeth forth into battle ; the skins of all beasts, and gems glittering with a light inhuman.

Within those walls stood palaces like cities, where instruments of music sounded in the drowsy noontide and in the silver night, where the wine-cup, chased with gold and set with turquoises, passed from hand to hand, where the torches shed their fire on the, darkness and the slave - girls leaped and danced beside the couches of their masters. All things were bought and sold in those streets and alleys : the wood cut in the forests of Assyria and the women brought from far, weeping, in the inexorable caravans; bricks, beams, and doors for twelve manehs of silver; oxen and asses, statues of the great god Bel, charms against evil fates and against mysterious maladies, artabs of corn and shields of copper, chariots wrought in bronze, coats of mail, and tablets of brick. There the hucksters cried their wares. There lurked the sorcerers in their mysterious dwellings, and the singing-women chanted upon the walls, and the watchmen looked forth from the towers. There, too, in the midst of a thousand pleasures, did the learned men whose fame travelled far to the four winds and to the four corners of the world, pursue their endless studies. The grave astronomers lived, like strange birds, high up among those stars whose faces they knew as a man knoweth the face of a friend. The sculptors toiled, bringing a beautiful and lifeless life to the hard substances that they loved. The librarians muttered together of the thoughts of men, that should be recorded for the observation of the heedless and of those who know not how to think. The mathematicians lost themselves in calculations, treading the mazes of a crafty region where only the clearest mind could go at ease. The irrigators planned the wanderings of artificial rivers, and the law-givers watched over the destinies of the uninstructed, and the quick-eyed men leaned over the tiny gems, engraving them with tools scarce visible, and the artists painted, and the weaver bent above his weaving. There, in sombre laboratories, the men of the healing art combined

their potions, and apart in their silent houses the
omen-givers drew up their treatises of divination,
their tables of dreams, their lists of the meanings
of those creatures that a traveller meets when on
his journey. If a blue dog enters a palace, that
palace will be burned. If a dog goes to a palace
and lies down upon a bed, that palace none with
his hand will take. If a man dreameth of bright
fire, there will surely be fire in his dwelling-place.
If a sheep bears a lion, the King of Babylon will
have no rival. And there the children cooed
and played among bright flowers, and the processions of Bel went by with the sounding of flutes
and of cymbals, and the scattering of the wine-red
petals of roses. And the priests abased themselves before the statues of the gods—of Merodach,
who smote the dragon ; Tihamter, and Anu, god
of the sky ; and Makhir, the god of dreams ; and
Adar, and Ana, god of heaven. And there
histories were inscribed in clay, and the men
passed through the ways carrying seals upon their
wrists, and hymns were sung to the seven wicked
spirits, and at gateways, chased with fine gold, the
eunuchs lay asleep. There human beings swarmed
like flies ; drovers and masons, shepherds and
soldiers, carpenters and builders of houses, poets
and bankers, scribes and silversmiths. And there
was the sound of music by night and day. And
through the mighty city flowed the great river
Euphrates, on whose shining bosom floated the
daring navigators and merchants from far
countries, borne along on rafts of skins, or in

boats fashioned of reeds and covered with bitumen. Grandiose was this city and grandiose its river. Men held their breath as they approached it. Women wept from the fear of it, or extended their longing arms to its fierce and complex charms. The voices of it clamoured to the skies, and the hearts of it beat like the beating in the world's heart. Its laughter was like the laughter of the gods, and its songs were like the choruses of the morning stars. And its wonder was more great than the wonder of all lands. And its terror surpassed the terror of the deep places beyond the mountains.

Even men of hardest nature were moved deep in their souls as they approached Babylon, and in this caravan, now travelling toward the western gate of the city, were two who spoke together but little, though they were companions, though—as one believed—they were even friends. For among the travellers, coming thus in the noontide to Babylon, were Jediah and Johanan. Strange was it that they should be together. It had fallen out in this wise. When the search for Elcia was all in vain, Johanan was well-nigh distraught with jealousy and with despair. Now he thought his wife dead in some hidden place ; now he believed her fled from him with some man who loved her. And when he could nowhere find her, he bethought him of the wicked city Babylon, and that, perchance, she had fled thither to find safe hiding among its teeming crowds. He told his thought to Jediah, and Jediah answered—

"It may be so. As thou knowest, I am thy friend. Stay thou here, for, peradventure, Elcia may return in sorrow to greet thee, and I will go up to Babylon to seek her there."

"Nay," said Johanan, "but I will come with thee. We will go together, and surely we shall find her there."

He held Jediah hard by the hand and looked into his eyes, as if for hope and consolation. But Jediah cast down his eyes and answered—

"Had'st thou not better stay by the tent? It is far to Babylon, and why should Elcia be gone thither, if, indeed, she liveth still?"

And as he spoke the words he was seized by a great terror, which seemed to shake his very soul, even as the leaf of a tree is shaken by the wild winds of the autumn time that come out of the desolate heart of the desert. If his sin should be discovered! If his black deed should be known! What then would be his fate? He, Judge and Lord in Israel—he, Jediah, son of Zoar, whom all men respected—would be stoned with stones until he lay dead before his father and his brethren. And a dream of horror came upon him and enwrapped him, until he was like unto one who walketh in darkness and in the night, companioned by a spectre that leadeth him into the dreadful places of the earth and unto the dwellings of the damned.

"Better she were dead than alive in sin," Johanan said, with bitterness. "But, Jediah, something telleth me that she is indeed in Babylon, and that thou and I shall find her there."

"Thou shalt never find her, if I have to slay thee to close those eyes of thine," muttered Jediah, beneath his breath.

He feared deeply the presence of Johanan in Babylon. Yet he dared not let him go thither alone. For, alone, he might indeed come upon Elcia.

So it came about that Jediah, unable to dissuade Johanan from his purpose, was at last resolute to accompany him to the city; and thus the betrayer and the betrayed now entered in at the western gate as friends, the one stern to hide that woman whom the other was so deeply purposed to find.

As they passed beneath the mighty gateway and entered at length fully into the teeming life of the city, they gazed about them with curious and almost awestruck eyes. The streets cut each other at right angles, and the houses, built of bricks painted in bright colours, were tall and massive and of an exceeding solidity. Even the lowest of them was at the least three storeys in height. Close by the entrance of the city were gardens and orchards, groves of palms, and even patches of land on which the corn was growing. All this within the walls. Here and there the land was intersected by broad canals, and here and there it rose in artificial hills, so artfully constructed that it seemed as if Nature herself had lifted them towards the sun. Upon the houses by which the caravan now passed, slowly threading its way among the swarming crowds who jostled it, were many paintings on stucco, chiefly figures of men and of

animals. Some of them seemed to be in action.
Some struck strange attitudes expressive of the
emotions. The cornices of these mansions, which
belonged to the wealthy Babylonians, were decor-
ated with bronze, some even with alabaster and
with- bright gold. Before the walls were many
gardens and plantations, and beneath the trees
stood seats and small tables at which the owners
ate when the weather was, as at present, hot
and fine. Jediah and Johanan perceived some
Babylonish families thus enjoying the air beneath
the shade, the while slaves agitated gigantic fans
to keep away the swarming insects that buzzed
and flew on all hands. These gardens and small
plantations were irrigated by tiny rivulets, fed by
water that was drawn in buckets and poured heed-
fully into them by slaves. Along these rivulets
grew vegetables, much garlic, also onions and a
sort of cabbage. Upon the tables beneath the
palms stood large vases filled with bright-coloured
flowers.

But now the sights of the streets attracted and
filled their eyes. Men and women buzzed, even as
the insects in the gardens, various in appearance,
in manner, and, most of all, strangely various in
attire. Some among them wore but one garment
and that a short one, but others were richly and
elaborately dressed in materials made in Babylon,
or in muslins and other fabrics imported from
India. They were robed in tunics of wool, or,
sometimes, of linen, fastened by girdles and reaching to the thigh. Above this was a long and

graceful robe, without sleeves and richly fringed, opening in front and exposing, as the wearer walked, the inner side of the left leg. Upon the head was a thick, quilted tiara, or a species of helmet, peaked and projecting forward above the forehead. It was, in some cases, ornamented with ribands shaped into the form of horns. Above the heads of many were spread large parasols to keep away the sun's rays, and from the wrists of the men hung seals. Those that were priests were attired in flounced robes falling to the feet, and carried upon their shoulders the skin of the sacred goat. The women wore ear-rings, necklaces, and bracelets of gold or silver; so also did many of the men, who went mostly barefoot, though some were shod with sandals, and one or two with shoes of soft leather. The water-sellers beat their cups, and the sellers of sweetmeats — round whom gathered the children—cried in high voices their wares. Here and there amid the throng a soldier passed, clad in kilt and skullcap, or a dandy, whose hair and beard, long and flowing, were carefully curled and drenched with strong essences. Cavalry soldiers, in tightly fitting breeches fashioned of plaited leather, and high boots, rode by mounted upon magnificent horses with streaming manes and tails. Their coloured saddles gleamed in the sunshine, and their martial bearing drew cries of admiration from the women who leaned out from the windows. Beggars and dogs swarmed on all sides. The blind, reckless of their infirmity, scrambled under the very feet of the camels and asses. The poor stretched out their filthy hands shrieking for alms. The cripples lay on the door-steps, demonstrating their diseases and discovering their sores. Here went by a man wrapped in the snakes he charmed, there a miracle-worker bearing his little boxes, his cups, and wands. A sand-diviner called to the crowd to learn their destinies, a maniac gibbered and sprang beneath a yellow wall in the sun glare. An old man, pale and malignant of countenance and girt with a black girdle, played upon a pale green pipe beneath a palm tree, and round his feet danced little boys in fluttering white garments. A throng of sheep, bleating to the shambles, mingled their hoarse voices with the lowing of a herd of oxen being driven to the city gate. And not only were the streets full of Babylonians, born within the walls of Babylon or come there from the neighbouring plains, but among the crowd might be discovered men from all the nations of the earth, lured thither by the greatness of the place, by its pleasures, by its glory, and, most especially, by its vast trade. At this period it was, in fact, at the height of its renown. Its luxury was immoderate. Its de-bauchery surpassed conception. In Babylon men gave their lives to joy as a child gives a flower to the dust. Women yielded their souls to the pass-ing hours. Effeminacy, bred of too great civilisa-tion, already began to increase upon the growing youths. The sun looked down upon a riot of pleasure such as the world had never seen. And at night, when the moon stole up above the mighty palaces, the monstrous walls, and the great brick towers, and the hanging gardens and the wondrous temple of the powerful god Bel, it shone upon strange scenes of ecstasy and of sorrow, of wild, even of frantic, dissipation and of profound superstition. For the people of Babylon, reckless in their sins, cowered like children before the predictions of a begging prophet, or the whispering voice of a dream, and gave vast sums to propitiate the gods, before whose altars they sank in abasement, after orgies whose violence echoed, surely, to the distant gates of heaven.

The two Israelites, Jediah and Johanan, were in amaze at the thronging people in the streets, at the cries and the music, and at the mighty buildings, and presently Johanan said—

"If Elcia be here, Jediah, how shall we come upon her? For here men are as the sands of the sea and the women cannot be numbered. Yet, while I have eyes to see and feet to walk upon, will I seek her."

Even as he spoke, a blind man, tottering upon a heavy stick, of brown wood, held forth his hand, crying with a sad voice—

"Help the blind!"

Jediah looked down upon him and then at Johanan, and he answered slowly—

"Thou wilt seek her, thou sayest, while that thou hast eyes to see. That is well, Johanan. Surely, if she be indeed here, she shall not escape thee."

Then he spoke no more until they reached a

wide space of ground, where the caravan stopped to unload the camels and to pitch the tents for the drivers and for the owners.   There they must set forth to seek a lodging for the night.   Johanan, who was possessed by but one thought, had no care for himself.   He gazed ever around him, examining the faces of all who passed by.   And he cried unto Jediah—

"Seek thou a lodging, Jediah.   I will go forth into the street.   Peradventure I may meet Elcia. At sundown I will come hither again to find thee. Farewell, O my friend."

And he turned away and mingled with the crowd that had gathered to see the coming of the caravan.

Jediah looked after him as he went, muttering in his beard—

" Help the blind ! "

Then he too turned to go his way to the house where Elcia lodged.   This was not in the wealthier quarter of the city, among the palaces of the great and the temples of the mighty gods, but near the eastern wall, where stood many small and poor-looking houses, at the base of one of the artifi-cial hills reared by the Babylonians to break the monotony of the flat plain in which the city lay. As he passed upon his road, thinking deeply,— for he was in most strange circumstances,—he came presently to a street that lay at a higher level.   In this street were many Babylonians offering their wares for sale—carpet merchants, sellers of embroideries and of dyed stuffs, of perfumes, amulets, sandals, and bronzes. Among them was a god-seller, who cried with a loud voice—

"Come hither, ye who would buy gods—buy them of me! I sell the cheapest gods in Babylon. Merodach, the General of all gods; he who can cure witchcraft and brain-sickness for one shekel! Ana, god of heaven, and Anatu, his consort, for two shekels. Bel, the great god Bel, who ruleth the evil of the south-west wind—who will give a shekel for Bel? Bel, who alone hath power to dispel the seven evil spirits who seize the body, who bring wastings and fevers, sickness of the head, sickness of the heart, sickness of terror; the ruler of the Seven! Who will buy him for only one shekel? Only one shekel for the great god Bel!"

There were some women passing in the crowd, and as Jediah, contemptuous of this superstition, like all Israelites, paused to listen to the loud cry of the god-seller, one of them stopped and said—

"Wilt thou sell me Bel for half a shekel?"

"Sell the great god Bel for half a shekel!" cried the huckster, making wild gestures of extravagant horror and surprise. "Nay, may the accursed Seven seize me if I will sell him for less than a whole shekel!"

"But a whole shekel is food for a week," replied the woman doubtfully.

"The great god Bel cures hunger for all time."

"But will he make my husband true unto me?" asked the woman, gazing at the little effigy of the god, which the huckster displayed most temptingly before her.

"There is no god like Bel for making husbands true," said the man, with a crafty smile.

"Then I will even take him," said the woman eagerly. "Here is my shekel."

"And here is the great god Bel," cried the huckster, as he took the money and handed to her the image.

Another woman who was standing near now approached and said, in a low voice—

"If indeed Bel keep husbands true, I too will buy him; but I would be sure, and, knowing my husband, I will buy two of the great god Bel. For, of a surety, it will take more than one to keep him faithful."

"Thou art a wise woman, and wilt prosper," said the god-seller, making the exchange.

"Come, child," said the woman to her little one, who was clinging to her robe with one tiny hand.

"May not I too have the great god Bel, my mother?"

"Nay, but thou may'st share mine until thou gettest a husband for thyself."

"But, my mother, I cannot get a husband until I get a lover." And, turning to the god-seller, she lisped—

"Will the great god Bel bring me a lover?"

"Nay, child," he replied, "he is too busy watching the husbands. If thou would'st have one to love thee, buy the goddess of all love, Ishtar."

"But what is her price?"

"Two shekels for Ishtar."

"And I have but half a shekel."

"Will not thy mother"—

"Nay, nay," answered the mother decidedly.

"Then," said the god-seller, "shalt thou have her for thy half shekel ; but, in thy supplications to her, tell her thou did'st pay her full price. Else will she be angry and reject thy prayers."

The child took the goddess eagerly, and she and her mother moved on down the crowded street, worshipping their images and breathing prayers to them.

Jediah, who had watched the scene with a smile of contempt, muttered to himself—

"If the great god Bel could make husbands faithless! Ay, if Johanan could forget Elcia with these women of Babylon, then would I too be like unto these people of superstition."

He regarded the god-seller for a moment, and the man, an evil-looking creature, catching his eye, extended towards him the reed panier, full of images, and began to cry aloud their merits and their powers.

But Jediah turned away and passed on into the crowd, seeking the dwelling of Elcia.

CHAPTER III

ELCIA was housed, for the moment, near the
eastern gate of Babylon, from which departed
the caravans which travelled along the great road
leading from Sardis to Susa. Here passed by
incessantly camels, oxen and asses, and mules
drawing carts and waggons loaded with all descriptions of merchandise. And the cries of the
drivers, the merchants, and the traders made a
continual music that seemed to reach the skies.
They travelled far away, from caravanserai to
caravanserai, to take unto other lands the exports
of Babylon, the marvellous carpets,—celebrated
through all the world,—the silks and the fabrics of
wool, broidered cunningly and woven with strange
designs and with figures of mythic animals, the
richly coloured Sindones and garments of all kinds,
also cylinders and many gems most curiously
engraved.

With some difficulty Jediah made his way
through the thronged and noisy thoroughfares till
he came to the dwelling where he thought to find
Elcia. It stood a little back from the public path,
and was built of bricks soldered together with
white clay. The walls were pierced with very

3

small windows, and in front of the house stood two or three meagre palm trees, whose great leaves, yellow around the edges, looked brittle and ready to crack under the fierce rays of the sun. Upon the door of this dwelling Jediah struck with his staff, and in a moment an elderly man, dressed in a long garment of wool, that flowed nearly to his feet, came and opened to him. Jediah was about to ask if Elcia was within, when she, who had, indeed, been watching anxiously from the house, came hurriedly to him, crying—

"Jediah, Jediah! art thou here at last?"

He took her swiftly by the arm and drew her from the door, glancing behind him as he did so.

"Thou must not be seen," he whispered. "Knowest thou that I have journeyed hither with thy husband?"

The cheek of Elcia grew pale, and she seemed like to fall.

"With Johanan?" she murmured.

"Even so. He careth not for thee, but he is wroth at thy going. And he seeketh thee now to kill thee. Have a care!"

For Elcia had stumbled upon the door-sill, and now swayed forward and must have swooned upon the ground had not Jediah sustained her. She was trembling as in a spasm of deadly fear as he laid her down upon the divan which ran round the room.

"Be not afraid, Elcia," he said, "for I am with thee, and Johanan shall not find thee. He shall go

back to the tents of our people and to the well of
Naomi even as he has come. There shall be no
blood upon his hands. Fear nothing."

But in his heart he said, "Shall Johanan indeed
go back? Shall he indeed ever see again the
tents of his people and Naomi's well?"

And he thought of the god-seller with his face
full of the shadow of evil things, who stood at the
street corner with his basket of images. In this
dim and poorly furnished room he seemed to see the
man, short, broad, with thick eyebrows meeting
above his nose, and long pointed teeth that stuck
out when he smiled upon the superstitious Babylonish women. Why did the vision come to
him? For he desired no image of the great god
Bel. But for the moment he put the thought
from him, turning to Elcia, whose beauty revived
in his heart the passion that was to lead him on so
strange a journey. She had opened her great
eyes, but her fair body was still shaken by a
spasm, and she repeated, with white lips—

"Johanan—Johanan here with thee in Babylon !"

Jediah endeavoured to calm her with fair
words.

" I swear to thee, Elcia," he said, " that within
three days thy husband shall be where he can never
set his eyes on thy sweet face again."

" But where, then, will he go? Nay, if he be
come hither, he will not depart. How knoweth he
that I am indeed in Babylon?"

" He knoweth it not; it is but his fancy. When
he hath searched in the public ways and findeth

thee not, he will surely lose courage and will
depart."

"And he will take thee with him, Jediah. Is it
not so? Ah, why came I hither? Why did I
leave the tents and my people to seek this strange
and terrible city, where the men look so cruelly on
women, and where the noise of voices is as the
noise of the sea, or of the wind that bringeth the
sand out of the desert! I am unhappy here. I
thought that thou would'st never come."

And she clung to him like a child that is afraid
in the night.

He embraced her, saying—

"Trust in me, Elcia. I will not leave thee, and
Johanan shall not set eyes on thee again. Have
no fear. Do not I love thee?"

Then she rested in his arms and dried her tears.
But ever, as she listened to the voices of the
Babylonians without, and to the snarling of the
camels, the rumbling of the waggons towards the
great highway in the plains, and the cries and
vociferations of the traders and drovers, there was
terror in her heart. This world was strange to
her, and seemed as if it would take her to itself to
keep her for ever and to do her injury.

But Jediah was a man, strong, even though with
a strength unholy, bold with women, and unyielding of purpose. He held Elcia fast in his arms,
and he whispered away the sounds of the city, the
cries of those without, even, for a moment, the
terror in the soul of Elcia. He taught her forget-
fulness as the twilight stole along the ways among

the tall houses. She gave up her lips to his lips. She yielded herself to his passion.

At the sunset hour Jediah left her and went forth to return to the caravan to find Johanan. He passed again the god-seller on his way. The man recognised him, and, turning from the women who were round about, intent on the buying of charms and gods, he said to Jediah—

"Cannot I do anything for thee, stranger?"

"Nay," said Jediah, "not to-day."

"To-morrow, then, stranger; I will see thee to-morrow. I have many things that will please thee."

"To-morrow, perchance," Jediah answered, looking into his crafty eyes as one that searcheth for the soul. "To-morrow."

And he went on his way, thinking deeply, while the god-seller turned again to his customers.

That night Jediah and Johanan lay in the house of an Israelite, in a street over against the "House of the Males," a monastic establishment which furnished the great temples of the city with servitors and with singers. They spoke together till far into the darkness, and Johanan unlocked all his heart to Jediah.

"I tell thee, Jediah, that Elcia is indeed here in this great city," he said.

"How knowest thou that, Johanan?" said Jediah, turning uneasily on his mattress, which was laid upon the floor, as was the custom in the poorer houses. "Hath anyone told thee, then?"

"Naught but my heart."

"The heart is the great liar, Johanan. It leadeth men in crooked paths."

And he turned again, as one that seeketh rest in vain.

"It telleth me the truth. She is here, hidden in some strange house of Babylon, and never will I leave the city till I do find her. Nay, Jediah, if I spend here all the days of the years of my earthly pilgrimage, yet will I linger till I see Elcia."

"Stay, then, for ever if thou wilt," Jediah answered. "But perchance thou wilt not see her, nevertheless. Now let us sleep."

And there fell a silence between the two men.

A great bat, which had flown into the room, beat about against the walls all through the night. It was like a spirit of evil, unquiet, and seeking a home. Jediah heard it, for he could not sleep.

In the morning he stood again in the street that was higher than the others, among the press around the god-seller. And the god-seller looked at him and said—

"Thou art come again, stranger. Of a truth thou seekest something of me."

"Peradventure I do. But I cannot tell thee here what I desire. Can I see thee by night?"

"Yea."

"Where dwellest thou?"

"Beside the eastern gate of the city, where go the caravans when they depart for Sardis."

Jediah started.

"Beside the eastern gate? Where is thy house?"

" I lodge with one named Agpul."

" Strange ! " murmured Jediah.

For it was in the house of Agpul that Elcia was bestowed.

" What is strange ?   Must not a man lodge in some house ?   Would you have me sleep here in the street with my gods ?   Is it decent to treat the great god Bel, and Merodach, and Ana, god of heaven, so ? "

" Nay, nay, I meant not that.   I will see thee to - night, after sunset, in the house of Agpul. Farewell."

The god-seller smiled till all the pointed teeth of his mouth peered forth between his thick lips. For he smelt money.   And money was his god. He cared more for it than for the great god Bel, or than for Ana, god of heaven.

That evening, at sundown, when, in the hanging gardens, the wonder of the world, the rich Baby-lonish women walked, attended by those Indian dogs that they so loved, and waited on by Nubian slaves, who fanned them as they looked forth across the city to the river Euphrates and the plain beyond, Jediah, having taken leave of Elcia in the house of Agpul by the eastern gate, stole craftily into the chamber of the god-seller, whose name was Migdapul.

He was not yet returned from his bartering, and Jediah lay down upon a mattress to wait his coming.   The chamber of the god-seller was mean and dark.   Two or three gaudy rugs lay upon the floor of brick.   Very little light entered through the two holes which served as windows. And the air was hot and well - nigh suffocating. On a rudely fashioned table in a corner stood an array of gods, made in cedar wood, bronze, and stone. They stared before them into the dimness with their sightless eyes, and it seemed to Jediah as if they looked into his heart and read the black thoughts that were crowding on his mind as he stretched his limbs along the hard mattress. Under the table that was their home stood a stone pitcher filled with water. Flies buzzed incessantly about the room, as if seeking something that they could not find. They came about Jediah in swarms, desiring to settle on his beard and hands and hair. They disturbed his meditations, and he sprang up angrily and paced to and fro upon the bricks, going softly, for Elcia was lodged near by, and she thought him gone into the city.

The darkness of night came on, and still the god-seller did not return. Jediah grew fiercely impatient, then numb and cold, then dull and heavy, passing through strangely varied changes. At the last, a sense of relief struck him. He suddenly paused in his walk, and, extending his arms, as if in a great sigh of thankfulness, said aloud—

"He cometh not! It is the will of God. He cometh not. I will go forth. I will not do this thing."

And, as he stretched forth his arms, a great load seemed to drop from him—a load that had lain upon his heart cold, heavy, and morose, the load of terror that lies upon the hearts of the wicked and of those who defy the sweet purposes of Heaven.

And there passed from before the eyes of his inner being the vision that had haunted them so long. In this vision he saw himself ever set, a Judge, before his brother Judges, who were become his accusers. He beheld his place upon the height of the Judgment Seat filled by another, who called upon the people over whom he had been lord to pronounce the sentence of his doom. And, looking forth over the sea of faces that encompassed him, he saw, in all the eyes that stared upon him, no soul of pity, no tenderness, no pardon. But the eyes looked death, and the lips cried death, and the souls desired death. Death by stones, cruel, horrible; the crushing of the image of God that should be beautiful, the fierce sending of the man who has done evil unprepared before the throne of the great Judge who will surely judge all the world.

Ah! the veil dropped from his heart. The vision passed. He seemed to see kind eyes and to be near tender hearts.

And he cried again, scarce knowing that words came from him—

" I will not do this thing!"

Even as he spoke, he heard a shuffling tread without. He stood still, listening intently. The step came nearer. The dirty covering at the doorway was pulled aside, and the god-seller entered, bearing his basket of images on his arm, and showing his pointed teeth in an evil smile of welcome.

"Thou art here before me, stranger," he said. And he set down the basket. "It has been an evil day for me. Only two Bels sold for a shekel and Merodachs all left upon my hands. Of a truth, I know not what is come to the people that they buy not my wares. But what desirest thou?"

"I know not if I desire anything," answered Jediah, hesitating and with the speech of a man affrighted.

The god-seller ceased from smiling, and his square face became grim and old.

"Then why comest thou here? For a charm against the wasting sickness?"

"I believe not in thy charms."

"Thou art an Israelite, like the maiden in yonder chamber."

"Hush!"

"Why? What meanest thou? Dost thou know her?"

"It is of her I would speak with thee—of her and of her husband."

"She is married? Then must she buy of me a spell to"—

"Nay, nay. She will buy naught of thee. But I"—

He hesitated.

"Thou wilt buy something? Shall I show thee my"—

But Jediah took him by the arm and whispered in his ear—

"Dost thou do aught save to sell thy gods to fools?   Dost thou not predict things for men?"

"I do.   And I would have thee to know that"—

"And dost thou not help thy prophecies to come true?"

"And what if I do?   Even the gods need the help of men."

"I know a man—draw near, and speak low—I know a man here in this city who seeketh a woman."

"There be many that do that."

"He must not find her."

"Is she in Babylon?"

"She is here in this house."

The god-seller made a gesture with his hand towards the room in which Elcia was lodged.

"The Israelitish woman?"

"Yea.   There be many blind in Babylon?"

"'Tis true.   And 'tis a good trade, better than god-selling.   I would I were blind, for then should I be richer than I am."

"Thou shalt be richer if — if"—

"If what?"

"If thou wilt give one more blind man to Babylon."

"Give a blind man to Babylon?   What meanest thou?"

"This man I told thee of, who seeketh the Israelitish woman, must not see her.   And yet he goeth in the streets, and he is not blind.   How, then, shall he not one day see her?"

Jediah and the god-seller looked at one another in silence. The room was growing dark, and in the darkness sounded the noise of the flies. Jediah bent down and whispered—

"Canst thou not give one more blind man to Babylon? Thou hast said it is a good trade, and better than the selling of gods."

The god-seller nodded.

"And the shekels?" he whispered.

"Thou shalt have much."

Jediah named a sum.

"Wilt thou show me the man?"

"Yea."

"When?"

"To-morrow, when thou criest thy gods in the street, ere the sun is high in the heaven. And now, farewell."

"Stay! The Israelitish woman — doth she know that thou art here?"

"She must not know."

They were in the doorway now, and the god-seller, with his skinny hand, was holding up the covering for Jediah to pass out. In the street they could hear a shrill voice crying with endless repetition one melancholy phrase—

"Help the blind! Help the blind!"

The god-seller smiled.

"Thou hearest?" he said. "It is an omen."

Jediah's face was very white, and he shuddered as if with cold.

"Art thou ill, Israelite?"

"Nay, nay."

Jediah, with a great effort, pulled himself up into an erect attitude. The voice of the beggar died away down the dark street. Then Jediah thought of Elcia, and he whispered into the ear of the god-seller—

"Within three days there must be one more blind man in Babylon."

"There shall be, if thou hast indeed the shekels," said the god-seller.

And letting the ragged covering drop, he turned back into the black chamber in which the flies were now buzzing more drowsily.

On the morrow, Jediah said to Johanan—

"Wilt thou even search for Elcia to-day, Johanan? She is not here in Babylon, be sure; for why should she come hither, and with whom?"

"That I know not, Jediah, but that she is here I know. And each day will I seek until I do find her."

"I will come with thee," answered Jediah, "since thou wilt go. Four eyes are better than two. And if Elcia is indeed here, peradventure I shall see her before thou dost."

"Thou art indeed my friend, Jediah. Let us go forth."

Jediah led Johanan towards the street of the god-seller.

"He is a strange man, who selleth images and charms," he said to Johanan. "And he is ever beset by the women. Peradventure we may find Elcia with him. For Babylon changeth faith, and Elcia is but a woman. She may desire to learn her destiny or to purchase some sorcery to protect her from the danger of the city — if she be here!"

"Ah, let us go thither.   If she be there!   Where is the god-seller, Jediah?   Let us hasten, let us hasten!"

And Johanan drew his companion on almost as one distraught.   For ever he hoped to meet with Elcia.   When they gained the high street, it chanced that Migdapul stood alone with his basket before him.   There were no barterers with him, and no women.   And it seemed indeed as if he had spoken truth when he said that the selling of gods was but a poor trade, and that the people of Babylon sought not after Bel and after Merodach, as in former days.

As they came towards him, Migdapul fastened his small dark eyes on Johanan.   He gave no sign of recognition to Jediah, but began to cry his wares in a loud voice.   And ever his eyes looked at the eyes of Johanan.

"She is not here, Jediah, she is not here," said Johanan.   "Let us go on, let us seek her.   Perchance she is at the eastern side of the city, where go the caravans to the great highway.   I have not sought there yet.   Let us go."

But Jediah laid his hand on Johanan's arm.

"Stay awhile, Johanan," he said.   "All the women of the city seek the god-seller, be it to-day or to-morrow, or be it yesterday.   Perchance he hath seen Elcia here in Babylon.   Demand of him, I beseech thee."

Then Johanan approached the god-seller with eagerness.

"Gods! cheap gods!" vociferated Migdapul. "The cheapest gods in Babylon. Merodach, who "—

"Nay, nay, I want not thy gods; but I would speak to thee a moment," said Johanan. "Thou seest many women? Is it not so?"

"All the women of Babylon come to me. For am not I he who can sell charms against all sickness? Cannot I, with my spells,—the cheapest spells in Babylon,—make the lame to walk and even the blind to see?"

As he spoke the last words he smiled curiously, looking towards Jediah. But Jediah turned away and gazed out over the city.

"I want not thy charms. I would speak with thee of a woman."

"Thou lovest one who is false to thee? Is it not so?"

"How knowest thou that?" said Johanan, starting.

"Cannot I, who live ever with the gods, divine more than other men? She is an Israelitish woman?"

"Yea, yea! Hast thou seen her in Babylon?"

"What like is she?"

"She is beautiful. She hath dark eyes, like the deep waters, but behind them there is fire. Her hair is black as jet, and she bears herself proudly. She is like a queen, more than common tall!"

"What is her name?"

" Elcia."

The god-seller affected a start of surprise.

" Elcia ! Elcia ! Nay, now, by the great god Bel, it seems to me that I—and yet "—

He paused, as one plunged in deep and anxious meditation.   Johanan regarded him with a terrible anxiety.

" Thou hast seen her !—thou hast seen her !" he cried out. " Tell me—where is she? Lead me to her, I beseech thee !"

But the god-seller, holding up his skinny hand, checked the fervour of Johanan.

" I do not say so," he answered. " But it seemeth to me that thou art right, and that there is such a woman here in Babylon."

He stopped.   Then he continued abruptly—

" Tell me, Israelite,—hast thou no faith in my spells, no belief in my divining power? For, if not, I cannot aid thee. But "—

" Yea—yea—speak on !"

" If thou hast faith, I may do what thou desirest. I may even find this woman for thee."

At these words Jediah turned round from gazing on the city, and his face was dark with anger and with fear. The god-seller reassured him with a glance, then continued to Johanan—

' But thou must come to me at night, and alone."

" I will come. But may not I bring my friend Jediah ?"

" Doth he desire to companion thee ? "

" Nay, nay, Johanan," said Jediah hastily. " Go thou alone, if indeed thou believest in the charms.

of a false religion. I will have naught to do with this."

"I must believe. I will," said Johanan.

Then he lowered his voice and said to Jediah apart—

"This man is not like unto other men. Did he not tell me I loved one who is false to me?"

"'Tis true."

"How should he know it if he be not of a truth a diviner? I will go to him, Jediah, by night and alone."

"As thou wilt, Johanan. But I will have naught to do with this thing."

"Whither shall I go, O god-seller?" said Johanan, "and at what hour of the night?"

"Meet me here when the sun goeth down, when the river Euphrates is red as with blood. And I will lead thee to the dwelling of a sorcerer who knoweth more of secret things than any man in Babylon. Together will he and I cast a spell and set the woman thou seekest before thee as in a vision. In a dream shalt thou see the place where she abideth."

"Thou art indeed a worker of miracles. I will be with thee at sundown."

Johanan turned to go. As Jediah passed by the god-seller, he whispered to him—

"Thou wilt do as thou said'st to me? Remember he is poor and cannot pay thee."

And the god-seller answered—

"Ere three days are over I will give one more blind man to Babylon."

4

And then, once more, he began to cry aloud the merits of his gods.

At sundown, when the great river Euphrates was red as with blood, Johanan bade farewell to Jediah and departed to seek the god-seller.

"I will see thee again ere the dawn cometh, Jediah," he said, in going.

And Jediah looked at him and said—

"Art thou sure of that, Johanan?"

"Or to-morrow."

Then an impulse of horror seized Jediah and he caught Johanan by the skirt and cried—

"Go not to the god-seller, Johanan. Thou knowest him not. He may be a man of evil, with his false gods and his sorceries and his divining that cometh surely from the Wicked One. Stay here, I beseech thee."

But Johanan answered—

"Nay, I must even go. For hath he not promised to show unto me Elcia in a vision, or in a dream of the night? Farewell, Jediah; I will see thee in the dawn."

And he drew his garment from the hand of Jediah and departed.

The sun was red in the sky. There was a noise of sailors' voices singing on the great river. Jediah stood in the door watching Johanan as he went down the street, and murmuring—

"I will see thee in the dawn. I will see thee in the dawn."

That night he did not close his eyes, but tossed on his mattress upon the floor. The great bat wheeled and circled about the room, stirring the hot air with its dusky wings. The sweat stood upon Jediah's brow and his eyes stared, as if he saw something terrible in the darkness. He dreaded the coming of the dawn. Horror invaded his heart, and he counted the hours till the air seemed to grow colder in presage of the morning. He listened, straining his ears. But there was no sound without. All Babylon seemed to be sleeping ; princes in their palaces and hucksters in their hovels, trader and noble, law-giver and law-breaker. It was deadly silent. Only the bat stirred and seemed to grow ever wilder in its flight. It beat the walls and uttered a remote and yet penetrating little cry that was like a cry of pain or fear. To Jediah it was as the cry of a spirit. His hair shifted upon his head and he sat up on his mattress, supporting himself with his hands. Why did he listen? What did he expect to hear ? The call of a man in the street without or the song of a woman by her window? No, he listened not for that. The air now seemed to him to become very cold, damp also, as wind that bloweth from a river or from the long marshes where the mists sleep in the darkness. He knew that the dawn was very near, and he thought of the words of Johanan, " I will see thee in the dawn." He was listening for the footfalls of Johanan. Each moment he expected to hear them, far away, at the end of the thoroughfare, passing before the portals of the " House of the Males." Now he saw a very faint glimmer in the narrow apertures of the wall and the grotesque shadow of the bat passing and repassing, swaying and darting. The glimmer grew, and ever as it grew Jediah listened more intently, leaning forward with lips apart and muscles braced and tightened till they stood up upon his body. And as the first beam of light appeared he did indeed hear a distant footstep. It was far away, but coming slowly onward, slowly, slowly down the street. It drew nearer and nearer, and Jediah muttered to himself, "It is he! It is Johanan!"

How loud it was now, beating in his ears like the drums beaten in the processions of the great god Bel. It deafened him. It sounded in his heart. He covered his ears with his hands, and his hands were cold and damp with the dews of terror. And the noise of the feet ceased. Surely Johanan was stopping before the house. He would strike upon the door with his staff now. He would strike. Jediah strained his ears. There came a hard knock upon the outer door, and then a voice, like the voice of one who wailed aloud in horrible despair, cried—

"Help the blind!"

Throwing his hands abroad as if to ward off a blow, Jediah sank back upon his mattress, burying himself in the coarse woollen covering, hiding his eyes from the light, closing his ears from the voice. But he still heard it pealing like a trumpet in his soul—

"Help the blind! Help the blind!"

CHAPTER IV

THREE months later Jediah returned alone to the tents of his people. His face was lined as with care, and he appeared to be already older by some years than when he departed from the well of Naomi with Johanan to seek Elcia in the great city of Babylon. So deeply doth sin weigh upon the shoulders of a man and steal into the secret places of his heart. Those months in Babylon had been ever fraught with anxiety and burdened with horror. Ever had Jediah heard the distant sound of footsteps, the beating of a staff upon a door, the terrible and despairing cry of a man that is blind. Even the pressure ot the arms of Elcia had not availed to keep out the sound that haunted him like a cruel echo by day and by night. Indeed, when he was with Elcia in the house the terror came more near, and he felt that the blind man entered and stood at his side, gazing upon him with eyes that were sightless, and that yet could see into his very soul Sometimes he cried aloud, and started up trembling. And Elcia was affrighted, and asked him—

" What is ill with thee, Jediah ? Thou starest as if someone were before thee."

And he answered her—

"And is there not indeed someone — there — there?"

"Nay, there is nothing. Turn thee, and sleep again."

And she laid her hand upon the dews of his forehead, and gave him to drink. But sleep came not to the porches of his eyes, and ever the horror gathered more thickly about his heart, till he could neither rest nor be at peace for a moment. Then he grew to hate the woman for desire of whom he had betrayed the man who trusted in him, and to hate himself when he was with her. He was cruel and bitter to her, till she trembled at his approach and would have fled at the sound of his voice. And at last he rose in the night, while she slept, and stole from the dwelling-house like a thief fearing discovery, and, finding a caravan that was setting forth from Babylon to gather in tribute from the captive Israelites, he joined it, and returned alone to the tents of his people and to Zoar his father. Zoar was glad at his return, for he loved him, and Naomi, the wife of Zoar, stepmother to Jediah and own mother to Lemuel, who was yet a lad and away from the tents, shepherd to an Israelite afar among the hills — Naomi wept with joy. For, though she loved best her own son Lemuel, yet she loved also Jediah, deeming him a man of great virtue, and one to whom the whole tribe looked as Lord and Judge. Yet soon she learned to fear Jediah, who was now ever stern and cold, relentless as law-giver and hard to those about him. Sometimes she asked Zoar—

"What has come to thy son Jediah, O my husband?"

And Zoar answered her—

"He that is Judge is not as other men. From him cometh the law, and he holdeth in his hands the scales of Justice. How, then, should he be soft in heart, inclining ever to mercy, as doth a woman?"

Then Naomi bowed her head in the tent, and said—

"Thou art right, O my husband. Jediah is not as other men, but a Judge in Israel."

Now in Israel there was a law which was thus written :—

"If a damsel be betrothed unto a man, and another man take her, then shall ye bring them both out unto the gate of the city, and ye shall stone them with stones, that they both die."

It chanced that, soon after the return of Jediah from Babylon, a certain Israelite had stolen from his own brother the maiden to whom that one was betrothed, and had taken her unto himself in love. Therefore the brother came up unto Jediah, demanding the punishment of these guilty ones according to the law of his fathers.

"Justice, O Jediah!" he cried aloud. "My joy is taken from me, my peace is broken upon the earth for ever. Give me justice!"

And Jediah answered him—

"Fear not. Thou shalt have justice while I am a law-giver in Israel."

Then he called together the Judges, and convoked all the people for a certain day to gather about the Judgment Seat that was set in the midst of the plain before the tents. And on the day appointed he went forth from his tent, wrapping his robe about him. His face was stern and cold. His lips were set in his beard, and his eyes, fierce as the eyes of a hawk when it falleth upon its prey, stared before him, looking neither to the right hand nor to the left. All those that saw him feared him that day, and even the little children shrank to the side of the way when he approached. When he came in sight of the Judgment Seat he saw that there was a great crowd about it, and he heard the murmur of many voices, like the long murmur of the waves of the sea upon the sand. For all the people had come in from their labours in the fields, and from tending the flocks and the herds, to hear the pronouncing of the Judgment, and to assist at the payment of the penalty, if indeed the sentence of the law should be given. Here were all the shepherds and the drovers, those that planted, and those that drove the asses and that laded the camels, old and young, men, women, and children — all were gathered about the Judgment Seat. There, too, was Zoar, with his wife Naomi. And with them there was a very young maiden, by name Elna, one of the most beautiful of all the daughters of Israel. Her hair was dark, and flowed down upon her shoulders almost to her feet. She had blue eyes, and her mouth was like a flower. But now her cheek was pale, and in her eyes the tears were gathering. For she had great fear of the terrors of the inexorable Law, and knew not what was to come. The Judgment Seat was a great seat of stone, and before it there was a step. And at the foot of this step, in the midst of all the people, watched by all eyes, spoken of by all lips, stood together the man and the woman who were to be judged. They looked not up, but cast their eyes down to the ground, longing to hide themselves from the press of the people, and from the gaze of those who regarded them so pitilessly. As Jediah drew near there was a murmur from the crowd, who drew aside to let him pass to join the other Judges. These stood together by the Judgment Seat, with the priest of the tribe, and with the elders of the people. Then the trumpet sounded, and the Judges mounted upon their seat, Zoar being in the midst, with Jediah upon his right hand. And the priest cried aloud—

"Blessed be the name of the Lord!"

And all the people answered and said—

"We praise His holy name."

Only the man and the woman were silent, trembling in the knowledge of their guilt and of the punishment that was to come upon them. And the tears welled up under the white lids of the eyes of the young maiden Elna, who stood with Naomi, and ran down upon her cheeks. For she was pitiful and tender-hearted.

Then rose up a Judge, and he said—

"Men of Israel, of the house of Zoar! If a man is betrothed unto a woman, and another man take her, what shall be their punishment?   What saith the law?"

"Their punishment shall be death."

And the Judge said, speaking with a loud voice that all might hear him—

"Shall they not be stoned with stones until they die?"

And all the people cried out—

"They shall be stoned with stones until they die."

Then the Judge said, turning to him that was betrothed to the maiden who was now summoned to judgment—

"Speak thou, Manael.   Testify the wrong that hath been done to thee."

And Manael, standing by the Judgment Seat, said with exceeding great bitterness—

"I, Manael, eldest born of my father's house, a tender of flocks and of herds in Israel, do testify and do swear that I was betrothed unto this maid, Martha, by my father Abirah.   Answer, O my father.   Did'st thou not indeed give this woman unto me for wife?"

Then Abirah, a man well stricken in years, testified and said—

"It is true.   I did give this woman unto thee."

Then the Judge said to the maiden—

"Answer thou, O woman.   Wast not thou betrothed unto this man, Manael, by his father Abirah?"

And the maiden bowed her head and said in a voice scarce audible—

"Yea."

Then the Judge said to the man—

' And thou—answer thou.   Did'st thou not know that this woman was betrothed unto thy brother?"

And the man answered—

" I did know it."

" And, knowing it, did'st thou steal her from thy brother and take her unto thyself in love?"

And the man answered—

" Yea."

Then the Judge, turning to his brethren upon the Judgment Seat, said unto them—

"What shall be the sentence of the law upon this man and this woman?"

And the Judges answered and said—

" They shall be taken out and stoned with stones that they both die."

Only Jediah answered not with the others.   His throat was dry and parched as the wind in the desert, and there was a singing within his ears. And it seemed to him as if he stood at the step of the Judgment Seat, and that all the people looked upon him and cried, " He is guilty!   Let him go forth and be stoned with stones until he die."

" Jediah, son of Zoar, thou that art a Judge in Israel, why answerest thou not?   What shall be the sentence upon this man and this woman?"

Then Jediah called upon his soul, and said in a low voice that the people could not hear—

"They shall both be stoned with stones that they—may—die."

And he sank back in his seat and put his hands

before his face. For he seemed to pronounce his own condemnation.

Then the Judge, for the last time, turned to the people and said unto them—

"What shall be done unto this man and unto this woman?"

And all the people answered—

"They shall be stoned with stones that they may die."

Then the Judge cried and said to the people—

"It is finished. Let justice be done in the name of the Lord."

And the trumpet sounded and the priest said in a loud voice—

"Praise the name of the Lord!"

And all the people answered and said—

"We praise His holy name."

Then all the Judges stood up in the Judgment Seat, and the people ran from every side; the elders and the fathers, and the men come in from the fields and from far off in the plains, the camel-drivers and the shepherds and many women. Yea, the women were in the forefront of the press. And they laid their hands upon the young man and the maiden who stood before the Judgment Seat. And they all cried aloud—

"To the place of stones! To the place of stones!"

Then the maiden screamed with terror, and cried for mercy; but the people heeded her not. But they seized and carried her, dragging her from the Judgment Seat. And they tore the young man from her, buffeting him and grasping him with their hands. And he too called for mercy, repenting of what he had done. And stretching out his arms to the Judges, who stood ever upon the lofty seat, he caught the skirt of Jediah's robe with his fingers, crying in a lamentable voice—

"Mercy, Jediah, son of Zoar! Mercy! mercy!"

Then Jediah leaned down where he stood, and tore away his robe from the grasp of the young man, and thrust him backwards down among the press of the people, and cried out—

"Not mercy, but justice!"

And all the people caught up the cry and shouted—

"Not mercy, but justice! Justice in Israel! Justice! justice!"

Only the young maid Elna joined not her voice with the others. She wept bitterly and clung to Naomi, hiding her face that she might not see the tumult and the seizing of these guilty ones. But when she heard this great shout, she, with her weak voice of a child, cried—

"Nay, nay. Mercy! mercy!"

Jediah heard her, and he turned him on the Judgment Seat and looked down to where she was standing. Her face, soft as a flower, was turned upward to him as if in appeal. The tears streamed down upon her tender cheeks, and when she saw that Jediah looked at her, she held forth her two little hands towards him and cried again with all her strength—

"Help them! Help them! Mercy! mercy!"

Her cry struck like a sharp blade of steel into his heart. He sprang forward as if he would arrest the throng who were hurrying towards the place of stones. But he was powerless. Already the guilty maiden, half dead with fear, was being borne beyond his sight. He saw her white face, like the face of a corpse, tossed upon the sea of humanity as a lily upon the waves of the stormy deep. He saw her arms hanging, her long hair, in which rude hands were thrust, flowing down among the trampling feet of the shrieking crowd. She fell, and was raised up again and carried onward to meet her doom. And behind her, the young man who had loved her to their undoing was hurried onward with blows and with scornful words. He too was pale, and his eyes stared before him, but there was courage in his face. Now that death was close upon him, he called upon all the strength of his heart. He bore himself as a man should, and there was even a sort of glory upon him, as if, by paying the penalty of his sin, he was purged from his sin and could look upward again to the great God of his fathers and say with confidence—

"Thou wilt pardon me!"

He disappeared from the eyes of Jediah. There fell a silence. And then there was the sound of stones dropping upon the hard ground. And then there was again a silence.

Jediah stepped down slowly from the Judgment Seat. His limbs were trembling, but his face was grave and stern as he came up to Naomi. The little maid Elna sprang towards him, sobbing and seizing his robe with her tiny hands. Hiding her face there, she cried—

"Oh, save them—save them! Mercy! mercy!"

And then she wailed bitterly. Jediah took her by the hand and lifted her in his arms. Her childish beauty spoke to his heart. Her bitter grief moved his stern nature.

"There is no mercy for the wicked," he said. "Knowest thou not that?"

The child only wept the more. Then it seemed as if a voice that he would fain have put from him spoke within Jediah, out of his soul, whether he would or no. And he said—

"The deeds that we do, whether good or evil, return to us again to give us our reward. They may tarry long on their journey, as tarry the great caravans that come from the desert. And per-adventure we may say unto ourselves that they will never come. But there surely dawneth a day when they do stand before us, and in their hand they do bear the gift—life for the good, death for the evil."

He ceased from speaking. And then suddenly a great fear came upon him. He put down the little maid from his arms, and he went away alone into the darkness of his tent.

And that night he wept sore. And his soul was full of terror.

CHAPTER V

FOUR years passed, with their sixteen seasons of labours in the fields and pleasures in the city, their births, marriages, and deaths. Elcia had never returned from distant Babylon to the tents of her kindred. Nor had Jediah again gone up unto Babylon. He knew not the measure of her fate. He had forgotten her beauty. The voice of his passion for her had long been silent in his heart. But the voice of his conscience was not stilled by the years. He was become a hard and a morose man, inflexible even to cruelty as a Judge, and reserved to those about him. Yet, although all tenderness seemed to have been driven out from his soul, the murmur of desire that is natural in man was wakeful in him as the murmur is wakeful in the sea; and when the maiden Elna, who had so wept at the bitter scene of the judgment in the plains, grew up into the first fulness of beauty, Jediah cast his eyes upon her and desired her to be his wife. She knew not love, being so youthful. Nor did she know at all what joy life can bring to a maid when she loves. So, when Jediah asked her in marriage, she knew not how to say him nay; and

Zoar, his father, betrothed them, as was the custom in Israel. Yet was Elna ever afraid of the hardness of Jediah and of the fierceness of his eyes, in which seemed to burn a light more pitiless than the light of any torch, and of the sound of his voice, which was cold as the night wind that blows out of the desert. Nevertheless did she look up to and respect him. For he was a Judge and law-giver in Israel, and a man of consideration to all his tribe. But respect is not love. And this Elna knew, to the sorrow of her heart, when she knew Lemuel, own son to Naomi and half-brother to Jediah.

This one, who had been long away from the tents, serving a master as shepherd of the flocks, returned to the tents of his father and of his mother soon after the betrothal of Jediah with Elna. He was now a man, strong of courage, stalwart and well-knit of figure, with a brave and open countenance and a heart fearless as a lion's. His brown hair clustered thickly about his brows. The muscles of his arms were as iron, his voice was clear as the voice of a bell, and his heart was hot with the fire of patriotism. He loved his country and his people with no ordinary love such as loses itself in words and in useless regrets. Their captivity in a land of bondage oppressed him as a sad and baleful dream oppresses a sleeper in the watches of the night. And the longing of his soul was to free them from this bondage in which they laboured, and to set them again in their own country.

5

Gifted with eloquence and with the power of moving the heart of crowds, dauntless in courage, shrinking from no labour, and careless of fatigue, Lemuel, although young in years, was already looked to by many as a regenerator and as a possible Messiah. He was known among all the Israelites. Men spoke of him—whispering low—in Babylon. Some said he was a prophet inspired by God. Others that he was a dreamer and a visionary. But all his people knew the courage that burned in him like a flame, and the single-purposed devotion that set him apart from his brethren. They loved him. And Elna, when she saw him, loved him too.

That was terrible to her. For now was she betrothed to his brother Jediah, and must not look at any other man. And Lemuel, deep in his soul, loved Elna, youth drawing instinctively towards youth and single heart to single heart. But he put the thought of the maiden from him, busying himself with his labours in the fields and among the brethren. For there was now a widely extending movement in Israel, secret and ever surreptitious, yet persistent and hopeful, towards freedom. Already there were men who looked forward to the end of captivity, and women who whispered to their little ones that they should not die—as they were born—in slavery. A strange hope ran through Israel, murmured from mouth to mouth, in the ways of Babylon and among the green corn in the fields, and on the waters of the river Euphrates, and in the silent places among the hills. A glowing confidence arose—how or why, men could not tell. Perhaps it came from the courage of Lemuel. For one man can set a spark to a torch that will light a world. One man that truly believes can create belief in a universe of men. And at the time now written of hope grew ever in Israel, and there were many secret conclaves both in Babylon and in the surrounding country.

One afternoon, towards the sunset hour, some Israelites were gathered about the well of Naomi. Hezron, a shepherd, seated upon a stone, was playing a melancholy air upon a reed pipe, cunningly fashioned and tinted a pale green. Ababa and other Israelites were lying upon the warm ground, fashioning packs for camels. Some women were drawing water from the well to fill the pitchers which they bore upon their heads, and three or four little children played gaily together among the palm trees. Their laughter and their merry shouting rang out in the evening air. They knew naught of slavery, naught of the grinding misery of those who dwell in bondage. They danced to Hezron's pipe and chattered together as happily as if they were in their own land, far from the whip of the taskmaster and from the voice of the oppressor. But their mothers often gazed at them with sorrow and kissed them with tears. And then, for a moment, they too looked sorrowful, wondering as children will, and sensitive to the grief of those about them.

Presently Hezron put down his pipe, as Sabaal, followed by three or four men bearing water-skins, came towards the well of Naomi, saying—

"Haste, haste! Hither, idlers! Help to fill these skins. The Lord Alorus is at hand with his taskmasters. If thou would'st not taste their whips, to work!"

Sabaal was a slave to Alorus, who was a great lord in Babylon, and was now come hither with his master, who was gathering in tribute from Israel.

"Nay, Sabaal," said Adoram, another Israelite, "let not the Babylonians use their whips on us. We are not the slaves of Alorus as thou art. We are free."

Sabaal turned upon him with a sort of fury, and his face, cunning and sinister, was dark with anger, as he replied—

"Free art thou! An Israelite, and free! Free! Ay, and for that thou payest tribute unto Babylon—in flocks, in herds, in corn, and in toil. Thou art free, O sons of Israel, and therefore thy best bone and sinew goeth to Babylon, to hew her stone, bake her bricks, and build her palaces, while thy fairest daughters are stolen to fill them! Free! Ay, even as Israel was free in Egypt before the prophet led her chosen people through the Red Sea out into the wilderness. Free! Babylon holds thee beneath her feet; ye are slaves—slaves—slaves! And ye sleep and rot in her chains. Will ye never awake?"

"Ay, Sabaal," answered Adoram, "ay, when

that a second Messiah doth come to tell us the dawn is at hand."

Sabaal paused by the well for a moment, as if in thought. Then he said in an under voice—

"Both prophet and dawn may be nearer than thou thinkest, Adoram."

"Prophet! Dost thou mean Lemuel?" said Adoram eagerly.

"Hold thy peace! hold thy peace!" returned Sabaal quickly.

He turned again towards the men with the water-skins, crying—

"Haste with those skins! Haste! haste!"

There was a bustle round about the well. The men bent to draw the water, filling the mighty skins till they swelled into strange and bloated shapes. While they were thus occupied, Sabaal, speaking aside to another Israelite, one named Ahira, whispered—

"Find a time to speak with me alone. I will place thee near me on our march. If thou art a true son of Israel, thou may'st help her prophet yet."

Ahira's dark face and brilliant eyes gleamed with a light of energy. He bent his head in response, but he uttered no word. And Sabaal, moving away from him, pushed the men with the water-skins from the wellside, crying aloud in a strident voice—

"Haste, men, haste! Thou—and thou!"

The men hurried at his bidding, and he drove them on before him towards the camp of the

Lord Alorus. Hezron, who had laid down his pipe and had risen from the stone on which he had been seated, watched the retreating form of Sabaal till it disappeared in the distance and the sound of his shouting voice died away into silence; then he turned to a woman, Tirzah, and said—

"That is a strange man, that Sabaal; strange and violent. He hath been much with Lemuel since the Lord Alorus brought him hither. Time after time among the palm trees have I seen them in close converse, and ever have they parted hastily when discovered."

"Nay, but that is a strange thing, Hezron," answered Tirzah; "for what can there be in common between Lemuel and Sabaal, slave to Alorus?"

"I know not," answered Hezron.

"It seemeth to me," said Ahira, who was seated on the fallen trunk of a giant palm, "that Lemuel desireth, peradventure, to learn news of Babylon, of her people and of her ways. 'Tis a dangerous and terrible city to the stranger within its gates. And they say that no man who tarrieth there for long ever returns unchanged."

While he was speaking, some women passed by towards the well, bearing their pitchers. They lingered, giving heed to the conversation as the sun sank lower in the sky.

"Nay," rejoined Tirzah; "but what of our Lord Jediah? In the years that are gone he went up to Babylon—ay, and he tarried there a long time."

“ And sayest thou that he returned to our tents unchanged, Tirzah ? ”

“ Nay, now I bethink me, he came back stern and hard, and, being Judge, showed himself the most severe and unrelenting in all Judea. But what could Babylon have to do with that ? ”

“ Ask Sabaal,” responded Ahira mysteriously. “ Trust him who hath fallen himself to be most unmerciful to others.”

All the Israelites who stood listening gathered more closely about the speaker, with exclamations of wonder and of excitement. And Tirzah cried out—

“ Fallen ! Jediah, our Lord and Judge, fallen ? What art thou saying ? ”

“ What I do know. Sabaal hath been long slave in Babylon, and he knoweth many in the city, ay, even the Babylonians. For he is a cunning man and full of craft.”

“ And what saith Sabaal, Ahira ? ”

“ When Elcia, wife of Johanan, fled our tents and went to Babylon, it was at the bidding of Jediah.”

“ Nay,” cried Tirzah, “ such a thing is not possible ! ”

“ Sabaal hath told me that it was so. He learned it from one Migdapul, a Babylonian, who selleth gods to the foolish women of the city.”

“ But Johanan went up to Babylon with our Lord Jediah.”

“ Ay, and what befell him there ? Someone in the city seized him, and, carrying him into a secret place, put out his eyes.”

"But why did they do this dreadful thing, Ahira?"

"That he might not find Elcia."

"And by whose order was it done?"

"'Twas never known. Some say it was the deed of Elcia."

"A maiden! Nay, nay; such work is not for women."

"And some say"—here he lowered his voice and looked cautiously around—"some say that Jediah himself was the cause."

"Better had they slain him at once," exclaimed Tirzah.

"True, but men fear blood-guiltiness."

"How horrible! How horrible!"

"Mayhap it was Johanan's sight against Jediah's life, and "—

"And 'if a damsel is betrothed unto one man, and another take her, then shall ye bring them both out unto the gates of the city, and ye shall stone them with stones until they die.' Thus saith the law."

"Ay," said Ahira, breaking into a grim laugh. "And yet, how men will risk even stoning unto death—when they do love! Now "—

He paused, looking at the women who stood near. They moved onward to the well, and he continued—

"Lemuel loveth his brother's betrothed, Elna "—

"What!" exclaimed Tirzah. "Hush! What art thou saying?"

"The very truth, I do assure thee. Hast thou

not eyes to see?   And Elna, betrothed unto Jediah, loveth Lemuel."

" Silence !   To say that is to endanger Lemuel's life and the hopes of captive Israel.   But lo! here cometh Elna.   If she should have heard thee!"

Indeed at this moment Elna came towards the well.   She was now a lovely maiden.   Her face was oval and fair-complexioned, with dark blue eyes under long lashes.   Her figure was tall and slim almost as a boy's, and her long curling black hair streamed down over her shoulders and made a cloud above her white and noble brow.   Her expression was innocent and tender, but rather sad, as if some secret apprehension oppressed her. Now, as she came forward to the two men, she said anxiously—

" What sayest thou ?   What danger threateneth Lemuel ? "

" Nay,   nay — heed   not,   Elna," said   Tirzah hastily.

The women from the well had once again drawn near.   Elna looked round upon them questioningly as she repeated—

" What danger unto Lemuel ?   Why do you all look so strange ?   What danger ?   Speak thou, Ahira."

" Nay, 'tis but maids' gossip," answered Ahira cautiously.   " But, in very sooth, Babylon is a dangerous place for one like Lemuel, who loves his people.   Our brothers groan in slavery under the Babylonish yoke—it may be, when Lemuel comes among them that they will turn to Zoar's son as unto a new deliverer. Is not that danger enough?"

"Alas!" said Elna, with agitation, "and Lemuel will not pause to think of danger."

"Lemuel is brave, reckless. He needs a friend to teach him caution," said Tirzah. "But is he indeed resolved to leave all and go to Babylon?"

"Yea, he is resolved," said Elna.

"Who goeth with him?" asked Tirzah.

"None. He goeth alone."

"Nay," interrupted Ahira, "he will go with Alorus, and Alorus is mighty in Babylon."

"Alorus may be his host," said Elna, still with great anxiety, "but Alorus is of the oppressors—not of our people. His hand would be raised against Lemuel, not for him, did Lemuel strive for freedom."

"Hush!" said Tirzah. "Here be Zoar and Jediah."

As she spoke, those that were gathered around her moved off to their work, but not ere Jediah, whose fierce eyes had seen their idleness, had cried out—

"To your work! Must the sun go down ere the herds be watered? Hence!"

Then he turned towards Zoar and spoke with him in a low voice.

Zoar was now become very old. His long white beard flowed down upon his breast. His gait was somewhat feeble, and his sight was growing dim. But his spirit was still proud and unquenchable, his heart still kind and just. He was respected by all, but—more—he was beloved. Jediah too was greatly aged in the years that had passed since his return from Babylon. His hair was streaked here and there with grey. His face had become more rugged and forbidding, his mouth hard and lined. But his tall figure was erect and his aspect commanding. He looked a man born to rule, and certain to rule cruelly. Now he gazed in surprise at Elna, who had fallen on her knees at the feet of Zoar, crying—

"A boon, my father!"

"What is thy need, my daughter?" answered Zoar tenderly.

She cast a frightened and abashed glance towards Jediah. Then she replied—

"I beseech thee, my lord, let not Lemuel, thy son, go forth to Babylon unattended."

"What matter is it of thine what Lemuel doth?" interrupted Jediah sternly.

Elna rose from her knees, but still gazed imploringly at Zoar, as she said—

"Is it not ordained that I wed his brother? And may not a sister "—

"My mother needs thee," Jediah said roughly. "My father and I have weightier matters "—

"What weightier matters than my brother's safety canst thou have, O my lord?" asked Elna, striving to control her emotion.

"The sons of Zoar are not wont to seek their safety at the hands of their women," said Jediah, casting a piercing glance upon her.

"But, tell me, daughter," said Zoar, sitting down

upon a tree trunk to rest his aged limbs, "tell me what peril threatens Lemuel."

"O my father, it is said among the people that our brethren who are slaves in Babylon may look to the coming of Lemuel as to a deliverer."

"That is but the gossip of the women," said Jediah. "Go hence, Elna."

But Elna, carried away by her emotion, heeded not his command. She seized the thin and wrinkled hand of Zoar, and reiterated in a trembling voice—

"Zoar, I beseech thee, hearken unto thy servant!"

"Go hence," said Jediah, more roughly. "Art thou betrothed unto me and dost not obey the words of my mouth?"

"But—but"—

She still hesitated, trembling but determined. And at this moment Lemuel himself entered, bearing in his mighty arms a lamb of the flocks that was sick and that he tended with all the care and love of a woman. For he was kind to all things that were weak and suffering. Jediah cast a dark glance upon him, and then said sternly—

"I have spoken!"

"Brother!" said Lemuel, looking with deep pity at the beautiful eyes of Elna, which were full of tears.

"Go hence!" exclaimed Jediah furiously, with a movement towards Elna as if to thrust her away.

"Elna," said Lemuel gently, interposing himself

between them, "my mother calls thee. Go to her."

Elna stood still for a moment, looking up into his face. Then she turned away to go, murmuring—

"My lord, I obey."

"Stay, Elna," said Jediah, taking a sudden step forward towards her, "stay! Tell us—whom dost thou obey?"

And he glanced jealously from her to Lemuel, who had set down the lamb under the shade of a bush and now stood with his bare arms folded and his eyes fixed ever on Elna.

The maiden hesitated, casting down her eyes.

"Whom?" reiterated Jediah.

"Him who is my lord," Elna replied at length, in a very low voice.

And then, without daring to lift her eyes, she turned away and disappeared among the trees, going towards the tents.

"Him who is my lord?" said Jediah. "Lord of what? Her body or her soul?"

And he looked at Lemuel, as if for an answer.

"Why speak so harshly to Elna, my brother?" said Lemuel quietly.

"I spoke to my betrothed wife. Must I fashion my words to please thee?"

Lemuel seemed about to make a hot reply to the sneering question, but with an effort he controlled himself, and, going up to Zoar, who still sat, resting, upon the tree trunk, said to him—

"Of what was Elna speaking, my father?"

"Of Babylon and of our brethren who are bond-slaves there, my son—and of their dreams."

"What are their dreams, my father?"

"They do dream of a deliverer."

"Ah!" said Jediah, with cynical bitterness. "They wait for a deliverer! Now, as ever, there is one to come who will restore Israel and make her again a nation. Dreams indeed! Dreams!"

"Dreams!" said Lemuel, and a great light came into his eyes, as if he saw some bright and beautiful vision afar off among the coloured clouds of the fair evening sky. "It may be, but so they dreamed in Egypt, and the deliverer came. Father! father! a new prophet hath arisen in the land, and he hath foretold the fall of the mighty—yea, even of Babylon—and the coming together of the tribes of Israel. Thus hath he spoken: 'He that scattered Israel will gather him, and keep him, as a shepherd doth his flock. And He will turn his mourning into joy, and will comfort him, and he shall come again from the land of the enemy.'"

"Dreams, I tell thee," said Jediah scornfully. "Dreams! dreams! Shall we go up against Babylon with our reaping-hooks and with our sickles? And shall her walls and her gates open at our approach? Shall the shepherd's crook indeed prevail against the sword and the spear?"

"So the shepherd David prevailed against the giant of the Philistines," answered Lemuel, with a brave enthusiasm. "Israel a nation!"

He clasped his hands together as if he prayed,

and his whole countenance was inspired with glowing courage and hope. But Jediah, crossing over to the well and taking in his hand a pitcher, answered coldly—

"Israel will be no more a nation. God's curse is upon the people."

He bent down his head to drink. Then, lifting himself up again, he added—

"Go up unto Babylon, brother. Behold her in her mightiness, and then return unto our tents to toil for her tribute."

"Tribute!" said Zoar feebly. "Ay, while ye are talking, the Lord Alorus waits for our tribute, and it is yet uncounted. Come, Jediah, thine arm. Lemuel, my son, put all these vain dreams from thee. Hearken not unto them. Be not deceived by the diviners and the false prophets that tell thee, 'Thou shalt not serve the king that reigneth in Babylon.' For it is the Lord's will. Even so doth He punish us for our transgressions. Submit thy neck to the yoke, my son. Submit in patience."

He rose up slowly and heavily, for he was old and weary. Then leaning upon the arm of Jediah, he walked away, repeating in a feeble voice—

"Submit, ay—the yoke—the yoke!"

But Lemuel remained alone beside the well, nothing daunted. For he was young and brave and strong. Life lay before him with all its shining deeds and golden promises — life, with its mighty struggles and its great achievements. How then could he fear?

"Submit!" he said to himself. "Nay, is not this submission itself a sin? Ever in bondage! As we served in Egypt, so now we serve in Babylon. And there is no strange nation that is not strong enough to make Israel a slave. But—but"— and he smiled with a proud confidence—"it is not for ever. It shall not be for ever. Ah, Sabaal! is it thou?"

Sabaal came to the well swiftly, and sat down at its edge, by Lemuel, who continued—

"Ah, Sabaal! is it but a dream, as my father telleth me? Are we born slaves? Is bondage our inheritance? Are my father and brother wiser than we, who counsel me to stay in the tents and forget this vision of freedom?"

"There are those who are born to serve and those who are born to rule. If thou art weak or afraid, turn back—stay by the knees of thy mother. Babylon, with its strife, is not for thee. Be thine the shepherd's crook and the harvester's sickle."

Sabaal spoke deliberately, fixing his cunning eyes upon Lemuel to note the effect of his words.

"Here, at least, there is peace," said Lemuel. "Peace and"—

"And Elna?"

"Elna! What sayest thou? Elna is betrothed to my brother Jediah."

"And therein lies thy peace? When Jediah espouses Elna, Lemuel will rejoice, and in Jediah's love Lemuel will find happiness!"

"Hush, Sabaal! hush!" said Lemuel, with a

look of pain. "Thou art indeed right. There can be no peace nor happiness for me where Elna dwells as Jediah's wife. But what further news?"

"At least a score of those who travel with us can be relied upon to strike for us. The road is dark over the desert. Knives are sharp and silent, and Alorus, the Babylonian, is our foe. Let the sons of Zoar strike where there are none to see."

And, while he spoke, he caught Lemuel eagerly by the arm and leaned forward, peering into his face. But Lemuel moved back as if in horror, and answered—

"Ah! is it thus that Israel is to be freed? In darkness and with the knife of the assassin? Nay! Our God is the God of battles, not of murder."

"But He hath delivered the Lord Alorus, who is our enemy, into our hands."

"No more, Sabaal! no more!" exclaimed Lemuel. "Alorus is our guest. He hath tasted salt with us, and his life is sacred."

"I counsel thee"—

"Thou counsellest according to thy wisdom," answered Lemuel, with decision, "I judge according to mine. I have spoken. To thy work!"

Sabaal had got up. He stood now, looking angered and cowed. Keeping his eyes on the ground, he said slowly—

"Those who await thee in Babylon will ask much of thee. Take heed, O son of Zoar, lest they weigh thee in the balance and find thee wanting."

Then he moved away, his head bent upon his breast, his thick lips curled in a malignant smile.

"Are these the instruments chosen by a righteous God to free His people?" thought Lemuel. "Is there no choice between murder and bondage for our race? Shall I forget the dreams? Shall I endure and stay in my father's tents? And Elna—Elna"—

Unwittingly he spoke the last words aloud. A soft voice answered him—

"Did'st thou call me, Lemuel?"

And he beheld Elna standing near him, with her great blue eyes fixed upon his face.

"Nay, my sister," answered Lemuel, with forced indifference. "Nay, I called thee not."

"Art thou angered with me?"

"No," answered Lemuel, moving away as if to leave her. "Why should I be angered with thee?"

"Art thou going?" asked the maiden, and she made a movement as if to detain him, then hesitated, and slightly retreated as if in confusion.

"Why should I stay?" asked Lemuel, pausing.

"It may be that I shall not speak to thee alone again—if, indeed, thou wilt go to Babylon."

"I must go thither. And, perchance, it will be better if we two speak not alone again."

Elna moved towards the well, saying softly—

"Why art thou so changed to me, Lemuel?"

"Changed? Ah, Elna, thou knowest that I am changeless. Thou knowest each thought of my heart."

"Once I deemed so," she replied, seating herself by the well and looking down into its deep and still waters, "but that seems long, long ago. And now "—

"Thou knowest them still. But I may never utter them, for that way waiteth dishonour and death. Let us part."

"Part thus?"

"How else?"

"Once thou wert kinder to me."

"Once I dared to be kind. That time is past."

"Why?"

"Remember thou art the betrothed wife of my brother Jediah."

"Yea, and I was betrothed as a child, ere even I knew myself and my own heart. Now I know I love him not."

"But thou art betrothed, and by the law thou art his."

"By the law of man, yes. But what of God's law? By His will my love was given unto thee. Shall I, knowing this, give myself to Jediah?— breaking the law of God to fulfil the law of man? Living a lie—a lifelong lie—degrading my body and forswearing my soul? No! Sooner than that, I would give back my soul to Him who made it!"

And as she spoke she drew from her bosom a knife, and ran her delicate fingers along the blade with a motion that was almost caressing. Lemuel looked at her for a moment with horror. Then he laid his hand upon the knife, took it from her, and exclaimed—

"Elna, my Elna! for pity's sake make not my task the harder! We must do that which is right and just. I will leave my father's house to-night —God of our people grant never to return to it ! There is no light, no day, no hope for me here, where thou livest, wife of Jediah. Away from thee there is but darkness, night, despair—and yet I must go. For the burthen of duty is heavy upon me. Help me to bear it, Elna."

And as he spoke he leaned down to her and took her two hands in his. She trembled, swaying towards him as if she would hide her face in his bosom. But suddenly he dropped her hands and sprang to his feet. He had seen Jediah approaching among the palms. And even at the same moment came the Lord Alorus with his friend Menanahim, and other Babylonians from the opposite direction. Jediah, his face white with anger, strode towards his brother, his arm upraised as if to strike him, but Alorus interposed, looking from one to the other with an amused smile.

"Stay!" he said, "stay!"

His eye fell upon Elna, who stood with her eyes downcast, while her lovely face was suffused with blushes.

"Ah!" he continued, "it is the beautiful Elna! Maiden, I am thy slave. Lemuel, how I do envy thee!"

"I do not understand thy words, my lord," said Lemuel, looking his brother full in the face.

"Nay, then thou art not quick-witted, shepherd. See, Menanahim, is not this a gem worthy of e'en a Babylonish setting?"

"A gem so rare is best unset," Menanahim answered, laughing. "It should be kept where none can gaze upon it save its owner. Such gems do make even the honest rogues. Now I, for instance, I am esteemed fairly honest, and yet —Ah, well, friend Lemuel, lock up thy gem."

And he gazed impudently at Elna, and turning, smiled significantly at the Babylonians who accompanied the Lord Alorus.

"My lords are pleased to jest," said Lemuel calmly, though his eyes shone with the light of anger. "Elna, wilt thou go and tell my father, Zoar, that the Lord Alorus waits."

Elna bowed her head and moved towards the tents, but Alorus stopped her, saying gaily—

"Nay, maiden, rob us not of thy beauty so soon. We will go and find him together."

"He comes hither, my lord," said Lemuel quietly, "and so spares our pains."

The aged Zoar indeed approached, accompanied and assisted by his faithful wife, Naomi, to whom Alorus inclined himself in half-satirical obeisance, crying—

"Here is the fount of beauty! Source of much loveliness, we are thy grateful slaves."

"How shall I answer my lord that understand not his speech?" answered Naomi, with quiet dignity.

"Do not thine eyes answer for thee," said

Alorus, "those eyes that are so like unto this maid's—thy child."

"Nay, my lord, Elna is not my child," said Naomi.

"She is like unto thee."

"She is the child of my dead sister."

"She is more than fair," returned Alorus.

Then going close up to Elna, and with the easy impudence of a conqueror among slaves, he said to her—

"Maiden, I pray thee do not hate me."

"Why should I hate my lord?" asked Elna, shrinking back.

"Because this night I do take thy lover from thee to Babylon."

"My lord!" cried Elna.

"Whom dost thou mean?" said Lemuel, stepping forward till he stood before Alorus.

"He is not her lover!" exclaimed Jediah. "The maiden is betrothed unto me."

Alorus started with feigned and exaggerated astonishment.

"To thee? A mistake indeed! A dull and stupid mistake! I crave pardon. I judged by— Ah, well, Lemuel, so much the better. Then thou art free—free to taste the sweets that wait for thee in Babylon."

Lemuel made no reply, but Naomi, with all the sweet anxiety of a tender mother, cried—

"Ah, sir, you will take care of my son! This Babylon of thine is, they tell me, as treacherous as she is beautiful."

" Treacherous she may be," replied Alorus, " but she is beautiful, sitting in glory upon Euphrates' banks.   Her streets are rows of palaces, towering terrace upon terrace, fragrant with flowers that perfume the whole air.   For Babylon doth Lebanon grow her cedars and sweet-smelling woods ; Assyria her grapes.   Tyre and Sidon exist only to weave our silks and samites.   Egypt toils in brass and in gold to deck our homes, our horses, and our own tenderly nurtured bodies ; while all the mines of Araby and of Ophir yield their tribute to deck our women.   Ah ! our women !   How lovely they are !   And foremost among them all ranks one who, like her fabled namesake, is a goddess, towards whom men's love doth flow as naturally as doth the river to the sea. Ishtar !   The fair and radiant Ishtar !   Jediah, did'st thou ever see Ishtar ? "

" Nay, my lord," answered Jediah.

" She came to Babylon some four or five years ago."

Jediah started slightly.   A strange thought had been born in his mind, he knew not why.

" She is like one of thy women," continued Alorus.   " Tall, with hair and eyes like the night and the shining stars, and the most cunning dimples about her mouth."

" Can it be Elcia ? " murmured Jediah to himself.

Aloud, and hastily, he said—

" My Lord Alorus, the tally of the tribute is here.   Wilt thou not verify it, and give thy receipt and seal ? "

" Nay, nay," answered Alorus, with dandified pettishness, as he arranged the great golden bracelets starred with uncut jewels that bedecked his arms. " These details I leave to Kedemoth here. Kedemoth, do thou verify it. Bring it with thee to the tents."

He looked again towards Elna. Then he said to Jediah—

" She is thy betrothed, sayest thou? Then will we leave thee with her. By thy countenance I divine that thou would'st speak with her alone. Hither, my people! Hither, Zoar!"

He burst into a laugh, and calling to those around him, turned away from the well, followed by the whole company. Elna seemed as if she would fain go with Naomi, but Jediah stopped her, saying—

" Nay, Elna, stay awhile. I would speak with thee here and now."

" Yes, my lord," she answered submissively.

When all the people were gone, Jediah said—

" Elna, this night Lemuel "—

But, ere he could say more, Elna, speaking with great agitation, said—

" My lord, thou hast heard what this man hath said of Babylon—the life he hath described. Shall Lemuel go forth alone?"

" It is his own desire to go," answered Jediah, with bitter coldness. " Lemuel is no babe nor girl. I went alone—why not he?"

" There are dangers for Lemuel that existed not for thee. Thou knowest what our people may expect of him.   Wilt thou let him go forth alone?"

"Why this concern for Lemuel's safety?"

"Is he not thy brother?"

"Brother!" exclaimed Jediah, with an angry gesture.   "Ah, most tender sister!   No other feeling moves thee—eh?"

"What other feeling could move me, my lord?"

"Love!   Thinkest thou, then, that I am blind, a child, bereft of sight, of reason?   Doth a sister tremble when a brother draweth nigh?   Doth her heart throb, sending the hot blood surging to her brow when a brother speaketh?   Or do her eyes brim over with gushing tears when a brother is absent?"

"And this"—

"And this I have seen and known in thee for Lemuel.   Even now thine eyes do seek the ground—the blush of shame is on thy cheek. Thy breath cometh quick.   All these things are truths that give the words thy tongue dare not utter."

"O my lord," cried Elna passionately, "if indeed all this be true—if in my heart there is no love for thee—if all that is pure and good and true calls out aloud in me against the law that gives me unto thee for wife—wilt thou still hold me to the bond?"

"Yea," said Jediah sternly, "yea, unto death."

"Ah! why—why?"

"Because thou dost love him.   Because I do hate him for this love of thine; and as I have suffered, seeing thy heart was his, so shall he suffer, knowing thy body is mine."

"I beg of thee, Jediah, hearken to me!" said Elna imploringly. "This union of our hands, which love doth not cement, can bring but evil unto thee and me. I beseech thee, give me back my troth—even though I ne'er see Lemuel more. Let me be free!"

"Thou shalt be that "—

"When? When, Jediah?"

"When that I am dead. Thou knowest our law—death to the woman who breaks her troth, death to the man with whom she is false."

"Ah! thou art merciless, pitiless, without bowels of tenderness or remorse. But thou art not omnipotent. Thou hast the law to aid thee, and all its power to enforce it on me. I stand alone, with naught but love to help me. Yet a woman's love hath proved ere now too strong for all the laws of man. What hath been may be again. Man's law can slay my body; it can never kill my love."

She spoke with all the vehemence of one completely carried away by a flood of emotion that rendered her careless of all save the necessity of expressing herself fully and completely. And, on the last words, she drew back from Jediah with a gesture almost of hatred, and hurried away towards the tent of Naomi. Her heart beat with a violence that nearly choked her. The blood coursed in her cheeks. But she no longer felt any sensation of fear. Indeed, a wave of almost wild courage ran through her, and, for the moment, she was careless of fate, careless of all save love alone.

And the fierce emotion that surged in Elna had not left Jediah unmoved. He too was carried out of himself, and, as she left him, he cried out in a loud voice to an Israelite who passed by, laden with packs for the camels of Alorus' caravan—

"Jozadah! Jozadah!"

The Israelite stopped. He was a lean and hungry-looking man, poorly clad and of an evil countenance. His eyes, which were unusually small for one of his race, were set near together in his head beneath projecting brows. And his gait was habitually gentle and cringing, like that of a dog which has been often beaten.

"Come hither, Jozadah," said Jediah imperiously.

Jozadah advanced a few steps.

"What is thy will, my lord?" he asked, in a whining voice.

"Jozadah," said Jediah, coming close to him, "thou art poor."

"My lord hath spoken. Would it were not so."

"Thou hast neither flocks, nor herds, nor fields, nor pastures."

"My lord knoweth these things are true."

While he was speaking the last words, Tirzah came into sight among the palms, unseen by the two men. As she was drawing near to them, Jediah said—

"And yet, Jozadah, beggar as thou art, thou hast set thine eyes and thy heart on Tirzah."

On hearing her name spoken, the woman, full of curiosity, hid herself behind the trunk of a tree, from which concealment she could hear all that went on without being observed.

"Tirzah is very fair," said Jozadah obsequiously, and casting his eyes upon the ground, "and my lord knoweth that even a beggar may have a heart like other men."

"Ay, but Tirzah's father is prudent; not like to give his daughter to a man whose whole stock of worldly goods is the few poor rags that cover him."

"All this thy servant knows."

"And," said Jediah, watching the beggar with his fierce and bird-like eyes, "dost thou know likewise that Lemuel, my brother, hath cast an eye of longing upon her?"

Jozadah started as if he had been struck with the lash of a Babylonish taskmaster, and Tirzah crept a little nearer among the trees.

"Nay, my lord," said Jozadah, and his voice was hoarse with passion, "I know not that."

But Jozadah put his hand upon the long knife that hung at his girdle of camel's hair.

"He shall not have her," he muttered. "He shall not have her."

"Why should he? To-night he goeth to Babylon. Babylon is a dangerous city."

"Ay, so they say."

"There are ever brawls there and strife. A dark night, Jozadah, a quick thrust of a knife," he touched the knife at the beggar's girdle, as if almost unconsciously, "one more body to fling into the waters of Euphrates."

" Ay.   And then, my lord, and then ? "

" Those fields that once were Ezra's, a score of cattle, ten score of sheep—and Tirzah to dwell in thy tent and share thy happiness."

Jozadah looked up under his thick eyebrows with unutterable cunning.

" And my lord sayeth that all these things are mine if—if "—

" If, by some chance,—such as happeneth in great cities,—I must e'en mourn a brother's death in Babylon."

" That were not difficult.   But the mind of my lord may change.   He will give his servant bond for the fields, the flocks, the herds ? "

" I shall not fail thee, Jozadah.   For I would fain see all men — and thee — happy, especially thee, Jozadah."

" My lord is good."

" But come — come to my tent ; there is but little time.   For thou art going up to Babylon to-night, I think ?   Is it not so ? "

" My lord hath spoken," said Jozadah.

And he smiled as he crept away after Jediah.

When they were gone, Tirzah came forth from her place of hiding.   Her face was pale with horror, and she gazed around as if seeking help. Presently she made a beckoning gesture with her hand, and, after two or three minutes, Elna appeared, running to her.

" What is the matter, Tirzah ? " cried Elna

anxiously. "How thou dost tremble! And the pale shade of death is surely on thy cheek! What ails thee?"

"Death's pale shade is indeed about me—and thee, my Elna. Even here—here doth he hover, ready to strike. Oh, Elna—Lemuel"—

She stopped. Her lips were dry and her tongue refused to speak. But Elna caught her by the shoulders with a wild anxiety, crying—

"What of Lemuel? Speak, and quickly!"

"Jediah hath promised Jozadah lands and flocks and herds and—and me, even me, to be his wife— if Lemuel dies in Babylon."

Elna turned as white as was Tirzah.

"God of our people!" she exclaimed. "He would have Jozadah slay him!"

"Even so. This very night Jozadah goeth to Babylon. Thou knowest what will come of this. For Lemuel goeth alone, with none to warn him or to watch over him."

"Alone!" exclaimed Elna, and her face was alight with a sudden resolution that made her look strong and courageous, almost as a man. "That shall he not! One, at least, shall be there who loveth him and who would die for him."

"One! Whom dost thou mean?"

"Myself, Tirzah, myself! Help me to fly hence to save the man we love. For thou dost love Lemuel, even as all must. Nay, there is no shame in love! Come, Tirzah, come! Love and the right shall conquer hate and wrong. Come with me! Come!"

And she drew Tirzah away towards the tents, moving almost joyously. For in action each human being can find solace for the sorrow that oppresseth and the dread that draweth nigh.

.   .   .   .

At the falling of night, the caravan which was to accompany the Lord Alorus to Babylon was ready to depart, and Alorus himself, standing before the tents, took ceremonious leave of the aged Zoar. The tribute was all collected. The heavy packs had been fastened upon the backs of the snarling camels. Now, through the soft air of the evening, rang the note of a steer's horn, giving the signal of departure. All the people of the tribe were gathered together to witness the going of the caravan and to bid farewell to Lemuel. Only Elna was not there. Naomi wept. For this parting from her youngest born was bitter unto her as death. Alorus and the Baby lonians of his train were assembled, and Alorus, speaking to Zoar, said—

"I hear the signal, and the night falleth. Farewell, Zoar."

"Is my lord content?" answered Zoar. "Have I paid him in full?"

"Indeed," replied Alorus, "thou art most liberal of all the sons of Israel. Trust me, Zoar; I hate to be sent hither to exact tribute of one who is so much my friend."

"Thou but doest thy master's bidding, my lord."

"Most true, Zoar. And yet, 'tis well when 'tis

over—and 'tis over now. My camels are loaded with thy wealth, and yet none can see that thou art the poorer. Such flocks hast thou, such harvests, such pastures — and such lovely maidens!"

"My lord will not speak of them in Babylon?"

"Nay, Zoar, not I. Why, she would swoop upon thee, and, like a herd of locusts, eat thee up. Nay, Zoar, thou hast proved my friend, and I will prove thine."

"My lord is good."

Alorus, after inclining himself before Naomi, walked towards the caravan, followed by his train. The horn again sounded, and Naomi, with a cry of anguish, clasped Lemuel in her arms.

"My son!" she murmured, sobbing, "my youngest born!"

Lemuel returned her caresses. He too was deeply moved, but he bore himself, as ever, bravely and nobly.

"My son," said Naomi, striving again to be calm, "thou goest among strangers, worshippers of strange gods. Thou wert ever obedient, loving, and faithful. Thou wilt not ever be tempted to forget the God of thy fathers?"

"Nay, my mother," answered Lemuel, and he fell at her feet.

She laid her hands upon his head, saying solemnly—

"My blessing be upon thee, O son of my soul!"

Zoar turned to the crowd that stood by, watching and strangely moved.

"Lift up your voices, O my people!" he said. "Sing ye His praises, and give thanks unto Him. Sing ye the hymn of parting."

The people obeyed with full hearts, and as the voices rang out Lemuel bade farewell to those he loved, kissing the little children who clung about his knees. As the music died away he came to his brother Jediah, who stood a little apart, with his eyes cast moodily upon the ground.

"Farewell, my brother," Lemuel said, holding forth his hand.

"Farewell," responded Jediah coldly, and without looking towards him.

Lemuel, as if chilled and hurt, hesitated for a moment. Then, coming close to Jediah and putting his arm around his brother, he said to him—

"Jediah, thou art the eldest born of our father Zoar, and unto thee is given the firstfruits of the land and the flocks, and—and the jewel of our tribe, Elna."

"Elna!" said Jediah sternly. "And what sayest thou of her?"

"Cherish her, my brother. Guard this jewel tenderly, as the apple of thine eye."

"I will surely guard her, Lemuel," answered Jediah, with a dark frown.

"Farewell, my brother."

"Farewell," said Jediah, drawing away from Lemuel.

Once more Lemuel knelt before Zoar and Naomi. The horn again sounded.

"Farewell, my father and my mother," he said,

7

and his voice was low from his emotion. "And may the God of Israel so deal with me if I prove not worthy of thee. Thy blessing, father."

The people that stood by bowed their heads reverently, and Zoar, spreading abroad his hands, said—

"The God of Abraham, of Isaac, and of Jacob be with thee and keep thee, my son, my son!"

It was now growing rapidly dark. Lemuel rose up. It was time to depart, yet for one moment he lingered, looking towards the tents. Jediah watched him, and knew well why he hesitated. But no one came from the tents. No shadowy figure stood in the tent door of Naomi. The tears rose in Lemuel's eyes. He turned away and walked slowly into the gathering darkness.

"My son! my son!" wailed Naomi.

"Come to the tent, my wife, and pray with me for the safety of thy son in the great Babylon," said Zoar. "Come, my people."

And, taking her by the hand, he led her tenderly away, followed by all those about him.

The darkness had fallen. The caravan was already on its way, when the slight figure of a boy stole softly by the well of Naomi, taking the direction of the caravan. The boy paused for a moment beside the well and looked up at the stars.

"Give me strength, O God!" he whispered, in a prayer. "Give me strength for my task! For where my love goeth there will I follow, even though he leadeth me into the valley of the Shadow of Death!"

Then he grasped his staff and set bravely forth into the night.

Lemuel, in the caravan, was heavy-hearted.

He knew not that Elna, casting aside all maidenly fear with the robe of a maiden, stole through the darkness, led by her love. Babylon, that great and mighty city, called her too, because it called him. Babylon stretched forth her arms and shone with all her torches, and murmured with all her voices. So, in a bygone year, had Babylon called unto another Israelitish maiden, even unto Elcia. She too had forsaken the tents of her people, and had heard the singing voices die in her ears as she fled away to the city of glory and of terror. And she too—but how differently!—had become a pilgrim through darkness and strange dangers, driven by the prompting of what she thought was love.

Elna would not fear the lights, the voices, the unknown people, or the unknown gods they worshipped. She was strong with love, the boy Elna.

And so the caravan journeyed, and far off in Babylon, Ishtar—who once was Elcia—slept in her palace upon the banks of Euphrates.

And the slaves lay about her feet, holding their instruments of music.

She slept, in the soft and sweet night — and dreamed.

And in the dream, her soul, released by slumber from the worldly bonds that held it fast by day, was again beside the well of Naomi. It stood with the soul of Elna beneath the stars, as if the soul that waked and the soul that slept met and mingled, as do the souls, most surely,—here or elsewhere,—of all loving women.

They touched hands and lips. Eyes looked into eyes. Heart joined heart in the mystery that is the mystery of longing and the mystery of pain. It was but for a moment—prophetic and quickly gone. Then Ishtar stirred from her sleep upon her couch of gold.

She raised herself up, thinking to see the long reeds rustle beside Naomi's well, the shadowy tents upon the dim and endless plain.

But, instead, she saw the gleaming of the river and the golden lights of Babylon. Then the tears fell from her eyes, and she cried aloud to her slaves—

"Sing to me. Sing softly. I would sleep again."

And as their soft and sad voices rose in the night, she saw the shadowy figure of a slim boy, with a maiden's eyes, bend above her where she lay.

She stretched forth her arms. But there was nothing.

And the slaves sang on, and played upon their instruments, until Ishtar dreamed again.

CHAPTER VI

WHEN Elcia was deserted by Jediah in Babylon, her great beauty became both her great danger and her worldly salvation. Had she been stronger in character than she was, she might have perished honourably of starvation, being left in poverty and utterly without friends in the great city of the strangers. Being at that time weak, and ignorant of the ways of a complicated and glittering life, she fell into the hands of Migdapul, the god-seller, and within four years became the famous Ishtar, the Queen of Beauty, at whose feet sat the Babylonish lords, the wealthy merchants and traders, and the effeminate dandies of the city. Her lovers and her friends knew not her history, whence she came or who she was. They scarcely cared to know. The power of her loveliness silenced all tongues. Men were content to look upon her and to worship. Some strove to look beyond her wonderful eyes, down into her heart. These strove in vain. Every woman is an enigma. Ishtar was more enigmatic than her sisters, and so more strangely attractive unto men, who love ever to beat out their hearts against that which they can never understand. If she had a heart, she allowed no one to hear its pulsation. She permitted no one to dwell within it. For her worshippers she had caprices, but no adoration. They said, at last, that she was without a heart, and this legend drew men to her. Each one, perhaps, hoped to create in her what she lacked. Each desired to win the favour denied to all his rivals. All failed. Ishtar remained mysteriously cold. And yet her face was passionate. Her eyes were full of sombre meaning. It seemed as if she must have felt and suffered once, perhaps very long ago, ere ever she ruled in Babylon. There was even about her a terror, as of night and of dead days. Her long black hair, in which the jewels shone, was like a cloud about her. Her cheeks were pale, like smooth ivory. And there was often a delicate weariness in her poses, and in her movements the subtlety of an eternal languor. She spent long hours reclining on the silken cushions of a golden couch beneath the trees of her palace garden, which over-looked the great river and the terraces of the city. And in those hours she seemed to dream, although her eyes were seldom closed in sleep. All the cries of the town, softened by distance into fairy voices, came up to her, and the sounds of distant music and the songs of the sailors of all lands upon the flowing river. She heard the far-off beating of drums as the religious processions went by to the temples of the strange gods, the clash of cymbals, the thin flutter of flutes. She heard the cool wind of night rustling in the palm trees above her head. And sometimes all these noises, mingling together curiously, died down and away, and there seemed to come over the city a mysterious hush. Then, in the silence, as she gazed upward at the blue sky, she heard the bleating of sheep and the chatter of women about a well. She closed her eyes and saw tents and long green pastures and everlasting plains. And in her ears there was the whisper of a shepherd's pipe and the trickle of a melancholy tune. Then her eyes filled with tears, and she turned to her slaves and cried—

"Play to me!—play! Sing me the songs, the love-songs of Babylon! Music! music!"

And she stretched out her lovely arms like one that is sick and desires comfort, but ever finds it not. The slaves obeyed her command. They fluted and plucked the strings of their lutes, and they lifted up their soft voices in singing. Then Ishtar heard no more the bleating of the flocks and the pipe of the shepherd. And the tears fled from her eyes, and she said to herself—

"I will be happy! For am I not a queen in Babylon?"

And she summoned her lovers, and she feasted, and called the dancing-girls and the sorcerers and the diviners. And there was revelry in the palace by the river. And all the people of Babylon spoke of the glory of Ishtar.

Migdapul, the god-seller, who combined many professions and knew many men and women of curious occupation in Babylon, was become a sort of paid servant of Ishtar. He was often at her palace, and he received many commands in secret from her and ministered to the pleasures with which she filled her life. The woman whose heart is sad often seeks to drown her sorrow in imperious caprices. So it was with Ishtar. Since no man really moved her, she was ever searching for some new lover, hoping to find in him that which was lacking in all the others. Migdapul, who learned what strangers entered Babylon, sought out those whom he thought might please Ishtar, and led them to the palace on the river bank. And so it came to pass that he, ever on the watch, took note of the arrival of Lemuel in the caravan of the Lord Alorus. Now, Lemuel, simple shepherd though he was, had more of manly beauty than falls to the lot of most men. He was untainted by city pleasures, untired by the dissipations that sapped the strength and tarnished the faces of the Babylonians. His bearing was noble. His eyes were clear and his cheeks glowed with the brilliant colouring of health. When Migdapul saw Lemuel, he thought "Surely this man would please the Lady Ishtar," and presently he sought an interview with her, to tell her of the arrival in Babylon of the beautiful shepherd.

Ishtar's palace, which stood on one of the artificial hills of Babylon, was built of enamelled bricks, rosy in hue and covered with a shining glaze that made them look almost like jewels. It was set upon a great platform of brickwork and was of vast extent, containing mighty halls and chambers crammed with exquisite furniture, with carved figures of black basalt, with architectural ornaments, with bronzes, inscriptions, silks, embroideries, and vessels of chased gold and silver, in many cases set with gigantic barbaric gems. The gardens were extraordinary, even for Babylon, the city of gardens. One of them, in which Ishtar generally reclined when she desired to hear music or to see the dancing-girls leap and posture, was square in form, nearly four hundred feet each way, and rested upon tiers of arches and on walls of colossal thickness. Trees and shrubs flourished here abundantly, growing to a great size, and affording a delicious shade from the heat of the sun, even at high noontide. Innumerable fountains cast their silver spray towards heaven, and long beds of flowers made patches of gorgeous colour. There was also an artificial reservoir, along whose banks grew aquatic plants and in whose depths fish floated to and fro like restless shadows. Set about this garden were couches and tables, made of carved wood and of precious metals, and great piles of embroidered silken cushions, on which the guests of Ishtar lay, eating sweetmeats from silver caskets, listening to the sound of citharas and breathing the perfumes and spices that smoked in vases of beaten bronze.

It was into this garden that Migdapul, the god-seller, was introduced by a black slave when he came to tell Ishtar of the arrival of the beautiful shepherd, Lemuel, in Babylon. The air was warm, for it was noon, and Ishtar lay upon a couch, fanned by two slaves who sat at her feet, waving slowly to and fro the feathers of huge birds set in staffs of gold. In sheer weariness of spirit she had dismissed her lovers, and when Migdapul entered, inclining himself obsequiously almost to the ground, she was alone, but for her attendants.

"Hail, beautiful Lady Ishtar!" said the god-seller, standing at a little distance from her couch. "Hail!"

And he bowed again with exaggerated servility. Ishtar scarcely turned her head towards him. She looked weary, and her great eyes were cloudy with discontent.

"Why art thou here?" she murmured indifferently. "On what foolish errand comest thou?"

"On an errand for thy pleasure, lady."

"My pleasure?" Ishtar reiterated, with a sigh of complete lassitude. "And how canst thou give pleasure to me?"

"Am I not ever zealous for thy delight?"

"It is seldom that thou delightest me. But tell me thy errand and be gone. I am not well to-day, and would be alone."

She leaned lower on the couch, stretching her delicate limbs and playing idly with the jewelled bracelets that covered her white arms. The slaves, with impassive faces, totally devoid of expression, continued to fan her with the regularity of machines.

"There is a stranger come to Babylon, lady," began Migdapul.

"That happens every day."

" He arrived in the train of the Lord Alorus. He is young and well-favoured."

" What of it ?   What is that to me ? "

" Thou hast seen many men in Babylon, lady, but none like unto him. For he is stronger than the strongest, and hath an air more brave than all the soldiers of the city. By the great god Bel, he is beautiful."

Ishtar closed her eyes. She had no air of listening to the god-seller.

He came close to her couch, and bending lower to her ear, he said—

" He is a youthful shepherd come in from the plains and from the tents of captive Israel."

Ishtar started slightly and opened her eyes.

" What is his name ? " she asked.

" Lemuel, lady."

Ishtar raised herself on one arm. The weariness had gone from her face, and a faint eagerness flickered in her deep eyes.

" Lemuel ! " she repeated. " It is a name of Israel, truly. Thou sayest this shepherd is well-favoured ? "

" By the great god Merodach, he "—

" Why hath he left his flocks to come up unto Babylon ? "

" That I know not, lady. Perchance he is tired of the simple life of the plains. In sooth I should love it not for my part."

" Thou ! Thou art of Babylon. Thou knowest naught else."

" There is much to know in Babylon, lady."

" Too much—too much," murmured Ishtar, with a bitter contempt.

" Or, perchance, the Lord Alorus took the shepherd to be one of his servitors."

Ishtar was silent for a moment. She seemed to be lost in thought. At length she said—

" Go to the Lord Alorus. Tell him I make a feast to-night, and bid him to come and to bring his shepherd with him. Dost thou understand?"

" Yes, lady."

Ishtar's lips curved in a smile that was not without cruelty. She struck a silver gong that stood upon a table by her side. . A eunuch, richly dressed in a silk robe covered with jewelled embroidery, appeared.

" I shall make a feast to-night," she said. " Command the musicians, the diviners, the Indian dancers."

The eunuch made an obeisance and withdrew. Then Ishtar turned again to Migdapul.

" We will show thy simple shepherd the glories of Babylon to-night," she said. And her eyes glittered almost fiercely. " He is come hither from the country plains and from hearing the voices of the flocks and the herds. To-night he shall hear my voice and the voices of the singers. He shall look upon the dancers dancing to the citherns. And his comely simplicity shall be enlightened. Poor Israelite!"

She laughed aloud.

" Go, Migdapul," she added. " Bear my message. And—stay—here is something for thee."

She took a ring from her finger and put it into his hand.   He burst forth into a torrent of thanks.

"Go," she said.   "Go—I am sick of thy babble."

And she turned her face from him and lay back as one who would sleep.

But when he was gone she did not sleep.   She called her attendants and gave orders for a great feast.   And when the evening came, she bade her slaves attire her in magnificent robes and bring forth the finest of her jewels to deck her hair and her bosom.

The night fell, and the sky was thick with stars above the great palace of Ishtar.   She came forth into the garden above the arches to await her guests.   She was clad in a sindone, a long garment of extremely fine muslin, of a deep red hue, with a delicate pattern of gold birds and a deep fringe of gold that fell about her feet.   In her black hair, on her neck and arms, gleamed enormous red jewels set in heavy gold, and in her hand she carried a gigantic fan of red feathers that sprang from sticks of gold.   Her face was pale as ivory, and her dark eyes shone with an unwonted eagerness.

In the garden the Persian and Nubian slaves had arranged many couches and divans of ebony, ivory, cedar wood, and other precious materials, on which lay piles of white, blue, and scarlet silken cushions, elaborately embroidered with curious patterns and with figures of mythical beasts and of birds.   Torches, flaming in bronze stands, flared forth upon the night, mingling their fierce lustre with the pale light of the rising moon. Upon the ground were spread rich carpets—those marvellous carpets for which Babylon was so famous. They were made of the finest wool, exquisitely woven, amazingly brilliant in colour, and covered with complicated and sometimes humorous patterns, representing griffins and strange beasts of Lower Asia. The air was heavy with the perfume of flowers and of frank-incense which smoked in vases of chased silver. The moonbeams glittered on the artificial water, and beyond the alabaster terrace wall could be seen a superb panorama of Babylon, gleaming with myriads of lights like a fairy city in a wonderful dream.

Ishtar approached this wall, and, leaning upon the balustrade, looked out over the city. The romance of it touched her far less than the wickedness of it. For she had learned to know it too well to think of it as a fairy wonder, as an enchanted abode of light and colour and artistry and pleasure. The glory of it rose up to her in the night like flame and smoke from the pit. The cries of it sounded in her ears like the cries of demons. And its music was melancholy and foreboding. The long lines of lights, stretching far out on every side into the shadowy darkness of the immense plain, were like terrible eyes of the wild and devouring beasts that haunt the waste places of the desert. And the wind that blew softly above the walls of the palaces and temples

seemed to her cold with the breath of some
coming unknown fate. Sometimes she wondered
why Babylon was so terrible to her, why she could
not be happy. She was rich. She was worshipped. Her name was great throughout the
city. Luxury surrounded her. All the hard
things of life were smoothed away before her
pretty feet. All the pleasures of the world
trooped around her in smiling squadrons. Her
lovers gave her passion ; her slaves, faithful servitude ; her musicians, exquisite melodies ; her
dancers, sinuous grace and the songs of gestures.
For her the diviners ruled the stars. For her
prayers were murmured in the temples of the gods.
For her men had suffered and had died. She
had her sacrifices like Merodach, and like Ana, the
god of heaven. She was more than a name to the
Babylonians. She was a superstition, and on the
"day of rest for the heart," the Sabbath of the
city, there were those who worshipped her as they
never worshipped the images that ruled in silence,
motionless above the shrines where superstition
fell to plead for worldly joys and everlasting
rewards hereafter.

And yet Ishtar's heart was desolate and full of
those mysterious and pathetic echoes which dwell
in solitary places, and Ishtar's soul was bitter with
an exceeding great bitterness. Only sometimes,
in wild dissipation, in the abandonments of passion, could she lose for a while her sense of despair,
the cruel sensation of lovelessness that filled her
world with blackness even when her lovers lay at

her feet upon the silken cushions, and the wine-cup passed from hand to hand.

To-night, even, as she leaned out from her hanging garden, her soul was heavy within her like a thing of lead. Her momentary excitement had died away, and tears rose in her eyes as she gazed at the lights of the city, till they swam in a blurred mist and wavered and faded. And she drooped her dark head upon her arms, and longed for peace and rest.

That dwelt far off, in the green plains, among the flocks and the herds, not here under the palms and cypress trees in which torches were fastened till they sparkled with shaded fire. Then Ishtar, with one of those great gestures that come from the soul, stretched forth her arms above the city, as if she called silently to the distant silence of the plain. The huge red jewels shone fiercely in the torchlight and the moonlight. The golden brace-lets gleamed. The long red robe, with its golden birds hiding their quaint and demure heads in the rich dimness of the folds, flowed out in the soft night wind, and the hanging sleeves of embroidery fell backward from the white arms. She stood there almost like some majestic and inhuman thing, and from the depths of her heart arose a great and voiceless cry: "Take me away — away — to the spaces of the stars, to the silver shadows of the moon, to the ebony solitudes of the night—where no men are—no voices—no hands to touch me— no lips to lie on mine! Take me away—away!"

She felt something that pushed against her robe,

and she dropped her arms with a sigh, and turned from the terrace.   One of her dogs, a Persian greyhound, was trying to attract her attention.   She bent down and kissed its narrow head, laid her hand on the silver collar that circled its neck, and led it with her to a couch, on which she sank, keeping the dog at her side.

"Let the instruments of music play," she said to a slave.   "Scatter red flowers upon the carpets. It is the hour for the feast."

The slave-girls plucked their citherns.   The flutes rose coolly from the shadows of the cypresses, and the psalteries quivered to her ears as a rosy cloud of scented flowers fell around her.   Then from the court of her palace, conducted by slaves, came the favoured Babylonians who were her guests of the night.   And, as they entered, from an open chamber of the palace rose the voices of girls singing—

> "Softly glides the moon along heaven's way.
> She draws her veil of cloud across her face,
> She doth not wish to pry where love doth wait.
> Be thou as kind as she, and close the gate."

A trumpet sounded loudly.   Then the voices rose more softly—

> "Yes, close the gate.
> Draw the curtains close
> And close the gate.
> Let love commune with love alone,
> And close the gate.
> Let no eyes see—let no ears hear;
> Guard well the gate."

The voices and the instruments faded away, as

8

if the singers and the players withdrew themselves to the inner courts of the palace. And as the last faint note sank into silence, Alorus entered the garden, surrounded by several magnificently attired Babylonish nobles and attendants, among whom was Lemuel.

Alorus, whose arms were covered with jewels, and whose thick black hair, which curled naturally, was elaborately knotted and decked with golden ornaments, advanced towards Ishtar with a jaunty and dandified gait, and bent low before her.

"Queen of the night," he said, "more lovely art thou than the silver moon, or than any star. I, like all men, am thy slave, and am here at thy gracious bidding."

Ishtar extended her hand to his lips, but her eyes were turned upon the throng of his attendants. She bowed to several of them, then, turning to Alorus, who remained beside her in an attitude of ostentatious submission, she said—

" And thy new attendant, the shepherd Lemuel?"
" Thou would'st speak with him, fairest lady?"
Ishtar bent her head.

"Lemuel," said Alorus, "the Lady Ishtar would speak with thee. Come hither."

Lemuel, who had been standing quietly behind the gorgeous Babylonians, obeyed the command of Alorus, and, moving from his place, came before the couch of Ishtar. Her greyhound fawned upon him instantly, and licked his hands with affection. Lemuel was simply attired in a white tunic that fell only to his knees, and was confined at the waist by a broad girdle of dyed wool. His arms were bare, and on his feet he wore sandals. His brown hair, which was not elaborately plaited, as was the hair of the Babylonians, clustered in curls about his broad and noble forehead, and his frank brown eyes looked, unabashed, into the great eyes of Ishtar. His whole person breathed a quiet dignity, mingled with a manly simplicity that seemed born of the very essence of fearlessness, and the obeisance that he made seemed rather the inclination of strength before beauty than of a slave before a queen of Babylon. Ishtar looked up at him, and a strange interest quickened in her eyes.

For when she saw, set in the midst of the coarse and laughing Babylonians, this noble and sincere shepherd, fearless, godly, and strong with a strength unsapped by deeds of evil, her heart went back to the days when she was happy and sinless, when she sat in the tent door and looked out upon the plain, shading her eyes to catch the first glimpse of her husband, Johanan, as he returned, singing, from his labours in the fields. How long ago that seemed! And o'er what a deep gulf did she gaze upon her lovely life of innocence!

"Thou art new in Babylon?" she asked Lemuel. And there was a quiver of strange emotion in her voice.

"Yes, lady."

"What of the city thinkest thou?"

"I know not yet, lady. Babylon is not learnt in a day. It hath surely many secrets."

As he spoke his eyes looked piercingly into hers, and she felt herself tremble. She cast down her eyes and said, with a forced laugh, to Alorus—

"Thou hearest what saith the stranger, Alorus?"

"Ay, and it is true. But what is a city without its secrets? Tame as would be a woman without hers, at which no mere man can even guess. Is it not so, Menanahim?"

"It is even so," said Menanahim, looking contemptuously at Lemuel. "Methinks our simple shepherd here would be surprised indeed could his wit of the plains understand the marvels and the mysteries of Babylon."

"Perhaps even his wit can understand the mystery of beauty that is like unto the sun in his glory," said Lemuel calmly.

And again he looked into the eyes of Ishtar. She smiled at him and answered—

"And darest thou fix thine eyes upon the sun? Fearest thou not blindness?"

As she spoke she rose up and stood before him in the light of the torches. Beneath her robe the voluptuous beauty of the curves of her exquisite limbs could be seen, half concealed, half revealed by the cunning arrangement and disposal of her falling draperies. A sort of insolence crept into her face, as if she felt the splendour of her own power, the glory of the spell of face and form before which all men made obeisance.

She lifted her hand to her veil of spangled golden tissue and seemed as if she would draw it before her face as she added—

"Shall the sun draw its veil of clouds across its face?"

"Nay," answered Lemuel; "let not all the land be dark. Spare us the light, and we will veil our eyes. Without the sun we perish."

"Ah!" said Menanahim, with a sneer, "there spoke the husbandman, brooding o'er his harvest. Our good friend Lemuel, as a born tiller of the land, is full of the sun and rain; without them must he indeed perish."

"So must thou, O lord of Babylon," retorted Lemuel. "Lacking Israel's flocks and harvest, even so fine a lord as Menanahim might, like unto a whining beggar of the streets, go clamouring for bread."

"Not at the heels of an upstart Israelite," said Menanahim fiercely.

"Take heed, O lord, lest thou find thyself not at, but under the heels of some upstart Israelite," returned Lemuel.

"Darest thou?" began Menanahim furiously, as he thrust his hand into his girdle and drew forth a jewelled knife.

But Ishtar touched his arm with a queenly gesture of command, and said—

"Enough, Menanahim! The retort was fair. Let be, I say. Even as the shepherd's wits are keener than thine, so may his steel be. Nay, I said 'Enough'!"

As she spoke the last words she stood up between the two men, drawing herself to her full height. Menanahim, scowling with anger, slowly returned the knife to its place, muttering to himself—

"Another time—another time, shepherd!"

Alorus and the Babylonians who stood around burst into laughter, and began to overwhelm Menanahim with mock felicitations. But Lemuel, who seemed totally unmoved, stood calmly in his place without a word. Only the muscles that started under the smooth skin of his arms betrayed his readiness for combat and the excitement that stirred within him. Ishtar looked at him with growing admiration, which she scarcely strove to conceal. For the libertine life of Babylon had stripped from her much of woman's beautiful and precious reserve. Then, seeing by the fury of Menanahim's countenance that the banter of his companions was likely to drive away his last remnant of self-control, she said, raising her voice—

"And now, my lords, I beseech you stand no longer as if you were about to leave me. Let us sit and see the dancing of the Indian girls and drink the wines that are brought from far."

She clapped her hands together.

"Summon the dancers," she cried, "and let wine be brought. Lemuel, hast thou ever seen the strange dancers from India?"

"Nay, lady."

"Hast thou drunk the purple wine?"

"Nay, lady, but the water from the well of Naomi beside the tents of my people."

Ishtar started, and for a moment her face was

contorted as if by pain.   Then, with a curious sort
of violence, she cried—

" Sit thou here at my feet on this silken cushion.
Thou shalt taste the wonders of Babylon ere ever
the moon mounts higher in the sky above the
cypress yonder.   Put thy lips to the wine-cup and
drink to the sun that shines upon thee ! "

As she spoke, one of the slaves, kneeling, handed
her a silver vessel in the form of a mythical dragon,
filled to the mouth with wine.   She touched her
own lips with it and then gave it to Lemuel.   He
feigned to drink, saying—

" To the sun, Lady Ishtar ! "

Then, handing the dragon to the Lord Alorus,
he reclined at the feet of Ishtar, who leaned towards him from the couch whereon she sank,
fanning his face with the great red feathers of her
fan.   The Babylonians disposed themselves around
her.   Some wandered away along the paths of the
garden.   Some walked aside, speaking to the
beautiful slave-girls.   Menanahim leaned alone by
a cypress tree, regarding Ishtar and Lemuel with
eyes that darted flame.   Alorus stood behind the
couch of Ishtar, resting one hand upon it, and now
and then, with an affected playfulness, touching the
red jewels that gleamed in the dark tresses of her
hair.   There was a moment of silent expectation,
then a strain of distant and melancholy music stole
through the garden, accompanied by the dull and
reiterated hum of a shrouded gong beaten far off
and the soft clash of cymbals.   In a dark court of
the palace, that opened on the garden through a

yawning arch, coloured lights began to twinkle. And presently through this archway floated a string of Indian girls, bearing tiny torches. Their thin robes of purple muslin, spangled with a silver design of conventional flowers, scarcely hid their slim forms. On their uplifted arms jingled quantities of loose bracelets of silver, and in their floating hair were purple flowers and dark green leaves.

Moving with a slow and undulating gait, they passed by the Babylonians, taking no sort of heed of their exclamations of admiration, and made their sinuous way to a gorgeous carpet that was spread before the couch of Ishtar. Then, arranging themselves in a sort of pattern, they began to dance one of those curious and almost terrible dances that seem to be handed on as a tradition from one generation of women to another in the curious and terrible countries of the East. In the light of the torches and of the moon, to the far-off beat of the barbarous music, they leaped and gesticulated, swaying their attenuated bodies, trembling their white arms, on which the silver bracelets jangled, with a cruel and clashing persistence. The expressions on their dark and unfathomable faces were intellectual and very sad, totally unself-conscious, like expressions of statuettes. But their movements gradually became more and more vehement, as if their bodies were full of excitement, while their minds remained watchful, cold, and reserved. They leaped high into the air with an incomparable activity beside the silver fountains, which leaped in emulation.

Their long dark eyes stared into the violet air of the night, as if they looked at something distressing and very far away. They were sombre as the black cypresses that cast long shadows upon the garden walls. They were cruel as fate is cruel. And the distant music which accompanied them was savage and sweet at the same time, yearning and unkind, like many passionate women.

The Babylonians leaned forward towards these leaping figures, fascinated. Their lips parted in their beards. Their hands mechanically beat time. Unconsciously they swayed their bodies to the soft clash of the cymbals. They forgot to pass the wine - cup. They forgot to speak or to laugh. Mystery ran over them like a wave. Even a sort of fear overtook them. And in the violet night they lay upon their cushions like engrossed men in a dream who will never cease from gazing at dancers who will dance for ever. Ishtar no longer moved to and fro the golden sticks and the huge red feathers of her fan. She, too, leaned a little nearer to Lemuel. Her eyes were fixed upon his face, and an expression of tenderness had come into them, of tenderness that was full of melancholy. Beyond the terrace wall the multitudinous lights of Babylon twinkled in the night. Lemuel looked at the dancers for a while, but rather with disgust than with any other sensation. Then he turned his eyes to the lights of the city, and his thoughts passed beyond them to the empty plain beyond, and travelled, as in some spectral caravan, to the tents of his people beside the well of Naomi, to the tent of the maiden Elna. There was his heart, so far away from Babylon and from the queen of its beauty, who leaned towards him, striving to read the meaning of his face. And a great sadness and oppression overtook him, helped by the gesticulations and mysterious faces of the dancers, and by the romantic loveliness of the night, and by the wandering tunes of the hidden instruments in the blackness of the palace court. His whole being cried out to Elna. All this music called to her. And then he thought of Jediah, her husband, holding her in unyielding arms, and a black bitterness flowed into his soul.

"Dost thou love the wonders of Babylon, shepherd?" whispered the soft voice of Ishtar in his ear. "Dost thou love its women and its winecups, its music and its moon? See how she mounts above the cypresses and the palms."

The moon was indeed now higher in the heaven, and her light, pouring over the garden, made the illumination from the quivering torches seem dusky and horribly artificial. All the staring faces of the Babylonians were touched with silver radiance, and the floating robes of the dancers looked like the gossamer robes of elves.

Lemuel, full of the bitterness of his thought, turned to Ishtar.

"Thy city is indeed beautiful, lady," he answered.

"And I, shepherd?"

"Thou art the most beautiful of its wonders."

Ishtar smiled.

"If indeed thou thinkest so," she said, lowering

her voice to a whisper, "why stay with the Lord Alorus?"

Lemuel looked at her with a sort of naïve surprise that she found enchanting.

"Why not stay here with me? E'en now I seek a new attendant. Wilt thou enter into my service? I have my court, as doth the King of Babylon. Wilt thou be among my courtiers and be lodged within the mighty walls of my palace?"

Lemuel glanced around him, at the Indian girls leaping in the moonlight, at the coarse faces of the watching Babylonians, at the slaves who reclined farther away upon the terrace. This palace, he mused, was a true centre of the life of Babylon. Hither came all the great men of the city to worship at the shrine of beauty; idlers, dandies, politicians, priests and merchants, actors and poets, the players of music and the sorcerers and diviners. Nowhere could he spy out the nakedness of Babylon, learn its ways and its secrets, its cruelties and its captives, more surely than here. In no other place, perchance, could he do his people greater service than here, within the courts of the most famous woman of Babylon. Rapidly these thoughts ran through his mind. He turned again to Ishtar and he said—

"Lady, if my Lord Alorus consenteth, I would stay here with thee."

"All the world consents to do my bidding," she answered proudly. "Alorus!"

"What desireth Ishtar?" asked Alorus, withdrawing his eyes from the dancers.

"Thy shepherd will stay here at my side and will be among the number of mine attendants."

The lips of Alorus curled in a smile that was full of meaning.

" As thou wilt, lady," he replied.

Then he bent down to her and whispered—

" Is the heart of Ishtar caught by simplicity ? "

"Or by truth," she answered, with an accent almost of emotion. Then she burst into a laugh, and cried aloud—

" Enough of dancing ! Bring more wine. And summon the charmers and the diviners. We will speed the night more merrily. Drink, my lords, and you, Menanahim—drink ye all to simplicity ! "

She lifted the wine-cup, and, with her eyes fastened on Lemuel, she drained it to the dregs.

That night Lemuel lay in the palace of Ishtar. But he dreamed of Elna and of the plains where rose the tents of his people.

CHAPTER VII

THREE days later, in one of the crowded streets of Babylon, not far from the great temple of Bel-Merodach and the Mound of Amram, Sabaal, the Israelitish slave of the Lord Alorus, stopped a water-carrier who was beating his cups together to attract the attention of the passing multitude, and, making a peculiar sign to him with the fingers, said to him in a low voice—

"Israel in bondage!"

The man instantly gave a counter-sign, replying—

"Israel free!"

"Your report, Elkanus," whispered Sabaal.

"Ten of the house of Josias, six of the house of Eleasor, four of the house of Joahaz."

"'Tis good. We meet to-night at moonrise, behind the house of Maalch."

"So be it," answered the water-carrier, and, in response to an imperative sign from Sabaal, he was about to continue his occupation, when suddenly he started and exclaimed—

"Look!—look yonder!"

"Guard thyself!" responded Sabaal angrily. "Have a care, lest we be suspected. What now?"

"Yonder! yonder!" said Elkanus. "Jediah, son of Zoar!"

"Jediah in Babylon!" exclaimed Sabaal hastily. "What meaneth this?"

And, gazing into the crowd, he saw Jediah slowly approaching, accompanied by Adoram. They were engaged in earnest conversation, and Jediah gesticulated as he talked, in the manner of a man excited and moved to anger.

"Is Jediah with us?" whispered the water-carrier.

"No, against us, and his coming hither bodes naught but evil. Go thy way. To-night!"

"To-night!" replied Elkanus. "Water! water! Clear water! Sweet water!"

He struck his cups together vigorously, and passed on through the street.

Meanwhile, Sabaal moved into the shadow of a gigantic archway through which lay the path to the riverside, and, leaning against the wall, prepared to observe the proceedings of Jediah. This one came on towards the arch. He was closely muffled in a burnous with an enormous hood, and his manner was cautious and watchful.

"Look upon them all," he said to Adoram; "let not one face escape thee. We shall find them. We must. Seek! seek!"

"These endless streets daze me," replied Adoram. "And the noise thereof deafens me. Let us give up the search."

And he paused, as one that is weary.

Jediah turned upon him furiously.

"Give up the search!" he exclaimed. "I tell thee that I will neither rest nor sleep till these guilty ones be found and, before all the people, dragged to judgment."

"To judgment!" said Adoram, in horror. "They two! Elna and thine own brother!"

"Brother! That bond is broken. Lemuel's life is forfeit, and I will exact the penalty—yea, even to the uttermost."

"But there may be some error," said Adoram; "she may not be with him."

Jediah made a gesture of contemptuous impatience.

"Seek Lemuel and learn," continued Adoram.

"Seek him in the house of Ishtar?" said Jediah suspiciously.

"Why not?"

"I know not," answered Jediah, dropping his head on his breast, "I know not. But they say this Ishtar is a dangerous woman, and hath many wiles for men."

"And thou dost fear to meet her?" asked Adoram, staring into the face of his companion.

"I have not said I fear."

"Nay," said Adoram, coming a little closer, "but surely fear is in thine eyes."

"Thou liest!" said Jediah, turning from him angrily. "Why should I fear this woman Ishtar?"

"I know not."

"Nor I," murmured Jediah to himself. "For why should Ishtar be— It is a foolish fancy."

At this moment there was the beating of a staff

on the stones near to them, and a lamentable voice cried with piercing yet mechanical energy—

"Help the blind!   Help the blind!"

Jediah started, as if he had been struck with a thong.   The cry recalled to him the night in which, years ago, he lay in a house of Babylon over against the "House of the Males" and listened in the dark hours to the beating of the great bat about the chamber.   He remembered how his heart waited in terror, as the dawn drew near, for a far-away step at the end of the street, for the tapping of a staff upon the stones of the way.   The bat, like some spirit of evil, uttered its thin and sinister note.   A pale light grew at the window.   He saw the wings of the creature, its grotesque shadow flying along the walls.   The sweat burst forth upon his forehead now, for it seemed to him that he was back in the past, that he heard the beating of a staff upon his door, and that this lamentable cry came from a voice that he knew, from the voice of one who had been his friend and who had trusted in him.

He turned sharply round and beheld a tall man, clothed in filthy rags.   His hair and beard were white, and he looked, at first sight, of a great age. Yet there was something in his gait and movements that seemed to betoken youth, disguised by sorrow, poverty, and the benediction of some terrible tragedy.   Where his eyes should have looked forth upon the sunlit world were two deep holes, like wounds, in which the flesh was discoloured and dry and horrible to gaze upon.   The

flies buzzed about these empty holes and settled
around their edges in multitudes. And the sound
of their hideous activity brought back to Jediah
the sound of the flies in the chamber of the god-
seller long ago, when he waited for the coming of
Migdapul while the darkness fell. The man beat
continually with his staff, and held forth one thin
hand, demanding alms.

"Help the blind! Help the blind!" he cried
again.

Jediah made a step backwards, involuntarily
thrusting abroad his hands. But Adoram, bending
to give the blind man alms, suddenly exclaimed—

"Why, let me look upon thee! Surely, surely
thou art Johanan, husband of Elcia!"

"Yea," answered the blind man, "I am Johanan
—blind, deceived, deserted Johanan. And who
art thou? Come hither. Nay, tell me not. Let
me pass my hands across thy face, and "—

He paused. Then, lifting his lean hands, he
stroked Adoram's face with a pathetic and trembling movement of anxious inquiry.

"I am "—began Adoram.

But Johanan stopped him.

"Ah, no!" he wailed. "Tell me not! Let me
learn for myself. I must teach myself. For I
seek one who is hard to find. Wait."

Again he passed his thin hands over the countenance of Adoram, sensitively, almost greedily,
laying his fingers on the Israelite's eyelids, on his
lips, on his hair and forehead. Then suddenly he
cried—

9

"I know thee!   Thou art of the tribe of Zoar. Wait awhile—wait!   Ah, yea—thou art Adoram!"

As he spoke, Jediah moved hastily, going backwards as if in deadly fear.   Johanan caught the sound.   He lifted one hand to his ear and listened. Then he said—

"Is it not so?   Art thou not indeed Adoram?"

"Yea, I am Adoram.   But what dost thou in Babylon?   And how camest thou into this sorrowful condition?"

"I seek my lost wife," said the blind man.   "I seek my Elcia."

Again Jediah moved a step away.

"There is someone with thee," exclaimed Johanan.   "Who is it?"

"Why"—began Adoram.

But Jediah suddenly caught him by the arm and thrust one hand over his mouth.

"Why doth he not speak?" continued Johanan. "Is he too of the tribe of Zoar?   He doth not answer!   Doth he fear to speak?   Ask him if he knoweth aught of the man who stole my Elcia from me, the wife of my bosom—of those who tore out my eyes.   Answer me, I say!   Who is by thy side?"

The blind man had become greatly excited. His suspicions were aroused by the strange silence of Adoram's companion.   And he now moved forward, spreading out his hands to grasp this presence that he could not see.   Adoram was about to speak, but Jediah dragged him away.   He resisted, crying—

"Art thou mad?   Art thou mad, I say?   What ails thee?"

"Silence!" hissed Jediah into his ear.   "Silence, I say!   Come, come!"

And he pulled him frantically on into the midst of the crowd.   But the blind man had heard his voice, despite his precaution.

"Jediah, son of Zoar, who was my friend!" Johanan cried.   "Jediah!   What doth he in Babylon? Why does he fear to speak to blind Johanan?"

"H'st! h'st!" said Sabaal, coming cautiously out of the shadow of the archway where he had been concealed.

"Who speaks?" said Johanan.

"That was Jediah, son of Zoar, who was here but now."

"What! Sabaal!   Yea, it was even Jediah.   I heard his voice.   But why doth he fear me?   I was his friend.   Dost hear?   His friend."

"I know not, but"—he hesitated, musing darkly, —"perchance I can make a guess.   But enough! Let thine ears be ever on the alert, Johanan. Thou goest sometimes to the palace of Ishtar to ask alms.   Is it not so?"

"It is so."

"If thou canst get speech with Lemuel, who abideth there, give him this cylinder.   It contains the names and the abiding-places of the leaders of the brethren."

He handed to him, surreptitiously, a cylinder. This was a sort of hollow tube, and within it, inscribed on a film of clay which, when wet, was used by the dwellers in Babylon as a writing material, were the names of the Israelites who were chiefly concerned in the movement for Israel's freedom.   Then he whispered—

"Thou understandest?   Be guarded."

"As of my life!" answered Johanan, concealing the cylinder swiftly in his bosom.

Sabaal hastened away, and Johanan, once more striking with his stick upon the stones of the street, lifted up his voice and renewed his melancholy cry—

"Help the blind!   Help the blind!"

Among the Babylonians who thronged the street, buying from the hucksters and talking gaily to the women who strolled along the shadowed side of the way or looked out from the windows, were Menanahim and some of the courtiers from the royal palace, which stood on an artificial mound to the north of the hill of Amram, with which it was connected by a broad causeway supported on arches.   And even as Johanan lifted up his voice, Meraioth, a rich woman of the town, came down the street with Lemuel, who was now richly attired in Babylonish garments and who wore upon his arms and neck golden ornaments presented to him by Ishtar.   As they came up to the place where Menanahim was standing, Meraioth said—

"And so, having wooed the man unavailingly, the lady bought him as her slave.   And then"—

"What happened then?" asked Lemuel simply.

Meraioth burst into a laugh, which was echoed by all the courtiers.

" What ever happens when a woman buys a handsome man ? "

The laugh rang out again, and some Babylonish women, who had gathered round, joined in it, responding impudently to the significant glances of the men.   But Lemuel said gravely—

" And thou canst laugh at this ? "

" And canst not thou ? " sneered Menanahim, with the dandified lisp that he affected.   " It is a merry jest."

" It is new to me to regard such things as jests," said Lemuel.

" Ah ! but thou art new to Babylon," said Meraioth.

" Indeed I am—and to the ways of her people. Pardon my simplicity."

" Nay," said Menanahim, " it is refreshing as the water-springs in a desert.   For simplicity in man, at least in Babylon, is so rare."

" As rare in her men as innocence in her women ? " asked Lemuel quietly.

Meraioth turned to Menanahim.   Her tinted lips curled in a smile of irony.

" Innocence ! " she cried.   " Ha, ha, ha !   What should a daughter of Babylon do with innocence ? "

" What indeed ? " echoed her companions.

" The daughters of my people regard it as a priceless jewel," said Lemuel.   " I have ever been taught to reverence it."

" Then, my simple shepherd," said Menanahim, playing with the seal that dangled from his wrist, " then thou hast much to learn, and hast been most vilely taught. Innocence! A mental blindness that leadeth its possessor into every moral slough and pitfall."

"Unless 'tis guided by the car of instinct."

"Instinct!" said Meraioth; "a woman's instinct! When did the instinct of a woman fail to misguide her to her natural enemy, man?"

"Man is woman's natural protector," said Lemuel.

"Is he, shepherd?" laughed Menanahim, bending with mock courtesy. "Is he? Then is he the most unnatural of created things. For never doth he follow nature's promptings. Ah! my poor, untaught guardian of the innocent lamb —study the elders of thy flocks, or, better still, go learn of Ishtar. Ishtar is just the tutor thou requirest."

And he looked jealously askance at the magnificent figure of Lemuel, which contrasted cruelly with his own meagre form and face lined with dissipation.

"I am content to learn at Ishtar's feet," said Lemuel, "and for that learning would risk my very life."

He spoke significantly, looking calmly around him at the tittering Babylonians.

"Help the blind!" cried the melancholy voice of Johanan, who still lingered in the street, and whose sharp cars had caught the sound of Lemuel's speech.

Lemuel looked round and saw the poor beggar, who carried his thin hand to his bosom, in which the cylinder lay hidden.

"Friends," he said to the Babylonians, "will ye not go on to the palace of Ishtar to await my coming there?"

"But why tarriest thou?" said Meraioth. "Hath our merry jest indeed shocked thee so much that thou would'st leave us?"

"Nay," answered Lemuel, "but I am in Babylon to learn her ways, understand her jests, and study her griefs. And I would be alone awhile to watch the crowd of those that pass."

"Oh, have thy way, shepherd," said Menanahim. "But thou wilt have jestings enough at Ishtar's feet and grief enough to give thee lifelong study, my poor simplicity! Do but sow rubies in Ishtar's field—thy crop of grief will surely follow."

As he spoke he made a profound obeisance before Lemuel. All the courtiers followed his example, as if saluting the king himself. Then, retreating backwards before him, they burst into a peal of laughter, and turning, strolled away down the street, talking gaily and making a thousand jests, saluting the pretty women and throwing alms to the beggars who thronged about their footsteps.

Lemuel looked after them, murmuring to himself—

"Perchance the grief will not be mine alone, fair Lady Ishtar."

"Help the blind!" cried Johanan, drawing near.

"Hold thine hands, father," said Lemuel, giving him an alms.

"Israel in bondage, son of Zoar!" whispered Johanan

"Israel free, Johanan, son of Elihud," whispered Lemuel, in return.

Then, going closer, he added softly—

"What is thy news?"

"Deign to place another coin in my hands," said Johanan.

And as Lemuel did so he secretly passed to him the cylinder containing the names of the chiefs of the brethren. Lemuel scanned them eagerly.

"The names of our friends and their dwelling-places," he said. "I thank thee."

"Guard well the cylinder," murmured the blind man. "It is charged with death and fate."

"It is in safe keeping," answered Lemuel, as he concealed it in his silken robe.

"Water, my lord! Cool and sweet for those who thirst!" cried the voice of Elkanus.

Lemuel turned from the blind man, saying—

"Thou here, Elkanus! Thy news?"

"The brethren murmur, O Lemuel."

"At what?"

"At thy constant presence in the house of that daughter of Babylon, Ishtar," exclaimed the voice of Sabaal, who suddenly stole out of the crowd to Lemuel's side, followed at a little distance by Jozadah, the hireling of Jediah. "Thy brethren groan beneath the lashes of this wanton and of her lovers, while thou art ever at her feet, hearkening to her lustful songs and joining in her shameless revelry."

While he spoke a number of wild-looking men

of the rabble, bearing staffs, had been gathering furtively round Lemuel, and as Jozadah added—

"Ay, he's a traitor and would betray us to the Babylonians! Kill him! kill him!" they rushed upon Lemuel, joining in the cry.

But Lemuel drew his sword, and seizing Jozadah and holding him fast with one powerful hand, he exclaimed—

"And hearken thou, Jozadah, spy and traitor! I am at Ishtar's feet for no love of her or of her kind. I have no love save one, and her I left by Naomi's well, never to see again. For that love's sake came I hither. It is strong enough to keep me undefiled even in that place of sin and lust, the house of Ishtar. Let the brethren be comforted ; I am at Ishtar's feet to drag our enemies to the dust. And amid all the glare of gems and of wanton beauty, there is in my brain and heart but one thought—Israel in bondage, and but one desire—Israel free!"

He flung Jozadah to the ground, while the crowd, changed already from enemies into friends, broke forth into cries of approval and admiration.

"Go hence!" he said to Jozadah, who lay trembling at his feet. "Go hence, ere I stain my sword with thy base blood!"

Jozadah, rising to his feet in terror, made off, throwing many a timorous glance behind him. Then Lemuel, putting aside the Israelites who thronged about him, strode away in the direction of Ishtar's palace.

He was already within sight of its monstrous

walls of gleaming red brick, when he encountered Menanahim, who was hurrying, breathless, towards him.

"Whom seekest thou, my lord?" he asked.

Menanahim stopped.

"Thee, O favoured mortal!" he answered, endeavouring to conceal the bitterness of his jealousy. "By the Seven, the all-powerful Seven, Zi-ana-ana be they conjured! but thou art the most favoured or unfavoured mortal. For I, after much seeking among women, I—I, Menanahim, versed in the ways of these our plagues and blessings, our slaves and despots, those whom we much despise and much obey, whom we fondle and fear, discard, yet cannot live without—even I cannot decide whether 'tis good or evil for thee; but sooth it is either because thou art new to them—and the newest toy doth ever catch the eye of child and woman—or for some other charm, but sooth it is that many of these, our daughters of Babylon, have looked upon thee with an eye of favour, and so—and so"—

"Take breath, my lord," interrupted Lemuel; "and if thou hast a message, pray give it to thy servant."

"I was travelling toward that — that same message."

"Hast thou not reached thy journey's end?"

"Almost, shepherd, but in sooth it is a weary road that a poor man doth tread that hath a woman at both ends and a third to watch him at the half-way."

"Well?—thy message?"

"Verily, O shepherd of Israel, these sheep, these lambs of ours,"—and he pointed to the towering palace of Ishtar,—"yea, even the choice ones of the flock of the lambs of Babylon,—do bleat themselves hoarse for thee.   Though, indeed, what they do in thee behold "—

"I come to them," said Lemuel, cutting him short.

And, followed by Menanahim, he mounted to the palace.

CHAPTER VIII

ALMOST at the same time that the events related
in the preceding chapter were taking place, in
another quarter of the city a great crowd of Babylonians had assembled to see a procession pass by
to the mighty temple of Bel - Merodach. This
temple lay to the north of the Mound of Kasr,
and was a huge pile of brickwork, of quadrilateral
shape, with an almost flat top and precipitous
sides. Millions of bricks had been used in its
construction. These bricks were made of the
tenacious mud found on the alluvial plains, mixed
with chopped straw. Before they became dry
they were placed on each other, and the heat of
the sun caked them together. They were cemented
often with a material composed of bitumen and
other substances, and covered with a glaze of rich
enamel, lustrous and brilliant to the eyes. The
gates of the temple were made of solid brass. But
the most remarkable of its features were its eight
towers, which were raised one on the top of
the other as if they would climb into the highest
heaven. On the outside of these towers a path
had been built which wound up and up round them
till it reached the summit. There were seats by

the way, on which those who were weary might rest and enjoy a magnificent view over Babylon. Below this temple, outside the vast precinct within which it was enclosed, there was a square, in which stood palm trees and flashing fountains, and here the people had assembled to see the procession of the god pass by. The little children were held up in the arms of their devout and superstitious mothers. The men raised themselves on their toes to see the better. The beggars, for the moment, forgot their sores and their necessities, and the whole mass of human beings was moved by but one impulse, the impulse of worship, as the great image, fashioned in pure gold that gleamed in the sunshine, was borne by. Before it came radiantly beautiful maidens, crowned with flowers and attired in rich stuffs, who sprang and danced as David may have danced before the ark, expressing religious enthusiasm by ardent bodily exercises, by fantastic gestures, even by cries and wild exclamations, which increased the excitement of the multitude. They scattered flowers along the path of the god, twisted like Dervishes, and were untiring in agility. Under the glare of the sun they seemed almost like radiant humming - birds, or birds of Paradise. Their long hair streamed down and floated in a cloud round their lissom bodies, and their little feet twinkled in the golden sandals which they wore instead of shoes. Behind them came the minstrels, playing on cymbals, beating drums, and plucking the frail strings of citherns. And behind them again the singers solemnly walked, uplifting their voices in a great chorus—

> " O Thou who reignest above the Seven,
> And rulest the evil of the South-West wind !
> Burn up our enemies, lead us to heaven ;
> In chains and torture thou our foemen bind.
> Keep thou the Namtar from us—wicked he
> Who would thy slaves assail and bring them woe.
> Oh, send thy sun to light and set us free,
> While to Arali let our foemen go."

The shout of the singers filled the sparkling air as they passed on through the mob, glancing neither to the right nor the left. Then came the priests, wearing the sacred skins of animals, and then the statue of the god, borne aloft on the shoulders of four men, and followed by more priests, singers, minstrels, dancers, and servitors of the temple. As it went by, all the people made obeisance, saving only the Jews. These turned aside or shrank away in horror. But few heeded them. For the Babylonians, though given over to money-making, to gluttony, and to dissipation of every kind, were intensely superstitious, and, in looking upon the effigy of the god, they had for the moment but one thought, one prayer—to be taken up at last, after death and the passing of the soul from earthly things, to the summit of the great mountain hidden in eternal cloud, the mountain of the East, the mountain of the world, where the apex of the firmament rested, and the golden stars hung round like the lamps in the temples of Babylon. Here would ascend only the souls of the great and of the good from the world of the dead which lay in dimness far below the earth, where all was darkness and terrible gloom, and the spirits flitted to and fro like bats, with naught to eat save dust alone. This dread region was barred by seven gates, and in the midst of it sat the rulers of Hades on a throne of solid gold, beneath which ran eternally the gushing waters of life. And Merodach alone—he who now went by to his temple with the great tower and the portals of brass—could raise up the spirits of the dead from darkness into the world of everlasting light. So all the people prostrated themselves, kissing the hem of the priests' garments, and bending their souls to prayer, while the music sounded ever, and the chorus rang out—

> " O Thou who reignest above the Seven,
> Burn up our enemies, lead us to heaven ! "

So engrossed were all the people in gazing upon the god and in murmuring their prayers to it, that but few noticed a pale and travel-worn boy who entered the square in the wake of the procession, leaning wearily upon a staff, and moving slowly as one exhausted with fatigue. This boy had a beautiful face lit by blue eyes, his hair was dark, and his mouth was red as a rose, while the delicate smallness of his hands and feet seemed almost like that of a girl. He looked very young, scarcely seventeen, and had a strange air of helplessness and of bewilderment in the throng and in the press of the multitude. Among all this multitude, at first only one human being noticed him, and this was a buxom fruit-girl who was seated upon the marble steps of a house with her big basket at her feet.   Her sense of religion did not prevent her from keeping an eye on her worldly prosperity, and, on perceiving this fatigued wanderer, she cried out in a ringing voice—

"Ripe fruit !   Sweet grapes !"

The boy hesitated, and looked eagerly towards her basket, in which the fruit lay temptingly surrounded by fresh green leaves.

"I parch with thirst," he murmured. "Child, are those costly?" he added, pointing to the grapes.

"Wert thou a daughter of Babylon, they would be," replied the girl gaily; "but since thou art but a stranger boy, and hast bright eyes and a face goodly to look upon, they shall not be costly unto thee."

And, as she spoke, she cast upon him a glance full of open admiration.

The boy drew forth a coin and gave it to her, saying—

"Will that suffice ? "

"For thee to pay?   Yea, sweet shepherd," replied the girl, handing to him a goodly bunch of purple grapes.

"How knowest thou me for a shepherd ? " asked the boy.

"Firstly, thou art timid, like the sheep ; then thou art not of Babylon, else had'st thou praised mine eyes and my form and face, as I even now praised thine. Thou art from the plains, art thou not ? "

"I am," said the boy more feebly, "and weary with my long travel."

The girl moved and made room on the step beside her.

"Sit thou here," she said coaxingly.

The boy obeyed.

"Hast thou come from very far?" the girl continued, looking closely into his white face.

"Yea."

"And did'st thou walk?"

"Yea."

"Art thou not an Israelite?"

The boy hesitated for a moment. ·Then he said—

"I am."

"A pretty boy, a stranger, and an Israelite," said the girl musingly; "beware lest they do sell thee into slavery."

"They will not dare!" exclaimed the boy, with a sudden flash of energy; "I am a free wom—"

"What?" cried the girl.

"I say I am free."

"'Twill avail thee but little to say thou art free, unless thou hast friends to protect thee. Our lords of Babylon look upon all Israelites as their lawful bondsmen. It was but yesterday we had a riot in the streets, and every Israelite who was at hand was taken and whipped and sold in the market-place."

"Alas!" cried the boy, trembling visibly and shrinking against the wall.

"Why," said the fruit-girl, "thou art trembling! Thou art a very timid boy, even for a shepherd."

"Nay, but I never saw a city like unto this

before, and the noise, the people, the great buildings—all do oppress me."

"But why did'st thou come to Babylon?"

"That I may not tell," answered the boy.

He hesitated. Then he put an arm around the girl's shoulder, and said more impulsively—

"And yet—let me look into thine eyes—yea, I will trust thee."

"Thou mayest," said the girl, "for I do swear I like thee well."

"I came, then, to seek one called Lemuel, son of Zoar, an Israelite. Knowest thou aught of him?"

"Who doth not?" exclaimed the girl. "Why, all the city speaks of him. Is he thy lord?"

"My lord? Ah, yes!"

"I saw him abroad in the city but this very morning."

The boy suddenly started up, exclaiming—

"Here? O Lemuel! Lemuel!"

"Well," said the fruit-girl, staring in amazement, "that's strange! So might a girl call out the name of her lover. This same Lemuel must be a gentle master, if thou dost love him thus."

"Yes, yes—he is, he is!" said the boy, still with excitement. "But whither went he? Who was with him? Where is he now?"

"Well, he went hence with some of Ishtar's fine lords and ladies."

"Ishtar! What is Ishtar?"

"One who maketh men mad with love — and who selleth her love to the highest bidder. That is the way in Babylon, shepherd."

“Can love be bought and sold?”

“Yea. And so Ishtar grows rich and queens it over kings and princes.”

“And—and Lemuel?” asked the boy.

“Is ever at her feet, and she, for a miracle, doth leave all others at a beckon from his finger, though he be but poor.”

“But—but he—doth not love her? Lemuel could not indeed love such a woman.”

“Ah, boy, when thou art older thou wilt be wiser. Men—and I speak who have met many, selling my fruit here in the streets—men are strange creatures and unaccountable.”

The boy’s white face grew whiter, and his delicate limbs trembled more piteously, as he cried in a lamentable voice—

“But he—Lemuel—could not! I know him. Ah, help! help!”

The fruit - girl sprang up, knocking over her basket.

“What aileth thee?” she cried. “The blood forsakes thy cheek!”

Even as she spoke, the boy wavered and dropped down at her very feet. The fruit-girl, in terror, cried aloud for help, and the crowd, now ready for any diversion, since the god had been borne within the precinct of his temple, began to gather round the prostrate shepherd, who lay to all appearance lifeless on the stones.

As they were all uttering exclamations and buzzing with comments, a loud and authoritative voice exclaimed—

"What hath happened?   Room, I say! room!
Stand clear there!"

And the Lord Alorus, accompanied by several
richly dressed attendants, pushed his way through
the throng.

"What is this, girl?" he said to the fruit-seller.

"This boy hath swooned," she answered piteously.

"The heat of the day "—

"Nay, my lord, I think not so.   'Tis something
concerning his master, Lemuel, so please you."

"Lemuel!" said Alorus.

And, bending down, he lifted the boy's head on
his arm, and gazed into the white face.

"By Baal!" he murmured, in astonishment,
"'tis the lovely Elna!   Give me some water!"
he cried aloud.

Elkanus, the water-carrier, pushed his way to the
step and handed him water in a gourd.   Alorus
put the gourd to the lips of Elna, who stirred and
stretched forth one hand, as if seeking help.

"'Tis a pretty boy," said the fruit-girl, "but
weak as a girl."

"Thou speakest truth," said Alorus, smiling.
"As weak as a girl, in very sooth."

At this moment Elna recovered her senses somewhat.   She sat up, stared wildly round, and, seeing
all the strange faces watching her, cried out in
terror—

"Ah, release me!—I have done no harm!   Let
me go!"

As she spoke she rose, trembling, to her feet,

and took her staff from the hands of a Babylonian who had picked it up.

"Thou art safe—boy," said Alorus, with meaning.

"Boy!" said Elna.   "Ah, yes,—I know now. But Lemuel,"—she passed her hand across her eyes,—"where is"—

She turned round and beheld Alorus smiling at her.

"Ah, the Lord Alorus!" she exclaimed. "How came I thus?"

"He knoweth thee, my lord," said the fruit-girl, in surprise.   "Dost thou know him?"

"Should I not, girl," said Alorus, laughing, "seeing that this boy is one of my slaves?"

"Slave!" said Elna, in terror.   "I—a slave! Nay, nay!"

Alorus went up to her, caught her by the arm, and whispered—

"Admit it! Own that thou art my slave, or thou art lost."

"Slave!" murmured Elna.   "Ah, Lemuel!"

And she looked appealingly at Alorus.

"Own it," he whispered, "and I will take thee unto Lemuel.   I am thy friend."

"I can trust thee?" said Elna, gazing at him doubtfully and with fear in her lovely eyes.

"Yes, yes."

'He turned to one of his attendants.

"Hither, Jael," he said.   "This boy is my slave. None have I of more value to me.   On thy head be it if he escapes thee."

As he spoke the attendants surrounded Elna. But she shrank away from them, crying—

"Let me go!—I can walk now. I shall not faint again. I can walk—but do not touch me, I pray thee."

And she took a few steps forward, moving with difficulty and with a wavering gait. The attendants, crowding about her, would have supported her, but, with feeble hands, she tried to thrust them away, exclaiming—

"No, no! Touch me not! I am well now—quite well!"

But even as she spoke the words she staggered again and would have fallen, had not Alorus himself caught her in his arms, and, lifting her up some steps that led to an archway on the eastern side of the square, disappeared with her towards his palace.

The crowd began quickly to separate and to resume their occupations, interrupted by the procession of the god and this subsequent incident. Soon the fruit-girl sat alone with her basket.

Her eyes were still fixed on the archway through which Alorus and the shepherd boy had disappeared, and she thought to herself—

"Poor boy! And he so dreaded slavery! Truly, Babylon is a cruel city."

Then, lifting up her clear young voice, she cried again and again—

"Grapes! Sweet grapes! Who will buy sweet grapes?"

CHAPTER IX

ON the evening of the same day, Ishtar's retinue
of slaves were arranging the silken cushions and
the golden and ivory couches upon the terrace of
her palace garden. Almost every night she held
a sort of gay court under the palms and the
cypress trees. The Indians, or the Babylonish
maidens, danced, the charmers of snakes ex-
hibited their reptiles, and the air was full of the
soft glimmer of distant music. Hither came all
the flower of the youth of the city, all the great
nobles, all the dandies, and, more strangely, perhaps,
many men of learning—astrologers, politicians, and
soothsayers. For Ishtar knew how to attract the
thinkers and the philosophers as well as the empty-
headed and the idly frivolous. Her face was
beautiful, but she was no mask without a brain
or soul behind it. And there were men who
worshipped her for her mind even more than for
her great eyes and her magnificent bearing.

The slaves were alone in the garden, for Ishtar
was within the palace feasting with some guests,
and the sound of far - away citherns and flutes
stole out to the shadowy spaces beside the water.
Down in the city the red and yellow lights were

beginning to twinkle, and the soft darkness of night closed rapidly round.

The slaves, as they went about their work, chattered among themselves of the doings of their lady, of the despair of her lovers, of the rich gifts that were ever being offered at her shrine, of a thousand things. Sometimes they broke forth into laughter, but the laughter was low and hushed, and even the chatter seemed submissive and surreptitious. As they were heaping up a pile of cushions by one of the fountains, Sabaal, the slave of Alorus, entered the garden by some marble steps that led to a lower terrace, and, coming upon one of the slaves, said to him—

"My Lord Alorus cometh hither. Where is Ishtar?"

"Ask where is Lemuel," the slave replied significantly.

Two or three of his companions laughed.

"Where is Lemuel, then?" said Sabaal.

"Even where Ishtar is," answered the slave, who was a captive Israelite. "This our deliverer! Ever at the feet of this daughter of Babylon, hearkening to her wanton love-songs and gazing upon her charms!"

An angry look crossed the dark face of Sabaal, but he answered—

"Thou wrongest Lemuel. He is here not for the sake of Ishtar but of Israel. Where can he so easily spy out the nakedness of the land as among these drunken lords who revel in Ishtar's palace? Lemuel is true, but we who are weak

must work by guile.   Trust him as thou would'st
trust thyself."

"Sayest thou "— began the slave.

But Sabaal suddenly whispered—

" My master!   Silence!

Even as he spoke the Lord Alorus approached,
attended by his slaves, and said to the slaves of
Ishtar, who bowed before him—

" Where is thy lady? "

"Within the inner gates, O lord," replied the
slave who had spoken with Sabaal.

"Go, tell her I have come as bidden," said
Alorus.

The slaves of Ishtar retired towards the palace
court, and Alorus, turning to Sabaal, said—

" Remain thou here, Sabaal, and be at my side
when the Lady Ishtar comes hither."

" I will be at my lord's bidding," said Sabaal,
with the deep servility that he always displayed
towards his possessor.

Alorus walked slowly along the terrace and
returned.   He seemed to be deep in thought.
Presently, he lifted up his head and said to
Sabaal—

" Sabaal, a new slave hath been added to my
household "—

He paused.

" Yea, my lord ? " said Sabaal.

" A boy," continued Alorus, " one—Amos.   He
hath gone to my palace under the care of Jael.
This — ah — this boy is precious in my sight,
although a slave.   See that he is well cared for

when thou returnest.   Let him have the chamber
next unto mine own.   Set him no task, but let
one of the handmaidens be sent to him.   He is
but young, and the rough ways of the men slaves
may affright him.   Dost understand?"

"I understand, my lord," answered Sabaal.

"As thou dost with him," said Alorus, with
emphasis, "so shalt thou win my favour.   If any
harm come to him, on thy head be it.   Remain
thou here.   I would be alone for a while."

And on the last words he moved slowly away
down one of the small and shaded paths of the
garden, still bending down his head as if in profound thought.   As he went, the whole demeanour
of Sabaal abruptly changed.   The servility died
out of his face and his bearing.   He half started
forward, with one strong arm raised as if to do
violence to his master, while he muttered between
his teeth—

"Thy favour!   Thine!   Ah, when my hand is
on thy throat, my knife in thy heart, thou wilt
grant me all the favour I care to take at thy hands
—thy dying groans, thou arrogant Babylonian!"

And then, as if fatigued by the rage that
possessed him, he flung himself down upon the
ground, beneath an immense cypress tree, and
buried his head in his arms.   To the murmur of
music within the palace of Ishtar was now added
the sound of song, very soft and distant, but clear
and tender in the night.   As Sabaal crouched
beneath the cypress tree, hot with the fury of his
wrongs and of his servitude, he heard the singing

as a man may hear echoes in an evil dream of the night. The voices seemed to him like the voices of devils, mocking his wrongs and the wrongs of his persecuted people. And, with a muttered imprecation on Babylon and on all within her mighty walls, he was about to thrust his fingers into his ears when he heard another sound beside the music, a cautious and hesitating footstep upon the terrace near him. He raised his head and saw, standing full in the light of the rising moon, the slight figure of a boy, who appeared to be listening to the music within the palace. This boy, after a moment's pause, stole very cautiously forward, as if intending to gain the archway of the first court of the palace. But Sabaal, starting up with the swiftness of a panther, intercepted him and exclaimed—

"Whither goest thou?"

The boy uttered a cry of surprise.

"Sabaal!"

Then he shrank away, concealing his face in the folds of the garment he wore.

"Whither goest thou?" repeated Sabaal roughly, coming towards him.

"What is that to thee?" answered the boy, without lifting his face.

"Who art thou?" continued Sabaal.

"I seek my master," said the boy.

"Who is thy master?"

"Lemuel, son of Zoar."

Sabaal made a movement of surprise. Then he said with caution—

"What wantest thou with Lemuel, son of Zoar?"

"I—I have a—a message for him," murmured the boy with obvious hesitation.

"From whom?"

The boy was silent for an instant; then he said, slowly and timidly—

"From my Lord Alorus."

"So! so!" exclaimed Sabaal. "Left'st thou but now the Lord Alorus?"

"But—but a short time since."

"And he sent thee hither with a message, thou sayest?"

"Have I not said?"

"Yea, thou hast—that which is false. The Lord Alorus hath sent thee with no message hither, for he is himself within."

"Ah!" exclaimed the boy.

And he turned suddenly as if to flee. But Sabaal caught him fast by the wrist, crying—

"Now let me see thy face!"

"No, no!" cried the boy.

"I will, I tell thee!" said Sabaal angrily.

And he seized the boy in his arms, swung him round, and tore the robe from his face, exclaiming—

"Thou fool! Let me look on thee!"

Then, as he saw the boy's face in the moonlight, he cried—

"Elna!"

"Yea," Elna answered, drooping her head.

"Mad, wicked girl! What brought thee hither?"

"Love," she answered, in a low voice, while her cheeks were stained with scarlet.

" Love for whom ? "

" My lord."

" Thy lord ?   Jediah ? "

" Jediah !—nay, Lemuel."

" Thou art here to seek Lemuel ? "

" Yea."

" And thou hast left our people to seek Lemuel in Babylon, and in a garb that, for a woman, is an abomination and a sin ? "

" I count naught sinful that I do to protect the man I love," answered Elna, with sudden firmness.

" Protect him !" said Sabaal, with contempt. " Foolish maid ! thou art more like to destroy him. Lemuel hath sterner work than dallying with a love-sick girl.   He is in danger."

" For that came I hither," said Elna proudly. " I will share it."

" Ay, and thou wilt double it," retorted Sabaal roughly.   "Get thee hence !"

But Elna stood her ground bravely.   All her timidity seemed to have left her.   She faced Sabaal now with fearless eyes, as she answered, unflinchingly—

" Not until I have looked on him for whom I have come up to this accursed city."

" Accursed, indeed !" said Sabaal, " and accursed be thou if thou dost hinder or destroy the work that Lemuel hath to do within its walls.   Wilt thou hence, I say ? "

" Not until I have seen him."

As he said the last words, unperceived of him or of Elna, Lemuel came forth from the inner court of the palace and advanced into the garden. Sabaal sprang upon Elna and laid his hands on her throat, crying furiously—

"Sooner than that, these hands shall choke thee!"

"Help!" she shrieked. "Help, my lord! help! Lemuel, Lemuel!"

"Silence, thou madwoman!" cried Sabaal, forcing her backward towards the steps that led to the lower terrace.

But Lemuel, hearing a voice cry out his name, and seeing the struggle between Sabaal and Elna, sprang forward, exclaiming—

"Who calleth upon me? Sabaal, let the boy go!"

"Nay, he is a spy, a traitor," returned Sabaal, still forcing Elna towards the steps. "Look not on his face."

"Let him go!" reiterated Lemuel, in a commanding voice.

"Nay, I will not!" cried Sabaal.

And he cast his cloak over Elna's face.

"I will see his face," exclaimed Lemuel, advancing.

"To look on him is death," said Sabaal.

But Lemuel, heedless of his words, caught him by the throat, and hurled him to the ground, saying—

"Did I not tell thee to let him go? Now, boy— Elna!"

Elna, who was panting from excitement and from the violence to which she had been subjected, made no reply. She could not speak. She could only stand before Lemuel with downcast eyes and heaving bosom.

“What hath brought thee hither?” exclaimed Lemuel, in profound amazement.

“My love for thee,” whispered Elna.

And she sank down against the alabaster wall of the terrace, resting her lovely dark head among a cloud of huge red flowers that climbed and clung there. Lemuel bent over her for an instant as if to take her in his arms. Then he controlled himself, and said to Sabaal—

“Sabaal, go hence and keep the Lord Alorus from coming hither.”

“And leave thee with this maid?” said Sabaal bitterly.

“Yea.”

“I entreat thee, Lemuel, think of thy danger!”

“I care naught for danger.”

“The sacred cause of Israel ”—

“No cause of Israel is more sacred than the honour of her daughters. Do as I bid thee. Go!”

Sabaal, whose eyes gleamed with fury and a rage of disappointment, clenched his sinewy hands together, as if he refrained but with difficulty from rushing upon Lemuel to do him violence.

“Accursed be the woman!” he hissed, “and thrice accursed be thou if, for her sake, thou dost betray those who have trusted in thee!”

Then, with an inarticulate exclamation that was almost like the snarl of some savage animal, he slipped away into the shades towards the palace.

When he had gone, Lemuel bent down and raised Elna up in his arms. She was gradually recovering, and now looked up more confidently into his face.

"How camest thou hither?" he asked her tenderly.

"I followed the caravan."

"And in this attire?"

"Yea," she answered.

"Unknown to my father?"

"Yea."

"And to my brother?"

"Even so."

"Dost thou know, my Elna, that to do this is a crime in the eyes of our people? A crime for which there is but one punishment—even death?"

Elna's thoughts flew back to that day when, as a child, she stood beneath the Judgment Seat and cried, with her pitiful little voice, to Jediah for mercy, while the stern crowd hurried the man and the maiden, taken in sin, towards the place of stones. She saw again, as in a vision, their pale and agonised faces. She heard the cruel stones falling—falling around them. Yet she answered and said to Lemuel, with no tremor in her soul—

"I fear it not."

And she spake that which was the truth.

"Death not alone to thee, Elna," continued Lemuel, "but to the man whom thou hast fled to."

"It was to save thee from death that I came hither," she answered. And now, indeed, there was fear in her voice.

" What meanest thou ? " asked Lemuel.

" Thy brother Jediah hath laid snares for thy destruction and hath plotted for thy death."

An expression of deep surprise came into the face of Lemuel.

" Impossible ! " he exclaimed. " Jediah is harsh and stern, but just—and I am his brother."

" And his rival, Lemuel. The night thou did'st depart for Babylon, Tirzah overheard him offer Jozadah a bribe to slay thee."

" Jozadah ! Ah, now I understand ! It was he who attacked me even this very day in a street of the city — who would have slain me ! "

Elna trembled in his arms.

" How horrible ! " she murmured. " Ah, Lemuel, - leave this accursed Babylon ! Let us go—now —now ! "

And she rose up, as if to flee. But Lemuel stood still, and, looking upon her with unutterable tenderness, said to her—

" And thou hast braved the desert, the perils of Babylon, and the penalty of the law to tell me of this treachery ? "

" Yea," she answered.

Then a shade came across her face, and she added—

" And to find thee at the feet of another."

" Thou too dost doubt me, Elna ? Dost thou— canst thou believe that I am in this woman's house for love of her ? "

" How else ? " she said, the suspicious thoughts

II

of a loving woman growing in her heart,—"how else? They have said "—

"And who are 'they'?" he interposed. "'They' are the murderers of reputations. 'They have said!' Trust not in them. I tell thee, I am here for the sake of our captive brethren."

"Thou speakest indeed truth to me?" she said, still with an accent of doubt.

She came close to him and, putting her small hands on his heart, gazed into his eyes.

"Dost thou doubt me?" he said.

"Ah, no!" she cried, laying her head against his heart. "I trust thee now and always."

But suddenly Lemuel loosed his arms from about her and put her back from him.

"Alorus cometh!" he whispered. "Stand away! Hide thyself!"

He motioned hastily with his hand toward some palm trees, and, quick as thought, Elna darted into the shadow. A crowd of Babylonians was indeed approaching from the palace, attended by numérous slaves who carried fans and torches. In the forefront of the crowd walked Alorus, with his usual affected and almost feminine gait, and as he drew near to Lemuel he said—

"Here is the truant! Verily, good shepherd, thou art bold to show this neglect of thine hostess. See where she doth come to bring thee to account."

The Babylonians drew aside, and a number of the female slaves of Ishtar advanced, scattering flowers for their mistress to walk upon. Ishtar herself followed them, walking slowly, like a queen.

She was attired to-night in a flowing robe of silk, purple as the clear sky at midnight, and embroidered with raised stars of silver, in each of which was set a glowing sapphire of enormous size and incomparable lustre. Round her superb throat was a great collar of various precious gems, and more jewels glittered on her arms, in her ears, and in the heavy masses of her hair; while her waist was girt with a chain of wrought silver, from which hung strings of pearls. Her wonderful dark eyes searched the garden as she advanced, and when she perceived Lemuel standing by Alorus in the glare of the torches, she said—

"Ah, thou art here! Why did'st thou leave the feast?"

"The wise man doth not seek to drain all life's happiness at one draught," answered Lemuel.

"Did'st thou hear that, Menanahim?" said Ishtar, with a smile, to the haggard courtier who was close at her side.

"Yes," he answered; "our shepherds are quick to learn."

"He is but a poor shepherd who hath not learned to know a sheep when he seeth one," said Lemuel to Menanahim.

Then, bowing low before Ishtar, while the slaves stood silently around her, he added—

"With such a tutor, who could be slow? To learn of Ishtar is but to follow instinct. As instinct leadeth the camel to the oasis and to the waters, so follow I man's instinct, which leadeth me out of the desert of common mortals to the oasis where dwelleth and reigneth the goddess Ishtar."

" Better and better," said Ishtar gaily. "'Twas well and sweetly said. But, alas!" and her face looked for a moment clouded, "thine instinct, or something less flattering to thy queen, led thee not to, but from my side. How interpretest thou that?"

" I feared to be drunk with too much joy. And I longed to walk apart, lady, and think on thee alone and in silence."

Ishtar extended her hand to him with a gesture of affection. "Thou thinkest ever on me?" she asked tenderly.

But ere ever Lemuel could reply there was the noise of a struggle in the garden. One of the slaves of Alorus had chanced upon the place where Elna lay hid, and now sought to drag her forth, crying—

" For what evil purpose art thou here? Why hidest thou thus among the trees of the garden? Come forth, I say,—come into the light."

Elna resisted, and, woman-like, cried out as the slave laid his rough hands upon her delicate flesh. And Ishtar, hearing the noise, exclaimed—

" What was that cry?"

At this moment Elna got free from the slave and rushed towards the steps of the terrace. But she was stopped by Alorus, who moved suddenly forward and intercepted her.

" Let me pass!" she cried desperately.

" Who is this boy?" said Ishtar. " Hold the torch, slaves! Who is he?"

" My slave, Ishtar," said Alorus, coming forward, still holding Elna fast.

" Thy slave ! " exclaimed Lemuel.   " Thou liest ! "

" Guard thy tongue, Israelite ! " said Alorus angrily, and putting his hand on the knife that hung at his girdle.

" She — he is no slave of thine," reiterated Lemuel, while Ishtar gazed from one to the other in growing anger.

" No ? " responded Alorus sarcastically.   " Let him decide. Answer, boy," and he turned upon Elna. " Tell these lords—art thou not my slave ? "

Then he whispered to her—

" Deny it, and Lemuel's death is sure ! "

He paused, but Elna made no answer.

" Art thou not my slave ? " he repeated, in a louder and more authoritative voice.

Elna cast a terrified glance towards Lemuel. Then she said in a trembling voice—

" I am slave unto my lord."

" What doth she mean ? " said Lemuel, as if half to himself.

" A pretty boy, indeed," said Ishtar to Alorus. " He is new to me. When did'st thou purchase him ? "

" Even this very day," replied Alorus. " He is from Israel, Lemuel. Knowest thou him ? "

And he pulled at his pointed and scented beard and smiled cruelly as he spoke the words.

" I know not all Israelites," said Lemuel.

" Strange thou dost not recognise this one ! "

" Are all who dwell in Babylon known to thee ? " retorted Lemuel.

Ishtar had now sunk down upon a couch. She leaned forward and tapped the arm of Alorus with the great fan she carried.

" What demon of discord hath entered, unbidden, to my feast to-night? Let us chase him hence. He loveth not good wine. Hither! Slaves, pass the wine-cup. Lemuel, come hither. Rest upon this couch by me."

Lemuel obeyed the command of Ishtar, and reclined upon the cushions at her side. But his eyes were still ever fixed upon Elna, to whom the Lord Alorus now said—

" Ay, and do thou, Amos,—that is thy name, is it not?—do thou stand by my side and wait upon me."

At these words Lemuel sprang up from the couch of Ishtar, exclaiming—

" Nay, that shall not be ! "

" Why not ? " asked Ishtar, frowning and pressing her white fingers so closely against the ebony sticks of the fan she carried that one of them broke in two. " Why not? What! shall Alorus not choose his own slaves ? "

" Yea, lady—but "—

" Well ? " demanded Ishtar imperiously.

" 'Tis scarce a compliment to the hostess to despise her servitors," answered Lemuel, striving to control his emotion.

" So do not I," interrupted Alorus, carelessly sprinkling himself with essence out of a silver bottle. " But this boy is an Israelite, and I take great interest in all things of Israel. Why, there was a dispute but now in the palace between Menanahim and myself as to the punishment of certain crimes against the laws of Israel. Amos shall decide who was in the right. Answer, boy. Is it lawful or no for a maid to put on man's attire ? "

And he turned to Elna and looked impudently into her white face. She cast down her eyes and stood in silence, trembling.

"Come," urged Alorus ; "surely thou dost know ! Answer."

"Let me answer, my lord," suddenly cried the slave Sabaal, fixing his piercing and excited eyes on Lemuel. "It is not lawful. And the woman is an abomination in the sight of the people."

"I spake not unto thee," cried Alorus pettishly. "Answer only when thou art questioned. This other thing I, too, would know. If a maid is betrothed unto one man, and another take her, what is the punishment for both? Thou canst not be ignorant. Come, answer."

"I will answer," said Lemuel, moving a step forward. "The punishment is death."

Ishtar, who had half risen on her couch, leaning upon one arm, suddenly fell back on the cushions, with a movement that was like a shudder. Her face, always pale, had become of a dusky colour, grey like the clouds before dawn. And her huge eyes stared like the eyes of one taken by fever.

"To one or to both?" said Alorus, facing Lemuel.

"To both," answered Lemuel. "They shall be stoned with stones until they die."

"I will no more of this," Ishtar cried sharply. "Who careth for these silly laws of a captive nation? Who heedeth them? Pass round the wine."

And, as she spoke, she shivered, as if with cold.

Alorus caught hold of Elna.

"Amos," he said, "do thou fill thee a cup and drink to thy master and to Babylon."

And he bent down over her till his beard touched against her delicate cheek.

"That shall not be!" exclaimed Lemuel. "Let be!"

And seizing Alorus in his strong hands, he flung him away from Elna. Alorus drew his knife, and crying—

"Insolent Israelite! Dost thou dare lay hands upon me?" was about to attack Lemuel, when Ishtar, starting up from her couch, exclaimed—

"What is this, my lords? Come hither, boy. I would look at thee more closely."

Elna reluctantly approached Ishtar, who took hold of her by the wrists, and cried to a slave—

"I command thee, hold a torch to this boy's face."

The slave obeyed, and Ishtar gazed long and fixedly into the face of Elna.

"Who art thou?" she asked at length.

"Amos, my slave," said Alorus, laughing affectedly. "Servant of my body."

"Thou liest!" said Lemuel.

Ishtar bent closer to regard Elna, on whose face fell the strong yellow glare of the torch flame.

"This his slave!" she cried suddenly.   "A woman!"

And she thrust Elna from her with violence. Then, glancing from Alorus to Lemuel, while her dark eyes flashed fire, she exclaimed vehemently—

"Ah, now I understand!   Verily, Ishtar is flattered that men should, at her feast, brawl over another woman!"

She turned again upon Elna.

"Who art thou, girl?" she demanded.

"I will tell thee," said Lemuel.   "She is Elna, of the tribe of Zoar, betrothed unto Jediah, my brother."

"What?" exclaimed Ishtar.

And on the word her voice rose strangely, in a sort of cry that startled even the impassive slaves who stood around immovably.

"I have said," answered Lemuel.

"Elna of Zoar!" repeated Ishtar unevenly. "Betrothed unto Jediah, thy brother?"

"Yea, lady," added Alorus, "and hither fled from Jediah with his brother, thy favoured shepherd— Lemuel."

"A faithful courtier to thee, indeed, lady," sneered Menanahim, with a triumphant smile of bitter satisfaction.

"She hath not fled hither with me," exclaimed Lemuel.

But Ishtar would not hear him.   She seemed to

tower above all those who stood with her in her wrath and astonishment.

"Jediah's betrothed fled to Babylon with another!" she cried, "and that other thee, O Lemuel! Verily, the simplicity and virtue of the plains doth somewhat confound the guile and vice of Babylon!"

Then, moving towards Elna with arm extended as if to strike her, she said with concentrated fury—

"O cunning Israelite! We are but children after all, we daughters of Babylon!"

At this moment one of the slaves of Alorus darted up the white steps of the terrace, and, kneeling before his master, cried—

"My Lord Alorus!"

"What now?" asked Alorus.

"Jediah of Zoar is at thy gate, craving instant audience. He bade me say that if the dwelling or abiding-place of Elna of Zoar be known unto thee, he prayeth that thou wilt direct him thither."

"Verily, he cometh at a goodly time," rejoined Alorus. "What shall I do, O Ishtar?"

The face of Ishtar had become cold and fixed as the face of a statue. Deep lines were cut in her broad forehead, and her eyes glittered with cruel fire.

"Let Jediah wait," she said, in a level and ringing voice, each word of which was clear, penetrating, and vibrant in the night. "Let him wait and suffer. Take thy slave, Alorus,"—and she thrust the trembling Elna towards him,—"she is thine handmaiden by the law of Babylon, to do with as thou wilt."

Then, drawing herself up to her full height, she looked towards Lemuel and exclaimed—

"So, simple shepherd, so doth Ishtar deal with thee."

But Lemuel sprang upon Alorus, crying fiercely—

" Let go, thou insolent Babylonian ! "

Ishtar clapped her hands together.

"Guards ! hither, hither ! " she called in a loud voice. " Protect me and my guests against that traitor."

In answer to her cry, the guards of the palace rushed forward, flung themselves upon Lemuel, and, after a short but sharp struggle, held him fast.

" So, for the second time, must Ishtar suffer degradation at the hands of one of the tribe of Zoar," continued Ishtar bitterly, " but this time not with meekness. Take this girl, Alorus. She is thy slave, thy chattel."   '

But Lemuel, though in the hands of the guards of Ishtar, was neither daunted nor conquered. His noble face was heroic with courage and with pride, as he exclaimed in a ringing voice—

" At his body's and his soul's peril let him take her ! Let but one hair of her fair head be defiled, and there is no guard, no lord, no prince, no king that can save the life of the defiler ! Limb from limb shall he be torn, and the dogs of the street shall lap up his blood."

"No dog of an Israelite shall lap up, or even spill, the blood of a Babylonian," retorted Alorus furiously. "Mongrels that ye are! Babylon in her might hath enslaved Israel, and in her might shall crush Israel for ever and ever!"

"Babylon may enslave but can never crush His people," said Lemuel.

A wild light had come into his eyes. It seemed to shine from the bright places of his soul. It was like a burning fire and like a great torch kindled by the hands of the angels. He stood up among the glittering guards of the stranger like a hero standing upon a throne, or like a prophet before an altar. And raising his voice till it rang through the night like unto the sound of a trumpet, he exclaimed—

"I tell ye all that Israel shall endure when Babylon and her might have passed away like a dream and are clean put away and forgotten."

The Babylonians, who pressed round Lemuel, burst into a roar of laughter, and Menanahim, seeing his rival held fast and unable to do him injury, approached him, spat on him venomously, and cried—

"Thou fool! Babylon forgotten! Hear this cur of Israel, my lords! Hear him, great Lady Ishtar! And look on Babylon! Look at her in her mightiness, the glory of kingdoms, the beauty of the Chaldeans!"

As he spoke he turned to the terrace wall of the garden of Ishtar, and with a gesture of dandified exultation he leaned forth over the mighty city which lay below, its thousands upon thousands of lights gleaming afar in the night like a sea of flame.   All the Babylonians instinctively moved forward.   Even the guards who held Lemuel could not resist the general impulse.   From this height the aspect of the city was magnificent, and its extent seemed endless.   The moonlight shone down on the gigantic palaces that were like unto towns enclosed within their solid walls — on the temples of the gods, with their vast courts and their sevenfold towers aspiring towards the stars —on the endless network of streets and gardens and squares and plantations—on the great river Euphrates, on whose waters swam the silver moonrays, where crowded the ships of the traders from all lands of the East, from India, Persia, and Arabia.   The voices of the swarming crowds rose up to the terrace like music in the night ; cries of children, songs of sailors, melodies of flutes and of citherns from the hanging gardens of the king, the beat of drums from the soldiers' quarters, the clash of cymbals from the houses where danced the beautiful girls, the shouts of those that feasted, the laughter of those that loved.   And the glory of the city, and of its marvellous life, and of its riches, and of its power, and of its joy, seemed to hang in the still air like a cloud of incense.   Could this pass away?   Not while the world hung in the firmament and the ocean roared in the bed of the world!   And again, looking down on their city and on its magnificence, the Babylonians laughed with triumph in the night.   But Lemuel, as if endowed with supernatural strength, suddenly broke from the guards that would have held him.

He sprang forward upon the terrace, and, lifting his arms towards heaven, he cried in a voice that surely travelled down to the multitudes below—

"I do look at Babylon, but through the eyes of the prophet of my people : and I behold her glory darkened, her beauty trampled in the dust, her walls thrown down, her gates of brass broken. I see her become as a wilderness where no man dwelleth, but the wild beasts of the desert dwell therein. Her temples shall be a house for dragons, her courts shall echo the roar of the winds of the desolate lands. She shall be a city where no man walketh, neither doth any son of man pass thereby. No king, no nation can oppress Israel's people and not be accursed. Thus hath He spoken, and what He ordained shall be. Hearken unto Him, O Babylon, for the days of thy might are numbered, and the hour of thy doom is at hand!"

As he spoke the Babylonians shrank and trembled, and when he ceased there was a deadly hush. All those who stood around him looked forth over the great and mighty city as if they expected to see fire come down out of heaven and consume it before their terror-stricken eyes. They listened, as if for the voice of its wailing and for the cries and lamentations of its despair. But the sound of its music rang on unaltered, its myriads of lights still gleamed along the plain. Then fury shook them. They turned upon Lemuel almost like wild beasts, and Menanahim cried—

"Strike the traitor down! Death to him! Death! death!"

The guards leaped forward, flashing forth their knives; but Ishtar rushed between them and Lemuel, and covering him with her purple robe, she cried—

"No! touch him not! His life is mine. I will that he goes free!"

CHAPTER X

JEDIAH was consumed with that passion which
corrodeth a man even like an acid, the passion of
jealousy. He had been in Babylon now for some
days, yet he had never set his eyes upon Elna—
nor had he seen Lemuel, for a strange fear kept
his feet ever away from the mighty palace of
Ishtar on the borders of Euphrates. Time after
time, indeed, had he clamoured at the portals of
the mansion of the Lord Alorus, but he had not
yet been admitted within the walls of the outer
precinct. His heart began to burn within him like
fire, and his soul was filled with a rage which ever
increased upon him. At night he could not sleep,
but paced to and fro in his chamber like an animal
pent within its cage. By day he walked ever in
the crowded streets of the city, scanning the
passers-by with wolfish eyes, and alarming many
of the women by his disordered gait and by his
savage gestures. He had encountered Migdapul,
the god-seller, and had inquired of him the truth
as to the famous Ishtar. But Migdapul, who was
now devoted to the service of the most powerful
woman in Babylon, and feared her anger, took
no heed of him, but called him "cursed dog of

Israel," and so departed about other business.
Jediah was near to being desperate. Sometimes
he bethought him of his words, spoken so long ago
to Elna: " The deeds that we do, whether good or
evil, return to us again to give us our reward.
They may tarry long on their journey . . . but
there surely dawneth a day when they do stand
before us, and in their hand they do bear the gift
— life for the good, death for the evil."

And then he trembled and was afraid. But
ever the hatred and the jealousy leaped up again
within him, and he was resolved to be avenged
upon Lemuel and upon his own betrothed.

Meanwhile, Elna was hidden within the palace
of Alorus, surrounded by immoderate luxury and
sick with terror of the future. Alorus dwelt at
some distance from Ishtar, not far from the immense palace of the king. His mansion, like
those of most of the great lords, was placed upon
a huge platform of brick, was of vast extent, and
contained every possible appurtenance of wealth
and beauty. Within the walls there were numerous courts, hanging gardens, chambers hung with
stuffs of all colours and with embroideries, furniture made of precious metals, masses of jewels,
ivory, exquisite carpets, rugs, and high vases in
which flowers bloomed, while fountains filled the
scented air with the ripple of a hushed music.
The retinue of his slaves was great, and he had
guards as magnificently attired as those of the
king himself. Yet, so far, all his power, all
his luxury, all his lustful devotion, all his pomp

and his pride, had made no impression upon the simple Israelitish maiden to whose fancy he had striven to appeal in every way that his passionate imagination could devise. And now, in the afternoon of one of the brilliant days of the hot and sultry season, he dismissed the slaves who waited in one of the halls of his palace, and calling unto him only Sabaal, said to him—

"Well, Sabaal? What tidings?"

"Nothing will move her, my lord," said Sabaal. "The maiden is resolute against my lord's demands. She is obdurate."

"She is a woman," replied Alorus, glancing at himself, with effeminate vanity, in a square of shining copper which served him as a mirror, "and a wise one. The woman who is not obdurate for a time is a fool."

He cast himself into a great chair hung with red silk, leaned his arm negligently upon a marble table, and continued—

"Elna is no fool. But she is a woman, and she will yield."

"She is a daughter of Israel, my lord, and not of Babylon," murmured Sabaal, with a travesty of modest submissiveness.

"She is a daughter of Eve, thou slave, and, be her birthplace Babylon or Judea, she will yield."

"My lord is master," said Sabaal, with a cringing obeisance, "but his slave would warn him against wronging the maiden Elna. Naught but evil can come to my lord, if evil come through him to Elna."

"Thy lord is master, indeed," returned Alorus proudly, "and heeds not the warnings of a slave. Thy lord is willing to risk the evil that may come through Elna."

"Yet let my lord beware "— began Sabaal.

But Alorus cut him short angrily.

"Thy lord will beware," he said. "There is the whip and scourge for thee as for others. Tell Elna that thy lord, and hers, awaits her here. Go!"

Sabaal hesitated for a moment. His face was fierce and forbidding, and his sinewy hands worked as if he longed to fly at the throat of his master. But with a great effort, controlling himself, he muttered "So be it," and crept out of the hall, going towards the chamber in which Elna was confined.

Alorus looked at himself again in the mirror with much complacence. He stroked his carefully washed and scented beard with his fingers, which were covered with enormous rings. Then he spread abroad his robe of white and gold silk, and smiled proudly.

"By Baal, but these Israelites are growing troublesome!" he said to himself. "They need more of the whip and scourge, and they shall have it. What now?" he said aloud, as a running slave entered and bent low at his fee

"One Jediah, son of Zoar, waits thy pleasure, my lord. He hath knocked on thy palace portals many times of late."

"Jediah! So let him wait. And tell this son

of Zoar that he shall know what is my pleasure later. Go!"

The slave vanished, going softly. Alorus muttered—

"Verily, the whole tribe of Zoar do gather round this maiden Elna, as doth a hive of bees about their queen. Ah!"

He did not rise from his seat, but lay back, half closing his sensual eyes as Elna advanced, bending down her blue eyes to the ground. She was dressed in a rich robe, forced upon her by the orders of Alorus. But she wore no trappings or ornaments. After standing before Alorus for a moment in silence, she said, in a low and scarce audible voice—

"What would you with me?"

Alorus raised himself upon the chair and leaned forward towards her, running his bold eyes over her fair form with admiration.

"A goodly sight, indeed!" he said. "A fairer one could not be found in Babylon."

"What would you with me?" asked Elna again.

"Where are the jewels that I did leave for thee?" said Alorus.

"Where thou did'st leave them," she answered, pointing to a large golden casket which stood on a table at a little distance.

Alorus rose up, went to the table, and opened the casket.

"Untouched!" he exclaimed.

"Yea."

" And unlooked upon ? " he asked curiously.

" And unlooked upon."

He put his hand into the casket and drew forth a great chain of emeralds.

" Look upon them now," he said, holding them up in the sunlight till they shone and glittered like things alive. " See, here are jewels that might have decked Sheba's fair queen—rubies beyond price—amethysts a Pharaoh might envy."

He advanced a step towards her, holding the chain of emeralds still in his hands.

" Let me clasp this round thy neck," he said coaxingly, and assuming a conquering look which he thought irresistible.

But Elna moved back from him.

" No," she said quietly. " I want not thy jewels. This robe I wear until I am free to replace it with one that more befits my race and needs. Only one other thing will I take at thy hands."

" What is that, fair Israelite ? " cried Alorus.

" My liberty," said Elna proudly. " How darest thou withhold it ? "

" Dare ! " exclaimed Alorus, bursting into a fit of laughter. " Dare ! Knowest thou that thou art my slave ? "

" I am not thy slave," she answered, with contempt. " And I demand my freedom. Justice ! justice ! There must be laws in Babylon, even for the daughters of Israel."

" There are laws in Babylon, fair Elna, especially for the daughters of Israel—laws that make their masters masters indeed. Thou art my slave,—by thine own admission,—slave to do my bidding, be that bidding what it may. Slave to toil and spin, to wait my word, or beck, or nod — to come and to go how and whence I will."

And, as he spoke, he came towards her, stretching forth his hands. Elna retreated before him.

"Thou art a man, at least," she said, "even though a Babylonian — and wilt not wrong thy manhood."

"Nay, fair Israelite," returned Alorus, "since first I saw thee in the tents of Zoar I loved thee."

"Loved me!" cried Elna, with bitter scorn.

"Well, desired thee, then,—if thou wilt have it so. Be wise. Force me not to use my power rather than yield to thine. There is naught that I cannot give thee out of my wealth— nothing that the heart of woman can desire shall be denied thee. Thou shalt be envied— ay, even by Ishtar herself."

"Ishtar!" cried Elna, and, on the word, she ran to the window, that looked out from a great height on to the court of the palace. "Ishtar! Rather than be like unto her, I would be as the leper without the gates."

And she pointed forth towards the beggars who sat for ever at the palace portals in hope of alms.

"I love!" she said, "I love!—but I love not thee. He whom I love loves me, and such as

I am—body, mind, heart, soul—are his and only his. I risked my life leaving him to whom I was betrothed. I would risk that life again and again to keep myself unstained and true to him I love. Let that suffice—and let me go."

"No!" exclaimed Alorus fiercely. "Sooner than lose thee, I would lose my life."

And he sprang impetuously towards Elna. But two strong hands caught him suddenly by the throat and forced him backward, while a voice said sternly—

"Take heed lest both be lost."

"Lemuel!" cried Elna joyfully.

"My guard!" gasped Alorus, struggling violently to release himself from Lemuel. "My guard!"

"Thy guard!" said Lemuel. "Can it be that the mighty Alorus is afraid?"

And, as he spoke, he released him, with a gesture of scorn. Alorus stood still for a moment, panting for breath and supporting himself against a huge vase of bronze that stood in the centre of the hall.

"Afraid!" he said at last. "Why art thou here?"

"Canst thou ask?"

"Yea; this is my house. It is the custom of Babylon to"—

"I know but little of the customs of Babylon," said Lemuel scornfully.

"True, shepherd,—and heed even less the customs of Israel."

"It is the custom of Israel to protect the honour of her daughters."

"And the law to slay their seducers," retorted Alorus.

As he spoke, Elna made a movement towards Lemuel, as if instinctively she sought to protect him.

"Even so," said Lemuel. "I do not seek to deny it."

"Then is thy life forfeit unto Israel's law."

"That shall be as Israel's Judges shall decide."

"Of whom thy brother, Jediah, is one," said Alorus, casting a malignant glance on Elna.

"Yea," said Lemuel.

And he too gazed towards Elna, with a depth of pity and suffering in his eyes. Alorus hesitated. A keen struggle was going on within his soul, a struggle between the evil and the good. He was not, by nature, entirely wicked, but he had been coarsened and corrupted by the foul life of Babylon, and his better self had been thrust down into the depths and scarcely allowed to look ever upon the light. And he desired Elna with all his body. At last he said slowly—

"Lemuel, I have no quarrel with thee. Go hence in peace."

"Not without this maid. If I go, she goeth too."

"This maid is my slave," said Alorus.

"She is no slave. For her and for all the house of Zoar tribute hath been paid. She is no more thy slave than am I. She is here against her will. Is not that so, Elna? Speak!"

"Yea, my lord," said Elna, moving a step nearer to Lemuel.

"And it is thy desire that thou should'st go hence with me?"

"Such is my desire."

The dark cloud came again upon the face of Alorus.

"One moment, Israelite," he said. "That it may not ever be charged upon me that I willingly resigned the custody of my slave, let me, at least, have a witness present who will testify for me hereafter."

"To that I agree," answered Lemuel.

Alorus smiled and struck a silver gong. A slave appeared.

"That lord who waited for me but now," said Alorus, "waits he still?"

"Yea, my lord," said the slave.

"Bid him come hither."

The slave made a low obeisance and departed. Alorus strode across the hall to a doorway over which was hung a heavy rose-coloured curtain. Holding the curtain up with one hand, he turned to Lemuel and said—

"Lemuel, I have no wish to harm thee. Even now thou may'st go in peace if thou wilt. Even for thine own good I beseech thee to go."

"And I tell thee," answered Lemuel firmly, "that unless this maid do go with me I will not go."

Alorus let the curtain fall. His face had again become hard and cruel.

"Then there is naught left for me but to call my witness hither," he said.

Going to another door, he cried in a loud voice—

"Jediah, son of Zoar, enter."

On hearing his words, Elna uttered a cry of terror. And when the wild and disordered figure of Jediah appeared in answer to the summons of Alorus, she shrieked—

"Jediah! O Lemuel, save me!" and clung to him for protection.

Jediah, whose face was pale as death, and whose eyes glittered like burning coals of fire, came forward slowly. He looked upon Elna and upon Lemuel. Then raising his hands on high, he said—

"Found! And together! God of my fathers, I thank Thee!"

He dropped his hands and stood in silence. But his terrible eyes never left Elna and Lemuel.

"Welcome, Jediah," said Alorus, with a jaunty affectation of geniality. "Welcome. As thou seest, thy brother is here before thee."

"So I perceive, my lord," answered Jediah.

"And this maiden, too, is kith of thine, is she not?"

"She is my betrothed wife, my lord," answered Jediah, with exceeding great bitterness.

"Ay. So thou did'st tell me when last I saw thee. This is a happy meeting indeed!"

"A meeting that I have desired," said Jediah. "Indeed, it was to ask my lord to aid me in my search for this maiden that I came hither."

"What would'st thou with me — and Elna?" asked Lemuel proudly.

"I do desire that thou—and this woman—do return with me—home," said Jediah, clenching his hands together.

"For what purpose?" asked Lemuel.

"Canst thou not guess?" said Jediah, still in the same cold and deadly voice.

"Knowing thee, my brother," replied Lemuel, "it is not hard to guess. It is well that thou hast come. I must indeed speak with thee."

He turned to Alorus.

"What I would say concerns not thee, my lord," he added, "so, by thy leave, we will withdraw."

"Thou hast my leave to go," said Alorus.

"Come, Elna," said Lemuel.

"Ah, no!" interposed Alorus. "I said thou— but not this maiden."

Lemuel's face was, for a moment, contorted with contempt and anger. But he quickly controlled himself, and said to his brother—

"Brother, this man—thy friend—doth claim Elna as his slave."

"Slave!" exclaimed Jediah. "His slave! What! Weary of thee too! And so soon! She is not slow, being in Babylon, to catch the Babylonish way."

"Brother!" retorted Lemuel, with difficulty restraining his rising anger, "thou hast been seemingly wronged, and thy wrath, perhaps, is just. But those words are cruelly unjust, and thou dost know it."

"Unjust? To whom?" said Jediah. "To the wantons of Babylon? If any suffer by the comparison, surely it is they. They make no pretence, at least, but ply their trade openly, and all do know it is their trade. But this woman acts the virtuous maid, and recking nothing of honour, love, wounded hearts, or broken lives, doth covertly, and with the guile of the serpent, steal from one man's arms unto another's. The traitress! the "—

"Stop!" exclaimed Lemuel.

He, as Jediah, was white with wrath. But he did not lose his self-control, although he clenched his hands together in his robe and his eyes shone with anger.

"Stop! Not even from thee will I hear one word of slander against this maid, who is as pure as when she left our tents, as when she left her mother's knee. Wrong is she in that she forsook thee and her people to come to this false city, but, on my life, her sin ends there."

"That shall be judged by Israel," said Jediah, trembling with passion. "By Israel and by Israel's law."

"She hath sinned against thee—indeed, against herself—but against no law of Israel," returned Lemuel.

"Israel shall determine that, and shall judge thee," said Jediah, "thou renegade from faith and trust and kin! Come, both of ye, to the home ye have outraged."

He made a step forward and stretched out his

arm as if he would drag Elna from the palace of Alorus. But Lemuel placed himself by the maiden's side.

"I have no fear," he said. "Elna, what sayest thou?"

"I hither came to Babylon to seek the man I do love," she answered bravely. "His command, and naught but his command in all this world, can send me home again. And not even at his bidding will I give myself unto another. I have said."

And she looked up into Lemuel's face with exultation, as if in this confession she released her soul from bondage.

"Thou hast heard, Jediah, my brother," said Lemuel. "Wilt thou still hold her to a bond so hateful?"

"Yea," cried Jediah furiously, almost as a man taken by a fit. "Yea, until the law hath done me justice. Justice! I call for justice! Justice on the adulterer and the adultress! Justice and the law! Death—death to both!"

"Who is it calls so loudly for truth and justice?" said a woman's voice.

Jediah started violently and laid his hand on the marble table by which he stood, as if he sought for support. Alorus, who had been watching the previous scene with an interest he did not attempt to disguise, turned hastily and bent low as if before a queen. Elna and Lemuel, side by side, did not move, but waited calmly, as if bravely prepared for any fate. And Ishtar, whose voice it was that had spoken, came forward slowly, till she stood in the midst of the hall.

"Who is it calls so loudly?" she repeated. "Can it be Jediah, son of Zoar?"

"Elcia!" whispered Jediah, under his breath.

Ishtar smiled coldly.

"Elcia!" she said. "Nay, Ishtar—Ishtar of Babylon. Is it possible that Ishtar, whose name is known throughout all the world, can be unknown to Jediah?"

"Ishtar—I—I"— stammered Jediah, with white lips.

"I am Ishtar," she replied. "Look on me."

In one hand she held her long veil of white Indian muslin, and she stood, straight and tall as a queen, facing this man, who cowered before her as if he would fain have sunk down into the ground.

"But thou, Jediah, did'st call for 'justice and the law.' Who in this company hath outraged the law?"

Jediah drew his breath huskily. He pointed, with a shaking hand, to Lemuel and to Elna.

"That man — and that — woman," he said hoarsely.

Ishtar gazed fixedly at Elna.

"What is this maid to thee, Jediah?" she asked.

"My betrothed wife," he answered, casting down his fierce eyes before her glance.

Ishtar burst into a peal of laughter and sank down upon a couch.

"Forgive me, Alorus!" she exclaimed. "Nay,

forgive me! But—but Jediah's betrothed wife a
fugitive! Jediah's betrothed wife flying from his
arms to seek her love in Babylon! How strange!
How very strange!"

She suddenly rose up again, and, addressing
Lemuel, said more gravely—

"And art thou — thou, the stern, unyielding
Lemuel—the guilty one?"

"There is no guilt here, lady," said Lemuel
calmly. "This maid hath been impetuous,
thoughtless, perchance—but she is, as I am,
innocent of the sin my brother hath charged
upon us."

"Innocent!" cried Jediah passionately. "A
lie! She and thou alike do lie! Ye are guilty
both! Think not to deceive me!"

"No," said Ishtar, turning upon him; "thou
must know too well the ways of those charged
with such a sin—being a Judge in Israel—to be
misled."

Jediah ground his teeth together. By his wild
bearing and contorted features it was easy to see
that passion was driving him on towards the con-
fines of madness.

"These twain must come with me!" he exclaimed,
in a choked voice.

"This maiden shall not go with thee against her
will," said Lemuel. "She shall not while I have
life."

"No, by Baal!" cried Alorus, "nor with thee
either, thou simple shepherd, while there is law in
Babylon."

Even as he spoke there was a clash of arms without, the curtain that hung over the great entrance door was thrust roughly aside, and a guard of soldiers entered, led by an officer of the king's palace.

"What means this intrusion?" said Alorus.

The officer signed to him to be silent, and, looking around him, said to Lemuel—

"Art thou Lemuel, son of Zoar?"

"I am," said Lemuel.

The officer turned to Elna.

"And thou—art thou Elna, the Israelite?"

"Yea," said Elna.

"My lord the king—may he live for ever—his signet and his mandate. It is the will of my lord the king that these two be cast into prison."

Alorus, Ishtar, and the Babylonians inclined their heads at the mention of the king's name. But Lemuel said quietly, and facing the soldiers unflinchingly—

"For what crime?"

"For treason," replied the officer. "It is bruited abroad through all the city that thou hast foretold the destruction of Babylon, the destruction of our mighty lord the king."

"But this maid is innocent," responded Lemuel. "Arrest me, if thou wilt, but let her go."

"The king's command is that I deliver both into his hands," said the officer. "His will is my law."

And at a sign from him the soldiers surrounded Elna and Lemuel.

Suddenly Lemuel put his hands to his breast. He had thought of the precious cylinder confided to him by the blind man, Johanan. In it were the names and abodes of all the brethren who were working for the freedom of Israel. These must not fall into the hands of the king, or all would be lost. In a moment his resolution was taken.

"Ere I go," he said to the officer, "I would speak with the Lady Ishtar."

The officer hesitated.

"What desirest thou "— he began.

But Ishtar stepped forward and said authoritatively—

"I will be answerable unto my lord the king. Let this man speak to me."

"Alone," said Lemuel firmly.

"Stand apart," said Ishtar.

The officer, awed by her beauty, instinctively obeyed her commands. The soldiers, at his order, stood back. Alorus moved away, wondering. Then Ishtar said softly to Lemuel—

"What would'st thou, Lemuel?"

"Lady," he answered, "wilt thou do me a great service in mine hour of need?"

"Teach me how," she replied earnestly.

He touched his breast.

"I have here a cylinder," he said. "On it are the names of many of my brethren, whose lives are forfeit if it be seen. I shall be searched, this tablet found. For their sakes take it from me and destroy it."

"But this is treason unto the king," she answered.

" I await my prisoner, lady," the officer cried.

" By thy love for me!" whispered Lemuel.

Ishtar stood in silence. Then she murmured—

" Give me the tablet."

Lemuel bent low as if to kiss her hand. As he did so Ishtar drew the cylinder from his bosom and hid it in her own.

The guards again surrounded Elna and Lemuel. Jediah stood watching, silently. He seemed exhausted with passion, and his cruel face was as if cut in stone.

Lemuel put his hand on Elna's.

" Be comforted, Elna," he said. " Thou art innocent. No harm shall come to thee."

" I have no fear," she answered, "so thy fate be mine."

Lemuel's hand closed on hers more firmly. Then turning to the officer, he said—

" Sir, I am ready!"

There was a clash of steel, a crash of marching feet, then Ishtar and Alorus stood alone in the palace hall.

Jediah had slunk away without a word.

CHAPTER XI

THE great dungeons of Babylon lay over against
the eastern wall of the city, and were of vast extent and of immense solidity. Within their con-
fines were courts in which the more favoured of the
prisoners took exercise, dwellings for the numerous
jailers, and endless rows of tiny cells, guarded by
stout doors provided with locks and bars and
pierced by small gratings through which but little
light and air could enter. To this gloomy abode
of crime and misery, of tyranny and torture, Elna
and Lemuel were now to be conducted by order of
the great king of Babylon. Two or three of the
jailers, Babylonians of the lowest order, uncouth,
unkempt, dissipated and drunken, were already
gathered together in the outer court of the prison,
awaiting the entry of the latest captives who had
fallen under the displeasure of the tyrant who
sat upon the throne. They rested upon a bench
of stone, and drank copious draughts of a cheap
sort of beer much loved by the people of the lower
orders. And while they drank they gossiped as
ever of the wretched prisoners in their charge,
and of those likely to be brought to the dungeons
in the near future. Said one, lifting his head, on

which the rough hair grew long, from the cup of
metal to which he had just been putting his thick
lips—

"Here's a goodly lot come in of late! Some for
the sword, some for the fiery furnace. Thieves,
murderers, and they that do refuse to worship the
golden image our lord the king hath provided.
Of a surety some are hard to please! Had they
been asked to bow the knee to an image of common
clay, now—but to one of gold! Of a height of
threescore cubits and a breadth of six cubits, and
sweet music prepared for them, too! Bah! what
can they want?"

"The great god Bel alone knows," returned
another. "But why do these men refuse to worship
the golden image?"

The first jailer shook his head, and a clumsy
and puzzled expression came over his red face.

"Why?" he ejaculated. "Eh, why? Well, because—because they are Israelites. Why else?"

"Is that a reason?" said his companion.

"Reason enough. They're a stiff-necked race."

"If they be stiff-necked and cannot bend, then
let them burn, I say."

The other burst out into a harsh laugh.

"Burn! Yea, frizzle—so we be rid of them and
get some peace."

He took another long draught from the cup,
smacked his lips, and passed his hand across them.

"If our lord the king"— he began.

But just then there was a loud knocking at the
prison portals. The jailer started up.

"Here be more of them!" he cried. "Ugh! there is no peace here."

He shuffled off to unlock the gate A guard of soldiers entered, conducting Elna and Lemuel.

"Lock these two prisoners in here, and come thou with me," said the officer of the king. "The governor will instruct thee further concerning them."

"But who are they?" asked the jailer, gazing in staring surprise at the lovely white face of Elna and at the noble figure and heroic bearing of Lemuel. "For what crime against the king are they come hither?"

"I will tell thee," said the officer, and he walked apart for a moment with the jailer, leaving Elna and Lemuel together. For the soldiers had fallen out of their ranks, and had departed to their quarters after conducting the prisoners within the court of the dungeon. Only two men remained on guard at the great door which opened on to the street of the city. Elna, almost overcome with grief and terror, stood with her beautiful head drooping, while tears that she strove in vain to repress coursed down her white cheeks. Lemuel looked upon her with a passion of pity.

"Nay, Elna," he said to her gently, "weep not. Thou wilt not falter! Thou hast been so brave until now."

"Yea, my beloved," she answered, through her tears, "for until now my heart was filled ever with the hope of finding thee, and that hope strengthened me. I found thee at last, light of my soul, and darkness fell from me as night flieth before the sun. But now that I must lose thee again, and may not have for my solace even the pleasant pain of seeking thee, my heart faileth me indeed, and my courage is well-nigh gone."

"Nay, Elna," said Lemuel, drawing a little closer to her, and glancing towards the two sentries, who stood immovable at their posts. "If thou hast been spared until now, thou wilt not now be cast down for ever. There is great might in love — more strength therein than in the swords of thousands, yea, even though they be wielded by the mightiest of the men of battle. Let our love uplift thee, O my beloved. Beyond these walls, Elna,—look, I see a land of plenty!"

As he spoke, that strange light of enthusiasm, which had so moved even the indifferent Babylonians gathered in the palace garden of Ishtar, flamed up once more in his eyes. And he seemed to see a vision afar off.

"I see a land of green pastures and pleasant vineyards, girt about with cedars and sweet-smelling trees—sweeter even than those of Lebanon— and orchards of ripe fruit, and gardens of bright flowers, and fountains of clear water. And the land is rich with harvests, with flocks and herds. And, Elna—listen! There is one who goeth down among her maidens to water the lambs and the young goats ; and behold ! though her hair is white, and she is well stricken in years, and her children and her children's children are with her and about her, she is upright, and her foot is fleet still as the young fawn's, and her eyes are bright, like twin stars in a dark sky.   And there is one who standeth at the door of his tent, and although he too is old the love-light is in his eyes as he watcheth his spouse ; and, for all his years, I know him!   It is Lemuel—thy Lemuel, O soul of my soul!—faithful and true unto thee, as he was and as he will be unto the end of time and the coming of the eternal !"

"Dost thou indeed see this vision?" she whispered.

And her face was transformed, as if she walked in the midst of a great light.

"Indeed and indeed," he murmured.   "And there is no prison here, for our life is yonder.   Nor can these walls divide us,"—and he pointed towards the gloomy cells,—" for our hearts and souls are one."

As he ceased to speak, and she turned towards him with a radiant gesture of courage and of confidence, the jailer returned from speaking with the officer.

"Come hither, maiden!" he cried roughly. "Thou shalt soon be where no man can see thy bright eyes and thy tender cheeks."

And, so saying, he seized her brutally by the arm, and led her away to one of the cells.   She made no resistance.   Only, as she turned to go, she cast one look of trust upon Lemuel.   Her courage had returned to her.   She was no longer fearful.   She looked beyond the present, and Lemuel's bravery renewed hers.

The heavy door of the cell closed upon her, and Lemuel stood alone.

" And now, come thou with me," said the jailer, returning. " Thou shalt have no further commerce with thy fair maiden. Here wilt thou lie, in this chamber, and other garments shall be found for thee and for thy companion."

As he spoke he unbarred the door of a low and filthy prison cell, and signed unto Lemuel to enter. The cell was full of black darkness, and ere Lemuel obeyed the jailer's command, he turned his eyes once more to the light of the sun and to the fair beauty of the clear blue sky. Then he moved to cross the lintel of the cell door ; but, even as he did so, the great portals of the prison opened, and a company of the king's guards entered, followed by a woman whose face was covered by a long white veil.

" Who art thou ? " exclaimed the jailer, with his hand laid still upon the door.

The woman, advancing quickly towards him, threw back her veil, and showed the face of Ishtar.

" Stay ! " she cried. " I have the king's authority to speak with thy prisoner, and alone."

" What ? " said the jailer, in perplexity. " Thou tellest me that "—

" Read and obey," said Ishtar imperiously.

And she held forth to him a tablet, on which was inscribed the mandate of the king.

" The king's seal ! " exclaimed the jailer.

He bowed low.

" Lady, I obey," he said, with a meek servility strangely unlike to his former rough and arbitrary brutality.

Then he retired, followed by the guards, leaving Ishtar alone with Lemuel. She stood in silence for a moment. Then she advanced towards him, and, with a gesture almost of pleading, she said—

" Lemuel ! "

" Lady ! " he replied.

" Lemuel," she said, " thou knowest that the king hath been informed of what thou did'st utter at my palace before my guests—that thou did'st prophesy the falling of Babylon and of her monarch. This he adjudged treason. Moreover, he hath learned that there is a plot among the Israelites captive in Babylon to rebel, and that thou art to be their leader. Is this true ? '

" I have naught to say, lady," he answered. " Let my accusers prove what they can."

" Dost thou know the penalty of such a crime ? " she asked him.

" Crime ! " he exclaimed, with sudden fervour. " That word better befits the deeds of the oppressors than the struggles of the oppressed. But —I know the penalty of such an act as thou hast described. It is death."

" Yea," she said ; " for he who lifteth his hand against our lord the king shall perish by fire. This fearful fate must surely be thine, unless "—

She paused, casting down her great eyes to the ground, while a warm flush slowly spread over her beautiful and tragic face.

" Unless what, lady ? " asked Lemuel.

" Unless one who hath great influence with the king doth plead on thy behalf."

"Who hath such influence?" said Lemuel, look-ing upon her searchingly.

"I have," responded Ishtar, in a low voice as of one ashamed. "But I may not go before my lord the king with empty hands, pleading for grace and mercy. Nor will he be content, even though the revolt be abandoned, to let the matter pass without some punishment."

"Dost thou mean that, unless I suffer, some other must?"

She did not reply directly to his question, but said, more quickly—

"Upon the tablet that thou gavest me are many names"—

"Hast thou not destroyed it?" exclaimed Lemuel.

"No," answered Ishtar. "Hush! Let me show the names unto my lord the king, under his promise to spare thee. Let him select three of the number, who shall be punished—and let thee go free."

But Lemuel turned from her with contempt.

"If I had ten thousand lives," he said, "and those three had but one, not by that one would I buy my ten thousand."

She laid her hand upon his robe, pressing nearer to his side.

"Lemuel," she said, and her voice was quick with passion and with excitement, "think — thy refusal will not save those others, if I give up the tablet."

He turned upon her and looked into her eyes.

"Will it save those others if thou dost destroy the tablet and I confess my guilt?" he said.

" It might," she answered.

"Then so let it be.   Go, make that bargain with your lord the king.   I will be the scapegoat for my brethren in bondage."

" Nay," said Ishtar, "let me answer thee after thine own fashion.   If each of thy brethren had twice ten thousand lives, I would not give thy precious one to save them."

Lemuel laid his hand upon hers to thrust her from him, but Ishtar clung to him, crying—

" There is yet another way to save thee, Lemuel."

" If it be so far from honour as the other, waste not thy breath to tell it me," he said.

" Stay, Lemuel!—heed me.   Thou—thou did'st ask me to take that tablet to prove my love for thee.   To hold that tablet one moment from the king maketh me in his sight a traitor, and my life too is forfeit.   Nay, thou shalt hear me!   Lemuel, I did gladly risk my life because I loved thee.   In all Babylon there is none richer than I.   Our lord the king doth look with favour upon me.   Were I to ask so rich a boon as mercy for thee and all thy friends—for Lemuel, a stranger, a plotter against our lord — 'twould be refused.   But did I ask it for Ishtar's husband, the king would surely grant it."

On the last words she clasped her hands more closely about his arm.   Her face was ardent with desire and with love, and her great eyes shone with excitement and with passion.

"Ishtar's husband?" exclaimed Lemuel, in a maze.

"Yea."

"That may never be," he said, striving to unclasp her hands. "Never—never!"

"And why?" she whispered. "Why, Lemuel?"

Her breath was hot on his cheek. Her stormy heart beat under the hand with which again he strove to put her from him.

"I love another," he said quickly.

"This Israelitish girl—this Elna?"

"Even so."

"But she can never be thine, even if thou wert free. She is thy brother's. Thou canst, by wedding me, save all these thy people, and thou wilt let them die!"

And she clung to him more closely, gazing into his face with a fury of anxiety.

"Woman," said Lemuel, "why wilt thou compel me to open my mouth and say that which is in my heart? Because thou hast avowed a love for me,—and the love that is unselfish, even of the vilest, a man may not despise,—because of this love, and for that thou hast done me a service, I have set a seal upon my tongue. For I would not hurt thee who art, whate'er thy sins, a woman. I have answered thee. Be thou content. This thing cannot be."

And with gentle but inexorable force he put her from him.

"Then shall thy people perish!" she cried.

" They are not my people who would buy their lives at such a price. By the laws of my people no man may wed with—with such as thou art—and live."

Ishtar cowered, as if struck by a blow. But her passion still drove her onward, and she answered—

" Remember, if thou dost refuse me, the tablet will I give unto the king; and they—and this girl Elna—all shall surely perish, and perish by fire."

A look of horror came into the face of Lemuel as she spoke Elna's name.

" No, no!" he cried. " She—Elna—hath no share in this thing. She is innocent of any harm, any sin. She hath only loved me. That is no sin."

" The sin is, in my eyes, that thou lovest her," said Ishtar. " She hath wronged thy brother. Let her atone. It may be, if he doth love her truly, that he would not exact the penalty of her fault, but would forgive her. Think not that her love for thee would last for ever. She would forget thee and find happiness in Jediah's love."

" In his love happiness for Elna!" said Lemuel. " Lady, thou hast answered thyself. She who did risk her life because she loved, could never save that life at the price of that love's constancy. Love hath the victory. Let death come! Love knows no fear save the one dread of parting. And we shall be united by the grave. She who was true to me, even at the risk of her life, shall find me true even unto death."

He turned from Ishtar proudly, and, raising his voice, he cried aloud—

" Jailer ! "

The jailer came in answer to the cry.

" This lady and I have nothing more to speak of," said Lemuel. " Do thy duty upon me. I am ready."

The jailer looked towards Ishtar, as if for her commands. But she stood with bowed head and spoke no word. Therefore he flung aside the door of Lemuel's cell, and said roughly—

" Enter, Israelite ! "

The heavy door closed with a crash. There was a rattle as the heavy bars fell into their places.

" Wilt thou go, lady ? " said the jailer to Ishtar. " What more desirest thou ? "

He stood still and looked upon her with a coarse curiosity. She made him a sign to leave her. He obeyed, muttering to himself, as he went about his business. When Ishtar stood alone, there seemed to be some great struggle going on within her, some tempest of the emotions, some fierce storm of the soul that shook and convulsed her, till she trembled and leaned against the stone wall of the cell where Lemuel lay in darkness. She pressed her forehead to the cold stone, and pressed her two hands to it, and stayed thus, with her eyes closed. Her lips were trembling convulsively. The tears burst out between her eyelids. All the heart of her wailed and fought, and was fierce and cruel, pitiless and pitiful by turns, as the waves of intense feeling surged through her. And now it was the nature of the great courtesan who had ruled in Babylon that triumphed, and a superb savage stood there, hating Elna and her lover, ready to watch them die in agony surrounded by the aspiring tongues of flame.   And now it was the nature of the woman who had been twisted and turned away from God's good purpose for a time that won the victory.   The battle was sore and bitter, and the woman went down as if into hell.   She was in thick darkness, and as if below the roots of the world.   But at last a light shone through the shadows of evil and of terror.   Her heart was shaken by a pulse of purity and of glorious self-abnegation.   And, stretching forth her hands to the cell where Lemuel sat alone in the blackness, waiting for death, she whispered to the stones—

"O brave, true soul!   Ah, had such a love been mine!   And shall he indeed perish?   Nay, not while Ishtar liveth and hath power to redeem —if but a little—the much evil she hath wrought. Can the past die?   Can the dead bury the dead? Light doth follow darkness.   Life doth spring from death.   Peradventure, with the light of this man's strong soul to guide her, even Ishtar may at last walk forth into the day!"

She bent down and pressed her soft lips upon the bar that lay across the door.   Then she drew her veil across her face, and turned and went out swiftly from the prison.

CHAPTER XII

WHEN Jediah slunk away from the palace of
Alorus, he was torn asunder by conflicting
emotions of so great violence that, as he passed
through the streets teeming with the population
of Babylon, he scarce knew that he was not alone.
He perceived those around him, indeed, but
vaguely, as people see through a thick mist
which distorts their actions and deadens their
voices.   For he was self-centred, self-engrossed,
preoccupied by two widely diverse sensations—
triumph and baffled despair.   The triumph came
to him from the thought that Lemuel was now
indeed doomed to die, that his brother must pass
on into the other world through the flaming
furnace heated by Babylon for the destruction
of all those who dared to plot against the king
and his glory.   Naught could save Lemuel now.
His days upon earth were surely numbered.   He
must go—even as all men at the last—to his own
place.   He must leave Elna.   He must resign his
dear hope of being the saviour of his downtrodden
nation.   Love and religious ambition, the hopes
of love and the hopes of glory—all had crumbled
into the dust.   And in that thought Jediah ex-

ulted. He clenched his hands together, and his fierce eyes blazed like the eyes of a madman, as he saw before him a vision of fire and Lemuel set in the midst of it. But then came to him that cold and deadly sensation of baffled despair, as he remembered Elna, and that she was surely passing beyond his reach. For death would surely be her lot also. Rather than that she should give herself up to Lemuel would Jediah have fallen upon and, with his own hands, strangled her. But if Lemuel should be slain and she live on! That would be sweet. For then would she have none to turn to save only to him who alone had the right to claim her and to keep her his for ever. And within Jediah there sprang up a fury of passionate desire, cruel, vindictive, and almost demoniac, to possess Elna—to have her at length for his own, for his chattel, his thing, on which he could wreak both his physical love and his mental hate, his passion for vengeance and his passion for power. Then he felt, indeed, that he could not let her go from him to the fire; that perhaps, after death, would she and Lemuel be united in the great region beyond, be granted there the fulfilment of that love which he had frustrated upon earth. And feeling thus, he raged as he walked, till the passers-by were terrified by his demeanour, and the little playing children ran, crying for fear, to their mothers, hiding hot little faces in their robes in order not to see any longer the distorted and wolfish countenance of this haggard Israelite, who stalked on unheeding them.

14

Thinking and thinking thus, Jediah presently became possessed of one dominating idea. How could Elna be saved ? The destruction of Lemuel was certain. Jediah wished it, exulted in the thought of it. But Elna ! She must be saved—saved for him, saved for the fate he silently prepared for her. She must be saved to be his wife, to dwell in his tent, sleep by his side, eat of his salt, and call him lord and master. Yes, she must be saved—saved. But how? All that night he brooded and pondered. But he could come to no conclusion. The sun shone in upon him as he crouched on his bed in the small chamber that he had hired in the eastern quarter of the city. The cries of the people going about their business summoned him forth. But he remained immersed in thought, and unable to come to any conclusion. It was late in the afternoon ere he left his chamber. He descended the street in which was set the house he occupied, and wandered on and on through the maze of the streets of Babylon, his head bent upon his breast, his eyes half closed, pondering ever how to snatch Elna from the fire in which Lemuel must burn and be destroyed. Towards evening, while he thus walked, like a man blind and deaf, enclosed in the narrow chamber of his thoughts, he heard—as from a long distance—two Babylonians who spoke together beside a water-spring, beneath a palm tree in a square of the city. Their voices pierced his dream and shook his soul awake. For one said to the other—

" Nay, and indeed the power of women passeth all knowledge and is beyond all reason."

" Why sayest thou so?" answered the other. " Hath thy wife, then, lorded it over thee, as is the way of women when they see that they are beloved?"

" My wife!—nay. But hast thou not heard of the doing of Ishtar in the palace of our lord the king?"

" Not a word."

Jediah stood still to listen.

" Well," continued the first Babylonian, " it seems that she hath set her eyes in love upon this self-same Israelitish shepherd, Lemuel, who hath falsely predicted the destruction of our mighty city and the end of the king's glorious rule."

" Is he of a goodly form and countenance?"

" I know not. For this treason of his, the king condemned the shepherd and the maid, one Elna, who had put on man's attire for love of him, to perish by fire."

" 'Twas rightly and well ordained."

" Yea. But Ishtar, having cast her eyes on this shepherd, liked it not. She went up into the palace of the king to plead for the revoking of his decree."

" These women are bolder than we men, of a truth."

" And with her words she so weighed upon the king that he hath yielded unto her entreaty."

Jediah moved a step towards the speakers.

" What sayest thou?" he cried harshly.

The two Babylonians looked at him in amaze.

"Who art thou, stranger, that speakest thus to those who know thee not?" asked he who was telling the story, haughtily.

Jediah bowed low.

"Thy pardon, sir," he said; "but I was so interested in thy strange tale of this Ishtar and the king that I could not help but listen. Forgive me, I pray thee."

The Babylonian smiled in gratified vanity.

"Bel hath given me the power of speech, I verily believe, stranger," he answered. "For all the town telleth me so. All praise to the great god Bel, in whose hands we are but as dust."

"Let me hear the end of thy tale, I pray thee," said Jediah. "Are these two prisoners to go free? Hath Ishtar indeed gained so great favour from my lord the king?"

And he shook, like a man palsied, with rage and fear.

"Nay," returned the Babylonian, "they shall not go free."

"What, then, is the sentence upon them? Tell me, I beseech thee."

"The king hath granted to Ishtar, whose beauty is indeed above the beauty of all other women "—

"And the king loveth well a pretty face," interrupted the other Babylonian.

"Yea—yea. He is a man, as all of us! The king hath granted to Ishtar that these plotters against his glory shall not die."

"They are to live?   Lemuel is to live?" cried Jediah.

"Yea—but both he and the girl Elna are to be sold into slavery."

Jediah uttered an inarticulate exclamation.

"They will be offered up to the highest bidder in the great slave - market to - morrow at noon," continued the Babylonian.   "All the city will be there, they do say.   For Elna, the maid, is beautiful.   And we of Babylon do love beauty in women, even if they be Israelites."

He burst into a coarse laugh.

"Dost thou love women, stranger?" he cried.

But Jediah turned from him without another word, and strode rapidly away.

This new turning of events threw Jediah into a paroxysm of fury and of excitement.   That Lemuel should, in spite of all, escape death, angered him to the verge of fury.   Even in slavery, in perpetual bondage, Lemuel might be happy.   He might be purchased by some Babylonian woman for the sake of his handsome face and noble bearing.   He might live in luxury, be petted and caressed.   In any event, he would escape the vengeance of Jediah—unless—unless—

Jediah spoke aloud to himself as he strode on. A determination was taking shape in his mind. He saw a possibility of the personal vengeance that his soul desired clearly before him.   If Lemuel and Elna were indeed offered for sale to the highest bidder in the slave - market of Babylon, why should not he—Jediah—buy his own brother, his own betrothed? He was rich. He would spend all his substance for revenge. He would give all—every foot of land, every sheep and goat, every grain of corn, the very robe that covered him, the gold chain which he wore about his neck—but he would have those captives for his. And, once he possessed them, he would drag them before the Judgment Seat of Zoar, in the plain beside the tents of his people. They should be tried. They should be condemned. They should be stoned to death. He laughed aloud in wild exultation, and he felt the stones grasped within his clenched hands. He saw the white faces of his victims. They should not escape him. Naught should save them from him. He would give the very flesh from his bones rather than that they should be sold to another. To-morrow! To-morrow at noon! All night he walked to and fro in the lighted streets till all men slept and the great city was silent. He paced upon the river bank of Euphrates, where lay the ships along the wharves, and the Babylonish guards slept beside the bales of merchandise from all lands. The moon lay on the river, and the grey of dawn came up over the water, changing it from silver to the colour of a mirror of steel. The sailors stirred from their dreams of seafaring men. The sun lay red in the golden couch of the east. But Jediah neither saw, nor heard, nor heeded. Like the madman, his mind held him in a vice. His soul was a prisoner in the chains of one idea. And the gay light of morning fell upon him and found him grey-haired, haggard, and with livid eyes of fire, still pacing up and down, still muttering over to himself as one who murmurs and who cries in slumber.

.   .   .   .   .   .

The slave-market of Babylon was an immense square, bounded upon three sides with tall houses, while upon the fourth side there was a public garden, shady with trees and bright with flowers. In the distance, beyond the garden, might be seen the watch-towers of the city and a glimpse of the river Euphrates. At the entrance to the garden, at the back of the square, stood one of the glories of Babylon, a gigantic statue of the god Bel, made of solid gold, which gleamed in the sun and could be seen from far. It stood upon a platform of alabaster, and was surrounded by flowers offered by devout worshippers to propitiate the god. In the centre of the square stood a rostrum, some six feet high, eight feet deep, and twelve feet wide, surrounded by a balustrade of marble. Upon this rostrum the slaves were exposed to the view of the crowd and were offered for sale. This market was usually humming with people, and was a centre of barter and of discussion. Here came the lowest of the Babylonians, drawn thither by the attraction of beholding the great nobles, who often bade for slaves in person. Here came the merchants and the traders, the auctioneers,—those who offered the slaves and cried aloud their attractions,—and all the young dandies of the day. These feasted their eyes upon the lovely girls who were bought for great prices, and sometimes, in sheer wantonness, sent up the bidding when they perceived some old and dissipated Babylonian busily intent upon a certain slave. And here, too, came many wealthy women to purchase handsome men for their palaces. For in Babylon the women were not veiled and secluded as in many countries of the East, but walked abroad in the daylight unabashed, showing their bold faces to all that cared to look upon them, and in very sooth rivalling each other in efforts to attract the notice of the passers-by.

The slave-market was habitually crowded, but to-day the concourse, drawn thither from all quarters of Babylon, was extraordinary, and showed plainly that some event of an unusual nature had very greatly excited the public mind. Not only was the whole square packed with people, but the crowd even overflowed into the adjacent streets. The windows of all the houses were beset with gazers, who also clustered upon the roofs. And upon every step, beneath every portico, stood knots of the curious. For Lemuel's denunciation of the city and prophecy of its passing away, the sentence of death by fire passed upon him, the errand of Ishtar to the palace of the king, and the subsequent revocation of the royal decree, had become known throughout the length and breadth of Babylon. All men and women spoke of it. Even the children babbled of it as they played about the doors of their parents. And everyone desired to look upon this shepherd, who dared defy the king and the gods, and who had won the love of the beautiful woman whom all men sought. There were, also, many who were fain to behold the maiden Elna, who had stolen into the city attired as a boy. For her sake came all the young dandies, and gossip about her flew from mouth to mouth. But there was another reason still for the assembling of this mighty concourse.

The Israelites in Babylon, who numbered at this time a considerable part of the population, were greatly moved and excited by the seizure of Lemuel, his condemnation to death, and the subsequent decree that he was to be publicly sold into slavery. For in Lemuel they had put their trust, on him they had set their hopes of freedom. They had begun to look upon him as their Messiah, from whom would come salvation. His fiery denunciation of Babylon, his prophecy of its fall, had appealed to their hearts and stirred their imaginations into a ferment of patriotic fervour. The thought of his fall, of his degradation, of his captivity, was bitter and abhorrent to them. Upon their excitement certain secret agents of the great cause of Israel's freedom had cunningly played, arguing that the hour had come to strike a bold blow; that if they allowed Lemuel to be borne away into bondage, the hopes of Israel would be dashed to the ground for ever. These secret agents, among whom was Sabaal, had worked with such passion and success that all Israel in Babylon had flowed forth to the slave-market, intent upon one thing only—the rescue of their shepherd-prophet, Lemuel. Wherever the eyes gazed might be discerned shrouded men gathered together in knots, watchful, silent, determined. And as the hour of noon drew near, these men closed up quietly towards the rostrum on which Elna and Lemuel were to be offered for sale. They were unnoticed by the gay and laughing Babylonians, who were too intent upon the prospect of seeing this famous shepherd and his love sold into bondage to think of aught else, and who, besides, felt far too secure and powerful in their great and prosperous city to dream of any attempt at rescue on the part of people whom they regarded with contempt as wretched dogs of Israelites, only worthy to pay tribute and perform the most menial services for their own greater glory.

Already, upon the rostrum in the middle of the market, various slaves were being offered to the critical buyers. The auctioneer in strident tones called aloud their beauties, their virtues, and their various capabilities. But the mass of the people scarcely heeded his voice. They were too much occupied in chattering among themselves, and in retailing a thousand pieces of scandal, many of which related to the doings of the famous Ishtar, whose name, at this time, was eternally upon the lips of Babylon. In the midst of the crowd, intent upon the making of money, stood Migdapul the god-seller. Although he was grown rich in the secret service of Ishtar, he still found occasion to continue, in propitious moments, his barter of deities; and now, above the roar of the people, he might be heard crying in a piercing voice—

"Come hither, ye who would buy gods! Buy them of me! I sell the cheapest gods in Babylon. Merodach, the General of all gods—he who can cure witchcraft and brain-sickness, for one shekel! Ana, god of heaven, and Anatu, his consort, for two shekels! Bel, the great god Bel, who ruleth the evil of the south-west wind—who will give a shekel for Bel? Bel, who alone hath power to dispel the seven evil spirits who seize the body, who bring wastings and fevers, sickness of the head, sickness of the heart, sickness of terror—the ruler of the Seven! Who will buy him for only one shekel? Only one shekel for the great god Bel!"

A handsome woman moved slowly through the crowd, and Migdapul was about to devote his special attention to her, when she stopped and said to him angrily—

"I did buy gods of thee, but I want my money again, for thy gods are useless, and thou thyself art but a cheat. Bel, so thou did'st tell me, would make my husband true unto me. And, to make all sure, I bought two images of the great god Bel."

"Well?" said Migdapul, with his habitual sturdy impudence,—"and what hath befallen thee?"

"Evil hath befallen me. While I was praying to the great god Bel to make my husband true, in came my husband. 'For what dost thou pray?' said my husband. 'To the great god Bel to make thee true unto me,' said I. 'Verily, that is good and wise of thee,' said my husband. 'But thou must pray from now until the sun goeth down if thy prayers are to be granted,' said he."

The crowd, who stood round about listening, began to laugh. And Migdapul winked at them merrily as he answered—

"A wise man, that same husband of thine. These things do take time—as most men know."

"A wise man!" cried the woman. "A cheat! a deceiver!"

"How, good woman?—how?"

"Why, it was then but noon, but I prayed until the sun went down, and my knees ached, and my head swam, and my voice grew weak with my supplications."

"And was he not true unto thee?" said Migdapul, while the curious people pressed ever more closely round to hear the end.

"True! True, forsooth!" exclaimed the woman wrathfully. "No. He got me to pray from noon to sunset to the great god Bel to make him true to me, that he might go unhindered to the wine-shop and make love to my handmaiden."

She burst into angry tears, and sobbed out—

"I want my money back! Give me my money back!"

"But thy handmaiden," said Migdapul, totally unmoved,—"she is tall and fair?"

"She is not!" cried the woman. "She is short and black — ugly creature! Give me back my money!"

" Short and black ! " ejaculated Migdapul.

He paused and seemed to muse.   Then suddenly, as if a light broke on him, he cried—

" The same !   Now I understand !   She, thy handmaiden, bought of me Merodach for three shekels, and thou Bel for but two.   And while thou did'st beseech Bel, at two shekels, to make thy husband true, she did beseech Merodach, at three shekels, to make him false."

The crowd laughed again at the adroitness of the god-seller.   But the woman wailed—

" What am I to do ? "

" Pluck up thine heart," said Migdapul, " and buy two of Merodach for six shekels, and triumph over this naughty handmaid who would rob thee of thy lawful husband."

" Six shekels ! " said the woman doubtfully. " Six !   For that I must sell this string of beads, this amulet, this girdle, and this raiment."

And she gazed down at her robe, which was of fine linen, gaily embroidered.

" Well, what of that," said Migdapul, with affected gravity, " if you buy your husband back ? Have a heart, good woman.   Wilt be wronged and deceived by this long white handmaiden ? "

" No, no—not long and white ; short and black, and most evil-favoured ! "

" Did I not say short and black—with her paltry three-shekel Merodach, when for the sacrifice of these few beads, this amulet, and this robe thou canst triumph over her for ever ?   Come, have a spirit ! "

He held forth his gods.

"Here!" he cried, "and here! Never falter nor dally! Hence with this long white—I should say, short black—handmaid! Come! come!"

"I will—verily I will!" exclaimed the woman, who was now becoming very excited at the thought of vengeance.

"Verily, thou shalt!" vociferated Migdapul. "Come! Haste! Off with the beads! Off with the amulet!"

He snatched them from her eagerly, while the people around laughed and applauded him.

"Off with the girdle! 'Tis well. Off with the— Nay, I am an easy man. Thou shalt keep this robe, for it becometh thee well. I make thee a present of thy gown, good woman."

And as the woman hurried away, holding fast the effigies for which she had parted from so much, Migdapul winked merrily at the crowd, then turning up his small eyes piously and showing his pointed tusks of teeth, he moved slowly away, ejaculating—

"Blessed be the gods, by whom alone I live! Blessed be the eternal gods!"

While the attention of many in the crowd had been attracted by the foregoing scene, Sabaal, who passed incessantly hither and thither, wriggling through the throng as deftly as some serpent of the desert, met with Elkanus, who, as usual, was beating his cups together and crying, "Water, water, sweet and cool!"

"Elkanus! Elkanus!" he whispered softly.

"Ah, Sabaal!" returned the other, with equal precaution. "What is thy news?"

"Have a care! These Babylonish eyes and ears are sharp. Lemuel is not to die."

"Nay, but to go into bondage."

"Lemuel is not to go into bondage," whispered Sabaal significantly.

"Not to go into bondage? But"—

"Not without a struggle. Lemuel hath been betrayed, but he hath not betrayed his people. Even so shall his people deal with him. Go among them—but with caution, Elkanus! Bid them stand close about the rostrum and await my signal. All our brethren are here in the crowd. We are many. We will strike a blow for Lemuel. We will rescue him, or die."

Elkanus nodded with assumed carelessness. Then he beat his cups together, and cried aloud—

"Come, ye who thirst! Water, water, sweet and cool!"

Some Israelites gathered round him to drink from his gourd. As he gave them to drink, he exchanged with them greetings and directions. Sabaal stole away through the crowd.

On its outskirts at this moment appeared Jediah, walking with the Israelite Adoram. Jediah was pale as wax. His long beard was untrimmed and ragged. His grey hair was disordered. Beneath his eyes were drawn those lines that grief, anxiety, anger, terror trace so clearly and so pitilessly on the countenance of man. He walked heavily, for all night he had not slept, and even now he had come up from the banks of Euphrates, where he had seen the bitter rising of the dawn.

"So this is the end!" he said to Adoram, as they moved on with difficulty through the seething mass of the people. "This new deliverer—this second Moses — sold into bondage like some common slave! He and his companion in sin, Elna. But they shall be mine. I will buy them both, Adoram, though it cost me all that I have in the world—this chain about my neck, this robe which clothes me."

"Thou wilt do this much for love, Jediah?" said Adoram.

"Love! love!" returned Jediah wildly. "No! for hate, for revenge! That I may drag them back in chains and punish them. That I may see them die the death of adulterers under the stones of the faithful and the law-abiding of our people. An eye for an eye and a tooth for a tooth; thus saith the law."

A hand plucked at his robe. He turned sharply and beheld his creature Jozadah.

"My lord! my lord!" cried the Israelite.

"Well, thou hast failed!" Jediah hissed into his ear. "Lemuel still lives."

"It is the fault of the king," said Jozadah. "He should have been slain by night as he was leaving the palace of Ishtar, but, as thou knowest, he was arrested by the king's command, and I "—

"Thou art helpless. I know it, slave. Stand close. I may have other work for thee. Stand close!"

The pressure of the crowd was becoming tremendous. All the citizens of Babylon seemed

to have assembled in the square. There were
Assyrians from the North—tall men, with regular
features of the Semitic type ; men descended from
the tribes of Elam and from the Accadians, Kassites,
Chaldeans from the South ; lithe youths from the
great salt marshes that spread around the sea-
coast ; Nubians black and lusty, with thick lips and
bulging eyes, like ebony with a yellow light playing on it; Arabians, Indians, Persians, walking
with a sinuous and yet solemn gait ; soldiers of the
guard of the king, exchanging coarse jokes and
following the women with bold looks of admiration ;
sailors and traders come up from the ships of the
river ; ragged boys wriggling through the throng
like eels; beggars, halt, maimed, and blind—among
them Johanan, urging lamentably his infirmity ;
money-changers, slave-dealers intent on purchases,
eunuchs,keepers of theharems,sorcerersand Semites,
priests and usurers. And all seemed talking at the
height of their voices, all seemed pressing forward
towards the rostrum in the midst of the market.
Presently a loud voice cried, above the hubbub—
"Room! Room for the Lord Alorus !"
Jediah heard the cry, and cast his haggard
eyes around. He perceived Alorus, magnificently
dressed, and accompanied by Menanahim, Meraioth, and some wealthy Babylonians, passing
slowly through the mob. They were talking ani-
matedly together.
"Well," exclaimed Meraioth, "I could almost
find it in my woman's heart to pity this Lemuel."
Menanahim burst out into a bitter laugh.

15

" Ay, pity him, and bid for him at the sale," he cried. " I hate the knave, and could know no sweeter pleasure than to see him thy slave, Meraioth. Ha, ha, ha! Poor fool! How thou would'st open the eyes of his understanding and knowledge of what it is to be a woman's slave!"

" I had not thought of it," said Meraioth, in no-wise offended ; " but, since thou hast spoken, it may be that I shall bid a talent of silver for the man. He hath a handsome head, and would make a right regal chariot-driver. He was thy friend, Alorus. Wilt thou venture for him?"

" By Bel, not I!" said Alorus. " Make way, slaves! Not I! I have knaves enough already. Let him go. Nay, my bid will be for the maiden who is with him."

" I had thought she was already thy slave."

" And so thought I ; but our lord the king, seeing her by the aid of Ishtar's eyes, and dis-posing of her by Ishtar's directions, made me think otherwise."

" Then," rejoined Meraioth, laughing, " we shall share the twain between us. Lemuel shall be my slave, and this maiden thine."

" The maiden shall, of a surety, be mine; but, unless Ishtar liveth no longer, all that thou hast will not buy Lemuel."

" What?" cried Meraioth. " Will she bid for him?"

Alorus burst into a roar of laughter that was affectedly echoed by Menanahim.

" Will Ishtar bid for Lemuel?" he cried. " Thou

shalt see—thou shalt see. Room, slaves—room, I say!"

They passed on towards the rostrum.

It was now close upon the stroke of noon, and the excitement and anticipation of the crowd were become intense. The windows of the houses were black with heads, and many women leaned so far forth that it seemed, indeed, as if they must fall into the midst of the multitude below. Cries and exclamations resounded on all sides. People strained their necks and raised themselves on their toes to see the better. The strong men jostled and pushed the weak. Old people fell in the press and were trodden under foot. Girls shrieked in fear, and none heeded them—not even their lovers. The soldiers struck the crowd with their fists, and even with the flat of their weapons, in order to make a path for themselves. And, with each moment that passed, the uproar became more terrific. The auctioneer, who was crying the merits of the slaves, could no longer make himself audible. And the business of the market came, perforce, to a standstill.

And now, just as the hour was at hand, there was suddenly a terrific roar of voices from the left side of the square, from which quarter ran the street that led to the dungeon. The crowd surged in that direction like a tide of a great sea. On every hand arose shouts—" Lemuel the Israelite!" " Lemuel, son of Zoar!" " See the prophet!" " The traitor!" " The denouncer of Babylon!" " Slay him! slay him!"

There was a clashing of arms, a glitter of spears. The crowd surged back as violently as it had surged forward. For the guards of the king, clad in helmets, coats of mail, leathern drawers, and high-laced boots, marched into the square, beating back all who obstructed their progress. Their helmets were of bronze, on which the sun shone bravely, and they bore stout shields of metal and tall spears tipped with bronze. But martial and brilliant as they looked, the people scarcely heeded them. For all eyes were turned to the two who walked in their midst—to Lemuel and to the maiden Elna.

Lemuel came first, walking with a firm step and holding himself fearlessly erect. He was clad in a coarse garment of wool given him to wear in the prison, and chains hung upon his mighty arms and upon his legs. His head was uncovered to the blaze of the noonday sun, and his luminous eyes met calmly the gaze of the multitude who thronged about him. Elna, who was also miserably attired, was veiled. She too walked with a firm step and seemed to take no heed of the excited uproar of the rabble. Now and then the procession paused, when the soldiers, for the moment, were blocked by the density of the crowd. During one of these moments, Sabaal found means to force his way close up to Lemuel.

"Be patient and watch!" he whispered.

Lemuel returned an almost imperceptible sign of understanding. A soldier brutally beat back Sabaal with his shield—the guard moved forward again, and at length gained the rostrum. As they did so, the Israelites pressed determinedly forward, and stood close around the steps which led up to the platform on which the slaves were exposed to view. Many of them leaned upon stout staves. Others clutched the long knives that lay hidden within the bosoms of their flowing robes. But the Babylonians heeded them not, being too intent upon Lemuel and Elna, who were now forced to ascend to the rostrum. As they did so, and appeared on high, visible to all that thronged the square, a sudden dead silence fell upon the people. Every voice was for a moment hushed, as every eye fastened upon them to behold their beauty and the strange courage which had surely come down to them from heaven itself. They stood there side by side, calm and resolute. Even Elna did not tremble or show the least symptom of terror. The slave-merchant, a swarthy Babylonian, stood half-way up the steps of the rostrum. The guards were beneath him, holding their shields and spears. A trumpet rang out. Then an official mounted the steps at the back of the rostrum softly, approached the place where Elna stood, lifted his hand and took from her face the veil which had covered it hitherto.

A cry rose from the crowd. The young dandies strained their eyes to see this beauty of which all Babylon had been gossiping. The rabble drew in their breath. The women murmured. And Jediah, laying his hand upon the arm of Adoram, uttered a hoarse ejaculation. For never had Elna looked more lovely, as she stood with her eyes cast down, the coarse garment that she wore half revealing the beautiful lines of her fair limbs, the chains hanging from her soft and delicate arms, and the flood of her magnificent black hair flowing about her. The whiteness of her face was still as marble. No terror convulsed it. Her soft lips were set together. And now, even while the multitude regarded her, she lifted up her eyes and fixed them upon Lemuel, with a glance of steadfast trust and deep love that moved even the coarse and hateful hearts of the dissipated Babylonians. A murmur of admiration ran from mouth to mouth, growing louder and louder. The young dandies strove to move nearer to the rostrum, but the rabble pressed them back, heedless now of rank or state. The guards extended their stout shields in a wall against the people who trampled about them, and the slave-merchant, from his post of vantage on the steps of the rostrum, lifted up his tremendous voice and cried aloud—

"By the will of our lord the king!"

"May the king live for ever!" shouted the people.

The shrouded Israelites pressed a little closer to the steps.

"This man and woman," cried the slave-merchant, "until now free, are to be sold to whomsoever shall bid the highest price; and whosoever shall buy them, it is by our lord decreed that they shall keep them in bondage to be their slaves so long as they may will it; and these their slaves shall be obedient unto them in all things, and obey them without a murmur, their masters having absolute dominion over them and power to punish, even unto death, their disobedience. This is the decree of our lord the king — may he live for ever! The woman is to be sold first. Who is there to bid?"

There was a moment's pause. All faces were turned towards the rostrum. Lemuel folded his arms and set his lips a little more firmly together. His eyes regarded Elna with a passion of brave pity and affection.

" Who is there to buy?" cried the slave-merchant again, in a voice of thunder.

And he looked around over the crowd.

Jediah raised his arm and forced his way with difficulty to the steps.

" A purchaser! a purchaser!" cried many voices.

Elna and Lemuel, noting the stir, looked down and beheld the deathly white face and fierce, glittering eyes of Jediah. And, for the first time, Elna trembled and seemed for a moment afraid.

" By the laws of Babylon," said Jediah, in a hard and distinct voice, "by the laws of Babylon, the purchaser hath absolute power over his slaves?"

" By the laws of Babylon," cried the merchant, "and by the will of our lord the king."

" Even unto death?" said Jediah.

" I have said," returned the merchant.

The excitement of the crowd was heightened by the sinister question of Jediah.

"Death?" they cried. "What meaneth he?
What would he with the maiden?"

Then again they were silent, to see what Jediah
would do. He stood leaning heavily upon his
staff, in silence.

"Wilt thou bid for this woman?" asked the
merchant.

Then Jediah raised his voice and cried aloud—

"I bid for that woman—an hundred pieces of
silver."

An exclamation broke from the crowd. The
slave-merchant chuckled with satisfaction.

"A noble commencement!" cried a voice in the
crowd.

All turned to the direction from which it came,
and beheld the Lord Alorus, who now made his
way towards the place where stood Jediah.

"A noble commencement!" Alorus cried again,
"but far below the maiden's price. I offer—five
hundred."

Jediah grasped his staff harder, and his livid face
took an ashen tint.

"Six hundred!" he cried.

"Seven!" responded Alorus, laughing.

"Eight!" shouted Jediah.

"Nine!" returned Alorus.

"A thousand!" Jediah said hoarsely.

"Two thousand!" replied Alorus.

A roar broke from the multitude, who pressed
against the shields of the guards. They were
fascinated by this contest and by the mention of
these great sums of money. It seemed as if the

beggars smacked their lips as a starving man does when he hears of the delicious food eaten by others.

"Two thousand!" reiterated Alorus, disdainfully returning the frantic gaze of Jediah, whose eyes glared like those of an animal.

"Two thousand pieces of silver have been offered by my Lord Alorus for this maiden," vociferated the slave-dealer. "Is this the end?—or doth any here bid more?"

There was an instant's pause. Then Jediah, speaking in a harsh and shaking voice, said—

"Two thousand five hundred!"

"Four thousand!" laughed Alorus, arranging the bracelets upon his arm. "Four thousand for this pretty maiden! Four thousand, Israelite!"

Jediah was now gasping for breath, like unto a man who is taken by a fit or who is well-nigh suffocated. The sweat broke forth upon his forehead. He tottered and caught hold of one of the guards for support.

"Four—thousand—five—five—hundred!" he stammered.

"My lord will pardon his servant," said the slave-dealer, bending down to him. "But my Lord Alorus hath offered four thousand pieces of silver for this maiden. The Lord Alorus is known to me and unto all Babylon. But thou art a stranger. It may be that thou hast not the means to pay the sum that thou hast named. Hast thou indeed as much with thee?"

"Alas!" groaned Jediah, "no. I have it not here with me."

"Then," returned the merchant, "the maiden is the property of my Lord Alorus, unless thou canst name a surety that thou wilt pay in full the sum that thou hast offered."

"A surety?" said Jediah, speaking as a man that is dazed. "A surety, sayest thou?"

"Ay," said the merchant. "Canst thou name one who will be thy surety for the full value thou hast offered?"

There was again a pause. Jediah bent his head upon his breast. He seemed to be considering deeply.

"Well?" said the merchant impatiently. "Well? Answerest thou nothing?"

Jediah lifted his head.

"I can name one," he said slowly, "and only one, who knoweth that I can and will pay the sum that I have named for purchase of this maiden."

"Who is that?" cried the merchant.

"My Lord Alorus," answered Jediah.

This answer struck surprise through all who heard it. Even Alorus was moved from his usual affected manner of contemptuous disdain. He clapped his hand on his girdle with a gesture of astonishment, exclaiming—

"I! By Baal! Shall I arm mine enemy that he may slay me?"

"Thou dost know me!" said Jediah passionately, "and what this maiden is to me. Thou dost seek to take her from me. Let the fight be equal. Be thou my surety!"

These words caught the sense of justice, the

love of contest that lives in crowds. The people pressed frantically round, vociferating—

"'Tis well said. The Israelite speaks truth. Be thou his surety. Let the fight be fair."

" Well," said Alorus, with a smile, " for one other bid I will, but not for one shekel more. The last bid was for four thousand five hundred pieces of silver. I bid five thousand. And for thy next bid, let it be what it may, I will be thy surety. Now—what sayest thou ? "

After he ceased to speak, the silence was intense. All the vast multitude stood as if under some spell, gazing at Jediah, who, in his excitement, had mounted upon the steps of the rostrum close to the slave-dealer. Elna never moved. She looked like some lovely statue of terror. For now her calm had left her. The fury of Jediah, his determination to spend all that he had so that he might wreak his vengeance upon her, shook the depths of her steadfast soul. Lemuel too was moved, but he bore himself calmly. Only the light in his eyes showed the strength of his excitement.

Jediah, clinging to the balustrade of the rostrum, shook like a man stricken with the palsy. He moved his white lips once or twice, but no sound came from them.

" Five thousand ! I have spoken ! " cried Alorus triumphantly. " The maiden is "—

Jediah raised his arms on high, in a frantic gesture, as if he would tear down Elna from the place whereon she stood, high above him.

" I bid five thousand five hundred ! " he shrieked.

"I can no more. Five thousand and five hundred!"

Alorus burst into a sneering laugh.

"Six thousand!" he exclaimed.

There was a wild roar from the crowd. Jediah staggered and must have fallen, had not Adoram caught him and held him up.

"What saith my lord?" asked the slave-merchant.

"I cannot—I cannot outbid this lord for her," said Jediah. "He hath surely all the wealth of Babylon. But I will buy him—the man"—and he pointed with his trembling hand to Lemuel. "He shall, at least, be mine. I can—no—more Water—give me water!"

Adoram handed him a cup filled with water. He drained it, and, dropping his hand, let the cup fall upon the steps of the rostrum.

"My Lord Alorus," said the slave-merchant, "the maid is thine."

"Lemuel," murmured Elna, "what am I to do?"

"For the moment, whate'er they bid thee," he whispered. "But have no fear."

"Now the man is offered," cried the merchant. "Who bids for the man?"

"I will," said Jediah to Adoram, "if it costeth me all mine inheritance. For where he goeth, there will she surely follow, if she doth live."

"Fifty pieces of silver!" cried a voice in the crowd.

"Two hundred!" exclaimed Meraioth, the Babylonish woman, who stood with the Lord Alorus.

" Three hundred ! " cried the voice.

" Five hundred ! " retorted Meraioth, gazing with favourable eyes upon the manly glory of the noble face of Lemuel.

" Six hundred ! " said Jediah, calling upon all his energy, and bracing himself to win in this final contest for revenge.

" Seven ! " cried the voice.

" Eight ! " said Jediah loudly.

" One thousand ! " said Meraioth, becoming greatly excited.

" Who is it that bids against us—against me and this Israelite ? " she whispered to Alorus.

" Nay, I know not," he said, turning to gaze upon the seething mass of people. " Some woman who hateth thee, perchance, or who loveth the shepherd."

" Two thousand ! " cried Jediah.

" Three ! " cried Meraioth. " Three ! — three thousand for the shepherd."

Jediah's countenance was contorted with rage. He turned on Meraioth like some wild beast.

" A thousand curses light on the Jezebel ! " he exclaimed furiously. " Three thousand five hundred ! "

" Four thousand ! " shrieked Meraioth.

" Five thousand ! " cried Jediah, in a voice that was hoarse and almost inhuman with rage and excitement. " Five thousand ! "

He leaned down from the balustrade to which he was clinging, and gazing with a desperate defiance into the face of Meraioth, snarled out again—

" Five thousand ! "

She fell backward a step towards Alorus, and murmured—

" I can no more ! "

Jediah heard the words. A terrible smile of triumph hovered on his lips, which were wet with blood where his teeth had bitten them. He turned to the slave-dealer, and, shaking one hand towards the place where Lemuel stood, he cried fiercely—

" He is mine—mine—mine ! "

But even as he spoke the words, the tall and majestic veiled figure of a woman came forward to the foot of the steps whereon he stood, all the crowd, as with one common impulse, making way for her. And a clear and imperious voice said, so distinctly that it was audible far off to the more distant crowd—

" Six thousand ! "

Jediah started as if he had been struck. He stared down at this mysterious opponent almost with terror, and the smile of triumph faded from his face, leaving it grey and old and appalling to look upon.

" Who is this woman ? " he whispered.

But nobody gave answer.

" Six thousand ! " repeated the woman, raising her voice.

" Seven thousand—seven ! " stammered Jediah.

" Eight thousand ! " said the woman inflexibly.

Exclamations broke from the crowd. A girl, over-come with excitement and emotion, staggered and fainted. No one heeded her. All eyes were fixed on this magnificent veiled figure that stood up like some strange and superb statue of resolution before the steps on which Jediah crouched, rent by conflicting emotions of passion and terror.

" Eight thousand ! "

Jediah tottered a step downwards towards where the woman stood, thrusting his head forward like a man who, despite himself, draws near to behold some horrible spectre that meets him on his path.

" I demand to know who is my opponent," he said, with a terrible cry. " Let her unveil ! Let me behold her face ! "

With a grand and sweeping gesture the woman cast back her veil.

" Behold it, then, Jediah, son of Zoar ! " she answered, in clear and ringing tones, that vibrated with an intense bitterness of scorn.

A blind man who stood afar among the crowd, seized hold of his neighbour with a wild exclamation. The man, a Babylonian, shook him roughly off, cursing him.

" Ishtar ! " exclaimed the people gathered close around the rostrum.

" The Lady Ishtar ! " cried even the guards of the king.

" Elcia ! " murmured Jediah, horror-stricken.

For one moment he seemed about to recoil, to turn away, to flee.

" The shepherd is Ishtar's," cried the Babylonians, " he is to the Lady Ishtar ! "

The cry ran from mouth to mouth, through all the vast assemblage.

"Ishtar's! Ishtar's!" shouted the people

This cry pierced to the very soul of Jediah. He glanced up at Lemuel. He gazed down at Ishtar, whose eyes were fixed upon him with a fire of intensity that seemed actually to burn as a flame. Then, gathering his forces for one last effort, he cried, like one demented—

"Ten thousand!"

"Twenty thousand!" said the cold and inflexible voice of Ishtar.

Jediah swayed upon the steps. His eyes were bloodshot. Foam broke from between his gnashing teeth. He extended his hands as if to clutch Ishtar by the throat and strangle her. Then, uttering a terrible, inarticulate exclamation, he fell senseless into the arms of Adoram.

The uproar from the crowd was now terrific. Men fought to gain a nearer view of the extraordinary events going forward around the rostrum. Women shrieked and struggled and were trodden under foot. The people who had been hitherto watching from the houses now descended from the windows and poured into the market-place, rendering the press and confusion more dangerous every moment. The slave-merchant, alarmed by the riot, hastily cried out—

"My Lord Alorus, the maid is thine. Lady Ishtar, Lemuel the shepherd is thine own, to do with as thou wilt. Come and give thy bonds! Swift, for the people grow dangerous. Soldiers, guard well your slaves!"

He turned to ascend the steps. As he did so,

Lemuel advanced to the balustrade and, placing his two hands upon it despite the heavy chains that hung from his wrists and almost crippled him, shouted in a voice that rang out above all the furious exclamations of the surging multitude—

"Sons of Israel! Will ye see this daughter of your race sold into infamy and slavery?"

An answering shout rose up from the Israelites who had crowded round the tribune, unheeded in the general excitement.

"Never!" they cried, as one man. "Never!"

"Strike, then," shouted Lemuel, "for the hour hath come! Strike for Israel—for her freedom and for thine own! To arms! To arms! To arms!"

In answer to his inspiring call, the Israelites drew their knives and grasped their staves and attacked with fury the surging Babylonians, who, utterly unprepared for the assault, driven hither and thither by their own comrades, scarce knew how to defend themselves. Sabaal, with many followers, sprang to the rostrum, covered Elna and Lemuel in two cloaks which rendered them unrecognisable and concealed their chains, and drew them hastily down into the midst of the crowd, where they were quickly lost to view. Having once sunk among the people, who were all in wild confusion, it was soon possible to convey them away unnoticed, and following the onrush of the fighting Israelites and Babylonians, and taking swift advantage of every opening that presented itself, to gain one of the verges of the square, and

16

finally to escape from it through the open space that lay beyond the golden statue of the great god Bel.

Meanwhile, the fury and terror increased in the market-place and extended through the city, assuming the proportions of a formidable and dangerous riot. The Babylonish soldiers were called out, and the king himself trembled within his palace. Many of the Babylonians, long accustomed to ease and to every form of refinement and debauchery, fled before the passion of the Israelites. The gates of the temples and of the magnificent mansions of the nobles were locked and barred. Women hid themselves in inner chambers. And the night fell upon a tumult that was almost like unto the seething of demons in the pit of hell itself.

The lower Babylonians, profiting by the general disorganisation, broke into the bazaars and shops, looted, plundered, and drank. Even the soldiers gave themselves up to the wildest excesses.

And Ishtar, leaning late upon the balustrade of her garden terrace, and looking out over the lighted city, from which rose confused shouts of fury, shrieks of despair, the clash of arms, the beating of the enormous war-drums, and the piercing calls of trumpets—seeing the flames leaping up from burning buildings and, mingled with volumes of smoke, mounting towards the stars—Ishtar said unto herself—

"Can it, indeed, be true? Are the days of Babylon indeed numbered? Is the God of Israel wroth with the heathen, and shall He send down His fury to consume this people? And I—I—Whither shall I go? Ah, Lemuel, Lemuel!"

She laid her forehead upon the cold marble, and as the flames from the burning quarters of the city sprang up still higher, as if they would reach the mighty walls of her palace, she wept at last as if all the troubles of the years came trooping about her in the night; as if her soul—which had struggled so long against despair, giving itself to the spectre called Lust, and to the phantom named Pleasure—could no longer strive, or fight, or hope, or disdain, but could only grovel in the dust, and faint in a hopeless desire of forgiveness and of peace!

CHAPTER XIII

THREE days had passed. The riot in the city had been, with difficulty, subdued. The flames of the conflagration, ignited by the refuse of the Babylonians themselves, had been quenched. Comparative quietude had been restored. Not yet was the prophecy of Lemuel in the palace garden of Ishtar to come true. Not yet was the mighty city doomed to destruction. But the rising of the Israelites, the rescue of their hero, the shepherd Lemuel, his escape—temporary, perhaps, but for the moment certain—all these events spread through Babylon a grave disquietude, a growing sense of uneasiness and of insecurity, which was accentuated by the fact that a large number of Persians inhabiting the city had joined actively in the revolt, and that the Babylonish soldiers had shown themselves cowardly and indifferent to the dangers of the king and of his capital. They too, like the nobles, the higher functionaries, and the priests, were undermined, body and soul, by indulgence and by pride. Believing themselves to be under the special protection of the great gods, and so invincible, they took little heed of discipline or of manly exercises at this period, but loved the wine-

cup and worshipped women. In a time of peace
they bore themselves brilliantly enough in their
shining armour. They had a martial outside, the
gallant swagger that imposes upon the ignorant
and catches the favour of maidens. But even this
rising brought their inherent weakness and rotten-
ness plainly to the view of all who were not blinded
by the tinsel trappings of an apparent glory, or
lulled in the radiant dreams that only come with a
sleep that is dangerous, if not deadly.

Far-seeing men were, however, rare in Babylon.
And already, in three days, the rising was almost
forgotten. A few Israelites had fled; a few had
been thrown into prison. But, owing to the riotous
behaviour of the Babylonians themselves, it had
been extremely difficult to discover the ringleaders
of the tumult. Already people talked of other
things. Already the great god, Pleasure, resumed
his interrupted sway, and in the palace of the Lord
Alorus—as in the other palaces of Babylon—there
was feasting and merriment as there had ever been.

It was afternoon. Within a magnificent chamber
of his palace, Alorus sat with his friend Menanahim,
drinking wine and gossiping of the events that
had been passing. Both men preserved their
habitual air of dandified complacence. Their calm
had apparently been in nowise disturbed. Their
gaiety was in nowise ruffled. Or so it seemed at
the first, as they talked lazily, while the silver water
of the fountains rose and fell on the scented air,
and the slaves, kneeling before them, cooled their
tinted faces with the waving fans of feathers set

in polished ivory.   Yet, now and then, a shadow crossed the impudent countenance of Alorus, and he moved a little restlessly upon his golden seat. And when, presently, a slave entered running, he turned and cried—

"Well, well?   And hast thou heard nothing further of these Israelites?"

"No, my lord," replied the slave humbly.   "The soldiers say they seemed to vanish into thin air."

Alorus struck his hands together with an impatient gesture.

"The soldiers!" he exclaimed.   "By Baal, and what do they know or care?   They think of naught save of feasting and revelry.   Go, go!   But be within hail.   Thou hearest?"

The slave made a low obeisance and softly retreated.   Alorus rose up from his seat and paced restlessly to and fro about the chamber.

"Any pretext!" he muttered.   "Any pretext to cover negligence!   A prisoner escapes.   Oh, he took unto himself wings—he disappeared in fire or vanished in a cloud."

"Nay," rejoined Menanahim, "the vulgar are ever superstitious."

As if struck by a sudden recollection, he jumped up hastily and made a fantastic inclination before some golden effigies of the gods of Babylon that stood upon an altar of marble in the chamber.

"May the great god Bel banish the Seven from thy house!" he cried, with an affected exaggeration of piety.   Then he added, resuming his former tone—

" The Lady Ishtar hath a hand in this."

" Thinkest thou ? " rejoined Alorus. " Nay, then, for hand say heart. And, truly, wonderful is the heart of woman. Like as the wind, it goeth where it listeth, and all in vain we seek the reason why."

" Reason ! " cried Menanahim. " He who seeketh reason in a woman seeketh his own confusion. As well seek to number the sands of the sea. Where women are concerned a man must take what the gods do give him, with much thankfulness and without question. I never question—and am ever grateful."

" I would be grateful too," said Alorus, still pacing up and down, " did the gods give me the woman I desire."

" Ah," said Menanahim, speaking now with an anæmic bitterness, " ah, desire no woman, but all women—so shalt thou escape much tribulation."

" For the sake of some women, tribulation becomes a joy," cried Alorus. " He who hath not seen such hath no sight. I have mine eyes, and mine eyes do guide my heart."

" P'f ! " sneered Menanahim ; " heart ! What is that ? Heart ? I deem that old Khasis-a-dra forgot to include those encumbrances among the strange things he took into his ark, and that the Deluge destroyed them."

A slave entered.

" What is it ? What desirest thou ? " cried Alorus impatiently. " Cannot I be left in peace even for one moment ? "

" It is the Lady Ishtar," said the slave submissively.

"Ishtar!" said Alorus.   "Go; escort her hither."

The slave withdrew.   Alorus turned to Menanahim, who had sprung up from the couch on which he had been extended by a table on which stood fruit, wine, and confections in boxes and trays of silver.

"Here cometh a woman," said Alorus, "who hath found that very thing—the heart—of which thou dost doubt the existence."

Menanahim's lips curled in a bitter sneer, but he said nothing, for at this moment there was heard the rustling of a robe, and Ishtar herself entered, attended by two female slaves.

"Hail, Lady Ishtar!" cried Menanahim, bending low before her.   "Hail!   Thou art radiant as Samas, the sun-god, himself!"

Ishtar bowed her head coldly.   She was dressed with an unusual simplicity in a robe of dull blue silk, that looked almost black where it fell into folds.   And she wore no jewels of any kind.

The two men regarded her with some astonishment.

"Where are thy jewels, Ishtar?" said Alorus.

"And where thy"— began Menanahim.

But she stopped him with an imperious gesture.

"I would speak with thee alone, O Alorus," she said.

An expression of gratified surprise came into the face of Alorus.   He cast a side glance towards a mirror of steel that stood near, and mechanically passed his ringed hands through his perfumed hair.

"Alone!" he exclaimed. "I am indeed highly favoured."

Menanahim scowled.

"Thrice-blessed Alorus!" he said, with a feeble attempt to conceal his anger.

He drew a little closer to Ishtar.

"Shall I tell thee, lady," he said, "what the Lord Alorus hath just said of thee?"

"Naught evil, I trust?" said Ishtar indifferently.

"It is a matter of doubt, lady. He hath told me that—that thou hast found that most rare of earthly things—a heart."

The look of indifference left Ishtar's face and was replaced by an expression of glorious pride.

"He speaketh truth," she answered, in a ringing voice. "I have found a heart indeed. And know, O Menanahim, that it is mine own!"

As she spoke she looked him full in the eyes, and she seemed almost like one transformed— like one who stood in some strange and glowing radiance. Never before had she appeared so wondrously beautiful. For now to the beauty of face and form, of deep eyes and exquisite limbs, of noble bearing and of incomparable grace, there was added a wonder of the spirit, a beauty of soul, an intensity of sublime emotionalism that uplifted her, and seemed verily to set her on high, as on some throne from which she gazed down upon the earth below. And yet there was no insolence of worldly pride in her now, but a species of thrilling humility, a white fire of modesty and of most delicate tenderness and patience. Menanahim gazed upon her with a kind of brutish wonder.

"Ishtar's heart!" he said slowly. 'Great Bel! What is its price?"

He looked at Alorus, and then back again to Ishtar.

"Emeralds and pearls can scarcely buy the lips of Ishtar," he continued. "What mine of rubies hath purchased her heart?"

"It hath not been purchased," said Ishtar. "Reckless, foolish merchant that I am, I have given it away."

As she spoke a beautiful flush crept into her white cheeks; and, for the first time, she cast down her great eyes as one half ashamed.

Menanahim regarded her with a growing irritation and amazement.

"Foolish indeed!" he exclaimed. "Take heed, fair merchant, that he who received the gift of thy merchandise doth not estimate its value at the price he paid for it."

And he laughed bitterly. But Ishtar answered, with a beautiful and profound melancholy—

"And if he did, who shall deny his judgment? For who would believe in Ishtar's love? Who would have faith in Ishtar's constancy?"

"At least I cannot," cried Menanahim, whose wounded vanity had never forgiven the slight Ishtar had put upon him when she preferred Lemuel to him, and bade Lemuel lie at her feet while the slave-girls danced in the moonbeams in the palace garden.

"Thou!" said Ishtar, with a scorn she did not attempt to conceal.

Menanahim opened his lips to speak. The red blood of anger rose beneath the dye with which his weak and sensual face was covered. He seemed about to make an angry rejoinder. But he checked himself, assumed a smile of contempt which could not conceal his disappointed jealousy, and caught up the flowing garment he wore with his white and effeminate hand.

"Ishtar's eyes are clouded," he said, with a travesty of dandified courtliness. "The moon is passing 'twixt the earth and the sun, and all the land is dark. I do not love the dark nor any creeping thing that is engendered by it. And so farewell, my Lady Ishtar."

He swept a bow, to which she scarcely deigned to respond by a slight inclination of her head. Then he cried out, with a sort of weak defiance—

"I go to other beauties! I go to seek the sun!" and walked airily out of the chamber, turning at the doorway to shoot one glance of bitter hatred at Ishtar.

She did not even see it. But as he disappeared behind the drapery that hung before the doorway, she said to Alorus, with a sigh as if of great relief—

"He seeketh the sun! So do all butterflies, and when they find it not they die or vanish."

Then turning to her slaves, who waited behind her, immobile as statues, she said unto them—

"Wait me without."

They saluted and obeyed her command, leaving her and Alorus alone in the chamber.

"What unaccustomed grace is here?" he asked, in growing wonderment. "For the first time I am alone with thee, Ishtar—a boon thou hast ever refused me until now."

"Because I have ever valued thy friendship," she replied slowly. "A man forgets all friendship when he finds himself alone with a woman."

She fixed her great and melancholy eyes upon him as if she would read his heart.

"Is it not so?" she asked.

Alorus felt uneasy beneath her searching gaze, he scarce knew why.

"Prove it," he answered. "We are alone. Ask of my—friendship any favour. What would'st thou, lady?"

Ishtar, with a sudden and swift movement, approached him and laid her hand upon his arm.

"I would have this slave-girl whom thou hast purchased," she said.

Alorus started with amazement.

"Elna?" he cried. "But she hath fled."

"That I know. But Babylon's arms are far-reaching enough to clasp her and to bring her back again to thee."

Alorus pursed his lips and hunched his shoulders.

"Truly," he said. "But—perchance a little de-creased in value. Her companion "—

"I understand," exclaimed Ishtar, interrupting him. "But then the less valuable, the easier parted with. Is it not so?"

"Not so fast, dear lady, not so fast," returned Alorus, smiling. "Less valuable doth not mean valueless."

"Is she, indeed, so precious unto thee?" asked Ishtar.

And there was an unwonted accent of pleading in her voice.

"Well, she will cost me six thousand pieces of silver at the least."

"If I refund thee the full price?" said Ishtar, with increasing insistence.

"Well," replied Alorus, "to tell the very truth, lady, I would rather thou did'st refund my slave."

Ishtar turned from him with obvious impatience.

"What is it governs a man?" she cried, stamping her foot upon the ground.

"'Tis hard to tell," said Alorus, with most unruffled composure and his most effeminate air of dandyism. "Say instinct. We are but brutes at the best."

Ishtar swept round upon him.

"And at the worst?" she cried.

Alorus bowed before her with suave mockery.

"Can Alorus instruct Ishtar?" he said.

For a moment Ishtar was deadly silent. Her cheeks flushed, then turned pale. Her lovely bosom heaved, and angry tears swam in her eyes. Then she lifted up her right arm with a magnificent gesture as of one invoking the judgment of Heaven itself, and said in a voice that thrilled with passion and quivered with intensity—

"Ah! accursed, thrice accursed be the man who made Ishtar what she was!"

Even as she spoke the words, the hideous form of Migdapul, the god-seller, appeared for a moment in the aperture of the doorway, then swiftly and silently drew back into the shadow.

"Was?" said Alorus. "And is!"

"Nay," cried Ishtar, with ever-increasing vehemence, "was—was—and never again will be."

Alorus threw himself down upon a couch and took up a fan, which he began to wave slowly to and fro.

"What hath changed Ishtar?" he asked, laughing lightly.

"A good man's pure love," she answered, with a grave sincerity, and lingering on the words as if they were dear to her lips.

"For thee?" cried Alorus. "For thee, most pure and innocent Ishtar?"

"Alas, no!" she said, heedless of the taunt. "Not for me. For another."

Alorus laid down the fan, took up a vase containing a perfume brought from the western region of India, and poured some upon his hands.

"And a good man's pure love," he said banteringly, "I marvel much what that is like! A good man's pure love—for another—hath changed proud Ishtar's life?"

"Doth not pure love exist in man?" she said.

"It did, doubtless, before the Fall."

"Alas for man's fall!"

Alorus heaved an ostentatious sigh, leaning back upon his cushions.

"Alas for the woman who did occasion that fall!" he said.

"The serpent was the cause," said Ishtar.

"Ah!" chuckled Alorus, "I have ever had my doubts as to the sex of that same serpent. But, at anýrate, lady, after the serpent, the woman "—

"The man should have resisted the temptation."

"Ah, women would have men resist all temptations—save only their own!"

"I am not come hither to argue such matters," said Ishtar impatiently, "but to implore thee— let me have this slave Elna as mine own."

"Thou askest much of me, Ishtar," said Alorus.

His manner suddenly became more grave. He rose up from the couch whereon he had been lying, and approached her.

"What givest thou to me in return?" he said significantly.

She moved a step backward.

"What would'st thou?" she said.

And in her voice, as she asked the question, there was a note of proud and impenetrable reserve.

"A fair substitute," he said, following her.

"Whom?" she asked.

"Ishtar!"

"Ah, no!" she said inflexibly. "Thou did'st

promise me a boon and would'st make a bargain. Give me this girl, Alorus."

"Thou hast the man—leave me the woman," he said, more coldly.

But Ishtar was strangely persistent.

"Nay," she said, "grant me this. Give me this maid, thy slave."

"What would'st thou gain by that?"

"Revenge," said Ishtar quietly.

Alorus looked into her face curiously.

"Why!" he said. "Would'st thou slay her?"

"Indeed, nay."

"And how, then, wilt thou compass this revenge?"

For a moment Ishtar stood silent. Then she said, with a grave simplicity—

"Even by giving Elna unto the man she doth love."

"To Lemuel!" cried Alorus, in astonishment.

"Even to Lemuel."

Alorus was so much amazed by this determination of Ishtar's that he was unable to speak. Twice he opened his lips, and twice closed them again without uttering a syllable. But at last, with a great effort, he cried—

"But thou lovest him!"

Ishtar bowed her head.

"Still would I do this thing."

"But—but why?"

"That when I am gone—as soon I shall be—he may think that the vile thing that once was Ishtar was, after all, a woman, and one who loved him better than her life, better than herself.   Give me this maid.   Oh, give her to me, Alorus!"

And she sank down upon her knees at his feet and bowed her proud head, catching his robe with her soft and beautiful hands, which had been clasped so often in admiration and in love.

"Give her to me.   For thee she is but a passing fancy.   For him she is the whole of life.   Grant me my prayer and give her to me—give her to me!"

And she laid her forehead against his knees, while great sobs shook her fair body.

Alorus stood looking down upon her.   He felt the feverish pressure of her hands on his, the touch of her forehead that was bent down like the forehead of some slave-girl who was his chattel. He saw the movement of that bosom on which all men longed to rest.   He heard the sound of her tears, the tears of her who was named the proudest woman in all Babylon.   And, despite himself, he was moved.   Some strange emotion stirred within him, some strange impulse of pity, of tenderness, of a devotion that was almost chivalrous, that seemed to come from the centre of that thing at which he had so lately laughed, which, by his life, he had ever striven to kill—a human heart.   He bent down to Ishtar, and, un-felt, unknown by her, touched her dark head with his lips.   Then he said, in a voice that shook slightly, though he strove to make it hard and gay—

"By Anatu and all the female gods! but I am

17

only half a man myself. Here are tears—and—
and— There! tell it not in Babylon, I beseech
thee, but thine example hath left me no course
but to follow it. Rise, Ishtar!"

And, as he spoke, he gently lifted her to her
feet.

"Rise. Thy prayer is granted, and Elna, my
slave, shall be thine."

"The God of Israel for ever bless thee!" exclaimed Ishtar, kissing his hand. "I am thy
grateful servant."

"The God of Israel?" said Alorus. "Can His
blessing avail aught? Well, maybe. But I still
look to Bel."

He bent and, in his turn, kissed the hand of
Ishtar. Then he said, more gaily—

"But, as thou art grateful, never remind me of
this. Let me forget that I could with so much
ease play the fool, like a raw youth unknown of
the town. Men love to be fooled by women, but
love not to be reminded of it when the fooling is
past and gone."

"Sign me the acquittance!" exclaimed Ishtar.
"Let me give them both their liberty, lest Jediah
do find them and some evil thing befall. Come!
come!"

And she moved towards the door.

"I come, I come," he answered. "I am but as
clay in the hands of the potter. Mould me as
thou wilt, but leave in the shaping a little to show
that this vessel was at one time—a man."

He turned to follow her, but ere they could

reach the doorway Migdapul suddenly appeared from behind the drapery where he had lain concealed.

" What dost thou here ? " said Ishtar.

Migdapul made a low and grotesque obeisance.

" I have obeyed thy commands, lady," he said. " I would have told thee sooner by some minutes, —for I am ever swifter to execute orders than all the other knaves of the city,—but I feared to interrupt thee and the noble Lord Alorus."

Alorus and Ishtar exchanged a glance, and Alorus shrugged his shoulders.

" What is thy news ? " said Ishtar.

" Lemuel and the maid Elna—forced thereto, as I believe, by Sabaal and other Israelites—have fled the city."

" Art sure ? " cried Ishtar.

" They escaped by one of the city towers — I myself saw them."

" In what direction went they ? "

" Towards the plains."

" Towards the plains ? " said Ishtar. " By what road ? "

" By the same road that taketh the noble Lord Alorus when he goeth to gather in tribute from the wealthy tribe of Zoar."

And Migdapul made a second obeisance to Alorus, showing his pointed tusks of teeth in an insidious smile.

" They are fled to the tents of their people," said Alorus to Ishtar.

Ishtar had become very pale, and she now laid

her hand upon the edge of the couch on which
Alorus had been reclining, as if she needed support.

"But if Jediah should "— she began.

Then she glanced at Migdapul, set her lips, and
was silent.

"Jediah hath also left the city, lady," said Migdapul.

"Following them?" she cried, turning swiftly
upon him.

The god - seller, as if startled by her flash of
emotion, recoiled a step or two, and his evil face
was overspread by a horrible expression of cringing
and servile cunning. Ishtar looked at him for a
moment in speaking silence. Then, struck by a
new idea, she advanced upon him and cried—

"How knew Jediah the Israelite which way
went Lemuel and the maiden Elna?"

"I — I know not, lady," stammered Migdapul.
"Thy slave is not a god. He — he can — cannot "—

"Thou did'st tell him!" exclaimed Ishtar, still
keeping her glowing eyes fastened upon Migdapul.

"Nay—indeed "—

"Thou did'st! I can read it in thy face. What
did he give thee?"

"Nay, lady, but three pieces of silver," cried
Migdapul lamentably. "He was ever a mean
man. Long ago, when I did lure Johanan "—

He stopped short. The expression that had
rushed into the face of Ishtar terrified him, long
used as he was to all crime and fear and agony.

"Johanan?" she said in a low and tense voice. "Speak! What dost thou say?"

"Naught, lady—naught. I will—even—go."

And he turned towards the doorway. But, with one bound, Ishtar planted herself in front of it and barred his egress with her outstretched arms.

"Speak, slave!" she said, bending upon him all the fiery and searching inquiry of her terrible eyes. "Thou—thou didst lure Johanan—whither, and for what purpose? I tell thee that I will have thee thrown into the dungeon—I will have thee slain, if thou dost not speak!"

Migdapul fell down upon the floor, grovelling before her.

"He—Jediah—forced me to it!" he wailed. "I was ever a kindly man—I would not hurt a fly, but—but "—

"But thou did'st "—

"I did but put Johanan in the way of a good trade, lady, of a trade that is of more profit than god-selling, as all Babylon doth know."

"A trade?" said Ishtar, with ever-growing horror. "What trade?"

"The trade of the blind man," groaned forth Migdapul.

With a hoarse cry, Ishtar fell back against the post of the door, grasping the silken curtain in her hands till it was rent in pieces. Alorus sprang forth to give her aid, but she put him from her.

"Nay—nay!" she gasped. "I am well. Heed me not."

She tottered to the window that looked forth to the outer court of the palace.

"Air!" she muttered. "I must have air! My breath—I have no more—breath—in me!"

Alorus hastened after her to support her. In a moment she seemed to recover. With one or two long gasps that were almost like sobs, she regained her voice. The terror of faintness left her. She turned round and looked into the chamber.

Migdapul had fled.

"Thou art better, Ishtar?" said Alorus. "Water —dost thou need"—

"I need naught," she said. "This is no time to take heed, and to be like a weak woman. Alorus, art thou indeed my friend?"

"Till death, lady!"

"Lemuel and Elna are gone to the tents of Zoar. Jediah doth pursue them to wreak his vengeance upon them. And well I know what will betide. My Lord Alorus, yet another favour!"

"Name it!" cried Alorus. "I am in the granting vein, Ishtar. Ask all I have."

"I go to save Lemuel and Elna. I may need thine aid. Wilt thou go with me?"

"A journey with the fair Ishtar! Who would not consent with thankfulness?"

"And thou wilt help me?"

"Yea, even to mine own undoing."

"Thou shalt have no cause to sorrow for this good deed. My friend, how I thank thee! Come, come! I must to the palace of the king."

"Wherefore?"

"As we go, I will tell thee.   Come, Alorus—come!   Ah, my friend, never wert thou more faithful unto manhood than in this hour!"

And, followed by Alorus, she hurried forth towards the palace of the great king of Babylon.

IT was even as Migdapul, the god-seller, had said to Ishtar. Lemuel and Elna had indeed escaped from Babylon. But Lemuel had, strangely, in falling between the hands of his friends, only passed from one captivity into another. His nobility of character, his dauntless courage could never have betrayed his people. He was not one of those smooth-tongued and ready orators who play upon the passions of a crowd, but refuse to share their danger when they follow the course of action urged by the fiery words of cowards. When he stood in chains upon the rostrum in the market-place, and cried, "To arms!" he desired to lead the Israelites against the Babylonians, to fight himself in the very forefront of the battle, to die, if necessary, for the cause of his country. But Sabaal, the slave of Alorus, was not of his mind. When the tumult broke forth, and the whole city was in uproar, Sabaal and those that worked with him caught Lemuel and Elna from the rostrum, huddled them in the immense loose robes that were commonly worn at that time, drew the great hoods forward before their faces, and sought to convey them, thus concealed and disguised, out of

the press of the rabble.   But Lemuel was of no
mind for such a flight, for such a desertion.

"Strike my chains from me," he cried to Sabaal.
"Give me my freedom to fight with and for my
brethren."

But Sabaal and his followers only surrounded
him the more closely, and sought to bear him
onward, crying—

"Keep silence!   Else will thy life be forfeit and
thou wilt be taken again into captivity.   Silence!
For each word thou utterest may mean thy death
and this maiden's."

"Then let me die," said Lemuel.   "Better so
than that I should thus desert them that trusted
in me.   Let me free, I say!   What! am I a
captive among mine own people?"

"Gag him!" whispered Sabaal to those about
him.   "Gag him and bear him onward.   It is for
the safety of Israel."

His followers obeyed, for Sabaal, by his unyielding ruthlessness of character and by his strength
of purpose, had, during his long slavery in
Babylon, gained great influence over the Israelites
within the city.   Lemuel and Elna, blinded by the
hoods that hid their faces, manacled in their
chains, and held fast in the grasp of the captors,
who were intent only upon their salvation, were
borne forward, unable to make any resistance, or
to take any part in the fight for freedom and the
tumult that raged around them on every side.
They could feel the buffetings of the surging
crowds that threw them this way and that.   They

could hear the dull roar of voices, muffled shouts and exclamations, the dim clash of arms and beat of war-drums and call of trumpets. But they could see nothing. They were as if in a prison, with no power of their own to perform any action or to take advantage of any circumstance. The journey through the mob seemed thus most endless to them, as must all periods of movement and of excitement in which one is bereft of power and paralysed of will. They were hurried onward and onward as if in some nightmare of storm and striving, of fury and of fierce combat. But, at length, the muffled noise of multitudes grew less. They were no longer buffeted and flung from one side to another. They moved forward more rapidly and more continuously, and peace grew about them. They could hear now the voices of the Israelites talking around them, and the strong tones of Sabaal giving commands.

"We must lie close this night in the city," he said. "For all the gates will be guarded. If our people do triumph over these cursed Babylonians, or be like to triumph, then will we let Lemuel forth to be indeed their leader and to inspire them to greater deeds. But if not, then must we get Lemuel in secret out of the city, to wait the appointed time. For he hath the ear of the people, and without him our cause will even be lost. His life must be preserved, let come what may. To the western gate—and warily. We must lie this night by the western wall and wait what may betide. To the house of Abimelech, friends."

"To the house of Abimelech!" returned the Israelites, hastening onward with Lemuel and Elna in their midst.

That night and the next they lay close within this house, under the shadow of the western wall of the city. Sabaal and others ventured forth from time to time, in order to learn the news of what was befalling, and at first their hearts rejoiced, and in exultation they spoke together, saying that the prophecy of Lemuel was already about to be fulfilled, that Babylon was already tottering to its fall. For they saw the guards of the king, whose duty it was to keep public order and to defend their ruler, rioting with the lowest of the people, drinking and dissipating with the women in the stews and in the infamous quarters wherein people lived like unto animals. And there was neither law, nor religion, nor order, nor peace. And they saw men feasting while the flames of burning houses rose up in the black night towards the sky, and girls dancing while the bodies of the murdered lay unburied, and robbers looting the shops of the merchants and pillaging the heavily loaded boats upon the river Euphrates, and the wealthy citizens pale with fear of their own slaves and servitors. And they heard of the king himself shuddering within the walls of his mighty palace.

Then they said unto Sabaal—

"The hour is come. Let us now send forth Lemuel to our people, and the city shall be ours. For—look—the Babylonians themselves do bring destruction upon Babylon. With their own hands do they set the torches to the buildings and spread terror among their own brethren. Soon shall the very temples of their gods crumble into dust. For the wrath of the God of our fathers is upon them, and the night of their passing away is come."

But Sabaal answered—

"Wait. The time is not yet ripe. Wait until the morrow."

On the morrow the tumult had already abated. The flames of the burning buildings had been quenched. The Babylonians, wearied by the wave of excitement that had caught them, fatigued by their excesses, were even now returning to the paths of reason from which they had strayed. And the revolt of the Israelites had been quelled.

So, on the coming of the third day, Sabaal and his followers, still bearing with them Lemuel and Elna as captives, escaped out of the city by the western tower, even as Migdapul had said, and made their way towards the plains, journeying towards the tents of the tribe of Zoar.

As it fell out, Migdapul, who had received the order of Ishtar to discover where Lemuel had lain hidden after his escape from the rostrum, perceived the shrouded figures of the captives, mounted upon camels, as they went forth from the city. Seeing that Sabaal was with them, and being well acquainted with him, as has already been mentioned, he accosted Sabaal, and whispered to him—

"Who are these thou bearest with thee, O Sabaal? And whither goest thou?"

Sabaal hesitated to reply, and at first endeavoured to evade the question.

"These are but women of Israel," he said, "whom we do escort to the tents of their people. For Babylon is no place for women when such riots do befall."

Migdapul showed his teeth in an incredulous smile.

"Nay," he rejoined, pointing to the mighty form of Lemuel. "If that be a woman, she is indeed well favoured of the gods and meet helpmate for one of those giants who, they do say, dwell in India. It seemeth unto me, O Sabaal, that the shepherd Lem—"

"Hush!" hissed Sabaal. "Keep silence, and I will give thee silver. Here—and here."

He pressed some coins into the greedy hands of Migdapul.

"And thou shalt have much more when I return. Moreover, if thou dost say aught, I have the wherewithal to bring thee low. Hast thou forgotten how, in thy cups, thou did'st tell me of the way to make blind men for the "—

"Enough! enough!" cried Migdapul hastily. "I have seen naught except these thy—women."

And he hurriedly mingled with the throng that beset the street, while Sabaal and his followers went forth in safety through the gate of the city and gained the open country, travelling with all speed towards the well of Naomi and the far-off tents of Zoar.

Now, while the crafty Migdapul was returning to the palace of Ishtar, hot with his news, and musing gladly upon the price he would be paid for it, by a strange chance—or, indeed, a stroke of Fate, as would say the superstitious—he fell in with Jediah and with Adoram. Even among the excited and perturbed people of a tumultuous city, Jediah stood forth as one on whom calamity had set a terrible stamp. He had recovered from the seizure by which he had been taken in the slave-market. He was now in reason, and could walk abroad. But he was so haggard, fierce, and old, in the aspect of his countenance and in the movement of his limbs, that he appeared, indeed, rather like some horrible spectre informed by the very spirit of Evil, than like a human being. He no longer thought, as other men, of the many passing concerns of life, of the gliding circumstances of the hours, of those about him and of the things his eyes looked upon, but lived in a dream of revenge, and was shut up within a prison of the soul. Where was Lemuel? Where was the maiden Elna? This question possessed him. He neither ate nor did he sleep at night, but ever he sought these two, who had been reft from him even as he thought to close his hands upon them and to keep them his—sad hostages to death.

He saw not Migdapul in the street, but the god-seller, whose eyes were ever glancing this way and that, intent on the service of his lust of money, perceived him, and, scenting further gain, stopped him, crying—

"Jediah the Israelite!   In the name of the great god Bel, and of Merodach, the god of all gods, whom seekest thou?"

Jediah snarled on him like some animal disturbed in its pursuit of a victim, and would have gone on his way, but Migdapul laid one filthy hand upon his arm, and whispered in his ear—

"Seekest thou not Lemuel the shepherd and the maiden Elna?"

Jediah stopped short, and glared into the evil face of the god-seller.

"Where are they?" he cried.   "Where are they? Speak, thou knave, or I will even tear the words from thy throat and throw thy carcase unto the dogs of the city."

"Nay," returned Migdapul, "I will speak no word without thou givest me my just reward for service.   I am no slave of thine, but of the great gods, who"—

Jediah caught him by the shoulders with hands like claws.

"Thou shalt speak!" he vociferated furiously, "or I will strike thee dead at my feet.   Thou shalt, I say!"

And he shook Migdapul till the creature's breath verily rattled in his throat.

"They—are—gone forth—by the—western—gate!" stammered Migdapul.   "Nay, let me go! Thou art mad!   Let—me"—

"The western gate?" cried Jediah.   "Adoram, they are fled to the tents of our people!"

He burst forth into a terrible laugh.

"They are run to meet their fate. Come thou with me, Adoram. We will pursue. We will take them. They shall come before the Judgment Seat. They shall be stoned with stones—with stones—hearest thou me?—until they die!"

He turned, like one demented, to be gone. But Migdapul caught him by the skirt of his garment, crying—

"Payment!—the payment for my service! Nay —nay—thou shalt pay me!"

"Take thy money and begone!" cried Jediah, throwing him some pieces of silver.

Migdapul flung himself upon the ground to pick them up. When he lifted his head again, Jediah and Adoram were gone from his sight.

CHAPTER XV

IT was late afternoon. Over the long plains where dwelt the tribe of Zoar the sunlight fell with a softened glory. The great palm trees shook as the delicate fingers of the breeze touched them, caressing them as the fingers of a gentle mother caress her child. Before the tents the little gay Israelites played, as of old, heedless of the troubles and the anxieties that ever rent their nation. And around the well of Naomi, where grew the tall reeds and the sweet-smelling bushes starred with yellow flowers, the maidens of the tribe chattered, as was their wont, while they drew the water to fill the tall pitchers that they bore upon their graceful heads. Among these women was Tirzah, she who had assisted Elna in her flight to Babylon. Tirzah joined but little in the talk about the well. She drew the water to fill her pitcher, placed the pitcher upon her head, and, walking with the peculiar freedom and majesty of the women of her tribe, took her way alone towards the tent of her mother. This lay rather apart from the other tents, and nearest to the Judgment Seat that stood up prominently in the plain. Now it chanced that, when Tirzah had set down her

18

pitcher within the tent, she came forth to the door and looked idly over the plain. Her mother was not within. She was quite alone. The day had been warm, but as the evening drew nigh, a cool breeze had sprung up. Tirzah, who was weary, enjoyed feeling it upon her face. She loved well this hour, when the silence seemed to grow around her, when the brass of the sky melted into many soft and beautiful colours, when the birds, full - throated, sang their last songs, and the flowers began to fold their delicate petals, and the children to droop their pretty eye-lids and gently long for rest. At this time a strange romance stole over these mighty plains in the midst of which dwelt the tribe of Zoar. It was scarcely palpable, yet Tirzah felt it. All nature softened, as softens a face when the mind thinks kindly and the heart is full of charity. The tall palm trees threw long shadows, and against the sky their outlines became romantic and sug-gestive of mysterious beauty and of haunted places far away. The long grasses waved and rustled, as if they talked together of quaint legends and of night imaginings. The noise of the stream surely changed. Its music became more peaceful, more naïve and infantine. A flight of big birds, like herons, passed overhead, flying towards the salt marshes that lay beside the distant margin of the sea. Their long wings were black like velvet against the lemon light. They dwindled to specks and disappeared. And their departure was full of mystery. The multitudinous insects that had their being in the rank herbage of the plain chirped less vivaciously. Their activities were lulled. Perhaps they crept to curious little homes beneath the plants that were to them a jungle, and gave themselves to dozings and to insect dreams. Never did there seem less cruelty in the world that God had made than at this hour of His day. So Tirzah often thought. And now, standing in the tent door, this idea came to her again. Why could not all men be ever kind, all women ever tender, all children ever happy and innocent? Why must there be violence on the beautiful earth, slavery and suffering, the wildness of passion and the haggard terror of pain? Nature was so lovely and so beneficent; the sun shone to ripen the grain and to prepare the harvests; the rain fell to give all flowers and plants the vital freshness of life; the winds blew from the distant deserts to cool those that were tired with long labour; the moon and the stars shone gently to guide the steps of the travellers in the night. And all these children of the Great God were kind. Did not the stars themselves sing together, the plants entwine their sister plants in sweet embraces, the winds go hand in hand, the stream give itself and all its music to the majesty and the music of the sea? The sun, in dying each evening, yielded beauty to the clouds that attended it. The purple of the sky was like a religion. Why, then, should there be pain and bondage, lust and violence, anger and despair, wherever men were gathered together, wherever women brought forth children?

Tirzah often pondered on these things in her simple way, as women before her had pondered, as women will ponder through all the ages of the world. For, in such evening hours as this, charity comes up from the heart of nature like a prayer and like a benediction. Tenderness hangs in the air, between the twilight and the darkness, as incense above the altars of the gods men worship. This evening, as she stood in the tent door looking forth towards the Judgment Seat, Tirzah's thoughts made their accustomed journey and then swept on to Babylon. Tirzah had never seen the great city that was the wonder of the world. She had heard men speak of its tremendous life, and women whisper of the things that were done in it. But ever it seemed to her like some city of a tale or of a dream. Even when those she knew went up to it, vanishing out of her sight and remaining long away, she felt as if they were gone out of the world rather than into a city that she herself might enter, did she join one of the passing caravans, with their company of merchants and of traders, of slaves and of water-carriers. And never did Babylon seem to her more legendary than at the hour of sunset.

Yet Babylon had taken into her fierce and evil embrace Lemuel and Jediah, and Elna and Jozadah. Then Tirzah thought of Lemuel, the shepherd who was like unto a king, the youth who had tended the flocks and who had the eyes of a seer and the heart of a prophet. Once Elna had said unto her that all women loved him. It was true that Tirzah's heart held some love for him, but it was wholly innocent, and asked for no return. Always she wished that Elna, whom she loved as a sister, might find peace and perfection in the strong arms of Lemuel. But ever she was haunted by a thousand vague fears for the safety of these two. And these fears had become more incessant, more clamorous in her soul since the departure of Jediah from the tents. She knew that he had followed the fugitive, the boy, Elna, to Babylon. She knew that he was intent upon revenge.

Now, she looked forth over the plain, and she strove, more keenly than before, to realise Babylon, to realise the doings and the fate of those she loved there. But even now the city, and their fate in it, became, as aforetime, dreamlike. For here she stood in silence, and it was the most charitable and tender hour. She could see no one upon the plain, and the world seemed empty. There was no sound of labourers singing, or of shepherds piping to their following flocks. There was no bark of dog, no murmur of chattering maidens. Was it indeed possible that evil passions existed anywhere, that anywhere there could be streets teeming with multitudes, buzzing with voices, that there could be cries of terror from dark houses in the night, and crimes committed secretly on those whose only fault was to love—on men like Lemuel, on women like Elna?

But now, listening intently to the loveliness of this twilight silence, Tirzah heard, far off, a tinkling of bells, a faint—a very faint sound of voices. And presently, at a long distance upon the plain beyond the Judgment Seat, she perceived something that looked like a long black serpent moving slowly towards the shadowy horizon. She knew that this must be a journeying caravan. It moved on and vanished. The tinkle of the bells faded, and silence gathered round once more. Presently, Tirzah woke from her dreaming with a sigh, and was about to turn and go into the tent, when her gaze was attracted by a black speck that was approaching the Judgment Seat from the direction in which the caravan had disappeared. It grew, as it drew nearer, until she could see that it was a man, moving slowly and with a curiously hesitating gait, frequently pausing as if to rest. This man came on until he reached the Judgment Seat. Then he stopped. A long time passed, and he did not move. Something within Tirzah's heart moved her to go towards this unknown stranger. She knew not whence came the impulse, nor at all why. But she obeyed it, left the tent, and slowly walked towards the Judgment Seat. When she was come near to it, she perceived a man, apparently old, with white hair and rough and tattered clothing, leaning against the mighty block of stone that formed its base, as if for support. He carried in one thin hand a stout staff. And as Tirzah approached him, and the sound of her movement through the herbage became audible, he turned his face towards her. The dying gleam of the sun fell full upon it, lighting up its white weariness, its lines, and two gaping holes where should have been his eyes. With a sense of deep and tender pity, Tirzah knew that he was blind.

"Who is that? Who cometh to me?" asked the blind man in a trembling voice, as Tirzah stood beside him.

And, as he spoke, he sank down wearily upon the steps of the Judgment Seat.

"I am one of the daughters of Israel, father," returned Tirzah gently.

'A daughter of Israel?" said the blind man sadly. "Yea, yea."

He paused, and let his head sink down on his breast, as if he lost himself in melancholy meditation.

Tirzah watched him with ever-growing sympathy. There was something infinitely pathetic in this face, the stamp, the signature of a great sorrow, a terrible tragedy. All the features were wasted, as if grief had fed through long years upon the very flesh of the man. The frame was big, and should surely have once been strong and lusty. But now it was feeble, and the bones appeared visibly through the flesh. The arms were like sticks, the fingers of the hands almost like the claws of some wild bird. Presently the blind man, returning from his morose meditation, lifted up his head again, and said to Tirzah—

"Why callest thou me—father?"

"Why?" she answered. "Because thou art old. Thy hair is white, and—alas!—thou art blind!"

'That I am blind 'tis true," said the man. "My

hair, too, is white, as thou sayest. Yet am I not old."

"How—not old?" cried Tirzah, in astonishment.

"My hair is whitened with suffering, mine eyes are darkened by cruelty, yet am I but young in years—but young in years."

And he shook his head mournfully and clasped his poor hands around his staff.

Tirzah was deeply surprised. It seemed to her incredible that this man could be young. Yet his words carried conviction to her heart. She felt that they were indeed true.

"Thine eyes were darkened by cruelty?" she said. "How can that be? Whence comest thou, stranger?"

"From Babylon."

Tirzah looked upon the stranger with even greater interest as he spoke the last words.

"From Babylon?" she said. "Ah! tell me—thou wast there but lately?"

"I am but just come from thence, maiden."

"And did'st thou see—?" began Tirzah eagerly. Then she paused, looking upon those horrible holes where should have gleamed the eyes of the man.

"I can see nothing," answered the man, "nothing."

"Forgive me, father," she said, kneeling beside him and taking one of his thin hands. "Forgive me that I spake without thought. And so thou art come from the great city whither goeth, surely, all the world?"

"Yea," said the blind man. "Yet am I not a

stranger in this land.   I went to Babylon to seek—
to seek no matter what.   I found it not until I had
waited and longed and suffered for years.   And
then, at last, I thought that I had found it."

He had grown greatly excited while he was
speaking, and now he grasped the hand of Tirzah so
tightly that she could scarce refrain from crying
out.

"And was it not true?" she asked.

'They said not," he answered.   "It was a voice
I heard, a voice I thought I knew, a voice I once
had loved—do you hear me?—had loved more
than all other voices upon the earth.   But they
told me I was mad.   They told me it was the
voice of a great queen in Babylon, that it was
Ishtar's voice.   Never had I heard Ishtar speak,
though often had I been up to her palace to ask
for alms.   But they told me it was her voice I
heard.   But shall I tell thee—shall I tell thee—?"

He bent mysteriously towards Tirzah.

"Yes, yes! tell me," she said, thinking to calm
and comfort him.

"I think it was some voice in my brain I heard,
some voice that never really spoke at all.   And
now—now—that same inward voice hath bid me
return hither."

"Yes, father," said Tirzah soothingly.   "This
place is sweeter than Babylon."

"Yea—and more silent.   'Tis, in truth, the plain
before the tents of Zoar, is it not?"

"It is, father."

"And this," he said, touching the stone whereon

he was seated with his thin fingers. "Tell me—what place is this?"

"The Judgment Seat, father."

Johanan, for it was he, started up.

"The Judgment Seat?" he cried. "An omen! A portent! 'Tis here that justice shall be done. The voice—the voice tells me so. I hear it even now."

And he stood with his hand to his ear as one that listens.

Then he said, more calmly—

"Come hither, maiden."

Tirzah approached him, and, very gently, Johanan passed his hands over her face and her hair.

"Thou art young," he said, "too young—thou would'st not know."

"Know what?" asked Tirzah.

"Tell me," he said. "Did'st thou ever hear thy people speak of one Elcia?"

"Elcia?" said Tirzah. "Yea—she fled the tents, she fled from her husband Johanan, and went to Babylon."

"To Babylon? Yea, yea!" said the blind man, trembling with excitement.

"And there she lived, they do say, with—with"—Tirzah paused, hesitating.

"With—with whom? Tell me, maiden, tell me!"

"With our Lord and Judge, Jediah," answered Tirzah in a low voice. She had not meant to say it, but there was something commanding about this blind man. He seemed to constrain her whether she would or no. As she spoke, a fear-

ful change came over the blind man. On hearing
the name of Jediah, he started violently, and seemed
as if he was about to fall. Then he straightened
himself up slowly, and into his face there came an
appalling expression of comprehension and of the
most vivid, the most vital fury.

As Tirzah looked upon him, it seemed as if he
became young in the depth of his wrath, strong in
the terror of his desire to wreak some strange
vengeance, as if he even saw, by a miracle,
some shape of one he had long ago known stand
before him.

"O father!" cried Tirzah, in fear at this transformation. "Tell me what ails thee! Speak, I
beseech thee!"

"Jediah! Jediah!" cried the blind man, lifting
up his arms towards heaven. "Fool that I was
not to see—*then*! Fool, more blind than now!
Was he not ever by our tent? Yet how could I
suspect our Lord and Judge? Now I know indeed!
Ah! great Judge of judges, give him into my hands!
Give him unto me!"

And, exhausted with passion, he sank down
at the foot of the Judgment Seat like a suppliant
prostrating himself before the throne of a mighty
king. Tirzah would fain have raised him up, for the
sun had now sunk behind the rim of the world, and
the darkness was falling. But he put her from him.

"Nay," he said. "Leave me, I pray thee, and tell
to no one the words that thou hast heard me speak.
Dost thou hear me? Swear that thou wilt say
naught."

"I swear, father," said Tirzah, to appease him. "But let me, I pray thee, lead thee with me, for it groweth dark and the winds of night blow coldly across the plains."

"They will not hurt me," answered the blind man.

"But thou art faint—thou art hungry."

"I have food here," he said, laying his hand on a species of wallet that hung at his girdle by a twisted rope of wool. "I shall neither starve, nor shall I feel any cold. Naught can hurt me now, I know. I live—I live till justice be done. Go, maiden—go, and say naught of me to thy people, I do straitly charge thee."

Reluctantly, Tirzah left him and went towards the tents. She turned once to look back upon him, but the darkness of the coming night had already swallowed him up from her sight.

That night, all her mind was turned from the blind man and from his strangeness and his story, for at the midnight hour, when already the people of the tribe of Zoar had been long within the tents, there rose the sound of voices calling out of the blackness, the long note of a horn blown from afar, the growl of camels and the shrill barking of wakened dogs. The weary men shifted upon their couches, and the women, half affrighted, sat up to listen. The voices grew louder, and presently one detached itself from the rest and cried out loudly—

"Wake, Zoar! Wake thou, Naomi! And give us welcome!"

"Verily, it is the voice of Sabaal, the slave of

the Lord Alorus," said one man to another. "Can Alorus be come hither in the night?"

"What may be his purpose?" returned his companion. "I like this not. There should be trouble afoot."

They hastened to the tent door. The night was very dark, and since evening a wind had arisen and was now blowing fiercely about the tents and whistling angrily among the palm trees, whose large leaves gave forth a desolate creaking note. Tirzah, with other of the women, had hurried forth at the sound of all this uproar, and even the aged Zoar came from his couch, attended by his faithful wife Naomi. Some of the men had hastily set fire to long torches of wood dipped in a species of resinous oil, and these now flared in the wind, blowing backwards as if they would fly away, like spirits, into the blackness of the night. Set in the wavering light of these torches, the people now saw several camels standing laden with packs, among which were perched hooded figures like enormous shadows scarce to be distinguished in the prevailing gloom.

"Who be ye," said Zoar, "that do call tired men from their slumbers in such a night as this?"

"Dost thou not know me, Zoar?" cried Sabaal, forcing his camel to kneel, and springing to the ground.

"Sabaal!" exclaimed Zoar. "What! Is the Lord Alorus come?"

"Nay, nay. Yet have I brought thee captives," answered Sabaal. "Set Lemuel free, Micah."

"Lemuel!" cried Naomi, hurrying forward. "My son! My son!"

Two Israelites now assisted Lemuel, who, by order of Sabaal, had been, during the march, a prisoner, to dismount, and drew back the long robe in which Elna had been muffled and disguised.

Lemuel stood once more in liberty. His face was very pale. His eyes flashed with passion. But he controlled himself, and, bending before his father and his mother, received their blessing. But to Sabaal he said—

"Thou hast done me bitter evil. Thou hast forced me to seem to play the coward."

"For the sake of the brethren," returned Sabaal, "I would do more than that. But for me, thou would'st now be still captive to the Babylonians or be laid in thy grave for ever."

Lemuel turned from him.

"And Elna?" he said.

"She is here," said Zoar sternly. "And with thee? What! art thou indeed guilty, as have said the brethren, guilty of this crime against thy brother Jediah?"

"There is no crime, father," said Lemuel proudly. "There is no guilt. Elna, come hither."

And he led her to Naomi, who was weeping, half with joy, half with terror.

"My mother," he said, "this maiden is innocent as when she left our tents to follow me that she might guard me from the danger that was plotted against me in Babylon."

Then Naomi opened her arms, and Elna fell, weeping too, upon her bosom.

All this time the violence of the storm was increasing, yet the Israelites scarce heeded it. From tent to tent, with the rapidity of the fire that licketh up the dry grass, had spread the news of Lemuel's return with Elna, and from every tent poured out men, women, and even children. Many of them carried in their hands torches, and there was a wavering and shifting blaze of light in the louring blackness. A ruddy glow fell upon the pale and weary faces of Lemuel and Elna, and upon the stern and rugged countenance of the slave Sabaal, who had dared so much in the cause of his people, driven by a zeal that could give him no rest nor ever let him be at peace.

"This is a strange tale," said Zoar gravely. "Where is thy brother Jediah? He went up to Babylon to seek this erring maiden, and is sworn to bring her hither that judgment may be done upon her."

"Let judgment be passed upon us both," answered Lemuel fearlessly. " My desire was to strike for my people against the Babylonians, and, when the issue of the revolt was certain, to come hither to face the Judges of our tribe. We have naught to fear, being innocent, and the judgment of the great God of Israel is ever just, for He holdeth in His hands the scales of justice and weigheth men according to their desert. But the revolt of our people against Babylon hath failed."

"And it must ever fail," said Zoar, with deep melancholy.

"Nay, not for ever," answered Lemuel, with enthusiasm, and the irrepressible hope and fervour of great-hearted men. "There will come a day when the Conqueror shall enter the gate of Babylon and the city shall lay its neck under the yoke of the destroyer. Even now it seemeth to me that I hear the roaring of the wheels of his chariots, the thunder of the footsteps of his legions in the wind."

As he spake, he stretched forth his hand as one that hearkens.

The Israelites, with their flaming torches, stood round about him, and—moved by the fire of his words and by the spell of his attitude — they listened too, wrought up to a height of strange excitement. But they heard naught save the long howl of the wind over the plain, and the voices of the tents, which strained in the blast like living things striving to be free. Then Zoar said—

"The hour is late, and men who labour must have rest and close their eyes in sleep. To your tents, O my people. When Jediah returneth, he will assemble ye, that the truth of the lives of this man and this maiden may be known to all."

"They are innocent, O my husband!" cried Naomi, with all the passion of a mother's love for her only son.

But Zoar answered—

"It may be so, wife. That shall certainly be known. For God is above all, and ruleth the doings of all men. Come thou to thy tent, and bring with thee this maiden.   She may need thy care."

And indeed Elna was half fainting from emotion and from the weariness of the long journey and from all the terrible excitement that she had endured in Babylon.   Naomi embraced her with tenderness, and led her into the tent of Zoar, and Lemuel lay apart in the tent of one of the tribe who was his friend.

He too was weary, yet he could not sleep, though he stretched himself upon the rugs and sought to lose his soul in the mazes of slumber. His brain seemed on fire with thought and his heart with passion.   And his hands were hot as those of a man to whom a fever cometh.   When he closed his eyes he saw in the darkness strange processions and wild scenes in Babylon.   He beheld the image of Bel going up to his temple, with the doors of brass, and the towers lifted towards the heaven.   Before the image went the dancing-girls.   They were crowned with flowers. He saw their scarlet robes set against the background of the night.   Their wild gestures were like the gestures of demons, and the roses that they scattered changed into charms of hell ere ever they fell to the ground.   The priests followed them, clad in their sacred skins of animals.   They opened their sensual mouths to sing a great hymn to the god whom they worshipped.   But from their lips came one cry, and one cry only, reiterated again and again—

"Babylon shall fall!   Babylon shall fall!"

The golden god, on his platform, seemed to lend

an ear to their cry and to be afraid, as if he knew that both he and his religion, the mystery that gathered about him and the worship, would sink into the dust. But he still glittered bravely in the light of the sun. And so he was borne up to his temple, and the great gates closed upon him, and Lemuel saw him no more. And then Lemuel beheld the hanging gardens of Ishtar's palace upon the banks of the river Euphrates. It was night, and the silver moon hung in the purple dimness of the sky above the myriad lights of Babylon. And he himself lay at the feet of Ishtar, and felt the softness of her touch, the light air stirred by the rose-coloured plumes of the fan she held. Round about them were the Babylonians who ever paid her court. And the pale and evil face of Menanahim stared in the night. There was a sound of far-off music, and the Indian girls, in their gossamer robes, spangled with silver, sprang and danced. And as they waved their slight arms the bracelets jingled coldly. Their little feet, in golden sandals, beat upon the gorgeous carpets, where strange animals of Asia lay embroidered in a coloured crowd. And how sad the faces of the dancers were, as if they too, with their dark and fatigued Eastern eyes, saw the dragons moving heavily through the crumbling temples and palaces of the great and glorious city, whose joy they were; as if they saw the everlasting sands rising, like a tide of the salt sea, to choke the streets that once were thronged with buyers and sellers, with gay women and laughing men. And then Lemuel heard again,

above the wind, the melodious magic of the love-
song, accompanied by flutes and by harps—

"Bind the cup with roses,
While thy love discloses
All the beauties she hath veiled from every eye but thine:
While the wine is flowing,
And desire is growing,
From the rose-wreathed, brim-filled cup drink to love and wine.

Have no thought of sorrow,
There is no to-morrow;
If there is, why, let it come, so we may love to-day.
Let care come hereafter,
Live to-day with laughter,
Let this moment bring us joy, the next bring what it may."

But their voices died, as if choked by sobs, and
the night was alive with cries of fear. War-drums
beat from the soldiers' quarters, and there was the
pealing of trumpets from the palace of the king.
Then these sounds were stilled, and it seemed to
Lemuel that a terrible and everlasting silence fell
upon Babylon, the silence of death and of eternal
desertion. The sentence of the God of Israel was
accomplished. Babylon had fallen. There were
no more love-songs in the gardens of the palaces.
There were no more prayers offered up in the temples
of the gods. The noise of feasting was over, the
joy of desire was past. The lawyers toiled no
more. The soothsayers prophesied no more. No
wise astronomers looked upwards to the stars, or
sought to read strange meanings in the white face
of the moon. No sculptors wrought soft clay into
the likeness of living men. The hucksters had

ceased for ever from crying their wares, and the watchmen from gazing forth from the towers. Still the great river Euphrates flowed on between its banks, but no ships glided upon its bosom, no merchandise was unladed upon its wharves. The dark-eyed traders from India and Persia, from the magical lands of the East, came up no more to Babylon. In distant markets and in thronged bazaars the name of the city was forgotten, and should be mentioned no more by the lips of them that bought and sold for ever. For in the market-places of Babylon the wild beast made its lair, and in the trembling temples the dragons laid them down to sleep. Where the women once walked with their lovers, the panthers crept on feet of velvet ; where the children had played, the serpent reared its slimy brood. And the wind that howled in the night was the wind of the wrath of God, and the wind from the furnace of His place of punishment.

It shook the walls of the tent in which Lemuel lay. It seemed to be a thing alive, with hands to tear and with a voice to speak. And it seemed to come straight from that far-off place where God sat watching everlastingly the doings and the thoughts of men. Then Lemuel knew that indeed the glory of Babylon must pass away, whether now or after a few more years had glided. And his heart was comforted for the failing of the last effort of Israel to break free from the yoke that the tyrant had laid upon its neck.

The night drew on, but still he could not sleep. Towards dawn the violence of the wind was abated.

It seemed to fold enormous wings and to long at last for rest. Then the visions of Babylon departed from Lemuel. He heard no more the music of the city and the cries of its people, and his mind shrank within itself and occupied itself with its own peculiar business. Generally, men who can do great things concern themselves not mightily with their own personal fate. Till now the heart of Lemuel, like some watching spirit, had hovered about the huge walls and towers of Babylon. Now it was with the maiden Elna, who slept this night in the tent of Naomi. What would be her fate and his?

Lemuel asked himself this question, running forward into the future. That seemed dark. For Jediah would certainly return to the tents of his people and cry aloud for justice. Perhaps he was even already upon the way, his soul hot with fury and with the desire of vengeance. And then, as Lemuel looked in the face of death, there rose within him the passionate love of life which is shared by almost all things living. And he, who had been so fearless in Babylon when Death reached out to clasp his hand in the midst of crowds and the shouting of many voices, trembled as he lay in the black tent while the wild wind sank to rest. Perhaps the romance of peace gathered about him, and the tenderness of olden days, and the dreamy magic of return. For here he first saw Elna, here among these tents, beneath the palm trees and by the well where the reeds rustled. Then Babylon was but a thought in his mind, love a reality in his heart. And even though that reality was sad, because Elna was betrothed to Jediah, yet it was sweet too, as love must ever be, howsoe'er frustrated, howsoe'er bound and harassed by evil fate. Already those days seemed very long ago. For Babylon stood like a horrible and mighty statue of evil between the past and the present, holding in her hand the flaming brand of sin. And the future was dark. Then Lemuel pondered upon the strange and mysterious purposes of the God of Israel. As a shepherd boy, tending his flocks among the hills, Lemuel had often been filled by an exultant sense of power, an overmastering and inspired joy—the joy and the ecstasy of the seer and of the prophet. As he sat alone on some green hillside, and played upon his pipe cut from a reed by the river, there came sometimes to him a certainty that he had been raised up to bring hope to his downtrodden people, to lead their souls to the patience that is the child of hope. There was no pride within his heart, but the nobility of youth, of faith, of dauntless courage, of iron resolution. He laid down his pipe and looked down at his flocks, scattered along the hillside, and he thought of the great Shepherd of Israel, who—perchance through him—would surely gather those whom He had scattered, would call again His chosen flock around Him in their own land. And then in such moments, led by the imagination, he would take up his pipe and call again to his sheep, and would whisper to his soul, " Thus and thus shall we gather to God at the last, when the time of our bondage is over, and the joy of our peace is come." And ever he had thought that, perhaps, he was chosen to be the earthly help of the Lord in this salvation. Inspired by this thought, he had put love from him, and had gone up unto Babylon, and had endured calmly both hate and the worship of Ishtar, fixing his eyes on greater things and a mighty, though hidden, purpose. But now, as he lay in the tent, while the wind sank and the dawn grew over the plains, a deep sorrow such as he had never known before shook him, and he wondered if the end had come. Then he understood indeed the feebleness of man, and that we are all in the hands of Him who directs the course of the stars and is afar off beyond the light of the sun. And he knew that there had been within him the seed of pride, from which might have sprung a great poison flower. For he had deemed himself, howsoever modestly, in some sort necessary for the working out of the purposes of God. But now he knew that no man is necessary.

He saw the grey light through the aperture of the tent, and he rose up softly and came to the tent door. The morning air was very cool, and upon the grass and upon the herbage lay drops of dew, waiting to catch the first beams of the rising sun. Lemuel wrapped his cloak about him and went forth into the plain. The wonder of the silence and of the cool dawn over the great spaces was very great to him who had grown accustomed to the roaring of the voices of Babylon, and to the tall houses and the mighty temples, on whose shining and jewelled walls the first sunbeams lay like tongues of flame. He felt once more that he was but a shepherd, a tender of the flocks and herds. And as a shepherd, humble, poor, peaceful, he longed to live. But he longed deeply to live. For life began to stir around him. The leaves, moved by the dying breeze, shook from them the dewdrops. The flowers opened their eyes. A bird sang. Nature herself was alive, too, in every plant and bush, in the thickets of the palms, in the thickets of the clouds that grew around the red sun on the horizon of the east, in the sun itself, which now stretched forth its fingers of gold to touch the smiling face of the world.

And, passing beyond the tents, Lemuel leaned against a tree trunk and searched the plain with his eyes. He thought that in its wide emptiness and silence it was like a vision of eternity, melting away on every side into the shadows where the night was swiftly retreating. But suddenly he started and clenched his hands together. For a beam of the sun had fallen upon the grim Judgment Seat that rose up in the plains, an emblem of the inflexible deeds of Fate rather than of the inflexible deeds of Justice. For Justice would raise no hand upon Elna, no hand upon Lemuel. But Fate? Would Fate stay her hand upon them? Exquisite was the peace of the plain, and exquisite the vision of the morning. The silence was breathing like a child that will soon awake, and a scented warmth crept about the happy earth. But cold was the great Seat of Judgment, stern and pitiless. Lemuel could not take his eyes from it. No crowd stood round about it now. No Judge mounted upon its steps of stone. No trumpet

rang through the air to proclaim the passing of
sentence. No prisoners shrank beneath its shadow.
Not yet—not yet !

But Jediah would return, soon or late. And an
unjust doom might indeed overwhelm two innocent
ones. For himself Lemuel now scarcely cared.
The coming forth into the morning, the vision of
the dawn, movement and sight had recalled the
courage within him, and chased away the fear that
had beset him as he lay within the blackness of
the tent. But tears rose to his eyes as he thought
of Elna, and that she might perish under the vengeance of Jediah ; that her delicate body might be
crushed with the cruel stones, her life beaten out
of her because she had, as all women, loved—
though she had loved innocently.

A figure rose up from the ground by the Judgment Seat. Lemuel, perceiving it from afar, sup-
posed it to be some shepherd on his way to tend
the flocks. He knew not that it was blind Justice
waiting the inevitable time. As he turned away
to return again to the tents, he saw, far off upon
the plain, coming from the direction of Babylon,
some moving specks, almost hidden by the mists
of dawn. They were so faint, so distant, that at
first he was hardly certain if indeed he saw them,
or if indeed they moved. He stood still to watch
them, and presently a certainty came upon him
that they were approaching. Doubtless, this was
a caravan coming from Babylon. It drew nearer,
actually with rapidity, though—since, at present,
it was so distant—it seemed to Lemuel to move
but with slowness and even with a sort of mysteri-

ous deliberation. The main highway for the caravans across the plain did not traverse the dwellings of Zoar and of his people, but was at some distance from them, upon the right, and nearer to the hills, which loomed, like faint shadows, far off upon the horizon. Lemuel now stood still to see whether the approaching caravan would continue upon the highway or would presently turn towards the tents, thus proving to him that those travelling from Babylon were coming thither to his tribe, to the habitations of his people. The thought in his mind was that this caravan might be Jediah and his followers, who had learned the news of his forced escape, with Elna, from Babylon. And, while he gazed, a flood of thought swept through his mind, as it sweeps through the mind of one who is drowning in the sea. He saw flashing visions of the past, heard words spoken that had been spoken long ago, felt again sensasations long forgotten. Yet, all the time, his eyes never left the moving specks that crept, like insects, upon the surface of the plain. They drew nearer and nearer, almost imperceptibly increasing in size to his watchfulness. Yet they were still at some distance from the place where they must change their direction, if they were indeed minded to gain the tents.

They were still at some distance, and Lemuel could have no certainty that they were not traders bearing rich merchandise from Babylon — embroideries, woven carpets, chased vessels, and engraved jewels. Or they might be slave-dealers, who had been up to the city from their distant homes to buy the captives who were almost daily offered for sale. Or they might be leading with them horses bred in the district around the city, and acquired in exchange for the products of foreign places where dwelt strange men and the land gave forth strange gifts to them that inhabited it. The caravan might well pass on, turning neither to the right hand nor to the left.

Yet already from Lemuel had fled the sense of peace on earth. No longer did he realise the loveliness of nature, for his soul was full of memories and of the cruel deeds of men. He could almost hear the clamour of voices around the Judgment Seat, the trampling of feet, the cries of women—even the bitter sobbing of his mother, Naomi, pleading for mercy and for the life of her only son. For something within his soul whispered—

"It is Jediah who cometh. His hands are swift to shed blood."

Now he thought that he could almost discern the camels and their peculiar gait, deceitful in its appearance of slowness, yet devouring the ground —that he could well-nigh perceive the hooded men rocking to the motion. The caravan was, indeed, approaching rapidly—Lemuel fancied with the rapidity of hatred, the speed of intense cruelty that journeys to its goal.

A bird rose from the grasses near his feet. It mounted into the clear air towards the sun, singing a song that was an ecstasy of joy.

The caravan turned from the highway and directed itself towards the tents of Zoar.

CHAPTER XVI

Then Lemuel knew that the great hour of his life was upon him. For one moment he stood still, turning his eyes away from the caravan, and fixing them, not upon the plain, now swimming in the glory of a golden haze, not upon the Judgment Seat, but upon the mounting bird, a quivering ball of feathers enclosing a heaven of music. It rose slowly in the air, trembling its tiny wings so rapidly that they seemed motionless. It grew smaller and smaller to his sight, and the sound of its song withdrew towards the blue spaces of the sky, fading, fainting, yet always intense with rapture, thrilling with a joy so perfect, so fiery as to be unearthly. And that song of the bird, sinking down from the purity of heaven, fell like a drop of magic liquid into the very heart of Lemuel. He trembled as if an angel had touched him, and his soul followed the bird in prayer.

Then, with a great brightness upon his face, he walked swiftly towards the tents.

There was a stir among them. The people of the tribe, roused from their slumbers, were preparing to go about the labours of the day. Men came forth drawing their long, loose robes about them, their eyes still cloudy and unobservant with sleep. Children rolled upon the grass, shouting and laughing with the gaiety engendered by rest. Women, lifting up from the ground their pitchers, posed them delicately upon their heads, and walked towards the well of Naomi. No one, as yet, had seen the approaching caravan. No one, as yet, knew that it was drawing near. Only Lemuel fancied he could hear the soft tread of the camels upon the rank herbage, the hum and mutter of the voices of the riders. And this was but an illusion of his senses. Instinctively, as he came to the tents, he looked towards the tent of his mother, Naomi. His father, Zoar, who was well stricken in years, still slept on, or, at least, reposed his aged limbs. But Naomi now came forth, and with her, embraced tenderly by her arm, she led Elna. Lemuel paused. His heart was very full as he looked on the face of Elna, so innocent and girlish, yet so resolute and strongly pure. His heart was very full of love, but it was no longer sad. For the bird's song was in it, and was mingled with the song of courage that is ever in the heart of the true man who has done no wrong to his neighbour.

Naomi lifted up her eyes and beheld her son. She loosed her arm from about the slender form of Elna, and came swiftly to Lemuel, and fell upon his neck and kissed him. And the tears gushed from her eyes upon his face.

"Nay, mother," he said gently, "why weepest thou?"

"From joy, son of my soul, and from terror," answered Naomi. "For thou art indeed returned unto me from the great and cruel Babylon—and I give thanks to the God of our fathers. But—but "—

And her tears flowed as she clasped Lemuel again to her breast.

"If thy brother — if Jediah," she murmured, "should return! But he may not. They say death waits for Israelites in Babylon. Nay, I am wicked. My heart is turned unto evil thoughts. I know not what I say. But oh! I cannot lose thee, my son, my son!"

"Mother," said Lemuel, "be not afraid. God watcheth over us, over thee and me, and—and this maiden. Elna, thou art not afraid?"

Elna looked up into his face. Perhaps she heard that song in his heart, or the light that shone in his eyes uplifted her soul. For she answered simply—

"I fear nothing, Lemuel. If thou livest, I would live with thee. If thou diest, I would die with thee. I fear nothing."

"May the God of Israel grant that Jediah may never return!" cried Naomi. "For if, indeed, he doth "—

"Mother," said Lemuel, clasping her trembling hand in his, "Elna—Jediah, my brother, will return. He is already near."

"Nay," said Naomi, "nay, Lemuel; that cannot be!"

But Lemuel answered—

"But now, as I looked forth upon the plain, far off I did behold a caravan of men journeying from Babylon."

Naomi trembled as if she would fall, but Elna moved not, nor did the shadow of fear come into her face.

"It is a caravan of merchants, my son," cried Naomi. "It is a caravan of traders going towards the east. They do ever pass, as thou knowest, upon the great highway."

"Do they turn aside from the great highway, my mother?" answered Lemuel.

Naomi's face was full of terror, but she replied quickly—

"Yea. Why not, my son? Perchance they do need to refill the water-skins, or to rest awhile, or to buy food from our people. Yea, yea, it is ever so. They have even turned aside to rest awhile, and afterward they will continue their journey. My heart tells me it is so."

And she smiled, but her sweet face was alive with a pitiful anxiety, and her lips were white as the dead ashes.

"Mother," said Lemuel, putting his arms around her, "my heart tells me these are no merchants or traders, but Jediah and Adoram. And it is better so. Elna and thy son are not guilty ones. Why, then, should we fear? Look up to the God of justice. Let us put our trust in Him, and men can do us no hurt. Hark! Dost thou not hear the caravan approaching among the palm trees?"

Even as he spoke there came to their ears the sound of voices urging forward the camels, and an Israelitish shepherd, who had been setting forth to drive the flocks to the pastures, rushed in among the tents, crying—

"Our Lord and Judge, Jediah, is come in from
Babylon, and with him are Adoram and Jozadah.
Jediah is at hand!"

Hearing his cry, the Israelites began to assemble themselves together. The children ceased
from playing, and stood silently staring with round
eyes; and the aged Zoar, rising up from the
couch within his tent, came forth folding his robe
about him and leaning heavily upon his staff.
Naomi uttered a cry of terror, but Lemuel clasped
her more closely with his strong arms, and
whispered—

"Mother, be brave. There is naught to fear."

Tirzah had now come up. She went to Elna
and took her hand. And thus they were standing when the caravan came in among the tents.

The camels were flecked with foam. They had
been driven ceaselessly onward through all the
dark hours of the night, and they were weary.
The men that rode them could scarce cling to the
rough packs used as saddles. Only Jediah, who
rode upon the first camel, sat upright, staring
before him as one that beholds his prey.

When he saw the group of Israelites before the
tents, with Lemuel and with Elna in their midst,
a wild cry of exultation broke from his lips. He
beat his camel down upon its knees, sprang off,
and stood before them, trembling. The people
were in amaze at the wildness of his demeanour,
and Zoar, stepping forward, said—

"Jediah, my son, be patient! Thy brother is
here before thee, as thou seest."

"And the maiden," said Jediah slowly, in a

thick voice. "God hath given them into my hands at last—at last!"

A smile of appalling exultation spread over his face. Naomi shrank against Lemuel's side, and her hand in his grew cold as the dew in the dawning. Zoar laid his hand gently, yet with authority, upon Jediah's shoulder.

"Thou needest rest, my son," he said. "Thou art weary with travel, and can indeed scarcely stand upright. Come into the tent. I would speak with thee alone."

" I am not weary, my father," Jediah answered hoarsely. "Summon the elders and all the people."

"Nay, but I will speak with thee," answered Zoar. " Follow me, Jediah, I do command thee."

And, with a strength almost superhuman in one of his years, he drew Jediah towards the tent. At the door he turned, and, speaking to the people, who were murmuring excitedly among themselves, he said—

"Wait, O my people. Shortly I will be with ye again."

Then he entered into the tent with Jediah. Once within its shadow, and concealed from the gaze of all, he placed his wrinkled hands upon the shoulders of Jediah, and, looking into his fierce and blazing eyes, he said—

"Thou hast found them, my son. But thou wilt not harm thine own brother?"

" I will have justice," said Jediah.

And his voice was cold as the water's voice when it falleth upon the rock.

" Thou wilt take the sin of Cain upon thy head, my son?" said Zoar.

" I will have justice," reiterated Jediah.

" Thou wilt break the heart of her who hath been to thee as thine own mother?"

" The Law shall strike for me," said Jediah. " The Law of Israel. And to that end will I call the people of Israel together."

" My son—thou wilt be merciful?"

" I will be just, O my father."

" Just?" said Zoar, with deep significance. " Can he be just whose heart's desire is vengeance? Can he be just who would spill the blood of his kindred and of the maiden whom he hath loved? O my son, hearken unto me. God is very pitiful. He forgiveth us many things, for He seeth into our hearts, and knoweth that we, and all men, are weak as water."

" I will not forgive. I will have justice."

" Nay — mercy! — mercy!" cried a trembling voice.

Zoar turned and saw the form of Naomi in the tent door. Her tender eyes were full of tears, and now, hastening forward, she caught Jediah by the cloak. In her agony she scarce knew what she did. She forgot that Jediah should show her reverence as the wife of his father. She forgot all save that her son, her only son, Lemuel, was in danger, perhaps of death. She fell down at the feet of Jediah and bathed his feet with her tears.

" He is innocent!" she sobbed. " Lemuel is innocent of all offence against thee. Let him go in peace, I beseech thee!"

Zoar was deeply moved, but Jediah seemed hardly to hear the cry of Naomi, hardly to feel the grasp of her hands upon his robe.

"Speak not to me of pity," he said. "I do live only for justice. Let the people be summoned, and let the Judges of our tribe be called together. I have witnesses to the guilt of these twain in Babylon. Let Israel's Judges decide betwixt us."

Zoar leaned down and tenderly raised up Naomi.

"Have courage, wife!" he whispered. "It must be. Put thou thy trust in God."

Naomi sobbed and hid her face against the breast of her husband. Then Zoar went forth to the tent door, and the people gathered around him. Jediah stood behind him, in the shadow of the tent, and Lemuel and Elna remained apart, awaiting calmly that which should be done.

"My people," said Zoar, and old though he was and well stricken in years, there was majesty in his aspect and his voice was clear and strong, "my people, Jediah, who hath come in from Babylon, doth demand that a cause shall be tried, and that the voice of the Judges of Israel shall be heard in a great matter, touching the truth and innocence of Lemuel, the son of my old age, and the maiden Elna, who is known to ye all. Go ye to your tents until the sun be but one hour higher in the heaven, and bend ye all the knee in prayer, to the Judge of all things, that indeed justice may be done and the truth for ever known before Heaven and in the sight of men. And when the trumpet shall sound forth, assemble yourselves together in the plain before the Judgment Seat. To your tents, O Israel—fall upon the ground and pray."

As he spake thus, he had solemnly uplifted his two hands towards the heaven. Now he let them fall with a gesture of dignified submission. And all the people, obedient to his voice, turned and went silently to their tents. Only Lemuel and Elna, apart from the others, fell down upon their knees where they had stood, and their lips moved in silent prayer. A great and mysterious quietude lay about the encampment. The voice of all activity was hushed while the sun mounted slowly up the sky. Only Jediah stole through the palm trees and called softly to him Adoram and Jozadah.

"The hour is at hand," he said unto Adoram. "Thou wilt not swerve or falter? Thou art prepared to swear before the Judges of the people that thou hast seen these two, Lemuel and Elna, together in Babylon?"

Adoram did not lift up his eyes, but looked down upon the ground as he answered uneasily—

"Yea, if thou dost reward me as thou hast promised."

"I will reward thee, be sure. Why dost thou doubt me?" said Jediah, with bitter impatience.

"I know not," answered Adoram. "Art thou in very truth assured that these two are guilty?"

"Thou fool, have I not told thee so? Thou craven heart—of what art thou afraid?"

Adoram was silent for a moment. In the silence these men heard from the tents a faint murmur— the voices of the Israelites offering up their prayers to the God of justice.

"I fear the wrath of Heaven—if indeed they are innocent," muttered Adoram.

Jediah uttered an imprecation.

"I tell thee they are guilty!" he cried furiously. "Did she not follow him to Babylon, having put on man's attire?"

"Yea, it is true. She must have sinned. Give me my reward, and I will testify as thou dost desire."

"And thou, Jozadah?" said Jediah.

"Yea, else why have I come hither?" Jozadah answered quickly. Then he added, with an indescribable greediness that was hideous, "I shall be paid—and I shall have Tirzah?"

"Have I not sworn it? See! the sun mounts in the heaven. The hour is at hand."

Even as he spoke, Zoar, calm and serene as one who puts his trust in the Ruler of all things, came forth from his tent, and said to an Israelite—

"It is the hour. Now go. Summon the heads of the people, the fathers and the elders. Call them from the tents and the fields. With the trumpet call them."

The Israelite obeyed the command, and now the silence that had lain about the camp was broken. The shrill note of a trumpet pealed forth again and again, now near among the tents, now far, softened and almost mysterious, as the herald of Justice passed on into the plain.

His call was heard by the blind man who sat alone in the shadow of the Judgment Seat. The blind man started to his feet and listened with a strained attention.

"Surely it is the call of Israel to judgment," he murmured. "It is to summon the Judges and the elders for some great matter."

He waited where he was. The warm sun fell upon him, for the morning was deepening over the plain. He heard the long note of the trumpet, now loud, now low, near and far, and excitement grew in him. For it seemed to him that the music called not unto the tribes of Zoar, not unto the men of the fields, to the fathers and the elders, but to him alone. It was like unto the voice in his own heart that had suffered so long and so bitterly, the voice that had bidden him to go out from Babylon and to return unto the tents of his own kindred. All sense of fatigue left him as he hearkened. The strength and the vigour of youth returned to him. And the trumpet note pealing through the warm air was like a blaze of fire springing up about him, and fire ran, surely, in his veins instead of blood. And he felt even as if fire glowed in those pitiful caverns where once, long ago, his eyes had looked forth upon the beauty and upon the brightness of the world. Thus he waited, braced and intense, like a man who is preparing himself for some great action of his life.

The sound of the trumpet died away towards the tents. There was a long silence, and then a distant murmur of voices, a distant tramp of many feet.

.   .   .   .

In answer to the cry of Zoar and to the sounding of the trumpet, the Israelites rose up from their prayers and came forth into the sun. The majesty of petition lay, surely, still upon their faces, for the men looked calm and grave, the women uplifted and serene. Only Naomi trembled, and in her eyes the fear lay behind the tears. And the children, holding the hands of their mothers, stared with round gravity and marvelled much what strange matter might be afoot. Two of them, of an age to comprehend, were crying gently. These were they whom Lemuel had taken up in his arms and kissed when he bade farewell to his people ere he went up to Babylon. They loved Lemuel, and knew that his life was in great danger, and terror came to them. They feared the harsh cry of the trumpet. They feared the gathering of the people. One of them pulled at the hand of the other, and whispered, under his breath—

" Let us go to him and kiss him, as ere he went away."

Then they ran to the place where Lemuel and Elna stood apart, waiting what might befall, and fell on his neck, and lifted their soft lips to his and kissed him.

And, at the sight, for the first time the calm of Elna went from her, and the tears rose up in her eyes. Lemuel put the children gently from him, and, as they ran back to their mothers, he said to Elna—

" Thinkest thou, Elna, that had we indeed been guilty, the children would have come to us ? Nay! for God often putteth truth into the hearts of little children when He hideth it for a while from the wise and those that are stricken in years. Let us, then, go forth to the Judgment armed, thou and I, by the love and the trust of little children."

Even as he spoke, the Israelites surrounded them to lead them forth into the plain. There was a silence upon all the people. They moved as men taken by a great awe, and their faces were stern with justice. They loved Lemuel well. They had learned to look to him as their saviour. But their sense of justice was graven on their hearts as a word may be graven on granite. It outweighed love and fear, and desire of release from slavery, and deep admiration of the bravery of a man. The laws of Israel were to them more than were ever their laws to the Medes and the Persians. And the man who offended against those laws, whatsoever his rank, his talent, his importance to his nation, must die. They had looked to Lemuel as to a Messiah. But justice was before all, and now justice must be done. So their faces were stern as they came about him silently to lead him to the Judgment Seat.

Jediah stood at a little distance, watching. With him were his witnesses, Adoram and Jozadah. Among the stern and calm Israelites, with their prayerful eyes and their silent dignity, his aspect of unbridled ferocity and blazing exultation seemed inhuman and horribly grotesque. His bloodshot eyes were fixed upon Lemuel and Elna. The fingers of his hands were twisted together like those of a man overtaken by a sudden shock of paralysis. There was foam about his bearded lips, and at moments his body was shaken as by a palsy.

"If thou wilt indeed accuse thy brother and thy betrothed," said Zoar unto him, "behold, the hour is come. Here be the Judges, the elders, and the people. Wilt thou that they go forth to the Judgment Seat?"

"I do will it," said Jediah hoarsely. "I do will it. I will have justice! They shall both die."

"That must first of all be judged," answered Zoar.

Then he returned to the people, and said—

"To the Judgment Seat, O my people. Lead forth the man Lemuel and the maiden Elna."

It was then that Johanan, where he stood afar by the Judgment Seat, heard the murmur of voices and the tramp of feet. For now the people broke through the strange and terrible silence they had kept. The excitement that comes ever upon crowds ran through them, from man to man, from woman to woman. And the noise of their many voices was like the deep murmur of the sea. It thrilled through the blind man's heart, and it was strange to him, for he could see nothing. Only he felt the sun upon him and the soft air about him, and heard the noise of the approaching multitude grow ever louder and louder in his ears. At first he could distinguish no words. All were lost in the dull and ceaseless murmur. But presently, as the crowd drew closer, he heard cries of "Justice! Justice before the God of Israel!"

And, standing there alone, he murmured beneath his breath—

"Justice! Justice before the God of Israel!"

The crowd came on across the plain. First walked the Judges and Zoar, supporting Naomi, who was faint with fear, and who walked as one in a dream, scarce knowing whither or for what purpose, but ever accompanied by darkness and by the horror of the dull sense that the world was heavy with some deep misfortune. Behind them came Jediah with his witnesses, to whom he spake in a low voice from time to time. Then followed the people, with Lemuel and Elna escorted in their midst. Near Elna walked Tirzah. Her face was deadly pale, and her lips moved ever in prayer. And as Elna drew near to the Judgment Seat her mind went back along the ways of the past, to the time when she was a child. She saw again the crowd gathered around a youth and a maiden who had been found in sin. She heard again the condemnation pronounced upon them. Then she had wept sore. She had cried out piteously. She had clasped the robe of Jediah. She had felt as if she herself went down to death and was murdered by the cruel stones. Yet now that such an hour had come to her, and that Jediah was to be her accuser, she neither wept nor did she tremble. Nor did she feel as one who walks to meet a great sorrow. For she bethought her of the words that Jediah himself had spoken unto her—

"The deeds that we do, whether good or evil, return to us again to give us our reward. They may tarry long on their journey, as tarry the great caravans that come from the desert, and peradventure we may say that they will never come. But there surely dawneth a day when they do stand before us, and in their hand they do bear the gift—life for the good, death for the evil."

If those words were indeed true, did death then wait, here by the Seat of Justice, for her and for Lemuel?

The crowd spread round the Judgment Seat as the sea beats round a rock. Johanan, the blind man, was swallowed up in it. But no one knew him, nor heeded him, for all the people were intent upon Lemuel and upon that which should be done. Upon the mound, in the view of all, were the Sanhedrin, or Council of seventy-two.

Unseen by them and by those around them, a caravan, travelling rapidly from the direction of Babylon, swept along the highway towards the plain. The riders urged on the camels at a frantic pace, beating them with whips and crying to them to hasten.

Being upon the Seat in the view of all the people, with Zoar in the centre and Jediah close upon his right hand, the Judges sat them down in silence. Then the priest of the tribe cried in a loud voice—

" Blessed be the name of the Lord ! "

And all the people answered—

" We praise His holy name ! "

Then there rose a Judge, and he said, stretching forth his arms to the people—

" Men of Israel, of the house of Zoar ! If a maid is betrothed unto one man, and another man take her, what shall be their punishment ? What saith the law ? "

And, as with one voice, the people answered—

" Death ! "

And Johanan, who stood over against the steps of the Judgment Seat, whispered—

" Death ! "

" Shall they not be stoned with stones until they die ? " cried the Judge.

And the people answered—

" They shall be stoned with stones until they die."

Then the Judge, turning to Jediah, said unto him—

" Speak thou, Jediah. Testify thou against this man and against this maiden."

The blind man drew a little closer to the steps of the Judgment Seat, and all the muscles of his body were as if turned to iron, and all the blood that ran in his veins was like fire that is hot in the furnace.

Jediah rose up in his place, and as the people gazed upon him, a hoarse murmur broke from them. For in the sun that blazed down upon his head, he looked gaunt and haggard and terrible as a spectre. The aspect of humanity, that is made in the image of God, had almost left him. His streaming hair was well-nigh like unto the mane of some animal of the forest. His eyes were as the eyes of a beast when it croucheth to spring upon its prey. His hands clenched and unclenched themselves. He gnashed his teeth in his beard. And the flames of an undying hatred seemed to emanate from him as, after a moment of silence, he said—

" I, Jediah, the eldest born of my father's house, a Judge in Israel, do swear that I was betrothed unto this maiden Elna by my father Zoar. Answer, O my father. Did'st thou not give this woman unto me for wife?"

Then Zoar bowed his head and answered—

"I did, my son."

Then Jediah said unto Elna—

"Answer thou, woman. Wert thou not betrothed unto me by my father Zoar?"

And Elna, lifting up her face proudly towards the Judges, said—

"Thy father Zoar did indeed give me unto thee. Yet was I but a child and knew not love, and knew not what I did."

Then Jediah said unto Lemuel—

"Answer thou, O Lemuel, that art my brother, son of my father and of his lawful wife, Naomi. Did'st thou not know that this woman was betrothed unto me?"

And Lemuel said—

"I did know it."

"And, knowing it, thou did'st steal her from me and did'st carry her with thee to Babylon?"

"No," cried Lemuel. "As my soul liveth, she went not forth with me to Babylon, nor knew I aught of her going thither."

"Thou liest!" cried Jediah fiercely. "Thou liest!"

"I do not lie," returned Lemuel proudly. "I speak the truth. No such plot was thought of by me, nor knew I aught of this maid's presence in Babylon until I found her in the palace gardens of Ishtar, claimed by our over-lord, Alorus, as his slave."

Even as he spake, and his words rang out clearly to all the people, who listened as if under a spell, the caravan that was travelling from Babylon turned from the highway, coming towards the Judgment Seat. The camels were stopped, and a woman, closely veiled, and attended by two men, dismounted from them, and came forward into the midst of the press of the people. No one heeded them, for all eyes were turned to the Judgment Seat, all lent ear to the words of Lemuel.

When Lemuel had ceased from speaking, the Judge said—

"Who can prove that these words are true?"

Then Elna called upon her soul and upon all her courage, and lifted up her voice and said—

"That can I. For I went up to Babylon unknown to Lemuel or to any man. He had conjured me by all we both held sacred to help him to be loyal to that man, his brother, who now seeketh to slay him. Unasked of him, I did confess my love for him, as here, before my Judges and my people, I, without shame, confess it still. In all else I am, as he is, innocent. If love, the strongest, purest, noblest love of which man is capable, be a crime, then is he guilty, but in naught else. He is true to his brother, to his nation, and to his God."

As she finished speaking there was a murmur of sympathy from the crowd, and Naomi clasped her hands together, while the tears rained down her face. It seemed unto her eager mother's heart that the answer of Elna must at once and for ever convince the Judges and the people of the innocence of her son. Already she saw him acquitted, set free, in her arms once more. But Jediah spoke fiercely in answer to the words of Elna.

"The evidence of his paramour doth not suffice," he exclaimed, with bitter sarcasm. "How should she, who hath betrayed all for him, not say that he is innocent? Her evidence is nothing worth. Who else, woman, can prove that thou did'st not go forth with him?"

"Who else?" murmured Elna, casting her eyes around upon all the eager, watching faces.

"Ay," cried Jediah. "There is no man—there is no man!"

"There is one man," cried a voice in the crowd. "The Lord Alorus. Who will gainsay his word?"

All the people turned, as with one accord, in the direction of the voice, and Alorus, dusty, travel-stained, and weary, but bearing himself, as ever, with a certain dandified gallantry and arrogance of demeanour, came forward to the foot of the Judgment Seat and stood looking upwards towards the fierce white face of Jediah.

"The Lord Alorus!" cried the people.

Sabaal, who was among the crowd, made a movement as if he would fain slink out of sight of the master from whom he had escaped. But Alorus had already seen him, and he now motioned to him to stay.

"What dost thou here?" muttered Jediah uneasily, casting his eyes hither and thither as if he feared some other presence.

"What do I here?" said Alorus. "I do stand here to say that, so far, the shepherd Lemuel hath spoken the truth. 'Twas I found this maid, who had fainted and lay as one dead in a street of Babylon. When Lemuel went forth with me from the tents of Zoar the maid was not with him."

The face of Naomi brightened, and she dried her tears.

"God speaketh even out of the mouths of the heathen," she murmured. "He speaketh for my son."

But Jediah's fury and determination for revenge were only increased by this unexpected opposition. His eyes glared wildly, but it was evident that he was making a mighty effort to retain his self-control as he said—

"Thou did'st claim her as thy slave, and in thine own house, O Lord Alorus, I did find her with this man. Is not that the truth?"

"That is the truth," said Alorus, with obvious reluctance.

"And even then," interposed Lemuel calmly, "in thy presence, O my brother, were we both arrested—I and this maiden—by the order of the king, in that we did plot for the liberty of the men of Israel held captive in Babylon."

At these words there were again great murmurs among the people, and a voice cried out—

"Shall we then kill with stones the man who would free us from captivity?"

"Thou utterest treason!" cried Alorus, turning in the direction of the voice.

"We will do justice on every man," said the aged Zoar proudly, " be he who he may."

"Brother," cried Lemuel, " have I not spoken that which is true? Answer thou, my brother."

" That is true," said Jediah.

"True, also, that I was sold," continued Lemuel, with passionate earnestness, "and with me this maid into bondage?"

" That also is true," said Jediah harshly.

" And that the brethren who had wrought with me in secret for their freedom did rise and put to the sword the guards, and did release me from the rostrum, and with me this maid. And then "— he turned proudly towards Sabaal—"then was I taken captive by mine own people, by thee, O Sabaal, and by thy followers, and borne away out of the city, bound and helpless—I, who should have fought with and for those brave ones who were ready to lay down their lives for my sake."

"Stand forth, Sabaal," cried Alorus, "and acknowledge thy treason unto me and unto my lord the king. Thou did'st help to stir up this revolt?"

Sabaal threw himself upon the ground at the feet of Alorus.

" It is true," he cried.

" And why did'st thou take captive thine own leader?"

" Lest he should be destroyed," exclaimed the slave.

" As now he shall be, if there is justice in the world," shouted Jediah.

21

"I thank thee, O my Lord Alorus," said Lemuel, "and thee, Sabaal, that have borne witness for me that I do speak the truth."

Cries broke from the people as Alorus turned away from the Judgment Seat. The Israelites were greatly excited by this narration of the events that had been taking place in Babylon. But Jediah's intensity of resolution was only made more fierce by these sounds and by the evidences of favour towards Lemuel. Raising his voice into a hoarse shout, he cried out, gesticulating wildly—

"All this I seek not to deny—it matters not. I have here two witnesses"—a hush fell upon the people, and the terror dawned again in the face of Naomi—"two witnesses that this man and this maid were together guiltily in Babylon. Thou did'st see them,"—he put forth his hand to Adoram, —"did'st thou not? Answer, O Adoram ! "

Then, in the dead silence, Adoram answered and said—

"It is true. I swear that I did see these two— as Jediah hath affirmed—together in Babylon."

"Answer thou, Jozadah," vociferated Jediah.

And Jozadah answered in a loud voice—

"I swear that I did see these two together in Babylon—as thou hast affirmed. And all the city knew it."

These words evidently made a deep impression on the Israelites, who guarded the chastity of their women as a most precious jewel. Murmurs adverse to Elna and Lemuel now came from many lips, and many of the women in the crowd cast looks of indignation upon Elna. Jediah saw that the tide of the feeling of the people was already turning in his favour, and he cried with passionate fervour—

"I claim justice! Hear these men—and all Babylon would bear them witness! I maintain that this man and this maid are guilty. I call for judgment and their death!"

A woman shrieked and fell, as one dead, to the ground. It was Naomi. Tirzah lifted her up tenderly. But Jediah took no heed.

"Grant me justice, O Judges!" he cried. "Let these two who have betrayed my honour and broken Israel's law be stoned with stones until they die."

Then the Judge who had first spoken stood up in his place, and his countenance was very stern. And he said in a loud voice—

"By the law given unto us by our fathers hast thou been tried, O Lemuel and Elna. What is the judgment, O ye Judges?"

And the Judges answered and said—

"They are guilty both."

"And their punishment?" said the Judge.

"Death," answered the Judges. "They shall be stoned with stones until they die."

Then the Judge turned to the people and said—

"Men of Israel, ye have heard the sentence of Israel's Judges. Take these two, and, as the law decrees, even so do ye unto them."

As he finished speaking, the crowd surged forward around Lemuel and Elna, stretching forth their hands to seize and bind them. But Elna, struggling violently, cried—

" Men of Israel, kill me if ye will, in that I did do wickedly in putting on man's attire and thus going up alone to Babylon. But spare Lemuel. Spare—spare him ! For he is innocent. Nay—nay—this is murder ! "

On the last words her voice rose in a piercing cry that was like a wail. And Jediah, answering her, shouted with fiendish exultation—

" Death to them both ! Death ! death ! "

As the crowd surged forward, Johanan, the blind man, had been caught in the press of it, and swept away some feet from the Judgment Seat. He struggled furiously to regain it as he heard the shout of Jediah, but for a moment his effort was in vain. A tremendous uproar broke from hundreds of voices, the cruel cry of " Death ! death ! " For the Israelites had stern hearts, and unto them the words of their Judges were as the words of God Himself. For the sinful woman, for the man who had led her into sin, they had no mercy. Guilt such as that attributed unto Lemuel and unto Elna was altogether abominable to them. Such guilt must be wiped out as a stain of blood is wiped out, or all the tribe would partake in the wickedness, and the wrath of God would surely come upon them. So now they took no heed of the wild cry of Elna. They took no heed of the patriotism of Lemuel. They thought no more of their own salvation from bondage, wrought for by him. They thought only of the punishment by their law decreed. And they bound the hands of Lemuel and the hands of Elna behind their backs, crying—

" Death !—death !—death ! "

Jediah stood above upon the Judgment Seat, and his white face was as the face of a devil exulting over the terror of a lost world. The crowd seized Lemuel and Elna to bear them forth unto the place of stones. Women shrieked aloud, and the roar of this human ocean echoed up under the glaring sunshine along the vastness of the plain. Then Jediah, leaning down, caught up the first stone and, with a cry of triumph, flung it at Lemuel. It struck him on the side of the face, and the blood gushed out. Jediah fell back upon the seat of the Judges, laughing triumphantly, and muttering over and over, like a madman repeating ever the one word that possesses him, "Death!—death!—death!"

But suddenly he caught the seat with his hands. His eyes stared. His voice died, strangled in his throat. For on high, above all the tumult, there rang out the imperious voice of a woman.

"Hold!" it cried. "Hold, men of Israel!"

And a woman's form, veiled, stood by the Judgment Seat.

The people, startled by this cry, which was thrilling in its passionate intensity, were silent and motionless. The Judges stood up upon their seat, and Naomi leaned forward in the arms of Tirzah.

"Hold!" cried the woman. "These twain are innocent!"

The crowd surged back, and Elna was seen upon her knees, resting her head against Lemuel, who stretched arms of protection above her to shield her from death.

"What would'st thou, woman?" exclaimed the Judge who had called for death.

"I would stay this judgment!" cried the woman.

"There is no power," shrieked Jediah, "no power to set aside the sentence passed by Israel's Judges."

"There is a power above Israel's Judges," said the woman. "A power to whom ye render tribute. He who reigneth in Babylon, my lord the king."

She held forth her hand. In it was a cylinder, stamped with the signet of the king.

"Here is his mandate and his signet," she cried. "It is the will of the king of Babylon that these two are to be set free, and that no harm or evil shall be done upon them."

Cries broke from the people, but the Judge said sternly—

"Who answereth for this woman that she speaketh indeed the truth?"

Then Alorus cried—

"I do. I, Alorus, thy over-lord and the servant of the king."

Then Jediah, beside himself with fury, and trembling like an old man, tottered down the steps of the Judgment Seat towards the woman who stood there, crying—

"I will not accept this message, nor will I heed this false decree."

But the woman caught his hand, and hers was like iron. And she said in his ear—

"Thou shalt! For I swear to thee, if thy brother and this maid die, they shall not die alone. They are innocent of the crime of which thou—thou and I are guilty. If they are stoned, I—Elcia—falsely called Ishtar, who was the wife of Johanan—at thy command made blind by this man "—

" There is no man "—stammered Jediah, pale as ashes.

But he looked, and lo ! Migdapul, the god-seller, stood by him. Then he fell back against the great stone of the Judgment Seat, and he heard in his ears a noise like the buzzing of flies in a dark place.

" I will proclaim myself and my sin—and thine —before all the people," said Elcia.

" Thou wilt not dare ! " he muttered.

" I have sworn it by the God of our fathers," she answered. " Call upon the people. Speak as I command thee."

And she lifted up her voice and cried aloud—

" Hearken, O ye people ! "

Then the people pressed close around them, and Naomi broke from the arms of Tirzah, and the blind man, Johanan, drew near to the sound of her voice.

" I have been unjust," she said, speaking unto Jediah, " and, in mine anger, have I sought the life of my brother."

And he, as one compelled by a spirit of truth and justice, lifted up his voice, that was piercing and shaken by the gusts of passion, and said, so that all could hear—

" I have been unjust, and, in mine anger, have I sought the life of my brother."

Then she said—

"I do here recall mine accusation "—

And he answered—

"I do here recall mine accusation "—

"And do plead to thee, my father Zoar, for these two—that thou wilt give this innocent maiden Elna unto my brother Lemuel, to be his wife."

But Jediah, on hearing these last words, shrieked out, like a man demented—

"No, no!   I will not say it!—I will not!"

"I say thou shalt!" cried Elcia.

"I will not!" he reiterated frantically.   "I will not!   Death shall possess her, but Lemuel never!"

And, drawing from his breast a knife that gleamed in the sunshine, he sprang towards Elna, who still kneeled upon the ground, fettered and helpless.   But Elcia, quick as thought, darted between Jediah and Elna, and, as Jediah struck, the point of the knife entered her breast and she sank down to the ground.   The people, who had stood as if turned to stone while Jediah uttered the bitter confession of his sin, now rushed forward to seize him, clamouring for his destruction.   But ere one could so much as lay a hand upon him, the blind man, Johanan, leaped up where he stood and caught Jediah by the throat, crying—

"At last!   At last!   Robber of my wife—my Elcia!   At last I find thee, O mine enemy!"

"Johanan!" gasped out Jediah.

"Ay," said the blind man.   "Johanan—whom thou madest blind.   Die, accursed one, die!"

And, on the last word, he pressed his hands

upon the throat of Jediah, strangled him, cast his body upon the ground at the very foot of the Judgment Seat that he would have polluted, and, with a cry as of a man who yields up his soul in triumph, fell dead upon it, as though to keep it his for ever.

Then a great awe fell upon the people. For Jediah had been their lord. And they gathered about his dead body and lifted it in their arms to carry it to the tent of his father.

But Lemuel and Elna they released, and Naomi fell, weeping, upon the breast of her son.

The Lord Alorus had supported Elcia and striven to bind up the wound in her breast. Elna, leaning over her, whispered—

" And thou—art thou hurt ? "

" But a little," Elcia answered.

" And thou," said Elna, " who hast saved us—who art thou ? "

Then Elcia drew back her veil and looked into the eyes of Elna.

" Ishtar ! " exclaimed Elna.

" Not Ishtar," answered Elcia, " but one more wretched—Elcia."

" Elcia ! " said Elna. " Thou art Elcia ! "

She bent down over Elcia and kissed her on the lips, and whispered—

" Sister ! "

A great light came upon the face of Elcia, and she lifted herself up, saying proudly—

" Sister ! That word repays me all."

Then she sank back in the arms of Alorus, and seemed for a moment as one dead. The heavy lids dropped over her great dark eyes. The colour fled from her cheek, and between her white lips the struggling breath came in gasps.

"She is dying," whispered Elna. "Lemuel, she is dying."

Elcia heard the words and opened her eyes. Already there was a strange and unearthly look in them, as if they beheld far-away visions, the faint and shadowy figures of some other world. She moved, and, stretching forth her hand, laid it upon Lemuel's, as he leaned over her.

"Is it true?" she murmured. "Am I indeed —dying?"

"Nay," he answered. "Nay, sister, that cannot be. I will fetch water."

He moved as if to hasten away. But she softly restrained him.

"Do not leave me—now," she said. "Stay—it will not be for long."

And she strove to come a little nearer to him. Lemuel made a sign to Alorus, and the Babylonian, with infinite care, loosed his arms from about Elcia and let her rest instead in the arms of Lemuel. This seemed to content her greatly, for a smile that was almost joyous hovered on her trembling lips, and she sighed—as a child sighs when it is given to its mother. She lay still for a moment. Then, suddenly lifting herself up in Lemuel's arms, she looked forth over the plain, staring in the direction in which—very far off—lay Babylon.

"I see—the city," she said in a thrilling voice. "There—there—but—but—the gods—they are fallen in the temples—the palaces—are desolate—

and in the chambers—serpents—serpents are sleeping."

"It is a vision," whispered Lemuel unto Elna. "The dying can behold the future and that which shall be done in the years as yet far off."

But already the light had faded from the eyes of Elcia. She nestled against the heart of Lemuel.

"Now let me sleep," she said softly.

With a last effort she put her arms about his neck, murmuring, so faintly that even he could scarcely hear the words—

"Let me sleep. The daughter of Babylon—is —avenged."

Her arms drooped down and fell. She sighed.

"Surely now she lies in the arms of God," said Lemuel. "Of our God and hers. For He forgiveth us all our sins and remembereth no more our iniquities."

And, bending down, he kissed the lips of the dead woman.

.   .   .   .

Lemuel, whose heart—wholly given as it was to Elna—beat ever in sympathy with his downtrodden people, was destined to live unto those days that beheld the passing away of the glory of the Babylonish conquerors. For, in the seventeenth year of Nabonidos, the tribes dwelling around the Persian Gulf revolted, stirred by the incessant intrigues of Cyrus. In the month Tammuz, Cyrus himself came up to the town of Opis and defeated the Accad army, and on the sixteenth day of the same month the Persians entered Babylon and captured the city, without striking a blow. The king was loaded with fetters and cast into a dungeon, and Kurdistan warriors guarded the mighty gates of the temple of Bel.

And in the cylinder of Cyrus may be read his record, a record of mercy and of joy. For one of the first acts of the king and conqueror was to restore the weary exiles of Babylonia unto their own lands, and to give them freedom after slavery.

So came the Israelites, and with them Lemuel and Elna, at last unto their own place in their own fair country. And there they rested from all their troubles, and served the God of their fathers in peace.

THE END

EDINBURGH: PRINTED BY MORRISON AND GIBB LIMITED

HASTINGS HOUSE,
NORFOLK STREET, STRAND,
February 1899.

Mr. John Macqueen's Publications.

Forthcoming Works.

The Daughters of Babylon.

By WILSON BARRETT, Author of "The Sign of the Cross"; and ROBERT HICHENS, Author of "Flames," etc. Crown 8vo, 6s.

Virtue's Tragedy.

By EFF KAYE, Part Author of "A Drawing-Room Cynic," "Her Ladyship's Income," etc. Crown 8vo, 6s.

A County Scandal.

A Story of King Midas and a Pastoral. By F. EMILY PHILLIPS, Author of "The Education of Antonia," "The Knight's Tale," etc. Crown 8vo, 6s.

The Secret of Sorrow.

Being the Confession of a Young Man. Edited by CECIL HEADLAM, Author of "Selections from the British Satirists," "Prayers of the Saints," "The Story of Nuremberg," etc. Crown 8vo, 6s.

Tom-All-Alone.

A Novel. By AMELIA M. BARKER. Crown 8vo, 6s.

Unholy Matrimony.

A Novel. By JOHN LE BRETON, Author of "Miss Tudor," etc. Crown 8vo, 6s.

Our Future King.

The Story of the Life of the Prince of Wales. By CHARLES LOWE, M.A., Author of "Prince Bismarck: An Historical Biography," "Bismarck's Table-Talk," etc. etc. Numerous Illustrations. Crown 8vo, 1s.

Natural History.

Lost and Vanishing Birds.

Being a Record of some Remarkable Extinct Species and a Plea for some Threatened Forms. By CHARLES DIXON, Author of "The Migration of Birds," etc. etc. Illustrations by CHARLES WHYMPER. Demy 8vo, 7s. 6d.

The Times :—"Mr. Dixon's latest work on 'Lost and Vanishing Birds' is a very attractive one. . . . Mr. Dixon's book is one to be enjoyed by all lovers of birds."

Pall Mall Gazette :—"Timely, and full of interesting information."

The Standard :—"Mr. Dixon's volume is full of interest."

London Review :—"Mr. Dixon has chosen a good subject, and has written well upon it. . . . We have read his book with great pleasure. Scarce any praise is too high for Mr. Whymper's drawings."

Country Life :—"A very fascinating, saddening, learned, and wise book."

Illustrated Sporting and Dramatic News :—"Everyone interested in the bird-life of our country ought to read this work, because it should cause an awakening of the public conscience, if there be such a thing, to the urgent need of making the Wild Birds' Protection Acts a reality and not a sham. Mr. Dixon is essentially a popular, as distinguished from a technical, dry-as-dust writer, and his productions are therefore eminently readable and entertaining alike to the student and the man in the street."

Works by J. H. Crawford, F.L.S.

All Illustrated by JOHN WILLIAMSON.

The Wild Flowers of Scotland.

Large crown 8vo, 6s. net.

The Times :—"Those who shrink from the hard scientific aspect and the cacophonous would-be Latinity of many works with titles of this kind, need have no fear that these pleasant, gossipy papers will be too severely botanical for them. . . . The reader will be hard to please, be he but a lover of nature, who does not find these pages interesting and full of charm."

The Spectator :—"Mr. Crawford, whose unconventional works on the natural history of Scotland have not undeservedly gained for him the reputation of being that country's Jefferies, has now followed up his previous successes with a volume on the wild flowers of Scotland. It is written with the same unstudied simplicity of style ; and its author shows the same pervading, rather than intense, love of his subject, or rather, subjects. . . . In short, while this book is not better than the others of the delightful series to which it belongs—all are equally good—it is the most enjoyable."

Country Life :—"A book of infinite grace and charm, from every page of which breathes the pure love of beauty in nature. . . . We commend this book without reserve to all persons, old and young, who love the fresh air, the mountain-side, and the low-lying valley. It will please them, it will not bray their minds in a mortar of science with a pestle of terrific nomenclature, and it will teach them a great deal."

Mr. J. H. Crawford's Works—continued.

The Wild Life of Scotland.

Large crown 8vo, 6s. net.

The Times :—" Mr. Crawford's skill in depicting various phases of nature and animal life ought to send his readers forth into the country with eyes ready to note and appreciate many things to which they have, perhaps, hitherto been totally blind. To read papers like ' Gulls and Divers' or ' The North Sea' on a July day in London is almost the next best thing to being in reality within sound of the waves."

The Spectator :—" This is a very delightful as well as informing book, which, in respect of style, recalls Thoreau rather than either Jefferies or Burroughes. . . Altogether this book, which belongs to the rare order that can be taken up at any moment and easily read in instalments, is by far the best and most convenient hand-book to Scottish Natural History—in the most comprehensive sense of the word—that has ever been published."

The Saturday Review :—" ' Wild Life of Scotland' is one of those delightful books which one places on the shelf with the Colquhouns and the St. Johns, nor is it possible to give it higher praise. . . . But we might go on indefinitely with our comments on a book which is a wellspring of enjoyment and a mine of information."

Summer Days for Winter Evenings.

A Series of Nature Idylls.　Large crown 8vo, 6s. net.

The Times :—" With Mr. Crawford's delightful sketches, sometimes telling alone of nature's aspects, sometimes with a thread of story to lend a touch of human interest, a reader must have little imagination if he does not speedily forget the tempest that beats against the casement, and fancy himself between green earth and blue sky, watching the kaleidoscope of the seasons and the changes of the year, and the ways of furred and feathered creatures which are so sympathetically described."

Pall Mall Gazette :—" A bright gleam of sunlight in this winter of our discontent comes from Mr. Crawford's ' Summer Days for Winter Evenings.' The author has already, in his ' Wild Life of Scotland,' shown himself a master in depicting the ever-changing phases of nature and animal life in an easy and graceful style— no slight art. This new volume of idylls on bird life in the hedgerows and fields during spring and summer should enhance his reputation as a colourman and decorator in words. Yet, for all his picturesque and dainty style, Mr. Crawford is an observant naturalist, one who discovers new beauties in things which every one of us must have seen thousands of times without ever having found them out."

Historical Works.

Cabot's Discovery of North America.

By G. E. WEARE, Author of "Edmund Burke's Connection with Bristol," etc. With numerous Maps and Illustrations. Large crown 8vo, 10s. 6d.

The Daily Chronicle:—"A most careful and painstaking account of everything which can be known or guessed at in reference to Cabot's life. Mr. Weare's account is the most complete which England has yet produced of the remarkable adventurers to whom she owes so much solid profit and immense fame."

A Narrative of the Boer War.

By T. F. CARTER. New Edition. Demy 8vo, 10s. 6d.

The Pall Mall Gazette:—"The best book on the subject."
The Sheffield Telegraph:—"This great work is history, exhaustive, impartial, and realistic."
The African Critic:—"The book is generally recognised as a standard work on the subject."

The Highland Brigade in the Crimea.

By Sir ANTHONY STERLING, K.C.B., a Staff Officer who was there. With Frontispiece and 18 Maps. Second Edition. Demy 8vo, handsomely bound in cloth, 7s. 6d.

The Times:—"These letters are evidently a faithful record of the great war waged by Great Britain, France, Turkey, and ultimately Sardinia, against Russia. The maps are drawn with skill and fidelity. No previous account of the war has contained so clear a map delineation of the terrain of the scene of the terrible sufferings of our soldiers and sailors during the Crimean winter, sufferings which, as everyone knows, might have been, and ought to have been avoided."

Gunner Jingo's Jubilee.

By Major-General TOM BLAND STRANGE (late R.A.). With Fifteen full-page Illustrations, Plans, Maps, and numerous Thumb-nail Sketches. Third Edition. Demy 8vo, 7s. 6d.

The Times:—"His reminiscences are full of stirring incident, told in a very lively, at times almost a boisterous fashion, which recalls the rollicking style of Lever in his earlier days."

The Court of England under George IV.

Founded on a Diary interspersed with Letters written by Queen Caroline and various other Distinguished Persons. Two Vols. demy 8vo, 25s.

The Daily Telegraph:—"There is all the usual Court and society scandal, not ill-naturedly reproduced, and a description of travel in Switzerland and of life in Italy. Moreover, there are interpolated, in the narrative, letters from the unhappy Princess Caroline herself, in which her vivacity, her spite, and her terrible loneliness are vividly depicted."

Miscellaneous Works.

Bismarck at Home.

By JULES HOCHE. Numerous Illustrations. Translated from the French. Demy 8vo, 7s. 6d.

The Times :—"Abounds in anecdote, and is written entirely without rancour. . . . Contains many interesting illustrations from engravings and photographs of places and scenes associated with Bismarck's career."

The Speaker :—"Is not without interest, for it gives some details worth having about the earlier and the latest periods of the Chancellor's life, and has some excellent engravings of the great man and his nearest relatives."

Sporting Dramatic News :—"A history of Bismarck by a French writer can scarcely fail to be amusing."

Army and Navy Gazette :—"The author has certainly written an interesting book, which has been well translated, and has a curious attraction . . . depicts a very interesting figure from a somewhat novel point of view."

Manchester Courier :—"It deals chiefly with the home scenes ef Bismarck's private life, but it is enlivened with many stories of his political and military adventures. . . . The numerous illustrations are nearly all very good. . . . The book is very interesting. . . . Admirably translated."

From "The Bells" to "King Arthur."

A Volume of Dramatic Criticism, dealing exclusively with the Irving Productions at the Lyceum, and containing the Casts of all the most important Revivals at that Theatre since 1871. By CLEMENT SCOTT. Fully Illustrated. Demy 8vo, 7s. 6d.

Truth :—"All playgoers, especially the enthusiastic Irvingites among them, will welcome the appearance of Mr. Clement Scott's handsome volume."

The Daily News :—"The book will be invaluable to those who are concerned with the history of the contemporary stage."

Indifference in Matters of Religion.

By the ABBÉ F. DE LAMENNAIS. Translated from the French, with a Preface by LORD STANLEY of Alderley. Demy 8vo, 12s.

The Spectator :— "The questions with which it deals still burn, perhaps with a greater heat than they did in 1817, when first the volume was published. It is impossible for an Anglican to accept all de Lamennais' statements, but he will feel, we venture to say, more in than out of harmony with him. The translation reads well."

The Catholic Herald :—"A thoroughly good and conscientious translation. The acute penetration, close reasoning, and lofty eloquence which characterise the best French writers, are to be found here in a high degree."

A Manual of Italian Literature.

By F. H. CLIFFE. Crown 8vo, 6s.

Mr. WILLIAM LE QUEUX, in *The Literary World* :—"Considerable thought and pains have been bestowed upon this book, for the critical estimates are, for the most part, sound, the examples of style are generally well chosen, and the biographical detail obtained from the best available sources. Mr. Cliffe gives a little too much prominence perhaps to his pet writer Leopardi ; nevertheless the work has few faults, and those of a trivial character. It is useful and may be relied upon, as well as being interesting."

Miscellaneous Works—continued.

Lesser Questions.

A Book dealing with the Principal Social Questions of the Day. By LADY JEUNE. Crown 8vo, cloth, 6s.

The Times:—"Not only are these great questions in themselves, but they involve, either directly or indirectly, some of the greatest of all the great questions of our time—nothing less than the social welfare and prospects of the whole body politic. On these questions Lady Jeune writes from direct experience and often with excellent judgment, with full sympathy, and yet not with unregulated enthusiasm."

Cheer, Boys, Cheer!

Memories of Men and Music. Portrait. By HENRY RUSSELL. Crown 8vo, 3s. 6d.

The Daily Chronicle:—"There is ample store of anecdotes in this cheap and handsome volume."

The Drama Birthday Book.

Compiled, by PERCY S. PHILLIPS, from the Works of the leading Dramatists of the Day. Fcap. 8vo, art linen, 3s. 6d.; morocco, 10s. 6d.

The Mark Twain Birthday Book.

Ninth Edition. Cloth, gilt edges, 1s.; leather, 2s. 6d.; morocco, 6s. 6d.

The Light that Lies.

By COCKBURN HARVEY. With seven Illustrations. Fcap. 8vo, 2s. 6d.

Westminster Gazette:—"A bright, clever little story. . . . The sketches of character are smart and amusing."

Scotsman:—"A jolly little story, which may be recommended to anybody as a cure for depression, or a stimulant to gaiety of mind."

Daily Chronicle:—"Amusing, brightly written, and easily read."

The Gordon Highlanders.

Being the Story of these Bonnie Fighters told by JAMES MILNE. Fully Illustrated. Crown 8vo, 1s.

Broad Arrow:—"There is nothing but praise to be said of this patriotic endeavour to bring into prominence the many deeds of valour performed, and the hard fighting which has fallen to the lot of the very gallant regiment."

Ye XIXth Century Horn Book.

Being an Alphabetical Record of the Anthropophagi, and other strange things existing at the close of that period of time : as set down by one WALLIS MACKAY. Demy 8vo, 1s.

Manchester Courier:—"It is an amusing pictorial satire of actors, brokers, chamberlains, dogs, etc., and the clever drawings and crisp comments accompanying the sketches cannot fail to amuse."

Lloyd's Weekly Newspaper.—"A satirically humorous production, touching on the men, manners, fads, and follies of the closing century. There is genuine fun in the book, and Mr. Mackay's pictures are grotesquely comic."

Newcastle Journal:—"For an hour's amusement one cannot do better than take up this little book. From the first page to the last it is very amusing, and the illustrations on every page are finely drawn."

Sporting Life:—"The original pencil of 'The Captious Critic' is seen at his best and raciest. Every pictorial page is a political or social cartoon pregnant with sly satire and full of fun."

Books for Young People.

For Boys.

Love and a Sword.

A Tale of the Afridi War. By KENNEDY KING. Numerous Illustrations by R. CATON WOODVILLE, W. B. WOLLEN, and others. Crown 8vo, gilt edges, 6s.

Manchester Courier:—"One of the most absorbing tales of adventure that we have read for some time. He (the author) narrates his incidents with vivid-telling force; his language is terse and well chosen . . . described with intense realism."

London Review:—"One of the most alluring stories of adventure we have come across this season . . . crowded from start to finish with excitement, and the reader is held almost breathless throughout. . . . Readers of all ages will be fascinated and held spell-bound in its perusal . . . forms a handsome Christmas present."

The Spectator:—"One forgets impossible things, however, in the rush of narrative, which is very effective in its way. Mr. King, like a good artist, also takes care to introduce actual historical incidents into his story. . . . The illustrations are almost photographic in their realism."

United Service Gazette:—"A thrilling story of the Afridi War. The book is really well written, and Mr. King is particularly happy in his descriptions and his pathos. The publisher has also done his duty well, for the work is handsomely produced and illustrated."

Belfast News Letter:—" . . . Of a character likely to commend itself very strongly to the young and rising generation. The style is attractive, and the story cannot fail to be exciting in the highest degree."

Dundee Courier:—"A book sure to engross the attention of every lad who take it up. . . . Throughout of a healthy, spirited nature."

Afloat with Nelson.

By CHARLES H. EDEN, Author of "George Donnington," etc. etc. With ten full-page Illustrations, by JOHN WILLIAM-SON. Crown 8vo, cloth, gilt edges, 6s.

The Spectator:—"A book that boys will gloat over."
The St. James's Gazette:—"One of the best of the sea stories recently published. . . . The sketch given of Nelson is a fine one."

Fairy Stories.

One Summer Holiday.

By Mrs. CHARLTON ANNE. Dedicated by most gracious permission to H.R.H. The Duchess of York. Numerous Illustrations, including a Collotype Portrait of the Duchess of York and her Children. Crown 4to, 5s.

The Gentlewoman:—"Deserves unstinted praise. To say the stories are excellent is by no means strong enough to convey the charm manifest in Mrs. Anne's writings. . . . All children will want to read it again and again until they know it by heart."

The Scotsman:—"Well written, well illustrated, and makes a capital story book."
Nottingham Guardian:—" . . . Told in a free and pleasant style, and possesses qualities which tend to improve the morals of children."

The Tablet:—"Simple in language and motive, and each manages to convey a lesson almost unconsciously, and certainly without raising any suspicion in the mind of the children that they are being lectured.'

B

Books for Young People—continued.

Stories the Sunflower Told.

By EVA M. HILDER. Illustrations by M. M. SUTCLIFFE. Fcap. 4to, 5s.

The Scotsman:—"Set forth in an interesting and entertaining way. . . . Nicely illustrated and attractive binding."

Lady's Pictorial:—"A charmingly pretty and fanciful fairy story for children. It is a particularly nice gift-book for imaginative children."

The Athenæum:—"Graceful little fairy tales pleasantly illustrated."

The Song of the Harp.

By RACHEL PENN, Author of "Cherriwink." Illustrations by JOHN WILLIAMSON. Fcap. 4to, 3s. 6d.

The Athenæum:—"A prettily written story, and will be popular."

Public Opinion:—"One of the most charming fairy tales we have encountered for some time. . . . The illustrations are very good."

Dundee Courier:—"A lovely story told in lovely language, and enchants the reader's attention to the very close. . . . It will be read with as much enjoyment by men and women as by children. The dainty etchings which illustrate the story make this charming book a most desirable acquisition."

Cherriwink.

By RACHEL PENN. Original Illustrations by MAUDE F. SAMBOURNE and M. JARDINE-THOMSON. Crown 4to, 6s.

Pall Mall Gazette:—"Such a delightful story has not been written this long time."

Glasgow Herald:—"A delightful and delightfully long and full-blooded fairy story . . . bright and airy as becomes a fairy tale, and it has the advantage of being most skilfully illustrated. A really beautiful book."

The Scotsman:—"These are quaint and fantastical ongoings, too odd to be coherently described, but not too odd to be amusing and pleasant to a reader with any fancy. The book has a number of charming illustrations."

Glasgow Evening News:—"This is one of the most charming books of the season for children."

The Englishwoman:—"The tale is charmingly told with graceful fancy and refreshing humour."

The Court of King Arthur.

Stories from the Land of the Round Table. By W. H. FROST. Twenty Illustrations by S. R. BURLEIGH. Crown 8vo, 6s.

The Scotsman:—"It is a cleverly written adaptation of the chief legends of the Round Table, done after Malory into simple language, and held together in a pretty framework of story of child life. The book is well illustrated by Mr. S. R. Burleigh."

New Fiction.

Six Shilling Volumes.

The Daughters of Babylon.

By WILSON BARRETT, Author of " The Sign of the Cross " and ROBERT HICHENS, Author of " Flames," etc. [*February 18th.*

The Secret of Sorrow.

Being the Confession of a Young Man. Edited by CECIL HEADLAM, Author of "Selections from the British Satirists," " Prayers of the Saints," " The Story of Nuremberg," etc.
[*March.*

A County Scandal.

A Story of King Midas and a Pastoral. By F. EMILY PHILLIPS, Author of " The Education of Antonia," " The Knight's Tale," etc. [*April.*

Unholy Matrimony.

By JOHN LE BRETON, Author of " Miss Tudor," etc. [*April.*

Tom-All-Alone.

By AMELIA M. BARKER. [*April.*

Virtue's Tragedy.

By EFF KAYE, Part Author of " A Drawing-Room Cynic," " Her Ladyship's Income," etc. [*April.*

A Girl's Awakening.

By J. H. CRAWFORD, Author of " The Wild Life of Scotland." With Frontispiece by JOHN WILLIAMSON.

The Athenæum:—" A pretty and idyllic study is 'A Girl's Awakening.' Mr. Crawford's feeling for Nature stands him in good stead, and the background of his picture in the Scottish village is as harmoniously fitted with the central figures, Alan Fordyce and his companions, as one of George Eliot's own drawing."

The Academy:—" In his works on the wild life of Scotland Mr. Crawford showed himself to be a writer of discernment. His novel fulfils the high expectations which were thus raised."

The Speaker:—" The story leaves an impression of vague charm, an aroma of romance and fantasy—all too rare in the fiction of the day."

The Sign of the Cross.

A Novel founded on the theme of the famous Play of the same name. By WILSON BARRETT. With a Preface by the Bishop of Truro. Sixth Edition.

Daily News:—" Few will read unmoved the concluding chapter of a story that has running through it something of the sense of haunting, overmastering fate that impresses one so terribly in Greek tragedy, while it inspires at the same time sympathy for the noblest ideals of humanity."

New Fiction.

Six Shilling Volumes—continued.

The Luck of the Native Born.

By J. A. BARRY, Author of "Steve Brown's Bunyip," "In the Great Deep," etc.

The Athenæum :—" . . . Really exciting and well told."

The Spectator :—"A rattling tale of Australian adventure by sea and land."

St. James's Gazette :—"The story is very cleverly told. It fascinates the reader from the outset, and holds him spellbound until the last page is turned. Mr. Barry is indeed to be congratulated upon a thoroughly sound and creditable piece of work."

Glasgow Herald :—"A very interesting story. . . . Mr. Barry knows Australia, and he knows the sea, and the reader goes with him to the Tarcoolta wool shed or the Coolgardie gold diggings, or follows him on board the *Compton Castle* or the *Aberbaldie*, with a feeling that he is being shown life pretty much as it really is."

The Gentlewoman :—"The book is full of 'go' and healthy sentiment, written in straight, honest English."

The River of Pearls; or, The Red Spider.

A Chinese Romance. By RENÉ DE PONT-JEST. With Sixty-one Illustrations by FELIX RÉGAMEY.

The Speaker :—"May be read with profit by anyone who wishes to realise the actual condition of native life in China."

The Scotsman :—"A Chinese romance of notable power and interest. . . . The object of the writer is to lay before the European reader an elaborate picture of Far Eastern life drawn from observation and experience. In this he has been completely successful."

The Gentlewoman :—"Has in it much that is charming and beautiful, and is written with a good deal of power."

Glasgow Herald :—"Full from first to last, of the most exciting incidents.'

Manchester Courier :—"The author has given us in it much that is extremely interesting regarding some of the laws and customs that prevail in China. . . A most uncommon and exciting book."

Jane Follett.

By GEORGE WEMYSS, Author of "'Tween the New and the Old."

The Speaker :—"The author has mastered the very important art of being interesting . . . very sympathetically told, with grace of feeling and charm of manner."

St. James's Gazette :—"A very powerful story. . . . The characters are finely drawn, and the novel is full of human interest and pathos."

Saturday Review :—"The idea is so well worked out as to be very successfully dramatic."

The Gentlewoman :—"George Wemyss has confirmed the favourable opinion of those who recognised the brilliant promise of his clever, romantic novel, 'Tween the New and the Old,' . . . a powerfully interesting human document, which should materially enhance Mr. Wemyss's reputation."

Manchester Courier. —" Mr. Wemyss gives us a lifelike sketch."

Esther's Pilgrimage.

By J. HENRY HARRIS, Author of "Saint Porth."

Academy :—"The story ripples like a pennon, and gives a pleasant insight into naval society on the Devon coast."

The Scotsman :—"The story has quite a number of capital characters, it has a breezy air of the naval port about it, and it is well and thoughtfully written."

New Fiction.

Six Shilling Volumes—continued.

Manders.

By ELWYN BARRON.

The Speaker :—" Bright descriptions of student life in Paris, sympathetic views ot human frailty, and a dash of dramatic force, combine to form an attractive story. The book contains some strong scenes, plenty of life and colour, and a pleasant tinge of humour. ' Manders' deserves attention as a novel. . . . It has grip, picturesqueness, and vivacity."

Literature :—" Is told in a quietly effective fashion and without offence to truth or taste. . . . more art and knowledge of human nature is displayed in the telling of it than is to be found in many a longer and more pretentious work. Manders is an original conception, and has been realised by his author with no little subtlety and force."

Daily Telegraph :—" . . . A sympathetic and ably written romance. The characters are marked by striking and sustained individuality. . . . Very high praise can be accorded to Elwyn Barron's brilliant word-sketches."

Manchester Guardian :—" One of the most readable books that we have seen for some time. . . . Madame Manders is Eve walking in the Garden of Eden, happy till she hears God's voice and knows that she is naked. Or she is the faun of Hawthorne's 'Transformation,' in whom a soul is born out of suffering and sin. Her development is described with admirable skill and knowledge of the human heart. The story possesses much of the quality of true tragedy. The heroine is caught in the web of fate. At any moment she might have gained happiness for the mere asking, but she was held in bonds forged by her own character. . . . The sympathetic insight of children is wonderful. . . . Florence Storey is a clever study, the cleverest, perhaps, but the least pleasing of the author's creation."

St. James's Gazette :—" A study of deep human interest, in which pathos and humour both play their parts. . . . The descriptions of life in the Quartier Latin are distinguished for their freshness and liveliness. . . . The story is full of surprises, which cause the reader to catch his breath, and fill him with delight at the development of each new phase of the plot. Moreover, the book is exceptionally well written, and, indeed, is likely to achieve considerable popularity."

'Tween the New and the Old.

A Tale of Three Lovers.   By GEORGE WEMYSS.

Daily Telegraph :—" Mr. Wemyss is to be cordially congratulated upon having written a story of striking originality and considerable power, remarkable alike for its thrilling human interest and dainty literary grace."

Manchester Guardian :—" Well thought out and cleverly executed."

The Scotsman :—" The reader will not willingly lay down the volume until the last page is perused. Mr. George Wemyss has written a clever story, and he is to be congratulated on his success. In character sketching, in dialogue, and in the creation of telling scenes, he reveals not only ability but the promise of even better work in the future."

A Son of Israel.

By RACHEL PENN, Author of " Cherriwink," etc.

Pall Mall Gazette :—" The scenes from the life of the Russian poor ring true to life, and are full of clever description. It is a bright and wholesome story, excellently told."

Newcastle Chronicle :—" A novel not to be missed."

Glasgow Herald :—" The influence which the good feelings of a woman may have upon her unborn child is sensitively worded and beautiful in its suggestions. Altogether Rachel Penn may be congratulated on this thoughtful and interesting story."

New Fiction.

Six Shilling Volumes—continued.

A Sinless Sinner.

By MARY H. TENNYSON, Author of "A Fool of Fate."

Saturday Review:—"An unusually striking plot . . . touchingly drawn."
Pall Mall Gazette:—"Well told and interesting."
St. James's Budget:—"A thrilling story of powerful and engrossing interest."

Possessed of Devils.

By Mrs. HAROLD E. GORST.

The Englishwoman:—"This clever psychological study is well worth reading. . . . That the author has succeeded in X-raying the soul of an egotistic, passionate, self-absorbed modern woman, revealing the tumultuous thoughts and emotions of this tumultuous child, no one who reads this human document will deny."

A Drawing-Room Cynic.

By LORIN KAYE, Author of "Her Ladyship's Income."

Miss GERTRUDE ATHERTON in *Vanity Fair*:—"Lorin Kaye makes a bid for the success of the season in 'A Drawing-Room Cynic,' and it will be surprising if she does not carry off one of the prizes, at least. Its atmosphere of unfailing smartness puts it in tune with the London of the moment. There is a possibility that the fascinating Cynic, la belle Americaine, and Lady Boulter will be met with at more than one dinner table. . . . It is to be hoped that the author will give us a novel every season, at least."

The Queen:—"A witty, cynical, whimsical writer is the author of this most captivating story. 'A Drawing-Room Cynic' is so much better a novel than the reader is likely to come across for some time, that he will find it advisable to begin it again when he has reached the end, for the book is a gallop from start to finish, and during the race he must miss some of the excellent things of which the story is full."

The Scotsman:—"To read 'A Drawing-Room Cynic,' by Lorin Kaye, is to experience a very great treat indeed. From end to end the story commands the keenest interest by the originality of the ideas, the skilful piecing together of the parts, and the raciness and often brilliancy and wit of the dialogue."

Miss Tudor.

By JOHN LE BRETON, Author of "Unholy Matrimony," etc.

The Right Hon. W. E. GLADSTONE writes:—"I find it to be of intense though most painful interest. Such double-dyed villains as Lamb are not, I hope, even in this evil world, to be found every day."

Mr. W. T. STEAD in the *Review of Reviews*:—"'Miss Tudor' is a novel with a purpose. Mr. Le Breton has an intimate knowledge of his subject, and also a heart which can feel for and sympathise with the sufferings of those whose experience he relates. It is a difficult subject to deal with, but Mr. Le Breton has handled it in a fashion which, while it can hardly offend the most sensitive, will appeal deeply to the sympathies of his readers. The tale is full of pathos, redeemed by many touches of kindliness and good feeling. Through the whole book there is an undernote of intense sympathy with the poor and oppressed, and of revolt against those who have inherited the good things of this world. The struggle for life in the little attic where Bessie has taken refuge is told with great feeling."

New Fiction.

Six Shilling Volumes—continued.

A Russian Wild Flower.

By E. A. BRAYLEY HODGETTS, Author of "In the Track of the Russian Famine," etc.

The World:—"Something absolutely new in fiction. This story is charming from every point of view; it makes the reader feel, when he closes the book, that he knows Russia as no other writer has ever enabled him to know the vast dim Empire of the Czars."

The Wooing of Avis Grayle.

By CHARLES HANNAN, Author of "Chin Chin Wa," "The Captive of Pekin," etc. etc.

The World:—"Since Sir William Brandon on the Bench was confronted by Paul Clifford in the dock by that master of romance, the first Lord Lytton, we have not had so strong a situation in the same order as that of the husband of Avis Grayle and his sworn friend."

Her Ladyship's Income.

By LORIN KAYE, Author of "A Drawing-Room Cynic." Crown 8vo. *[Fourth Edition in the Press.*

The Times:—"One of the best novels of the day. The author has more wit, reading, and intellect than the best advertised of the risky school, and she has much less affectation and *préciosité.* Her skill is most remarkable. . . . Her ability is incontestable."

The Daily Chronicle:—"The brightness and smartness of the style is perfectly captivating, and yet withal, when a deeper note is struck, there is discovered a thoughtfulness and grasp which show that the writer has something very much more than a superficial knowledge of men and things."

Denys D'Auvrillac.

A Story of French Life. By HANNAH LYNCH, Author of "Daughters of Men," "An Odd Experiment," etc. Crown 8vo.

Miss GERTRUDE ATHERTON, in *Vanity Fair:*—"'Denys D'Auvrillac' is a new character in English-written literature . . . the importance of this book is indubitable . . . the distinguished style gives this novel the air of a classic—a classic which must stand quite by itself in English literature."

The Athenæum:—"'Denys D'Auvrillac' may be honourably distinguished from the rank and file of current fiction."

Pall Mall Gazette:—"It is by intrinsic quality of a superior order that this book excels."

Miss Cherry-Blossom of Tôkyô.

A Japanese Novel. By JOHN LUTHER LONG. Crown 8vo.

Saturday Review:—"Miss Cherry-Blossom is the first view of Madame Chrysanthème as the New Woman, revolutionising Japanese immemorial custom by her love-making with a young Englishman . . . she is charming. The graceful end to the romance comes all too soon."

Daily Chronicle:—"Smart and pretty, and sets forth in a very charming way the joy of life in the land of the art-loving Jap."

MR. DOUGLAS SLADEN, in the *Literary World:*—"A really Japanese novel. . . . A fresh, artistic love story, full of human interest."

New Fiction.

Three and Sixpenny Volumes.

A Flirtation with Truth.

By CURTIS YORKE, Author of "Once," etc. etc. *Third Edition.*

The Athenæum:—"A very smartly written novel. . . . There are no dreary passages of retrospect, no explanations of things that do not need to be explained, and no merely aimless conversations. . . . The workmanship with which it is presented is excellent."

Faith, Hope, and Charity.

By JOHN LE BRETON, Author of "Miss Tudor."

The Christian World:—"These are three strong stories, decidedly uncommon in themselves, and told with power. They deal with the irony and tragedy of life, but without that pessimistic conclusion which is the commonplace suggestion of un-original and one-sided minds."

The Scotsman:—"A powerful book, which can scarcely fail to interest and to impress everyone who reads it."

The Red Painted Box.

By MARIE CONNOR LEIGHTON, Author of "The Harvest of Sin," etc., Joint-Author of "Convict 99," etc.

The Scotsman:—"It is only at pretty long intervals that stories so full of baffling mystery and powerful interest as 'The Red Painted Box' issue from the Press. With cunning art the author weaves her plot, and the reader follows its windings with absorbed attention, spurred on from point to point by the pleasant but deluded belief that he or she has solved the mystery."

Abbé Constantin.

By LUDOVIC HALÈVY. Translated from the French by THÉRÈSE BATBEDAT.

The Globe:—"Very welcome is the English translation of Ludovic Halèvy's 'Abbé Constantin.' The story is, as all the world knows, very charming, and should in its present shape find many English readers."

My Dear Grenadier.

By SYBIL BEATRICE REID.

The Daily Telegraph:—"A charmingly sprightly story."

You Never Know Your Luck.

By THEO. IRVING.

The Daily Telegraph:—"A *fin-de-siècle* society novel of considerably more than average merit, smartly written, replete with interest."

The Lighter Life.

By WILLIAM WALLACE. Frontispiece.

Daily Chronicle:—"Witty with that wit of which 'the readiness is all,' the wit of the smilingly malicious thrust, and the parry alert but debonair, the wit of the dramatic situation, changing with every turn in the talk—witty after that fashion Mr. Wallace's dialogue certainly is."

Poetry.

The Selected Poems of John Stuart Blackie.

With a Portrait after the Painting by J. H. LORIMER, A.R.S.A. Edited, with an Appreciation, by his Nephew, ARCHIBALD STODART WALKER. Crown 8vo, 5s.

The Scotsman:—"A fairly representative selection, with an introduction delightful to read. . . . The book will be welcome to many."

The Daily News:—"This book will abide, or should abide, for the sake of its introduction."

The Love Philtre, and other Poems.

By HELEN F. SCHWEITZER. Small fcap. 4to, 5s. net.

The Scotsman.—"There will be little disagreement among those who read it as to the sweetness and natural kindness of its feeling and its harmonious graces of expression."

The Manchester Courier:—"This latest contribution to the legends of King Arthur's Court is delightful, but all too short. . . . Displays unwonted vigour and earnest appreciation of the highest ideals of humanity."

The Bristol Mercury:—"'The Love Philtre' is a fine poem. It contains some exquisite passages of description, and the story told in it is interesting. . . . She (the author) feels deeply the glory and beauty and wonder of the world. She gives expression to this feeling in sweet, melodious verse."

Sonnets and Poems.

By the late EARL OF ROSSLYN. With a Portrait of the Author. Second Edition. Crown 8vo, 7s. 6d.

The New Day.

Sonnets by Dr. T. GORDON HAKE. With Portrait of the Author from a painting by ROSSETTI. Crown 8vo, 5s.

Old and New Poems.

By WALTER HERRIES POLLOCK. With a Portrait of the Author. Crown 8vo, 5s.

Vestigia Retrorsum.

Poems by ARTHUR J. MUNBY. With a Portrait of the Author. Crown 8vo, 5s.

Yggdrassil, and other Poems.

By JOHN CAMPBELL. Bound in limp leather, small fcap. 4to, 5s. net.

Catalogue of Publications.

Abbé Constantin.
By Ludovic Halèvy. Translated from the French by Thérèse Batbedat. Crown 8vo, 3s. 6d.

Afloat with Nelson ;
Or, From Nile to Trafalgar. By Charles H. Eden, Author of "George Donnington," "Queer Chums," etc. etc. Ten full-page Illustrations, by John Williamson. Crown 8vo, cloth, gilt edges, 6s.

Among the Apple Orchards.
By Clement Scott. Fcap. 8vo, 1s. 6d.

Anne, Mrs. Charlton.
One Summer Holiday. Crown 4to, 5s.

At the Sign of the Cross Keys.
A last Century Romance. By Paul Creswick. Crown 8vo, 6s.

Banshee's Warning, The.
By Mrs. J. H. Riddell, Author of "The Head of the Firm." Crown 8vo, 6s.

Barker, Amelia M.
Tom-All-Alone. Crown 8vo, 6s.

Barrett, Wilson.
The Sign of the Cross. Crown 8vo, 6s.
The Daughters of Babylon. Crown 8vo, 6s.

Barron, Elwyn.
Manders. Crown 8vo, 6s.

Barry, J. A.
Steve Brown's Bunyip. Crown 8vo, 3s. 6d.
The Luck of the Native-Born. Crown 8vo, 6s.

Bismarck at Home.
By Jules Hoche. Numerous Illustrations. Demy 8vo, 7s. 6d.

Blackie, John Stuart, Selected Poems of.
Portrait. Edited, with an Appreciation, by his Nephew, Archibald Stodart Walker. Crown 8vo, 5s.

Boer War, A Narrative of the.
By T. F. Carter. New Edition. Demy 8vo, 10s. 6d.

Bound Together.

By HUGH CONWAY, Author of "Called Back." Tenth Thousand. Crown 8vo, 3s. 6d.

Cabot's Discovery of North America.

By G. E. WEARE, Author of "Edmund Burke's Connection with Bristol," etc. etc. With numerous Maps and Illustrations. Large crown 8vo, 10s. 6d.

Cardinal Sin, A.

By HUGH CONWAY, Author of "Called Back," etc. Ninth Thousand. Crown 8vo, 3s. 6d.

Cheer, Boys, Cheer !

Memories of Men and Music. Frontispiece. By HENRY RUSSELL. Crown 8vo, 3s. 6d.

Cherriwink.

A Fairy Tale. By RACHEL PENN, Author of "A Son of Israel," etc. Illustrations by MAUDE F. SAMBOURNE and M. JARDINE-THOMSON. Crown 4to, 6s.

Chesney, General F. R., Life of the late.

The Colonel Commandant Royal Artillery, D.C.L., F.R.G.S., etc. By his WIFE and DAUGHTER. Edited by STANLEY LANE-POOLE. Portrait and Map. Second Edition. Demy 8vo, 12s.

Conway, Hugh.

Cardinal Sin, A. Crown 8vo, 3s. 6d.
Bound Together. Crown 8vo, 3s. 6d.

Court of England under George IV., The.

Founded on a Diary interspersed with Letters written by Queen Caroline and various other Distinguished Persons. Two Volumes, demy 8vo, 25s.

Court of King Arthur, The.

Stories from the Land of the Round Table. By WILLIAM HENRY FROST. Illustrations by SYDNEY RICHMOND BURLEIGH. Crown 8vo, 6s.

Crawford, J. H., F.L.S.

Wild Life of Scotland, The. Large crown 8vo, 8s. 6d. net.
Wild Flowers of Scotland, The. Large crown 8vo, 6s. net.
Summer Days for Winter Evenings. Large crown 8vo, 8s. 6d. net.
Girl's Awakening, A. A Novel. Crown 8vo, 6s.

County Scandal, A.

A Story of King Midas and a Pastoral. By F. EMILY PHILLIPS, Author of "The Education of Antonia," "The Knight's Tale," etc. Crown 8vo, 6s.

Daughters of Babylon, The.

By WILSON BARRETT and ROBERT HICHENS. Crown 8vo, 6s.

Denys D'Auvrillac.

A Story of French Life. By HANNAH LYNCH, Author of "Daughters of Men," etc. etc. Crown 8vo, 6s.

Diderot's Thoughts on Art and Style.

With some of his Shorter Essays. Selected and Translated by BEATRIX L. TOLLEMACHE (Hon. Mrs. Lionel Tollemache). Crown 8vo, 5s.

Diogenes' Sandals.

A Novel. By Mrs. ARTHUR KENNARD. Second Edition. Crown 8vo, cloth, 3s. 6d.

Dixon, Charles.

Lost and Vanishing Birds. Demy 8vo, 7s. 6d.

Double Ruin, A.

A Novel. By Mrs. A. HART (Sophie Kappey), Author of "A Modern Martyr." Crown 8vo, 3s. 6d.

Drama Birthday Book, The.

Compiled from the Works of the Dramatists of the Day. By PERCY S. PHILLIPS. Fcap. 8vo, art linen, 3s. 6d.; morocco, 10s. 6d.

Drawing-Room Cynic, A.

By LORIN KAYE, Author of "Her Ladyship's Income." Crown 8vo, 6s.

Dream's Fulfilment, A.

A Sporting Novel. By H. CUMBERLAND BENTLEY. Second Edition. Crown 8vo, 3s. 6d.

Early Bird, The, and other Drawing-Room Plays.

By BEATRIX L. TOLLEMACHE (Hon. Mrs. Lionel Tollemache). Crown 8vo, 2s. 6d.

Esther's Pilgrimage.

By J. HENRY HARRIS, Author of "St. Porth." Crown 8vo, 6s.

Etelka's Vow.

A Novel. By DOROTHEA GERARD, Author of "On the Way Through," "Orthodox," "Lady Baby," etc. etc., and Joint-Author of "The Waters of Hercules" and "Reata." Third Edition. Crown 8vo, 3s. 6d.

Faith, Hope, and Charity.

A Novel of the Graces. By JOHN LE BRETON, Author of "Miss Tudor," etc. etc. Crown 8vo, 3s. 6d.

Fate of Woman, The.

By FRANCIS SHORT. Crown 8vo, 3s. 6d.

Flirtation with Truth, A.

By CURTIS YORKE, Author of "Once," "A Record of Discords," etc. Third Edition. Crown 8vo, 3s. 6d.

From "The Bells" to "King Arthur."

By CLEMENT SCOTT. Fully Illustrated. Demy 8vo, 7s. 6d.

Gerard, Dorothea.

A Queen of Curds and Cream.   Crown 8vo, 3s. 6d.
Etelka's Vow.   Crown 8vo, 3s. 6d.
On the Way Through.   Crown 8vo, 3s. 6d.
Orthodox.   Crown 8vo, 3s. 6d.

Girl's Awakening, A.

A Novel. By J. H. CRAWFORD, Author of "The Wild Life of Scotland." Crown 8vo, 6s.

Gordon Highlanders, The.

By JAMES MILNE. Fully Illustrated. Crown 8vo, 1s.

Gorst, Mrs. Harold E.

Possessed of Devils.   Crown 8vo, 6s.

Gunner Jingo's Jubilee.

By Major-General TOM BLAND STRANGE, late R.A. With Fifteen full-page Illustrations, Plans, Maps, and numerous Thumb-nail Sketches. Third Edition. Demy 8vo, cloth, 7s. 6d.

Halèvy, Ludovic.

Abbé Constantin.   Crown 8vo, 3s. 6d.

Catalogue of Publications—continued.

Harris, J. Henry.
Esther's Pilgrimage. Crown 8vo, 6s.

He Went Out with the Tide.
By GUY EDEN, Author of "The Cry of the Curlew." Crown 8vo, 6s.

Headlam, Cecil.
The Secret of Sorrow. Crown 8vo, 6s.

Her Ladyship's Income.
A Society Novel. By LORIN KAYE, Author of "A Drawing-Room Cynic." Fourth Edition. Crown 8vo, 6s.

Hichens, Robert.
The Daughters of Babylon. Crown 8vo, 6s.

Highland Brigade in the Crimea, The.
By Sir ANTHONY STERLING, K.C.B., a Staff Officer who was there. With Frontispiece and 18 Maps. Second Edition. Demy 8vo, handsomely bound in cloth, 7s. 6d.

Hilder, Eva M.
Stories the Sunflower Told. Fcap. 4to, 5s.

Hodgetts, E. A. Brayley.
A Russian Wild Flower. Crown 8vo, 6s.

Horn Book, Ye XIXth Century.
By WALLIS MACKAY. Demy 8vo, 1s.

Indifference in Matters of Religion.
By the ABBÉ F. DE LAMENNAIS. Translated from the French, with a Preface by LORD STANLEY of Alderley. Demy 8vo, 12s.

Infant, The.
A Novel. By FREDERICK WICKS, Author of "The Veiled Hand." Illustrations by A. MORROW. Large crown 8vo, 6s.

Italian Literature, A Manual of.
By F. H. CLIFFE. Crown 8vo, 6s.

Jane Follett.
A Novel. By GEORGE WEMYSS, Author of "'Tween the New and the Old." Crown 8vo, 6s.

Jeune, Lady.
Lesser Questions.   Crown 8vo, 6s.

Kaye, Eff.
Virtue's Tragedy.   Crown 8vo, 6s.

Kaye, Lorin.
Her Ladyship's Income.   Crown 8vo, 6s.
A Drawing-Room Cynic.   Crown 8vo, 6s.

King, Kennedy.
Love and a Sword.   Crown 8vo, 6s.

Kreutzer Sonata, The.
By COUNT LEO TOLSTOI. Translated from the Russian by
H. SUTHERLAND EDWARDS. Paper covers, 1s. Thirty-
seventh Thousand.

Lady's Impressions of Cyprus in 1893, A.
By Mrs. LEWIS. With Map. Crown 8vo, 5s.

Lamennais, The Abbé F. de.
Indifference in Matters of Religion.   Demy 8vo, 12s.

Le Breton, John.
Unholy Matrimony.   Crown 8vo, 6s.
Miss Tudor.   Crown 8vo, 6s.
Faith, Hope, and Charity.   Crown 8vo, 3s. 6d.

Lesser Questions.
By LADY JEUNE. A Book dealing with the Principal Social
Questions of the Day. Third Edition. Crown 8vo, 6s.

Lighter Life, The.
A Series of Dialogues and Sketches. By WILLIAM WALLACE.
Frontispiece. Crown 8vo, 3s. 6d.

Light that Lies, The.
By COCKBURN HARVEY. Illustrated. Fcap. 8vo, 2s. 6d.

Literary Recollections.
By MAXIME DU CAMP, Member of the French Academy. Two
Volumes, demy 8vo, 30s.

Love and a Sword.
A Tale of the Afridi War. By KENNEDY KING. Illustrations by R. CATON WOODVILLE and others. Crown 8vo, 6s.

Love-Philtre, The, and Other Poems.
By HELEN F. SCHWEITZER. Fcap. 8vo, 5s. net.

Luck of the Native-Born, The.
A Story of Adventure. By J. A. BARRY, Author of "Steve Brown's Bunyip," etc. Crown 8vo, 6s.

Lynch, Hannah.
Denys D'Auvrillac. Crown 8vo, 6s.

Manders.
A Novel. By ELWYN BARRON. Crown 8vo, 6s.

Mapleson Memoirs, The.
Forty Years of Operatic Management, 1848–1888. By J. H. MAPLESON. With Portrait. Third Edition. Two Volumes, demy 8vo, 10s. 6d.

Mark Twain Birthday Book, The.
Tenth Thousand. Cloth, 1s.; leather, 2s. 6d.; morocco, 6s. 6d.

Memories of the Mutiny.
By Colonel FRANCIS CORNWALLIS MAUDE, V.C., C.B., who commanded the Artillery of Havelock's Column. Two Volumes, on special paper, with Maps and Illustrations, demy 8vo, 30s.

Mighty Toltec, The.
A Story of Adventure. By S. J. ADAIR FITZ-GERALD and S. O. LLOYD. Frontispiece. Crown 8vo, 6s.

Miss Cherry-Blossom of Tôkyô.
A Japanese Novel. By JOHN LUTHER LONG. Crown 8vo, 6s.

Miss Tudor.
A Novel. By JOHN LE BRETON, Author of "Unholy Matrimony," etc. etc. Crown 8vo, 6s.

Mrs. Fenton.
A Sketch. By W. E. NORRIS. Third Edition. Crown 8vo, 2s. 6d.

My Dear Grenadier.
A Novel. By SYBIL BEATRICE REID, Author of "Sweet Peas." Crown 8vo, 3s. 6d.

New Day, The.

Sonnets. By Dr. T. GORDON HAKE. With Portrait of the Author by ROSSETTI. Crown 8vo, 5s. Rosslyn Series.

Norris, W. E.

Mrs. Fenton. Crown 8vo, 2s. 6d.

Old and New Poems.

By WALTER HERRIES POLLOCK. With a Portrait of the Author. Crown 8vo, 5s.

On the Way Through.

By DOROTHEA GERARD, Author of "A Queen of Curds and Cream," and Joint-Author of "Reata" and "The Waters of Hercules." Crown 8vo, cloth, 3s. 6d.

One Summer Holiday.

A Fairy Book. By Mrs. CHARLTON ANNE. Dedicated by most gracious permission to H.R.H. the Duchess of York. Illustrations by R. HOLLIS and others. Crown 4to, 5s.

Orthodox.

By DOROTHEA GERARD, Author of "Lady Baby," "On the Way Through," etc. Third Edition. Crown 8vo, 3s. 6d.

Our Future King.

By CHARLES LOWE. Crown 8vo, 1s.

Penn, Rachel.

A Son of Israel. Crown 8vo, 6s.
Cherriwink. Crown 4to, 6s.
The Song of the Harp. Fcap. 4to, 3s. 6d.

Phillips, F. Emily.

A County Scandal. Crown 8vo, 6s.

Pont-Jest, René de.

The River of Pearls. Crown 8vo, 6s.

Possessed of Devils.

A Novel. By Mrs. HAROLD E. GORST. Crown 8vo, 6s.

Queen of Curds and Cream, A.

A Novel. By DOROTHEA GERARD, Author of "Lady Baby," "On the Way Through," etc. Fourth Edition. Crown 8vo, 3s. 6d.

Red Painted Box, The.

By MARIE CONNOR LEIGHTON, Author of "The Harvest of Sin," etc., and Joint-Author of "Convict 99," etc. Crown 8vo, 3s. 6d.

River of Pearls, The ; or, The Red Spider.

A Chinese Romance. By RENÉ DE PONT-JEST. With 61 Illustrations by FELIX RÉGAMEY. Crown 8vo, 6s.

Romances.

E. EGLANTINE. Cover designed by JOHN WILLIAMSON. Crown 8vo, 1s. 6d.

Russian Wild Flower, A.

By E. A. BRAYLEY HODGETTS, Author of "Round about Armenia," "In the Track of the Russian Famine," etc. Crown 8vo, 6s.

Saxe-Coburg-Gotha, Memoirs of Duke Ernest of (Brother of the late Prince Consort of England).

With Portraits of Prince Albert and Duke Ernest. Four Volumes, demy 8vo, cloth, 55s.

Scott, Clement.

From "The Bells" to "King Arthur." Demy 8vo, 7s. 6d.

Among the Apple Orchards. Foolscap 8vo, 1s. 6d.

Secret of Sorrow, The.

Being the Confession of a Young Man. Edited by CECIL HEADLAM, Author of "Selections from the British Satirists," "Prayers of the Saints," "The Story of Nuremberg," etc. Crown 8vo, 6s.

Shakspeare's Historical Plays: Roman and English.

With Revised Text, Introduction and Notes, Glossarial, Critical and Historical. By the late Right Rev. Bishop WORDSWORTH, D.C.L., LL.D. New Edition. Three Volumes, crown 8vo, 15s.

Shakspeare's Knowledge and Use of the Bible.

By the late Right Rev. Bishop WORDSWORTH, D.C.L., LL.D. Crown 8vo, cloth, 5s.; full calf, 8s.

Shilrick the Drummer; or, Loyal and True.

By JULIA AGNES FRASER. Three Volumes, crown 8vo, 31s. 6d.

Sign of the Cross, The.

A Novel. By WILSON BARRETT. With a Preface by the Bishop of Truro. Crown 8vo, 6s.

Sinless Sinner, A.

By MARY H. TENNYSON, Author of "A Fool of Fate." Crown 8vo, 6s.

Sixty Years of Recollections.

By ERNEST LEGOUVÉ of the Académie Française. Translated with Notes by the Author of "An Englishman in Paris." Two Volumes, demy 8vo, cloth, 18s.

Sketches of the Future.

By HAROLD E. GORST, Author of "Without Bloodshed." Small fcap. 8vo, limp cloth, 1s.

Son of Israel, A.

By RACHEL PENN, Author of "Cherriwink," etc. Crown 8vo, 6s.

Song of the Harp, The.

An Original Fairy Tale. By RACHEL PENN, Author of "Cherriwink." Illustrations by JOHN WILLIAMSON. Fcap. 4to, 3s. 6d.

Sonnets and Poems.

By the late EARL OF ROSSLYN. With Portrait of the Author. Second Edition. Crown 8vo, 7s. 6d.

Steve Brown's Bunyip.

By J. A. BARRY. With Introductory Verses by RUDYARD KIPLING. Fifth Edition. Crown 8vo, 3s. 6d.

Stories the Sunflower Told.

By EVA M. HILDER. Illustrations by M. M. SUTCLIFFE. Fcap. 4to, 5s.

Summer Days for Winter Evenings.

A Series of Nature Idylls. By J. H. CRAWFORD, F.L.S., Author of "The Wild Life of Scotland." Illustrations by JOHN WILLIAMSON. Handsomely bound, in uniform with Mr. Crawford's other works. Large crown 8vo, 6s. net.

Sweet Peas.

By SYBIL BEATRICE REID. Crown 8vo, cloth, 2s.

Thoughts of a Queen.

By CARMEN SYLVA (Elizabeth, Queen of Roumania). Translated into English, with Special Permission, by H. SUTHERLAND EDWARDS. Fcap. 8vo, cloth, 1s. 6d.

Tollemache, Beatrix L. (Hon. Mrs. Lionel Tollemache).

Diderot's Thoughts on Art and Style. Crown 8vo, 5s.
The Early Bird. Crown 8vo, 2s. 6d.

Tom-All-Alone.

By AMELIA M. BARKER. Crown 8vo, 6s.

'Tween the New and the Old.

A Tale of Three Lovers. By GEORGE WEMYSS. Crown 8vo, 6s.

Unholy Matrimony.

By JOHN LE BRETON, Author of "Miss Tudor," etc. Crown 8vo, 6s.

Veiled Hand, The.

By FREDERICK WICKS. With Illustrations by JEAN DE PALEOLOGUE. Fourth Edition. Crown 8vo, 3s. 6d.

Vestigia Retrorsum.

Poems by ARTHUR J. MUNBY. With Portrait of the Author. Crown 8vo, 5s.

Wemyss, George.

'Tween the New and the Old. Crown 8vo, 6s.
Jane Follett. Crown 8vo, 6s.

Wicks, Frederick.

The Veiled Hand. Illustrated. Crown 8vo, 3s. 6d.
The Infant. Illustrated. Large crown 8vo, 6s.

Wild Flowers of Scotland, The.

By J. II. CRAWFORD, F.L.S., Author of "The Wild Life of Scotland," etc. Illustrations by JOHN WILLIAMSON. Handsomely bound, in uniform with Mr. Crawford's other Works. Large crown 8vo, 6s. net.

Wild Life of Scotland, The.

By J. H. CRAWFORD. With Illustrations by JOHN WILLIAMSON. Large crown 8vo, 6s. net.

Windabyne.

A Record of By-gone Times in Australia. By REGINALD CRAWFORD. Edited by GEORGE RANKEN. Crown 8vo. 2s.

Wooing of Avis Grayle, The.

By CHARLES HANNAN, Author of "Chin Chin Wa," "The Captive of Pekin," etc. Crown 8vo, 6s.

Wordsworth, The late Right Rev. Bishop.

Shakspeare's Historical Plays. Three Vols. 15s.
Shakspeare's Knowledge and Use of the Bible. 5s.

Yorke, Curtis.

A Flirtation with Truth. Crown 8vo, 3s. 6d,

You Never Know Your Luck.

A Novel. By THEO. IRVING. Crown 8vo, 3s. 6d.

Standard Library of Foreign Classics.

Cheap and Popular Reprint of the Standard Foreign Authors in the Original Tongue. Fcap. 8vo, handsomely bound in cloth. Edited, with a Critical Preface, by W. H. SONLEY JOHNSTONE.

Vol. I. *THE COMEDIES OF MOLIÈRE.* 1s. 6d.

Vol. II. *MAXIMS AND REFLECTIONS OF LA ROCHE-FOUCAULD.* 1s.

Mr. Macqueen's Publications

Arranged according to their Prices.

55/-	Saxe-Coburg-Gotha, Memoirs of Duke Ernest of. 4 Vols.		Demy 8vo.
31/6	Fraser (Julia Agnes) . .	Shilrick the Drummer. Three Vols. . .	Crown 8vo.
30/-	Camp (Maxim du) . .	Literary Recollections. Two Vols. . . .	Demy 8vo.
	Maude (Colonel Francis Cornwallis)	Memoirs of the Mutiny. Illustrated. Two Vols.	Demy 8vo.
25/-	Court of England under George IV., The . . .		Demy 8vo.
18/-	Legouvé (Ernest) . .	Sixty Years of Recollections. Two Vols. .	Demy 8vo.
15/-	Shakspeare's Historical Plays, Roman and English. Three Vols.		Crown 8vo.
12/-	Chesney (General F. R.), Life of the late . . .		Demy 8vo.
	Lamennais (Abbé F. de) .	Indifference in Matters of Religion . . .	Demy 8vo.
10/6	Carter (T. F.) . . .	A Narrative of the Boer War	Demy 8vo.
	Mapleson (J. H.)	The Mapleson Memoirs. Two Vols. . .	Demy 8vo.
	Phillips (Percy S.) . .	Drama Birthday Book. Morocco . . .	Fcap. 8vo.
	Weare (G. E.) . . .	Cabot's Discovery of N. America. Illustrated.	L. cr. 8vo.
8/-	Wordsworth (The late Right Rev. Bishop)	Shakspeare's Knowledge and Use of the Bible. Full calf . . .	Crown 8vo.
7/6	Dixon (Charles) . . .	Lost and Vanishing Birds. Illustrated . . .	Demy 8vo.
	Hoche (Jules) . . .	Bismarck at Home. Illus.	Demy 8vo.
	Rosslyn (Earl of) . . .	Sonnets and Poems .	Crown 8vo.
	Scott (Clement) . . .	From "The Bells" to "King Arthur." Illus.	Demy 8vo.
	Sterling (Sir Anthony, K.C.B.)	The Highland Brigade in the Crimea . .	Demy 8vo.
	Strange (Major-General Tom Bland)	Gunner Jingo's Jubilee. Illustrated . . .	Demy 8vo.
6/6	Mark Twain's Birthday Book. Morocco . . .		Small 4to.
6/- nett.	Crawford (J. H., F.L.S.) .	Wild Life of Scotland .	L. cr. 8vo.
	,, ,, .	Wild Flowers of Scotland	L. cr. 8vo.
	,, ,, .	Summer Days for Winter Evenings . . .	L. cr. 8vo.
6/-	Barker (Amelia M.) . .	Tom-All-Alone . .	Crown 8vo.
	Barrett (Wilson) . .	The Sign of the Cross .	Crown 8vo.
	,, ,, . .	The Daughters of Babylon	Crown 8vo.
	Barron (Elwyn) . . .	Manders . . .	Crown 8vo.
	Barry (J. A.) . . .	The Luck of the Native Born	Crown 8vo.
	Cliffe (F. H.) . . .	A Manual of Italian Literature	Crown 8vo.

6/-	Crawford (J. H., F.L.S.)	A Girl's Awakening	Crown 8vo.
	Creswick (Paul)	At the Sign of the Cross Keys	Crown 8vo.
	Eden (Charles H.)	Afloat with Nelson. Illustrated	Crown 8vo.
	Eden (Guy)	He Went Out with the Tide	Crown 8vo.
	Fitz-Gerald (S. J. Adair)	The Mighty Toltec	Crown 8vo.
	Frost (William Henry)	The Court of King Arthur. Illustrated.	Crown 8vo.
	Gorst (Mrs. Harold E.)	Possessed of Devils	Crown 8vo.
	Hannan (Charles)	The Wooing of Avis Grayle	Crown 8vo.
	Harris (J. Henry)	Esther's Pilgrimage	Crown 8vo.
	Headlam (Cecil)	The Secret of Sorrow	Crown 8vo.
	Hichens (Robert)	The Daughters of Babylon	Crown 8vo.
	Hodgetts (E. A. Brayley)	A Russian Wild Flower	Crown 8vo.
	Jeune (Lady)	Lesser Questions	Crown 8vo.
	Kaye (Lorin)	A Drawing-Room Cynic	Crown 8vo.
	,, ,,	Her Ladyship's Income	Crown 8vo.
	Kaye (Eff)	Virtue's Tragedy	Crown 8vo.
	King (Kennedy)	Love and a Sword. Illus.	Crown 8vo.
	Le Breton (John)	Unholy Matrimony	Crown 8vo.
	,, ,,	Miss Tudor	Crown 8vo.
	Lloyd (S. O.)	The Mighty Toltec	Crown 8vo.
	Long (John Luther)	Miss Cherry-Blossom of Tôkyô	Crown 8vo.
	Lynch (Hannah)	Denys D'Auvrillac	Crown 8vo.
	Penn (Rachel)	Cherriwink. Illustrated	Crown 4to.
	,, ,,	A Son of Israel	Crown 8vo.
	Phillips (F. Emily)	A County Scandal	Crown 8vo.
	Pont-Jest (René de)	The River of Pearls. Illustrated	Crown 8vo.
	Riddell (Mrs. J. H.)	The Banshee's Warning	Crown 8vo.
	Tennyson (Mary H.)	A Sinless Sinner	Crown 8vo.
	Wemyss (George)	Jane Follett	Crown 8vo.
	,, ,,	'Tween the New and the Old	Crown 8vo.
	Wicks (Frederick)	The Infant. Illustrated	L. cr. 8vo.
5/-	Anne (Mrs. Charlton)	One Summer Holiday. Illustrated	Crown 4to.
	Blackie (John Stuart), Selected Poems of		Crown 8vo.
	Hake (Dr. T. Gordon)	The New Day	Crown 8vo.
	Hilder (Eva M.)	Stories the Sunflowers Told. Illustrated	Fcap. 4to.
	Lewis (Mrs.)	A Lady's Impressions of Cyprus in 1893	Crown 8vo.
	Munby (Arthur J.)	Vestigia Retrorsum	Crown 8vo.
	Pollock (Walter Herries)	Old and New Poems	Crown 8vo.
	Schweitzer (Helen F.)	The Love-Philtre	Fcap. 8vo.
	Tollemache (Hon. Mrs. Lionel)	Diderot's Thoughts on Art and Style	Crown 8vo.
	Wordsworth (The late Right Rev. Bishop)	Shakspeare's Knowledge and Use of the Bible	Crown 8vo.

3/6	Barry (J. A.) . . .	Steve Brown's Bunyip .	Crown 8vo.
	Bentley (Cumberland) . .	A Dream's Fulfilment .	Crown 8vo.
	Conway (Hugh) . . .	A Cardinal Sin . .	Crown 8vo.
	,, ,, . .	Bound Together . .	Crown 8vo.
	Gerard (Dorothea) . .	Etelka's Vow. . .	Crown 8vo.
	,, ,, . .	On the Way Through .	Crown 8vo.
	,, ,, . .	Orthodox . . .	Crown 8vo.
	,, ,, . .	A Queen of Curds and Cream . . .	Crown 8vo.
	Halèvy (Ludovic) . .	Abbé Constantin . .	Crown 8vo.
	Hart (Mrs. A.) . . .	A Double Ruin . .	Crown 8vo.
	Irving (Theo.) . . .	You Never Know Your Luck . . .	Crown 8vo.
	Kennard (Mrs. Arthur) .	Diogenes' Sandals . .	Crown 8vo.
	Le Breton (John) . .	Faith, Hope, and Charity	Crown 8vo.
	Leighton (Marie Connor) .	The Red Painted Box .	Crown 8vo.
	Penn (Rachel) . . .	The Song of the Harp. Illustrated . . .	Fcap. 4to.
	Phillips (Percy S.) . .	The Drama Birthday Book. Cloth . .	Fcap. 8vo.
	Reid (Sybil Beatrice) . .	My Dear Grenadier .	Crown 8vo.
	Russell (Henry) . . .	Cheer, Boys, Cheer ! .	Crown 8vo.
	Short (Francis) . . .	The Fate of Woman .	Crown 8vo.
	Wallace (William) . .	The Lighter Life . .	Crown 8vo.
	Wicks (Frederick) . .	The Veiled Hand. Illus.	Crown 8vo.
	Yorke (Curtis) . . .	A Flirtation with Truth .	Crown 8vo.
2/6	Harvey (Cockburn) . .	The Light that Lies .	Fcap. 8vo.
	Mark Twain's Birthday Book. Leather . . .		Small 4to.
	Norrris (W. E.) . . .	Mrs. Fenton . . .	Crown 8vo.
	Tollemache (Hon. Mrs. Lionel) . . .	The Early Bird .	Crown 8vo.
2/-	Crawford (Reginald) . .	Windabyne . . .	Crown 8vo.
	Reid (Sybil Beatrice) . .	Sweet Peas . - .	Crown 8vo.
1/6	Eglantine (E.) . . .	Romances . . .	Crown 8vo.
	Molière, The Comedies of .	. . . . .	Sm. cr. 8vo.
	Scott (Clement) . . .	Among the Apple Orchards . . .	Fcap. 8vo.
	Sylva (Carmen) . .	Thoughts of a Queen .	Fcap. 8vo.
1/-	Gorst (Harold E.) . .	Sketches of the Future .	Sm. fc. 8vo.
	Lowe (Charles) . .	Our Future King. Illustrated . . .	Crown 8vo.
	Mackay (William) . .	Ye XIXth Century Horn Book. Illustrated .	Demy 8vo.
	Mark Twain's Birthday Book		Small 4to.
	Milne (James) . . .	The Gordon Highlanders. Illustrated . . .	Crown 8vo.
	Rochefoucauld, Maxims and Reflections of La . .		Sm. cr. 8vo.
	Tolstoi (Count Leo) . .	Kreutzer Sonata . .	Fcap. 8vo.

LONDON : JOHN MACQUEEN,

HASTINGS HOUSE, NORFOLK STREET, STRAND.